CW01502225

Ex Libris

This Book belongs to ~

_____

The Hag-Stone : A stone with a naturally weathered hole through the centre. An efficient tool in warding off assaults from nocturnal entities and also a favoured means utilised by Seers to view the Otherworldly races.

Strange Lands

A Field-Guide to the Celtic & British Otherworld

Revised Edition

From ghoulies and ghosties and long-leggety beasties
And things that go bump in the night,
Good Lord, deliver us.
Anonymous Scottish Prayer.

With Special Thanks to pStan Batcow,
Karl Shuker, Kevin Morrow, Ian Topham,
Otto Rapp, Andrew McGuigan, Andrew M.
Hopcroft, Folk Horror Revival
and to Durham Art Gallery
for keeping the Strange Lands alive.

With Lots of Love to Erin Sorrey x

© 2010 Andrew L. Paciorek.
The book author and artist
retains sole copyright to his contributions to this book.

Foreword © 2010 Karl Shuker
www.karlshuker.com
http://karlshuker.blogspot.com/

The Blurb-provided layout designs and graphic elements are copyright Blurb
Inc., 2010. This book was created using the Blurb creative publishing service.
The book author retains sole copyright to his or her contributions to this book.

dremour
press~

FOREWORD
By Dr Karl P.N. Shuker, 5 January 2011.

Think of any major stage or screen musical, and the chances are that it will have been written by a composer/lyricist partnership – Rice & Lloyd Webber, Rodgers & Hammerstein, Gershwin & Gershwin, Lerner & Loewe, Sherman & Sherman, Schoenberg & Boublil, to name for a few. There is, however, one very significant exception – Cole Porter, a uniquely gifted individual whose talent for composing wonderful, melodious music was matched equally by his ability to pen complex, witty lyrics. But Cole Porters are few and far between.

The same principle applies in the world of books. There are countless talented writers, and countless talented illustrators, but individuals able to accomplish both to a suitably high standard are an extreme rarity, to be treasured and appreciated like a Renaissance Old Master or an exceptionally fine vintage of wine – which is why I am so impressed by this book and, most of all, by its creator.

I first came to know Andy Paciorek through Facebook, and was immediately captivated (mesmerised, even) by his extraordinarily detailed, imaginative artwork – and also by the prodigious quantities of it. Andy seems able to create his spectacular illustrations as easily as the rest of us draw breath, and yet every single one is as meticulously crafted as all of the others. Indeed, when viewing his numerous albums of artwork on his Facebook page and his various art websites, I have often been reminded of the famous quote by Edward Bulwer-Lytton:

"Talent does what it can; genius does what it must".

Unquestionably, Andy is a man whose life is driven by a passion for creating art – but when he sent me the manuscript for *Strange Lands* to read through, I was shocked to discover that his art was just one side of a coin whose very existence I had not even suspected before.

Long before I had finished reading it, I had discovered that Andy is not only a supremely talented artist, he is also a remarkably adept writer and researcher! Right from a child, I have always been fascinated by mythology and folklore, especially the rich corpus originating in the British Isles, and I have read very extensively on the subject. However, I can say in all honesty that *Strange Lands* is one of the most comprehensive single volumes on British mythological entities that I have ever encountered. Even Dr Katharine

M. Briggs's essential tome, *A Dictionary of Fairies*, universally acclaimed as the standard work on such beings, now has a rival in terms of the sheer diversity of examples documented.

And where *Strange Lands* effortlessly outpoints even that classic work is of course in its illustrations, which are truly breathtaking in their beauty, intricacy, and vibrancy. Moreover, especially with regard to the more obscure examples, Andy's may well be the first illustrations of such entities ever executed. Certainly, in addition to all of the well known examples of British (and Breton) supernatural being, there are numerous far less familiar ones included and illustrated here too – everything, in fact, from muryans, hyter sprites, the Lob, bwbachs, the Coranied, duergars, fir darrig, foidin seachrain, and the memorably-named wag by the way to the lunatishee, brown men, the dark men of dreams, hobyahs, bull beggars, merrows, gwrach-y-rhibyn, grugach, and many more!

An abridged version of *Strange Lands* has been available online at its very own website - http://www.batcow.co.uk/strangelands/ - for quite some time, but if ever there was a manuscript crying out to be produced in book form, with its spectacular illustrations reproduced in large format, this was the one. So I am absolutely delighted that Andy has now done so, and I am very honoured to have received the opportunity to pen for it this foreword – or, as I see it, a well-deserved paean of praise for what will unquestionably become a standard work of reference as well as a true thing of beauty that will indeed be a joy forever.

On his Facebook 'Like' (formerly Fan) Page, Andy includes the following quote from Charles Baudelaire:

A frenzied passion for art is a canker that devours everything else.

Much as I hesitate to question the viewpoint or tamper with the words of such an esteemed literary figure as Baudelaire, in Andy's case I feel that a more apposite wording of that quote would be something along the lines of:

A heartfelt passion for art is a fire that warms, nourishes, and sustains the life that it feeds above all else.

Certainly, I cannot ever imagine Andy existing even for a moment without his eternal fervour for art coursing through his veins like divine, fiery ichor. And long may it continue to do so – I for one am already eagerly awaiting his next published art project!

Introduction

"Once upon a time in a land far, far away ..." and so begins many a familiar fairy-tale. But just where is this land and how far away exactly ? Millions of miles or right on our own doorstep ? Not that that matters to a child listening intently to the unravelling drama, for it is the action, environment and characters that capture the imagination rather than the exact geography. However in the compilation of a guide-book pertaining specifically to the supernatural denizens of the regions of the world that are still touched by a distant Celtic tradition (namely Ireland and regions of Britain and North-Western France), it is imperative to try and discover just what is said to be where. To even speak of a 'Celtic ' world or Otherworld is ambigious, as there were no Celts as such but a number of tribes of similar habits but different names. To the invading Romans these were the Keltoi or Celts - the Secret People.

Though many of the most renowned fairy-tales were originally translated from foreign languages, a number of similarities exist with the native folklore and legends of these isles. It should be remembered however, that particular details will inevitably change over time and that exposure to other cultures will draw new influence, the vast majority of fairy-tales owe a considerable debt to the older myths and folk-tales. These in turn often refer to actual events either in literal or symbolic form. Therefore it is a task to determine which creatures were rumoured to have been encountered locally and which only made it to these shores on the lips of overseas travellers. Some fantastic creatures may be embellished on numerous British Coat of Arms, yet actual encounters with these creatures might not have actually been reported within the wilds of these shores. Their inclusion in heraldry and medieval bestiaries most probably occurred as a result of the descriptions given by overseas explorers, though many other strange beings were reportedly encountered at home.

As with the entirely natural heritage of these isles, the richness and diversity of its supernatural occupants (native or introduced) is often underestimated, and though the spread of towns and cities could be accused of perhaps diluting the traditional rural lore, industry and technology has also caused some entities to evolve and even created new ones. Some people, rather unfairly, may consider the native 'conventional' flora and fauna to be somehow less interesting than the exotic, foreign species that they may encounter only on television or perhaps in zoos. Whilst the unusual and unfamiliar do certainly offer a sense of exhilaration, the native wildlife is by no means bland. To encounter any of the elusive supernatural denizens of these isles however, would not likely provoke any feeling of security. For as familiarity can breed contempt, excitement often stems from unpredictability and the unknown, and the supernatural inhabitants of the

Celtic world certainly offer this in abundance. Sensations of risk and thrill could at times escalate into revulsion, fear and danger during such an encounter however and often with good reason.

So do these supernatural creatures actually live in these green and balmy isles ?

To even use the term 'supernatural' may provoke question, for if anything actually exists then it must be natural. Granted, but here we are dealing with a nature that we can barely comprehend and seemingly far less prove (at least so far at the time of writing). It is a nature of such magical intensity that to witness it in person would probably inspire such awe that adequate words to describe the event would surely be hard to find. Other words such as 'unnatural', 'preternatural' and 'paranormal' would be as efficient and as faltering to use, but although the word 'supernatural' may not be strictly accurate it does indicate that we are not dealing with the everyday or commonplace.

But that does not answer the question - do these creatures, call them what you will, live in the Celtic-influenced lands ? Well, just to momentarily digress again, the term 'exist' is perhaps more valid than 'live'. Certain supernatural creatures such as the various phantoms and Vampires are not 'alive' as such but are apparently active despite already being what we would call 'dead'. Encounters of some corporeal creatures such as Wyverns, for instance, have not been reported for so long that it could be contemplated that they are now possibly extinct ... that is, if they ever truly lived. Some of the semi-astral breeds we would call Fays or Faeries may not inhabit these isles in the conventional sense. (The terms 'Fay','Fairy' and a variety of very similar words are notably generic and are often used to describe quite an array of strange creatures.) The word 'Faerie' and its equivalents came into British use after the Norman era, the Bretons use the word ' Fete', the Anglo-Saxons used the word 'Aelf' and its Elven equivalents, whilst the Celts used the word Sidhe and other terms particular to individual tribes. Quite confusingly as well as appearing in our world, it has been suggested that the Faerie-realm lies in another dimension that exists parallel to earth. It could be compared to a semi-transparent sheet being laid over a photograph. Invisible to our eyes at most times, the Faerie world may on occasion converge and mingle with our world at certain locations and under particular circumstances. Much of rustic Britain, Ireland and Celtic France may coincide with the Faerie domain (or the Otherworld / Underworld as it is sometimes known).

Certain locations including Dartmoor, Glastonbury, Anglesey, Craig-y-Ddinas in Wales, the Isle of Man, Brociliande in Brittany, Munster, Tara in Co. Meath, New-Grange, Aberfoyle, the Eildon Hills and the Scottish Highlands and islands are said to be blessed (or cursed) with an especially strong Fay presence, but they may still turn up in the most unlikely places also. Some Faerie kingdoms such as Annwn, Avalon (Isle of Apples), Tir Nan Og (Land of the Young or Blessed), Mag Mell (the Pleasant Plain), Hy Breasil and the Fortunate Isles may lie at most times submerged or invisible at various points in the lakes, seas and channels around the Celtic isles. Other Fay kingdoms such as Elfhaime may lie under or within great forests or deep underground like Saint Martin's Land. The sunken kingdom of Ys is said to lie off the coast of Brittany. Only at rare times may they become apparent. Gateways to the hidden lands may also lie inland and such auspicious portals may be marked by standing stones, grassy knolls, hills, wells, waterfalls and certain trees. Likewise they may lie beyond fog, mist or even the clouds. The doors may open on particular days of the year such as the solstices and equinoxes (especially Midsummer night) and the ancient Celtic festivals of Beltain (May day) and Samhain (Halloween). Such places and moments where the Supernatural becomes apparent have been described as being 'Thin' or in Welsh as 'Fou' or alternatively as being 'Windows', 'Thresholds', Mist-Gates or 'Liminal Zones' . Though the Faerie denizens apparently possess the power to enter our existence whenever they so wish, the Fays may be looked upon only if they desire it or if they have been careless. Characteristically sensitive humans such as psychics, practitioners of the esoteric arts and many children, however may see the 'good folk' more frequently. Many of our ancestors considered that the Fays and all supernatural creatures for that matter, were better not seen at all. Frequently charms, talismans and superstitions (many of which still exist to this day) were employed with the specific aim of keeping such shadowy figures at bay.

Again, the question remains unanswered - have any of these creatures existed at any time, in whatsoever shape or form within these isles ? And if so, do they still ? Rumours of encounters with supernatural creatures have drifted down the centuries to us and purported sightings do on occasion still occur, though confrontations with particular entities are increasingly infrequent. Suggested reasons for this include the obvious destruction and depletion of many natural habitats, and also the general swing of mankind's psyche away from its fundamental (perhaps even spiritual) connection to the world and towards greater cynicism and isolation as a species. However due to the very essence and unpredictability of such encounters, substantial and verifying proof remains of course extremely ambiguous.

Observers of such strange sights in our times may often remain silent about their experiences, so as to avoid the risk of being ridiculed. They may scrutinise their minds in search of rational explanations and even begin to question their own eyesight or sanity. Do they exist then? ... maybe ... maybe not, but if you the reader just happen to hear an unfamiliar, blood-curdling sound or see something very strange indeed, perhaps only out of the corner of your eye, then it is hoped that this guide book will help you identify the encounter. Happy searching and good luck ... you'll need it.

NOTE: 16th July 2019
For this the revised edition of Strange Lands, I have taken the opportunity to include a new chapter - New Breeds. This looks at some of the new entities of folklore that have come into being in the 20th and 21st Century. Whilst most of these do not have Celtic origins as such, they are included because their influence has been felt within the British Isles.

Since the initial publication of Strange Lands I have been informed that the work of folklorist Ruth Tongue was not always the most diligent and some of the beings described by her (which feature in this book) may lend more to her personal imagination than to lore. I have not removed such entities from the book as in itself this is an example how lore develops with thoughts taking form perhaps like tulpas or conjurations of chaos magick. For instance initially Fairies were in bygone times rarely described as tiny winged creatures but following the popularisation of this form capturing the public information, many modern reported Faerie sightings describe such beings.

The Faerie Courts
(Also known as ~ Heroic Faeries. Noble Faeries. Courtly Faeries. The Sida.)

The Faerie Courts are stately communities reigned over by Kings and Queens, which in turn are answerable to a high King and Queen. They commonly inhabit the interiors of the perfectly curved grassy hills and ancient tumuli, which then become known as Fairy Hills, Bruth, Raths, Shi-en or Sidh amongst other names. They are occasionally sighted on solemn processions, with many of them riding handsome Faerie horses. This cortege is known as the Faerie Rade or Cavalcade. They indulge in pursuits such as hunting and sports like hurling, and many of their number are astounding musicians and craftsmen. However despite their refined culture, they are not human and their values and morals can sometimes differ greatly to what we may generally consider acceptable. They are known to cast powerful spells of illusion known as Glamour (or as Pishogue in Ireland). Some courts such as the Welsh Plant Annwn and the Irish Daoine Sidhe are commonly thought to have originally been worshipped as Celtic Gods (the Daoine Sidhe being associated with the Tuatha Danaan - the Children of Dana) but are thought to have lost their divine status in the advent of Christianity. They came also to be regarded by some as Fallen Angels, Neither loyal to God nor Lucifer in the War in Heaven , they were considered not evil enough for Hell yet not good enough for Heaven. As such they were either cast to earth or another intermediate place - the Otherworld. The Faerie Courts do not always exist in harmony on this world either, for a war between two rival Fay factions was reported in Kilkenny, Ireland in 1800. So violent was this conflict that the thorn trees stretching miles around were said to have been drenched in Faerie blood (alas though the colour of the blood was not stated, for some claim that Faerie blood is white rather than red). Though they may be a great wonder to behold, like all Fay breeds the Courtly Faeries must always be considered potentially very dangerous.

Range of the Faerie Courts -
Daoine Sidhe (People of the Hollow Hills) - Ireland
Seelie Court (also known as The People of Peace and the Sith) - Scotland
Tylwyth Teg (Fair Folk), Bendith y Mamau (Mother's Blessing) & Plant Annwn - Wales
Sleigh Beggey (also known as the Feathag, Squinters and Mooinger Veggey) - Isle of Man

Trooping Faeries

(Also known as ~ Gregarious Faeries. Shee-og. Macara-Shee. Sia Bhrugh. Sioghbhrugh. Siobhrogh. the Fatara. Fee / Feetauds. Fayules.)

Trooping Faeries bear some similarities to the Faerie Courts though they are often less aristocratic. Troops are to be found across the British Isles and though a few may bear allegiance to a major Court, many are independent. Some troops have their own King and / or Queen, though not all. Faerie Troops are renowned for being extremely territorial and feudal, and as the name suggests they do also troop. Their processions generally appear less majestic and more militaristic than the Courtly Faerie Rades. They tend also to be on foot rather than horseback. Manx Faeries such as the Hillmen, Hogmen and Ferrishyn are particularly thorough in their trooping, even to the extent of carrying their abode in its entirety (including the hill) on their shoulders, to new locations. (Many Faeries however use magic rather than manual labour to move home etc. The words " Horse and Hattock" or "Borram" apparently are frequently used by Fays to invoke flight and transportation.) Faerie Troops commonly follow established routes and would not hesitate to cause havoc or even physically move human buildings constructed on their path. People who pry impertinently or try to hamper the progress of the Trooping Faeries may find themselves inflicted with Strokes, insanity or other unpleasant conditions.

Appearance : Depending on individual Troops, can range between crude and elegant, though rarely reaching the grandeur of the Courts. Likewise manners and looks can vary from boorish to charming. Often subtle or obvious deformities or quirks are apparent. Shape-shifting abilities frequently evident. Certain tribes often sport particular colours. Some individuals may be winged.

Size : Variable, from a few inches tall to human proportions.

Diet : Again dependent on particular Troop. Many steal grain, milk, liquor and honey from human supplies. Others feed on essences, the plant silverweed (7th Bread) or other strange and perhaps unpleasant victuals. Some are rumoured to get drunk on flower nectar.

Habitat & Range : Faerie-hills, woods and caverns across the British Isles, Ireland and also in Brittany (where the females are known as Fees and the males as Feetauds).

The individual Faerie Troops are known by many different names (e.g. Farisees, Processionaries etc.), depending on their locality, habits or distinguishing features).

Merry Dancers
(Also known as ~ Fir Chlis. Na Fir Chis. Faerie Dancers. Toadstool Faeries. Perry Dancers. Moon Dancers. Nimble Men.)

At night it is sometimes possible to be drawn to or chance upon Faeries engaging in a fervent and beguiling dance. The music and motion is incredibly intoxicating and could likely entrance and entice the human viewer into participating. To do so could likely prove to be a dangerous folly. Those who do join the dance could find themselves gyrating in circles for far longer than planned. They may dance for eternity unable to stop themselves, or otherwise collapse in exhaustion, only to awaken where they fell in company but now to find the spot deserted. To them only a single night will have seemed to pass, but they shall soon discover that perhaps many years have in fact transcended and their life, possessions and loved ones may now be no more than distant memories. Even the merest encounter with a Faery dance could possibly provoke ennui, melancholy and wasting diseases. Therefore, anyone seeking out such a ceremony would be well advised to engage the services of a well ear-plugged companion to hold their coat tails and prevent them putting more than a single step into the soiree.

It is not certain whether the Faerie dancers belong to a particular Troop (Courtly festivities commonly occur within the hills) or are various Troops / Solitary Fays meeting up for festivities. Some Scots believe the Merry Dancers or Fir Chlis are the souls of Fallen Angels. (These names have also been used to refer to the Aurora Borealis or Northern Lights, the shimmering waves of colour sometimes seen in the night sky. This natural phenomena was also once regarded as Fays dancing in the dark or dusky sky.) Therefore depending upon individual or particular Fay species, the Merry Dancers could either be beautifully radiant or somewhat uncanny. Either way their music and festivities could often prove to be dangerously enticing to mortals.

The boundaries of the dances are marked on their circumference by a growth of either lush or withered grass, or alternatively by a ring of mushrooms or toadstools. These are known as Fairy Rings. To wilfully destroy such a ring was thought not only to be futile as in time it will likely regenerate itself, but also foolhardy as to do so was believed to invite grave misfortune upon oneself. Some megalithic stone circles may also mark the boundaries of Faerie dances.

dancers considerably smaller.

Habitat & Range : Commonly in meadows and wooded glades across Britain, Ireland and Brittany.

Muryans and the Teulu

Fay species are not necessarily immortal though their life-span is thought to out-measure human longevity by centuries rather than years. Ultimately many grow old and die, therefore mournful funeral processions may be observed on occasion. Usually the Fays inter their dead at infinitesimal size and carry their deceased on a leaf. The visionary English artist, William Blake recorded his observations of such an event, yet some Faerie-watchers believe that the Faeries are indeed immortal but either way their funerals are nothing more than mockeries of human grieving. In Wales, such phantasmal processions involving either diminutive Fays or man-size spectres occurred on occasion enough for them to be known as the Teulu or Goblin Funeral. The word 'Teulu' can be taken to mean 'a train of attendants' whilst the 'Goblin' funeral can equally be applied to Phantoms as to Fays or actual Goblins. Frequently they were perceived to be a prophecy of a real funeral soon to follow. On Dartmoor in Devon, Otherworldly funeral processions may be seen conducted by Headless Ghosts and Hooded Entities, more generally considered to be Phantom Monks rather than Faeries. Separate visitors to the moor related seeing such doleful processions both in the regions of Wistman's Wood and Fox-Tor Mire. A similar sight involving maudlin black caped figures was reputedly beheld by several children on Clonmillan Hall near Edenberry in Ireland and members of my own family have told of a vanishing collective of souls in Victorian mourning-attire seen in County Durham.

In Cornwall however, it was deemed unlucky to knowingly kill an ant, for these familiar insects could in fact be Fay folk in their final living form. These insect-fays are known as Muryans (or Meryons) and their appearance is a consequence of their youthful shape-shifting. Each time a Faerie transforms it expends astral energy known as Prana, and as a result each shift will cause its original form to diminish. Prolonged bouts of maintaining an assumed form can be extremely stressful to Faerie health; for instance on the very rare occasions that a Faerie has willingly adopted a human guise and lifestyle in order to be with a more mortal lover, they could only do so for a year at a time. To do so for even an additional day could prove fatal. The youngest and fittest could sometimes compensate by alternating between a year in the human domain and a year's rest in the Faerie realm. This however would still shorten their life-expectancy somewhat.

Ultimately though the shape-shifting Faeries may eventually be reduced to the unalterable size and shape of an ant. The form in which they will end their days. Other theories claim that the Muryans are actually

the souls of deceased humans that have been consigned to Purgatory or the souls of Druids condemned for not embracing Christianity or the souls of unbaptised children and therefore it is similarly unfortunate to tread on them. This however did not prevent Herbalists in other regions crushing ants and their eggs and mixing them with other ingredients to produce remedies that hopefully would cure ailments such as deafness, warts and broken hearts.

Whilst the Cornish word for 'ant' is 'Murrain', it is possible that the name 'Muryans' was a colloquial euphemism (translating into standard English as 'Merry Ones'), intended to placate the Fays, even in this deteriorated state. However it may also be noted that the colony of ants that were transformed into men by Zeus in Greek myth were known as Myrmidons.

Pixies
(Also known as ~ Piskies. Pigsies. Puggies. Pechs. Pichs. Dusters. Grigs. Colepexies.)

The Pixies share numerous similarities to the Faeries, but are actually an individual and separate Fay species. They are very territorial and in some locations the Pixies have entirely driven out the Faeries. Buckland St. Mary in Somerset was reputed to have been the site of a great battle between the Pixies and red-clad Faeries. The Pixies were hailed to be the victors of this conflict and claimed all land west of the River Parret to be Pixie territory.

Pixies tend also to inhabit grassy hills, which in these instances are known as Pixy-mounds. Commonly only male Pixies are usually sighted, though it is sometimes claimed that they are ruled only by Queens. The numerous peculiarities of this species include stealing or capturing ponies and horses and riding them to exhaustion around grassy circles known as Gallitraps. A Gallitrap is very similar to a Fairy Ring and for a human to step inside one could lead to entrapment or enchantment. Some folk felt that Gallitraps were more aptly called "Gallows' Traps". This is due to the belief that a person entrapped within its boundaries would be destined to eternally wander in circles unless a priest and a judge were brought to the scene. The minister would then break the spell through the power of prayer and the magistrate would then judge the man be hanged. Presumably the beguiled victim received such a harsh sentence due to the notion that they were now tainted and corrupted beyond redemption by their supernatural encounter. The Pixies can also cause humans to become entirely lost in normally familiar surroundings; a process known as being Pixy-led (see also Shellycoats. Ignis Faatus and Stray Sods.). Local people employ various folk-remedies to prevent or counter this and also to deter the Pixies from entering houses and throwing pots and pans around. Pixies are usually mischievous rather than outright malevolent and in Cornwall it is considered lucky to see one, but care should be taken around their haunts as they are potentially dangerous and their mischief sometimes borders on the malicious.

Some people think that the Pixies may be the souls of children who died before they were baptised or alternatively that they are the living folk-memories of native Pictish tribes.

Pixies are travellers or nomads and that they move around the country holding 'Pixy-fairs' (various Faerie Troops also hold 'Markets'.) The discovery in fields, of a fine scattering of phosphorous or metallic dust may be indicative of a Pixy presence.

Pixie Breeds

The Geancanach are a similar species known in Ireland and also the Hebrides.

Cornish coastal Pixies are known as Bucca.

Grigs are a closely related species to Pixies, though are more likely to be foundfrequenting apple orchards.

Similar, though slightly more Dwarf-like, creatures known as Derricks frequented the moors of Devon, Berkshire and Hampshire. Whilst the Home County Derricks would point a lost human traveller in the right direction, their West Country cousins would be more likely to deliberately give erroneous and perhaps even hazardous guidance.

Elves.

(Singular ~ Elf . Also known as ~ Wood-Elves. Mannikins. Ouph. Alfs. Alfar. Alps. Aelfs. Ellyllon. Ellylldan.)

The term 'Elf' has oft been used to describe a woodland Faerie or a particularly troublesome Faerie, but this is a misnomer as Elves are a different and separate Fay species. Whereas it has been suggested that in the far distant past the Faeries originally emigrated to these isles from the Mediterranean and Middle East; the localised colonies of Elves resident in Britain and Ireland initially had their roots in the Scandinavian and Germanic lands (where they are known as Alfs or Alps). Indeed in those lands the Elves actually prohibited the general spread of the Faerie breeds. Whether these Elves arrived in these lands with the Anglo-Saxon and Viking invaders or actually came earlier upon their own volition is uncertain. Elves also tend to live in communities reigned by Kings and Queens. Though in their native lands Elves can inhabit a variety of habitats, the British colonies exclusively dwell in wooded areas. They are known to be phenomenal musicians, weavers and jewellery-makers.

There are Light Elves and Dark Elves, which relates both to their colouring and to their general character. The Light Elves occupy the crowns of tall trees and are often the music makers whilst the Dark Elves may work metal in forges beneath the tree roots. In the colonies several shades between light and dark likely exist, though in their native lands they rarely mingle. In the Scandinavian territories their main kingdoms respectively were Alfheim and Swartheim. At their most extreme, the Dark Elves share more in common with Goblins than with the Light Elves (though Elves and Goblins were traditionally considered unfavourable towards the other). The immigrant Elven hierarchy within Britain is uncertain, but it is often thought that they held a monarchy. Leaders of the true Teutonic/ Norse Elves were said to include the nefarious Erlking (or Erlkonig) the regent of the Germanic Dark Elves, and also Holda (or Frau Holle). This Elven queen (who formerly may have been regarded by humans as a Goddess), wavered between being kindly and malicious towards mankind. All Elves in these isles however, are not particularly fond of humans though some may take pleasure in making their lives especially difficult. Amongst various pranks they are known to weave knots (Elf-locks) into human hair and horse manes which are enchanted to cause bad luck if untangled. Often however they will generally try to avoid mankind whenever possible.

Generally, solitary Elves are more malign than the individuals belonging to Troops. Humans who particularly displease the Elves, either knowingly or unwittingly, tend to be thoroughly dealt with. They could become injured, demented or even killed by being struck with cursed flint projectiles known as Elf-shot or Elf-bolts. Otherwise the touch of an Elf's long slender fingers can induce a detrimental medical condition once known as Elf-stroke, now often simply called Stroke. Light Elves have pale skin, blue eyes and fair hair; whilst Dark Elves have black hair, black eyes and either pale or dark skin. They can be either short and plump or slender with delicate sharp features, slanted eyes and pointed ears. Many have two small bumps on their foreheads above the eyes, which may be due to their acute psychic ability.

Stone Faeries
(Also known as ~ Stone Spinners. Ladies of Stone. Pyrenees.
Watchers. Saresyns.)
Scattered across the British Isles and Ireland are many megalithic monuments such as stone circles, dolmens, cairns and solitary standing stones. Many are the work of ancient architects and were designed as sites of sacred worship, burial grounds, route markers and agricultural /astronomical clocks. Others however may be the Stone Faeries frozen in time and space by the prayers and curses of certain Saints. Their stony fate decreed by their refusal to give up their wayward, heathen dancing. Some of the dancers may have been human in their natural lives yet others were already of Fay genealogy. The Devil himself played the fiddle (or some say pipes) at Stanton Drew, causing a normally god-fearing community to continue dancing into the Sabbath. Beguiled or willing they paid the price of sin by being transformed into a circle of standing stones.

During the day they maintain their silent and eternal vigil, entombed in their rock coffins, yet sometimes at night and especially under the rays of the moon, the Stone Faeries may again feel the freedom of their limbs. Though of course they resume their dance with enthusiasm, some also are to be found weaving the fabrics of time itself upon huge stone wheels - hence their alternative name of 'Stone Spinners'.

Come the rays of dawn, the maidens are again consigned to their grave destiny. In either form they propound the suggestion of fertility, and barren women were once prone to visit these stones in the hope that they may then conceive.

Similar tales of stones that once bore flesh and breathed air can be found across the length and breadth of the British Isles. Noteworthy examples include the Wookey Witch, a stalagmite to be found in a cave near Wells, Somerset and the Whispering Knights, part of the Rollright Stones close to the Oxfordshire – Warwickshire borders. Whilst the Wookey Witch was said to have been petrified by a Glastonbury coenobite sprinkling holy water upon her in response to her spiteful selfish ways : the Whispering Knights were pious men who had been condemned by a local Malefactor. Even as megaliths the Whispering Knights may be heard to some ears to be quietly muttering about events yet to pass.

During daylight they appear as cold stone monoliths and only give the rare fleeting suggestion of a melancholic sigh or expression. In the lunar rays, the transformation is profound as they appear as pretty young women with pale, iridescent complexions and soft long hair.

Hyter Sprites
(Also known as ~ Hyters.)

Hyter Sprites are an unusual and very localised Fay breed, who metamorphose from a small but humanoid frame into the form of birds. They may either be encountered in small groups or congregated in flocks of considerable number and are generally shy or indifferent to human presence. At times though they may swoop at people either out of mischief or as a defensive manoeuvre. Either anthropoid , avian or in a form that is a conglomerate of both, they are most active at late afternoon or early evening. The Hyter Sprites have been claimed at times to show a beneficent side by leading home lost human children.

In some parts of Norfolk however, the Hyter Sprites bore a more unpleasant reputation as some folk believed that they would lead people woefully astray in deep woods with their nocturnal chirping. Others still thought these creatures would spirit away naughty children or at least led their offspring to believe so in a bid to attain better behaviour. Some people said that the Hyter Sprites were prone to invading and vandalising any home that still bore Christmas decorations after the 12th Night (January 6th - the Epiphany).

Appearance: They range from small, spindly-legged , pointy-nosed Fays to complete Avian form (though many may maintain a more anthropomorphic face). In England they assume the form of Sand Martins (their foreign counterparts may also sometimes be more similar to larger birds such as Buzzards and Vultures). Their eyes are commonly green.

Size: In Britain, rarely larger than 5 inches (13 cm) tall.

Diet: Uncertain.

Habitat & Range: In Britain, local only to East Anglia, England (though the Suffolk Ferier Trooping Faeries have also been claimed to occasionally take a similar bird form).- Hyter Sprite type creatures have also been reported overseas in Spain and Mexico, so there may be a possibility that they are seasonally migratory.

Spriggans
(Also known as ~ Ghost-giants. Speryson.)

Though their music is often appealing, the same cannot be said for the Spriggans' behaviour and appearance. These coastal Fays keep themselves busy by looting human houses, abducting children, blighting crops, infecting or stealing livestock and by causing destructive storms. They viciously guard hoards of treasure which they hide in hills and caverns. In times past they would watch and wait as pirates and smugglers hid their booty in sea caves and as soon as the human rogues vacated the area, the Spriggans would claim the ill-gotten gains for themselves.

Spriggans gained their alternative name of 'Ghost-giants' from their unsettling ability to grow from tiny to massive proportions. This made some observers think that they were actually witnessing the ghosts of dead giants. The psychological effects of such a transformation were heightened when performed en-masse by fully armed Spriggan guards as they trooped. By altering their size as they marched the Spriggans would thus alter the laws of perspective and cause disorientation and confusion amongst their quarry. Despite their coastal habitat the Spriggans cannot touch salt-water, so in the event of such an encounter, a retreat into the sea (preferably by boat) is best advised.

Appearance: Unkempt and ugly. Rough, often bristly skin of varying dour, earthy hues. Leery, mean and shifty faces. They wear coarse, weather-beaten clothing and may carry daggers, coshes, slings or other weapons as well as Jew's-harps, reeds and other musical instruments. Many of them wear red caps. The females are very rarely seen but are no prettier.

Size : Extremely variable on a whim, from several inches to colossal heights.

Diet : Whatever they can steal or scavenge, probably including alcohol.

Habitat & Range: Caverns, hills, ruins, standing stones, cliffs and beaches, predominantly on or near Selena moor and the Cornish coast, England and localised smaller colonies in Ireland.

Spriggans were also sometimes apparently encountered roaming inside the Cornish tin-mines (see also Kobolds and Mine Spirits).

Korred

(Also known as ~ Korreds. Korregs. Specific Breeds include ~ **Couril. Kourils. Korriks. Carikines. Korrikaned. Korandon. Couretes. Chorriquets. Gwazig-Gon. Corics. Hommes-Corrus. Poulpikens. Korrs. Kores. Jetins. Kerions. Korrigans. Sauvageons.)**

The Korred are the dominant Fay race of Celtic France and are chiefly associated with ancient megaliths such as the standing stones of Carnac in Brittany. Some people believe that the Korred were the architects and constructors of all the ancient monuments and earthworks, and that they now dwell beneath these stones guarding them from physical and spiritual damage. It is also sometimes suspected that the Korreds are also protecting hordes of treasure that may be buried beneath the soil and slabs. Humans that venture near the sacred stones do so at their own risk for some Korred breeds such as the Korrs and Korriks will defend the site with formidable enthusiasm.

However should a person approach with due respect then they will much less likely be manhandled. Furthermore, for the right price the Korred could prove to be of benefit to mankind. If a blunt knife or other tool were to be left, alongside a coin, overnight at a known Korred haunt, then come the morning the implement may be found well-sharpened and the money gone. However anyone who lingers nearby with the hope of looking upon the Korred at work will likely return home with a dull blade and either no sighting or nips and bruises for their troubles. Also should a farmer allow his livestock (especially pigs) to graze near a Korred dwelling, then the animals should be well tended by the Korred, upon the understanding that they will receive a generous piece of smoked fat when the beasts come to be slaughtered.

The Korred are also extremely fond of feasting and dancing especially on Wednesdays which they deem sacred (the first Wednesday in May is apparently of particular importance to them). Their frenetic dancing may scorch the earth beneath their feet or fungi may fruit where their feet once trod (see also Merry Dancers). Should the opportunity arise, humans are ill-advised to partake in a Korred dance for men-folk are liable to collapse and die from exhaustion whilst women may suddenly fall pregnant. There is a strange humour to the Korred magic furthermore, as when the lady gives birth nine months later, the child will bear a striking resemblance to some man living in the same village as the woman. Though both may swear denial or ignorance of any intimate liaison, suspicion and speculation will surely arise, as may all manner of associated problems. Good-looking children were often considered at risk from being kidnapped and replaced, by the Korred.

The Unseelie Court
(Also known as ~ The Unseely Court. The Host. The Sluagh. Fiah Ri. Oisteag Sluaigh. Slua-Si. Sluag. Adh Sidhe. Unsele Wiht. The People's Puff of Wind. The Faerie Wind. The Faerie Horde. The Fair Eddy. Wicked Wichts. Farish. Guillyen Veggy. The Spirit Multitude. Sheen-ny-Feaynid. The Sounds of Infinity.)

The Unseelie Court are a motley collective of Faeries banished from the Seelie Court (a less malevolent Faerie community), for breaking their code of conduct, assorted Bogies and Goblins and even the souls of evil dead humans. As ' Seely' is an archaic word meaning 'Blessed' or 'Joyful', it becomes grievously apparent that 'Unseely' creatures are anything but that. The Unseelie Court are all murderous and vile, yet perhaps most petrifying to behold are their number that appear as the Sluagh or Host. These manifest as an ominous and sinister black cloud moving in from the western sky. It is only when it gets far too close for comfort that the individual members become apparent; their cruel, lecherous faces contorting with loathsome pleasure and their twisted bodies all mingling and transforming. By then it is probably too late for the human observer to make their escape. They are likely to be severely dragged into the air and carried for many miles, all the while being roughly manhandled and forced to indulge in their abhorrent pursuits, including the torture of animals and other humans with the use of Elf-shot (see Elves).

If the human survives such an ordeal they will probably be driven into babbling insanity. Otherwise their broken and battered body will be discarded without dignity a long distance from the site of capture. If of questionable character anyway, then their soul will be absorbed into the writhing mass of the Host.

If a foreboding dark cloud is seen moving rapidly eastwards, then it is wise to get indoors instantly or if this is not possible then to cling tightly to a tree or whatever, and to start praying. Sometimes the declaration of "God Bless You" may be enough to protect both yourself and to cause the Host to release any unfortunate that they may have also recently spirited away. Some also thought that to hurl your left shoe at the Host before it claimed you or to wear a sprig of Rowan fixed to the clothing, may also be effective remedies against the ill wind. The Unseelie Court and other associated malevolent Faerie Hosts, may wander near or far at twilight, (one tale describes how the host finally released a captive as far away as North America).

On the Isle of Man the Host are known as The Sounds of Infinity, due to the bloodcurling sounds that they emit.

The Fomorii
(Also known as ~ Fomors. Fomorians. Fomoire. Fooar. Sea-gods. Old Gods. _Sea-Devils. Sea-Demons. Children of Domnhu. Tuatha de Domhain.)

The Fomorii were a race of semi-aquatic fiends that would leave the sea at night to wreak havoc, extortion and slaughter upon the land. Perhaps the most fearsome member of this extremely weird army was the warrior giant known as Balor of the Baleful Eye. So malignant was the gaze from his one functional eye that it could cause crops to wither and brave warriors and their horses to shrivel and burn. It took several of his vile henchmen using ropes and pulleys to hold open Balor's eyelids during prolonged battles. Balor's grandson, Lugh Lhamfada - the Celtic Shining One who was of mixed Fomorian / Danaan blood, later managed to blind his grandfather in battle, thus disabling the deadly prowess of the eye. Following the Fomorii's defeat at the hands of the Tuatha de Danaan and the execution and beheading of Balor, their survivors scattered near and far. It is possible that certain supernatural creatures such as some Water Ogres, Wraths, Foawrs and Muardhuachas may have evolved or descended from the disbanded Fomorii.

Other notable Fomorian fiends were the dreadful female Fomorian warrior - Lot, who had hungry mouths situated on her breasts and four extra eyes in her back, and Searbhan - a one-eyed, one-legged, one-armed giant. Despite his apparent shortcomings, Searbhan was a considerably fearsome warrior.

Appearance: Extremely variable, but all were described as being twisted and deformed, often missing a single or several features or limbs (though this did not prohibit their savage warmongering). Their skin texture varied from slimy to scaly, leathery to hairy and they were often composed of hybrid animal parts.

Size : Balor was the largest, possibly standing between 20 - 100 ft (6 - 30 m) tall.
The other Fomorii varied from stunted halflings to immense proportions.

Diet : Varied - fish, flesh and probably alcohol. they may also have derived intoxication from drinking human or Fay tears drunk from chalices or scooped-out skulls.

Habitat & Range: Originally settled in and around Ireland, with smaller colonies in the Scottish Highlands and the Isle of Man. Individuals may have later moved further away. Before their downfall the stronghold of Balor was said to be Tory Island off the coast of Donegal.

Firbolgs
(Also known as ~ Bag-men. Bog-men. Bog-trotters.)

The Firbolgs were fairly primitive marsh dwellers who escaped to Ireland from a life of slavery in the east. Though they ruled Ireland for a short time it wasn't long before the were oppressed by the Fomorii. However they allied themselves with the tyrants in the war against the Tuatha de Danaan. The Firbolgs though were defeated and dispersed before the fall of Balor. Several individuals likely remained in hiding in the quagmires of Ireland, though others fled or were driven out of the land and likely took up scattered residence around the British Isles. Whilst some Firbolgs were enslaved by the conquering humans or served as mercenary warriors in their armies, others dispersed into the shadows and dark places. The bitterness of their conquest possibly caused them to become darker and more loathsome both in appearance and behaviour, gradually evolving into Ballybogs, Peat Faerys, Mudbogs, Bog a Boos, Boogies, Bogles and the other foul and similar swamp species.

Appearance: Dark and hairy, stunted with heavy brows. Filth encrusted and often foully odious.

Size: Originally, rarely over 5 ft (1.5 m) tall , the suspected evolved species are often smaller.

Diet: Initially they likely hunted and farmed. After their ostracism, they may have resolved to eating rats, frogs, slugs, carrion and other meat they could steal or slaughter. It is uncertain whether they actually ate children, or whether this was just a scare story to keep kiddies away from the obvious real dangers of marshland. Also likely to steal more generally palatable foodstuffs such as vegetables and milk whenever possible.

Habitat & Range : In and around fen-land. Originally emigrated to Ireland from Thrace (now Bulgaria /Greece). Possibly moved later into Britain and beyond. It has been suggested however that some of the Firbolgs who lingered in Ireland took to living inside Raths (prehistoric hill Forts) and even adapted to wearing more modern clothing ...well at least as up-to-date attire as that worn by 18th Century peasants.

The Coranied
(Also known as ~ The Coranians. The Coritani. The Koraneid.)

As the gruesome race of Fomorii sought to possess Ireland in ancient times, so too did a strange supernatural race seek to enslave Wales and Southern England. This mysterious race was known as the Coranied, and so awesome was their esoteric knowledge that they yielded the power to hear upon the wind any word spoken by man, no matter how low the whisper.
The Coranied invasion of South Britain was thwarted by the efforts of two brothers, Llud and Llevellys. Their means of avoiding conquest involved the crushing of certain unspecified insects into water and spraying the resulting bug-brew upon the Coranied. This concoction was to prove lethal to the invaders whilst remaining entirely harmless to the ancient Britons.

The Coranied are shrouded in mystery partly due to early commentators' lack of detailed description but also to the ambiguity of their origins. Some authors have compared them to the Korrigan (in the broader sense of Breton Faeries also known as Korred or Korregs, rather than specifically to the Loathly Ladies). And indeed the Coranied were reputed to use Glamour in the deceptive manner of some Fays and Witches - e.g. to give dry leaves the appearance of gold coins. However other Welsh text has alluded to the Coranied originating in Arabia. Therefore the Coranied could have been Arabian Sorcerer-Warriors of human lineage or if they were actually of an entirely supernatural bloodline, then perhaps they could be comparable to the Arabian Demons called Djinn (also known as Jinni or Genies). These creatures that possessed great magical abilities were borne from fire or the lustre of gems and like the Coranied bore a special relationship with the wind. However whilst certain comparisons can be drawn there is not enough specific material concerning the Coranied currently available to say for sure whether desert–dwelling Djinn did indeed descend on the lush Welsh valleys in ancient times.

Changelings

(Also known as ~ Plentyn-Newid. Change-Children. Crimbils. Sibhreach. Sharg Bairns. Faerie-children. Killcrops. Sithbheire.)

Many Fay and Gnomic breeds are notorious for abducting human infants from their cribs and cots. The reasons for doing so can vary; it could be to genetically diverse their bloodline or to pay a Teind or Tithe to Hell. This is a sacrifice that the Devil demands of many of the Social Faerie communities and is usually due every seven years, but how this arrangement originally came about and of what benefit it is to the Faeries is not certain. Other breeds may snatch children for capricious, broody or malicious ends but many will leave a substitute in its place. This is known as a Changeling and can either be a Fay child or alternatively an extremely old individual. The Changelings are glamorised to closely resemble the original human infant, yet there is always something not quite right that provokes suspicion. They could be jaundiced, wizened or otherwise somehow peculiar or sickly looking. Likewise they could be extremely demanding or foul-tempered.

Most commonly the abduction or exchange of a human infant for a Fay replacement would occur entirely unseen. However in some accounts from the Welsh valley of Ebury Fawr, alarmed parents were reputed to have witnessed their babies being spirited into the air by a clutch of visible or invisible Faerie hands.

There were various options open to parents that were suspicious that their offspring had been replaced. These methods could either trick the Changeling into revealing their true identity or pressurise the Fays into retrieving their progeny and restoring their own child to its proper home. As some of the more extreme procedures included beating or burning the suspected Changeling, this was unfortunate and dangerous to any child that was actually human but somehow 'unconventional'. It is conceivable that in more medically-unenlightened times, children born with conditions that produce pronounced physical characteristics may have fallen under suspicion of being Changelings. (Extreme and fatal remedies for Changelings and Stocks account for several murder / manslaughter trials, particularly in Ireland and not always in so distant a past as one may assume.) The few Changelings to grow into adolescence or adulthood in a human habitat were commonly somehow retarded or unhealthy, though rare individuals would become extremely creatively-gifted and particularly sensitive to the natural, supernatural and psychic world. Again though they would likely be unusual in both manner and appearance, and would often be dreamy outsiders.

Prize cows were sometimes also swapped for sickly, senescent Changelings.

Stocks

Adult humans would also on occasion be taken by the Fay folk, often for similar reasons to the child abductions, but also sometimes due to infatuation and desire (and if bygone clergymen are to be believed, sometimes also for persistently missing mass on Sundays). Some would willingly enter the Faerie realm perhaps to embark on a romantic affair, whilst others would become trapped by tasting Faerie food and drink or by participating in their dances. Others may have been taken as servants, midwives or slaves. These would often vanish without trace never to be seen again, at least not in their original form or not for many, many years. On seldom occasions individuals were rescued and retrieved but many of them found their normal life now exceedingly difficult to cope with. Other human adults however were suddenly and unwittingly spirited from their homes and beds. These people were not replaced with Changelings, but instead with Stocks. (Occasionally a child taken by the Faeries would also be replaced with a Stock.)

Stocks initially closely resembled the human victims, but would soon grow very ill, immobile and take to their beds. There they would languish and waste away often becoming increasingly paralysed and vacant minded. They would not live for long, but as death approached strange details became progressively apparent. The texture and colouring of their skin became wooden to sight and touch. They would begin to rot but not in the meaty way of a normal cadaver, instead they would smell and look like a decomposing piece of timber; for indeed the Stocks were actually glamorised wooden effigies.

On 4th July 1895, a man by the name of Michael Cleary was found guilty by the court of Clonmel in South Tipperary, Ireland of the manslaughter of his wife Bridget Cleary and was sentenced to 20 years imprisonment. Superstition was the cause of the woman's maltreatment and eventual burning to death at the hands of her husband, for all was initially well in their household. This changed for the worse as his wife began to sicken with something and influenced by the words of local Wise-folk, Cleary became convinced that the feeble specimen in front of him was not his betrothed but in fact an Otherworldly clone substituted by either the Faeries or Witches. The desperate measures that Michael Cleary finally found himself resorting to, did not see his 'true' love returned to him but instead marked him as a killer and caused also the loss of his freedom for two decades.

Fir Darrig
(Also known as ~ Fear Dearg. Red Men. Rat Boys.)

These very strange creatures will seek out human presence and though not evil as such, do delight in scaring people and playing practical jokes upon them that they are highly unlikely to find amusing. To show the Fir Darrig polite (if contrived) respect and especially to offer him food and gifts may inspire him to partake in conversation. Whatever he says however should be taken with a pinch of salt as truth or lies are of no real consequence to him and may be treated as just another game. There may though be some wisdom in his words, as he sometimes claims that he was once human but that his current countenance is due to years spent trapped in the Faerie kingdom. Whether he went willingly, through entrapment or abduction may differ in his accounts, though he will commonly and quite ironically remind the human listener of the dangers involved in encountering Fay beings.

Appearance & Attire: The Fir Darrig are most peculiar. Their pointy ears and shifty eyes peek out of the shadow cast by their tall hats. They often have big dirty, grey or ginger beards and straggly hair. Their skin is brownish - red and bristly and their noses often resemble a rodent's snout. A long rough tail, rather like that of a rat, protrudes from beneath a lengthy, patch-worked and commonly red trench coat. Their feet can grasp as efficiently as their hands. They may be seen carrying a shillelagh (Black-thorn wood walking stick) that is mounted with a human skull. Only males are usually sighted.

Size : Generally under 1 ft (0.3 m) tall.

Diet: Especially fond of rotting fish, they scavenge amongst carrion and rubbish for tasty tit-bits. They will also gladly scrounge or steal a human's food.

Habitat & Range : May be sighted in a variety of environments including riverbanks, refuse tips and sewers. In rural and urban areas particularly those near the coast, mainly in Ireland and to a lesser extent Scotland. on occasion they have also been known to enter houses uninvited and seat themselves by the fire.

Urisk
(Also known as ~ Uruisg. Peallaidh. Ourisks.)

Despite being distantly related to the Greco-Roman Fauns and Satyrs, the Urisk does not share its Mediterranean cousins' legendary sense of hedonism. In a sharp contrast to the Bacchanalian feasts of wine, women and song; the Urisks are more likely to be observed sitting in contemplative solitude by lonely sylvan pools or taking leisurely woodland strolls. That is not to say that the Urisks are anti-social creatures, for they will often try to engage human ramblers in amiable conversation. However unfortunately for the Urisk, its enthusiastic approach and its startling appearance more often than not will cause any potential new friends to flee in terror. The alternative name of Peallaidh can specifically refer to the Urisk, but also is a generic term for other supernatural creatures that frequent Scottish bank-sides, such as the Shellycoats. The term Uruisg is sometimes used alternatively to refer to a similar creature that frequents waterfalls and is of a more dangerous disposition.

The Pilosi of Celtic Gaul were a similar looking race yet they did not share the Urisks' bashful gentleness. More akin to the Satyrs or perhaps to the Woodwose, these goat-footed wild-men were loud, brash and fond of wine, women. and food.

Appearance : The upper parts of the Urisks' bodies are commonly human-like, though often scrawny with slightly over-large heads and frequently hairy, dappled skin. They often have small horns and downy beards. The lower body parts are like those of goats. Any sightings of female Urisks remain uncertain, however it is possible that their women may actually be the species known as Glaistigs.

Size : Of slight human proportions.

Diet : Unknown.

Habitat & Range : Commonly close to river banks and fresh-water pools, in remote woodland in Scotland.

Ghillie Dhu
(Also known as ~ Gille Dubh.)

The Ghillie Dhu value their privacy very highly and do not appreciate the intrusion of prying eyes. Their habits and attire enable them to generally remain well-hidden amongst the foliage of the trees they frequent. They are extremely wary, perhaps even paranoid of human presence and seem to regard us all as unwelcome intruders. Should they consider a human to be scrutinising or pursuing them, then they have the power to cause the fronds and under-storey growth of the woodland to writhe up and bind them fast. As the captured human is left to the mercy of the forest, the Ghillie Dhu would make their exit. In contrast however, the Ghillie Dhu were sometimes said to ensure that lost human children would remain safe from harm.

Appearance & Attire : They are pale, dishevelled and clothed in garments rendered from leaves, moss and foliage.
Size : Usually of slight human proportions.
Diet : Unknown.
Habitat & Range : Birch woods and copses in Scotland.

Bugul Noz
(Also known as ~ The Night Shepherd.)

Being the last of his kind, the sad and lonely Bugul Noz has too much time to brood and think. Occupying much of his thought is the matter of his appearance, though far from being vain the Bugul Noz is rather preoccupied with his ugliness. Though he may subconsciously long for company he is deeply afraid of the rejection, repulsion and terror that his looks may cause. Therefore for this reason the Bugul Noz only ventures out under the cover of darkness. Should anyone approach him then he will seek a hiding place from which he will order people to be on their way home for the night is no time to linger outdoors.
Some people say that even animals recoil in horror at the Bugul Noz's appearance, yet others insist that tends to flocks of sheep, hence his alternative name of the Night Shepherd.

Yann-An-Od
(Also Known as ~ Yan-An-Od. John of the Dunes.)

It has been suggested that Yann-An-Od was once the King of a Faerie Court and therefore possibly also once recognised as a Celtic God; but it is unknown what happened to his family, kingdom and subjects as he now wanders alone, the last of his kind. Despite his solitude, he does not seek the company of mankind and will often vanish should anyone approach him. He may however holler a warning from the seashore, should any sailors appear to be navigating their vessels too close to the reefs or shallows. Like the Bugul Noz, he may also sometimes take it upon himself to instruct humans caught wandering at night to get back indoors. Unlike the Bugul Noz, Yann-An-Od has been known to shriek at and even slap those who do not heed his advice.

Appearance : Yann-An-Od is a Shape-Shifter who may appear as a Dwarf, a Giant or man-size. If encountered by the coast then he frequently appears as a fisherman dressed in oil-skins, leaning on an oar and gazing out to sea. If however he is observed inland, then it is often in the shape of an elderly shepherd with a long white beard and dressed in lengthy robes.
Size : Variable at will.
Diet : Unknown.
Habitat & Range : Shores, meadows and pastures in Brittany.

Urchins
(Also known as ~ Hedge-hursts. Hurgeons. Prickly-back Orchuns.)

At first glance they may very closely resemble regular hedgehogs (which are sometimes also known as Urchins in local dialect). However on closer inspection, several distinct differences are noticeable; their limbs or facial features may appear strangely anthropomorphic and their eyes may be unusually coloured or betray a keen intellect. They may even be wearing a cap or neckerchief, for these are not conventional hedgehogs by any means. The people of England's West Country consider the Urchins to be transformed Pixies and will therefore show them the same cautious regard. In Ireland they have a darker reputation perhaps, as they are suspected to be human Witches who have transformed themselves thus in order to spy on folk and to suckle milk directly from cow and goat udders. It is sometimes claimed that the Urchins are also adept thieves and pickpockets. Although they are usually mischievous rather than malicious there is a possibility that some would rub their spines in the toxic secretions of toads as a defence against predators; therefore handling, as with all supernatural creatures is ill-advised.
They are known to the Scottish gypsies as Hedge-hursts . A travellers' tale oft repeated around fireside gatherings in times past, recollected the birth of such a creature to entirely human parents as a result of a Faerie curse. This particular specimen was said to have twinkling blue eyes and would ride around on the back of a cockerel.

Appearance : Brown and very spiny, very similar but disquietingly different to regular hedgehogs.

Size: 1 ft (0.3 m) long or less.

Diet : They show a particular fondness for milk.

Habitat & Range : Most common in South-west England (where they could be classed as Social rather than Solitary if they are actually metamorphosed Pixies, and not a separate species. However Urchins are most frequently spotted singularly).
Also known in Scotland and Ireland, perhaps Urchins occur elsewhere in the British Isles and have been overlooked as being common hedgehogs.

Jimmy Squarefoot

Though he means no harm, the appearance of Jimmy Squarefoot customarily has the effect of causing fearful humans to speedily head in the opposite direction. He may even prove to be an interesting companion if only given a chance, but his odd combination of human and pig parts is just too frightful for most folk. He hasn't always looked this way however, as the older accounts of his presence reported him as being a huge but otherwise common enough looking pig. Well, not that conventional perhaps, as in those days he frequently had a boorish Giant or Foawr riding upon his back! At some point over the years, Jimmy lost his unkindly bare-back rider (it is sometimes thought that the gigantic oaf went off alone, searching for his estranged wife, who left her husband due to his habit of lobbing boulders at her.) Left alone, Jimmy developed more human attributes of his own (though still maintaining a significantly porcine demeanour) and took to wandering the Isle of Man.

Though perhaps not Jimmy Squarefoot himself, a similarly heavily built humanoid with a porcine head was reputed to have severely pestered the building of a church on the main land at Church Stowe, Northamptonshire (See also Church-Grims). After dark this beast-man would wreck work done during the day and pilfer materials, however when another nearby location was instead chosen for the church construction, the pig-headed creature let the labourers continue their toils unhampered.

A race of tiny Faerie Pigs known as Arkan Sonney or Lucky Piggies have also been reported in the Isle of Man and are considered to bring good fortune if captured. Litters of Phantom piglets usually led by a ghostly sow, have been reported from various British locations. This includes the strange brood from Widecombe in Devon, who were reputedly to be heard repeatedly grunting "Starvin" and "Dead 'Oss" as they roamed eternally in search of the remains of perished horses.

Appearance & Attire : A large swine's head , complete with ferocious looking tusks, sits atop the pot-bellied body of a man. His arms are comparatively long and his feet are peculiarly square-shaped. His torso is often bare, though he wears a pair of braced breeches, stockings and makeshift shoes.

Size : He commonly stoops, though even then he reaches the height of a man.

Diet : Uncertain. Possibly Truffles and when unavailable, other fungi and acorns, etc.

Habitat & Range : Jimmy Squarefoot roams around the path-ways of the Isle of Man.

Fachan
(Also known as ~ Peg-Leg Jack. Direach. Dithreach.)

This very strange character is unpleasant both visually and in his behaviour. Extremely antisocial, the Fachan carries a mighty spiked club or mace in his single strong arm. He also only has one leg with which he can hop considerable distances at a surprising speed. It is uncertain whether he is a single individual or whether there are several Fachan and his history is hazy, yet he bears certain resemblance to the fiends known as Hai-Uri or Sciopods encountered in African deserts, or the creatures known in the Yemen as Nasnas (though the Fachan is considerably smaller). The Fachan is notoriously fierce and prone to attack humans without much provocation, and therefore it comes as no surprise that they are accredited with being able to cause heart failure. As well as despising mankind, the Fachan are also reputedly none too keen on birds either.

A curious suggestion concerning the appearance of the Fachan is the theory that this being derives from a folk-memory of Celtic Seers : for some of these visionaries were said to adopt the position of standing upon one leg, with one eye closed and a single arm outstretched, whilst in trance or communion with the Otherworld.

Appearance and Attire : Basically, very ugly. The Fachan has a squat black or dark-coloured body with a single, centred leg and arm. They are often described as generally being half-formed or possessing only single features. A plume of blue feathers sprouts around the neck, shoulder and back of the head. Their clothing never amounts to more than a rudimentary wrap of buckskin. They carry either a wooden bludgeon armed with a single spike in its head or a flail tipped with poison apples.

Size : Usually approximately 1 - 3 ft (0.3 - 0.9 m) tall, but are thought able to increase size to colossal proportions at will.

Diet : Unknown.

Range & Habitat : The mountain and hill regions of the Western Highlands and Argyllshire in Scotland. Possibly also in Ireland.

Stray Sods
(Also known as ~ Lone Sods. Foidin Seachrain.)

This Fay breed is so efficiently camouflaged that a person may not realise they have encountered one until it is too late. A clump of grass or wild flowers sprouts so proficiently from its soil-coloured body, that a human rambler can easily tread on one. This does not hurt the Stray Sod but instead provokes a profound magical reaction.

In a situation very similar to being Pixy-led (see Pixies), the person will suddenly become extremely disorientated and lost even in a small and usually familiar field. They will aimlessly wander round in circles and proceed in the total opposite direction to where they were initially heading. The Stray Sod's influence also extends to making stiles and guide-posts appear extremely elusive. This frustrating and progressively distressing scenario could last for hours , but the spell can usually be broken if the victim turns and wears their coat inside out. Whistling may also help break the enchantment, but this can be hazardous as it may attract the attention of (or even annoy) other supernatural beings. The sudden twisting or turning of walkers' ankles on relatively even terrain, has also been suggested as being as a result of a Stray Sod encounter. In Ireland there may also be some connection between Stray Sods and the Fear-Gerta (see Alp Luachra & Buttery Sprites) as some patches of greenery known by some as Hungry Grass (or quite confusingly also as Fear Gerta or Fear Gortach), are said to cause stupor and wasting disease if trod upon. Some folk believe that this is due to Fay mischief whilst others claim that such symptoms indicate that a human corpse had lain on the patch some time in the past.

In areas of the south-westerly English County of Devon, the plant Bog-Cotton was once known as Pixy-Grass. This name arose from the belief that this plant was utilised by the Pixies with the intention of fooling people into thinking that solid ground lay before them when it was in fact a treacherous mire. Ferns also once held the reputation for causing anyone who happened to tread upon them to become entirely lost and confused.

Appearance : Small, earthy humanoid bodies which are vaguely seen due to the varied foliage sprouting from the back, neck and shoulders. Not all Stray Sods are sentient beings however, as some are regular enough clods of earth that have been enchanted by Faeries, to have the same effect should a human step upon them.

Size : The body has the proportions of a clod of earth and the total height varies according to the particular plant growth.

Habitat & Range : In fields and meadows, particularly in Ireland but probably localised across the British Isles.

Alp Luachra and Buttery Sprites
(Alp Luachra also known as ~ Joint Eaters. Just Halvers. Shotten Herrings. Jack 'o' Lents.
Buttery Sprites also known as ~ Abbey Lubbers.)

The Alp Luachra have a potent connection to food and are most frequently observed whilst they are eating. However in sharp contrast to this they are extremely skinny, or at least that is how they are described by those with 'Second Sight'; for they are frequently only visible to humans who are psychically-gifted. Whether observed by the clairvoyant or going entirely unnoticed, these scrawny Fay beings will enter human households, sit invisibly by their unwary hosts at mealtimes and partake of their victuals. Though their appetite may at times seem voracious, the actual mass of food consumed is so meagre it may remain completely unnoticed. It is possible that they may ingest only the foyson or toradh - that is merely the intangible essence or goodness of the food. As Jack 'o' Lents and Shotten Herrings, they symbolised the Lenten Fast (see Easter Bunny) and scrawny puppets would traditionally be made to represent these spirits and then beaten with sticks and burnt before Easter.

The Buttery Sprites are a similar species, however their appetite and presence may often be somewhat more apparent. They commonly attach themselves to older homes, inns and also places of religious abode such as abbeys and monasteries. Normally their presence is most noticeable by the continuous disappearance of butter from the kitchen or larder. However if the Buttery Sprites consider their human house-mates to be dishonest, unscrupulous or hypocritical (particularly if they are lodging with monks or priests), then they will make their presence ever more apparent by causing disruption and nuisance at every possible opportunity.

Another emaciated Irish Fay is the Fear-gerta or 'Man of Hunger'. This famine faerie is visible and active along country roads, particularly in hard times. Poor people would face a dilemma in encountering this creature as he would ask them to share their meagre provisions. If they agreed they would go hungrier at that time, but may be rewarded with a future upturn in fortune. If they refused , then they would eat that day but their predicament could likely continue or worsen.

Gwyllion
(Also known as Gwyll. Mountain Faeries. Goat Faeries.)

Amongst the hills and mountains the Gwyllion may be encountered tending to goats, which are their favoured animals. It is sometimes claimed that they will themselves assume the form of these creatures, perhaps as a means of camouflage or to enable them to traverse rough terrain more efficiently. Otherwise they appear as strange women who most commonly are sighted , either alone or in small groups sat amongst the rocks on either side of mountain paths. Here, from this remote vantage point and under the cover of darkness (for they fear sunlight), they will silently and disturbingly stare at human passers-by. Sometimes it is said, the Gwyllion are inclined to lure travellers off their path and perhaps into potentially life-threatening territory. Conversely though, they may attempt to seek shelter in nearby human dwellings during a storm. It is possible to drive them out of the abode with a knife made of iron however, for as well as sunlight and storms the Gwyllion also fear this metal. If they are allowed to quietly sit out the thunder and lightning in the home, then the Gwyllion will from then on cast a protective eye over the roads to the house and also on any livestock belonging to the owners.

With regard to Welsh Fays in general there seems to be a strong connection to animals with many of their kind reputed to keenly shape-shift into goats, sheep, greyhounds and other creatures. The notorious Social Fays of Wales, the Tylwyth Teg or Fair Folk would reputedly make a habit of combing goats' beards every Friday evening.

Appearance & Attire : Feral and coarse in comparison to most of the Welsh Fays. The Gwyllions' hair is thick and wild. Also their skin may appear quite swarthy or hirsute and they may emit a musty, animal-like odour. Only sightings of female Gwyllion have been reported and they do not tend to speak, so it is not known even if there is a male of the species.

Size : Generally smaller than 5 ft (1.5 m) tall.

Diet : Probably goats' milk and cheese. It is unknown whether they supplement their diet with any other foodstuff.

Habitat & Range : Mountains and hills in Wales, especially in the area of Aberystwyth.

Grey Ladies
(Also known as ~ Well Spirits. Well Guardians.)

The Fay maidens that watch over the oldest of wells and springs, should be approached with utmost caution. Although they are intrigued with mankind they don't seem to understand us fully; or at least our inability to breathe underwater for prolonged periods of time. They may genuinely play with children around the water-holes, but should a child tragically fall into the depths these guardians seem to do little to save them. Also, what may be intended as an affectionate embrace may lead to the drowning of an unfortunate mortal. They can however also cause harm wilfully, should they consider someone to be disrespectful or destructive towards their fount. It is advisable to wear or carry a suitable charm if intending to approach a well.

In contrast some Well Spirits are believed to be of benefit to mankind. It is an enduring superstition that to cast coins or other worthy tokens into a 'wishing well', may cause its guardian to share their powers of enchantment and hopefully grant their deepest desires. Other wells are associated with certain Saints of the Celtic and Saxon Churches (the predecessors of the Roman influenced Christian church we know today). They perhaps sprung from the spot of their death and many are believed to hold healing properties. To tie a piece of cloth (known as a Jawn' or Clootie) around the branch of a tree growing close to a well, particularly a Hawthorn if one is to be found, was another old superstition believed to draw good health.

Some wells were considered to possess other strange powers which would manifest in exchange for specific tokens. For instance various storm-wells were believed to ensure fair weather upon the offering of white stones or quartz crystals, whilst the Silver Well of Otterburn, Northumberland was thought to convert sundry items into precious metal upon the payment of Pine-cones. There has also been association drawn between certain wells and the Celtic Head Cult. This connection materialises in several ways; initially by the conviction that the severed heads of enemies cast into a well would invigorate the water within with healing properties but furthermore that the water drawn from a Healing well would be enhanced by it being drunk out of a human skull.

The sudden flowing or drying up of a holy well in times when neither flood nor drought were respectively apparent was often taken as an omen of impending death or calamity.

Votive offerings to the Romano-Celtic Goddess Coventina, discovered in a well at Carrawburgh along Hadrian's Wall in Northern England included coins, pearls, pins, incense-burners, a carving of a horse, a carving of a dog and a real human skull. More sinister though was the reputation of St. Elian's Well at Llanelian-yn-Rhas near Colwyn Bay in Wales. Alternatively known as the Cursing Well, up until at least the 19th Century people would cast lead boxes into its water with the intent that the information contained within would be transformed into a hex aimed at that person's enemies.

Wag by the Way
(Also known as ~ Wag-at-the-Wa'.)

The Wag by the Way is a curious cat-like Fay, that may enter a household and curl up by the fireside. It rarely if ever, bothers to use the English or Celtic languages and unlike the Brownies and Hobs, it will not concern itself with assisting with domestic chores. Though visitors to the home will often be greeted by the Wag with scratches or even a barrage of hurled pots and pans, it will frequently treat its human cohabitants with a regard almost bordering on restrained affection. However like conventional cats, it may suddenly just decide to leave and never return.

It is possible that accounts of the Wag provided inspiration for the fairy-tale character the 'Mewing Man': Described by Enid Blyton as a little cat-like man who uses a whistle or flute to entice cats into a sack. If no cats are forthcoming he will conjure some kittens from the buds of 'Pussy' Willow trees. Either way it is suspected that he sells on the captured cats to Witches (see Familiars).

Alternatively he could be the 'King of the Cats'. Cats were worshipped by several ancient cultures world-wide and it has been considered that they may be a Fay species rather than *conventional* animals. They may have realised the convenience of their pleasant form and the occasional show of affection in ensuring a warm comfortable place to sleep and frequent meals, but they also maintain a certain aloofness and attend to their own enigmatic agenda on their nocturnal excursions. If that is so, it could also explain why Elves and Brownies are often more reluctant to enter a house already inhabited by a territorial Fay, i.e. a cat.

(See also Cats and Alien Big Cats.)

Appearance & Attire : The Wag is a little old man (females have not been reported) with cat -like attributes, most notably a long supple tail which he wags if irritated. He may wear rather smart clothing, which might often be covered in cinders. It was often claimed that he also wore a night-cap, which he tended to pull down over his cheek in order to try and soothe a persistent toothache.

Size : Approximately 1 ½ ft (0.45m) tall or less.

Diet : Fond of milk, and possibly other food favoured by cats.

Habitat & Range: May be encountered in houses or exploring other habitats, particularly in the Lowlands of Scotland, the Borders and Northern England. Pearlin Jean is another feline-like Fay of Scottish folklore. This cat-eyed Faerie Hag is most active at Halloween.

Gnomes
(Also known as ~ 'Irish Elves'. Little Fellers. Wee Folk. Nains.)

The Gnomes are possibly the most compassionate and conservative of the humanoid supernatural creatures, which is a sharp contrast to their relatives the true Dwarves. Gnomes are neither wholly social nor solitary, but instead tend to live in small scattered family groups. The males are the most commonly encountered, either taking a relaxing stroll or attending to the odd bit of work. It is sometimes claimed that their wives pride themselves on keeping a good home and that is possibly why they are seen less frequently.

Gnomes speak all of the woodland languages and they concern themselves with caring for injured or distressed birds and animals. Though they may steer well clear of healthy owls, weasels and other creatures that may attempt to eat them but should they see any of these beasts in trouble it is in their character to still try to help. Gnomes do not readily communicate with humans as often as they once might have, for they are deeply concerned about mankind's general swing towards disregard and exploitation of nature. If they are encountered by people who show respect for the environment, then the Gnome is more inclined to offer a polite 'hello'. At times they may also assist organic farmers and gardeners, or even traditional craftsmen such as cobblers and shoemakers if they appear to be struggling with their labours.

Perhaps the weirdest encounter with Gnomes to date, was the case reported at Woolaton Park near Nottingham in 1979. A group of youths earnestly claimed that they had witnessed about 30 diminutive red and white bubble-cars drive out of a clump of bushes. Apparently seated in each of the wee automobiles were a pair of wrinkly-faced Gnomes all sporting long white beards tipped with red. Being Gnomes it is assumed or at least hoped that they were driving on environmentally-friendly fuel.

Their association as protectors of nature, has seen some people place plaster or plastic (sometimes overtly mawkish) replicas of Gnomes in their gardens. However despite their general pleasantry as a species, some individual Gnomes may show less benevolence and perhaps display even malice towards mankind therefore (as with all Supernatural breeds) vigilance and caution should always be retained if ever in their company or habitat.

Dwarves
(Including ~ Pygmies. Troglodytes. Gwarchells. Yarthkins.
Dweorgs. Earth-Men.)

The term 'Dwarf' in this context applies to a particular race of beings and not to the humans who are of diminutive stature due to the condition known as Dwarfism. Rather similar in appearance to the Gnomes but often of a more unfriendly character, Dwarves are most common to the lore of Scandinavian and Germanic nations (both of which historically invaded these isles).

One theory relating to the origins of Faeries suggests that they are the descendants of an aboriginal Pygmy race that were resident in these lands before the coming of the Celts. In the face of invasion and the possible subsequent life of slavery, they were thought to have retreated to coves and underground canyons. Certainly the more unsightly Fay species, such as Spriggans and Trows could be comparable to the Troglodytes - a misshapen race of cave-dwelling Pygmies common to the lore of various nations. There is however a school of thought that separates Dwarves and their ilk from Fay species, instead suggesting that they belong to the Gnomic domain.

Like the Goblins, Dwarves in these isles tend to be solitary (such as the Duergars) or belong to a further sub-species such as the mine-dwelling Black Dwarves or the other Koboldic races that habituate coal and ore seams. (However these Koboldic races more specifically seem to exist somewhere between the bloodline of True Dwarves and True Goblins.)

There is however at least one tale in British folklore that mentions Trooping Dwarves of a kind most similarly found within Norse and Teutonic myth. This story involves King Herla (himself a candidate for the role of Midnight Hunter - see The Wild Hunt) but the Dwarves which he encountered showed similar characteristics to the Trooping Faeries. Inviting Herla into their abode, within the heart of a large hill on the Welsh / English borders, he presumed that he had spent only three days in their company but upon his return to the outer world he discovered that 200 years had actually passed.

Dwarves tend to be stouter than Gnomes with noticeably larger heads, hands and feet. Their feet may often display varying levels of deformity (even to the extent of resembling ducks' feet).They tend to be heavily bearded and in comparison so do the rarer females of the species. To avoid sunlight Dwarves may shapeshift into the forms of Toads. Though Dwarves are thought to have a natural life-span of several centuries or more, the juveniles tend to reach maturity considerably early.

Kobolds and Mine Spirits
(Also known as ~ Mine Goblins. Subterraneans. Main species ~ Knockers. Coblynau. Black Dwarves. Blue Caps. Old Men.)

The Fay creatures most commonly encountered underground are the Mine Goblins or more correctly the Kobolds. (The term Kobold is often used to specifically refer to the blue-skinned malignant mine-goblins of Germany, whilst the British breeds are most commonly known by their species name e.g. Knockers and Coblynau. All Goblins are sometimes stated to belong to a super-family called the Koboloids.) Dwarves and Phantoms have also been reported in some mines.

The Knockers probably most resemble the Germanic Kobolds, but they are only rarely as vicious. The noises they make (from which their name derives) can lead miners to rich veins of ore, but they can also be most unfriendly especially if displeased. They object to cross symbols being used as markers, which led some people to suspect that they were the ghosts of archaic Jewish miners. Like other Mine Spirits though, they also loathed swearing and whistling and any offending miners would likely be showered with a hail of pebbles. The solitary Cutty Soams of Northern England and the Knockers of Chaw Gully in Dartmoor, Devon were altogether more nasty however. They were commonly believed responsible for the deaths of miners and it has been said that rich seams of minerals and precious ore were left unmined because of their vile presence.

The Coblynau (also known as Cobyln or Koblernigh) of Wales similarly could lead to rich pickings and held the same taboos, but they were generally reported of being of a more cheerful nature. Sometimes they were also observed above ground participating in strange, manic Morris-dancing.

The Koboldic races were often replaced in the north by Black Dwarves. Their name relates not to their pigmentation (though their skin was often stained with the grime of their environment) but to their general character. They mined for themselves and were not keen on human presence but were not beyond claiming the humans' bait or coal as their own. The Black Dwarves were also unwelcome on the surface as they were prone to rustling farmers' sheep.

Other Mine Spirits would appear to warn of impending disasters, such as those of Northeast England who could take forms as diverse as phantom pit-ponies or the rarely seen Death's-head Hawk moths.

Blue Caps (also known as Blue Bonnets) could at times be inclined to assist miners with their work and were reputedly phenomenally strong despite their tiny stature. They would manifest as small blue flames if pit-collapse, gas or other dangers ensued.

Leprechauns & Portunes
(Portunes also known as ~ The Gentry. Wish-makers.
Thumblings. Hop O' My Thumbs. Portuni.
Leprechauns also known as ~ Leith Bhrugan. Lieth
Bhrogan {Shoemakers} Luacharama'n. {Pygmy} One-Shoe-
Makers. Loghery Men. Luricaunes. Luricans. Lurachmains.
Leprechans. Lubberkins. Lubricans. Lurikeens. Luricans.
Lurigadauns. Lurigdhans. Langremen. Luchorpains.)

The Leprechauns are strange and distinctive little men of a jovial
but crafty demeanour. They are renowned for being able to grant
wishes, for burying crocks brimming with gold and for knowing
the whereabouts of other hidden treasures. Therefore many humans
would hope to capture a Leprechaun and coerce him into granting
desires or revealing and relinquishing his precious hoards. However
the Leprechaun would likely treat such a confrontation as a game
and they love a battle of wills. Because of their greater guile the
Leprechaun is most likely to come out best in such a tryst. On one
such occasion an Irishman caught a Leprechaun unawares and held
him by his collar until he revealed the hiding-place of his treasure.
The Leprechaun indicated that the gold was to be found buried
under a particular plant in a field brimming with Ragwort. The
man released the Leprechaun and before heading home to fetch his
shovel tied his red neckerchief around the lucky plant. Upon his
return to the field the man was however dismayed to find that
every single one of the thousands of Ragwort plants growing there
had an identical piece of cloth tied around them.
Leprechauns are extremely dapper in their attire and are excellent
shoemakers ; however their talents are of little use (except perhaps
for a Fachan, and they are not known for their footwear) as they
will only craft a single shoe and never a pair. The Leprechaun is
inherently Irish, but has often followed human emigrants from the
emerald isle across the world, particularly to North America. The
smaller but similarly dandy Portunes of England are known for
their gardening prowess and horse-riding skills, and are possibly
descended from or related to the Leprechauns. Both species are
generally solitary but will mingle and gate-crash parties. It has
been suggested that the Leprechauns are descended from Lugh the
Irish-Celtic God of Light and Arts & Craft, who was also the
grandson / slayer of Balor the Fomorian.

Clurichauns
(Also known as ~ Cluricaune. His Nibs. Clobhair-Ceann.)

The Clurichaun closely resembles the Leprechaun and may even be the same species differentiated only by habit and habitat. This little man (for again, no females have been reported) take it upon themselves to become the sentinels of wine and beer cellars. Here they will keep all the kegs and bottles in order, prevent leakage and contamination, as well as seeing off any intruders. They do this on the understanding that they can then help themselves to any tipple they so desire. However as they have a notoriously tremendous thirst and are sometimes taken to neglect their self-appointed duties at night (to often instead indulge in drunken rodeo-riding on the backs of local dogs and sheep) some landlords and wine-keepers do not appreciate their presence. If they attempt to deny the Clurichaun access to the cellar or alcohol however, then he will cause them a great deal of fuss, chaos and damaged property.

The Clurichaun is quite distinguishable from the Thrummy Cap or Ruindie; another supernatural species that may also be encountered in cellars (particularly in Northern England). These tiny spirits wear clothing made from fluff that gets caught in the corners of cobwebs, and bonnets crafted from the off–cuts of weavers' looms. This species is also thought however to enjoy more than the odd tipple of ale or spirits.

Appearance & Attire : Clurichauns' noses are ruddy and their cheeks gin-blossomed. They may go hatless or instead wear three-cornered hats, but they may favour reds, browns, russet and plum colours rather than the traditional greens and blacks of the Leprechauns. Despite their constant inebriation and revelling, the Clurichauns generally manage to retain a well-groomed appearance.

Size : 0.5 to 2 ft (0.15 - 0.6 m) tall.

Diet : It is not known whether the Clurichaun bothers with solid foods, but his liquid diet is legendary. Wine, ale, stout and spirits are all quaffed with vigour.

Habitat & Range: Wherever drinking-alcohol is stored, especially in the cellars of old inns, traditional pubs and the wine vaults of manor-houses in Ireland. There may also be localised immigrants around Britain, particularly in Scotland.

Dunnshenchas
(Also known as ~ Dinnshenchas.)

The Dunnshenchas are an archaic breed of Dwarf-Faerie that are nearly always reported as being female, though they can reputedly shape-shift into many forms. They are associated with the ancient Irish Goddess, Aine, and commonly tend to cattle, the most sacred of her beasts. Like the Grugach, the Dunnshenchas may protect cattle from malevolent or troublesome supernatural powers such as the Buachaileen (also known as Little Boys or Herding Boys); red-capped, shape-shifting Fays who delight in rustling or leading sheep and cattle astray. Frequently they may assist dairy-maids with their duties and will more readily befriend human females as they have an inherent suspicion of men-folk. At times they may use their shape-shifting abilities to avenge women or girls who have been mistreated by males.

The term 'Dinnshenchas' also has the alternative Gaelic denotation meaning the 'lore of prominent places'.

Appearance & Attire : Usually the Dunnshenchas appear as small homely women wearing rustic garments. They can shape-shift into whatever form best befits their needs.
Size : Variable at will, naturally below 2 ft (0.6 m) tall and sometimes tiny.
Diet: Uncertain.
Habitat & Range: Pastures and dairy farms in Ireland.

Duergars

The localised and unpleasant Dwarf species known as Duergars, are thought to have perhaps originated in France and to have possibly first come over to Britain with the Normans. The Duergars seem to regard mankind with utter contempt, yet their original grievance may have long since been forgotten. They do not tend to attack out right but instead cause a great nuisance of themselves by removing and reversing directional sign-posts, blocking paths and even trying to guide humans over the edges of cliffs and crags. They sometimes also elect themselves as the guardians of Faerie, though whether the Fay folk actually bother to have anything to do with them is unknown. Either way, at times they will chase people and animals off Faerie paths or will sit close to the hollow hills keeping a solemn watch. Although the Duergars are strictly nocturnal, it is not known whether they assume the forms of Toads during daylight hours as is the habit of several European earth breeds.

Duergars are almost always encountered in isolation, yet on rare occasions they have been said to congregate in packs in the vicinity of the Simonside Hills near Rothbury in Northumberland, with the intention of leading human-folk off the beaten path and into grave danger. However it is possible that these malicious entities were actually small troops of the very similar Black Dwarf species rather than the more isolationist Duergars.

Appearance & Attire: Wrinkled, yet hardy. They are quite frequently what we would consider ugly, and their countenance is always grim. They commonly wear lamb-skin jackets, green caps and mole-skin shoes. Females remain unreported.

Size : 3 ft (0.9 m) or less.

Diet : Unknown, but likely unpleasant.

Habitat & Range : They are known to build small huts, often from rocks or rubble; but it is possible that they have no permanent abode and instead tend to tramp around. They may be encountered at night near hills, lonely paths, moor-land, quarries and even coastal cliffs, but generally only in Northern England.

Trows and Hogboons
(Trows also known as ~ Hill Trows. Land Trows. Trowies. Drows. Night –Stealers. Grey Neighbours. Creepers. Peeries. Henkies. Ferries.
Hogboons also known as ~ Hog-boys. Haughbondes. Bu-Men. Cattle-Men.)

The Trows are the only firmly established British variety of Troll and are limited in their range to the far north of Scotland. Trollers Gill at Appletreewick in North Yorkshire, England is however rumoured to harbour a small colony of true Nordic Trolls. Dwelling within dismal, foreboding caves, these malodorous, murderous fiends may have accompanied the Vikings to these parts centuries ago and lingered long after the age of invasion. Big-nosed and hairy, the Appletreewick Trolls have been blamed for numerous nefarious crimes including common theft, assault, kidnap and the butchery of human flesh. The Tolcarne Troll of Cornwall was apparently a solitary Phoenician immigrant.

The Trows differ to the Icelandic and European Trolls in several ways however. Whilst not all Trolls are large, some can grow to above 11 ft (3.3 m) tall but the Trows would rarely reach more than quarter of this height. Trolls commonly are solitary or live in very small groups, whereas the Trows live in larger communities or tribes often within hollow hills and sea-caves. Like the Trolls though, the Trows may at times snatch away human infants; but unlike them they tend not to abduct mortal women as captive brides. Also like the Trolls, they have a strong aversion to sunlight but perhaps not quite the same degree of sensitivity. Some have also displayed a deep dislike of fresh running water. The Trows often display sharper cunning and wit than their European cousins however and display some similarities also with Fay species.

The Trows have a curious code of conduct, as they will regularly raid farms and cottages and take whatever they can, however should a Trow steal so much as a wooden spoon from one of its own kind, then it does so at the risk of becoming completely isolated and banished from its clan. Trow music is reputedly exquisite, yet their dancing (known as Henking_ or Haltadans - the limping dance) is bizarre and clumsy. They are often also said to hop rather than walk, and if they become aware of a human looking at them it is claimed that they will bend down, grab their knees and shuffle away backwards. Though they can speak the tongues of men, their own language is said to sound like the chirping of birds.

Chieftains of Trow clans were known as King-Trows or Kunal-Trows.

The Hogboons are or were very similar in size and appearance to the Trows and the casual observer could very well mistake the two. However if given the treatment they expected, the Hogboons were of a more amiable character regarding mankind. In exchange for milk or ale, these scruffy, grey folk would assist humans with manual tasks and tool maintenance. However should their earth-mound homes be disturbed or if they should feel insulted, undervalued or exploited then the Hogboons could prove themselves to be every bit as menacing as the Trows.

Wraths
(Also known as ~ 'True' Giants. Hugboys. Atach. Gawr. Ents. Childes.)

The Wraths are the biggest 'supernatural' entities ever recorded in these isles or anywhere on this planet for that matter. Though essentially humanoid these big folk can vary somewhat in both appearance and character. Whilst many are extremely belligerent towards mankind, others would actually quite like to be our friends. However the sheer clumsiness of their nature could prove potentially hazardous to smaller creatures and any friendships would likely prove to be awkward or arduous. Wraths are generally solitary or live in small family groups, and encounters with others of their kind could often become confrontational. Either out of natural habit or deliberate antagonism, Wraths also frequently became the enemies of humankind and Giant-killers would oft be sought to dispose of them. A great source of consternation was food. Obviously something the size of a Wrath would need to eat a considerably large amount of food (though actually proportionately little in comparison to body size, unlike many much smaller creatures who consume several times their own body weight on a daily basis). However much of the Wraths' diet was grown or reared by the humans, otherwise belonged to the humans or in some cases were the humans. Another problem with the largest specimens was caused by the fact that it took so long for the food to move through the considerable length of the gullet. This meant much of it would have rotted before it had been digested and obviously the gastric ailments of a Giant were not pleasurable for any of their neighbours. The Scots term Atach was used to refer to Giants but equally could also be applied to other terrible (but sometimes less tall) monsters such as the Headless Trunk and the Cearb etc.

Medieval historians endeavouring to chronicle the early inhabitants of Britain have claimed that England was initially populated by a race of Giants. Their maternal parents were a group of Grecian Princesses who exiled from their own homeland, settled in Britain. Led by Albina (from whose son 'Albion' the poetic name of Britain was derived), these women found an absence on these shores at that time and instead coupled with the demonic beings known as Incubi. The Giant race were born from this union and in time initially reproduced themselves by impregnating their own sisters and mothers. (An apocryphal biblical equivalent is told of how the human women who had lain with the Angels known as the Grigori or Watchers, at the dawn of mankind gave birth to a race of Giants called the Nephilim.

The incestuous Wraths of Britain apparently ruled these lands until the arrival of the Trojan Warrior Brutus (from whom the name 'Britain' was thus derived). After Corineus, (a warrior of Brutus' army and the first Lord of Cornwall), cast the body of the Wrath overlord Gogmagog over the cliffs following a tremendous battle, the humans gained control of the country.

The Wraths varied considerably both in size and appearance, though most were thick-set with sloping brows and disproportionately long arms (to aid balance). Wraths had an insulating coat of body hair, whilst others made patchwork clothing comprised of animal furs and hides, foliage and turf and clothing or bedding etc. stolen from washing lines. Some Wraths also evolved efficient natural camouflage. Female Wraths were similar, though generally smaller, more intelligent and rarer.

Like the Faeries were said to inhabit several of their own Otherworldly kingdoms, so too in legend did the Giants have their own domain. Therefore it could perhaps be claimed that the Giants may now boycott our world in favour of Ysbadden - the Land of the Giants, that was said to lie within Wales (but across the supernatural borders). This land was named after Ysbadden Penkawl (or Yspadden Pencawr), a brutish Wrath of Celtic and Arthurian legend. The Yorkshire Giant, Wade was credited with the construction of numerous earthworks and structures in that county.

Cyclopes (Singular ~ Cyclops)

The Cyclopes are a distinctive variety of Giant, easily distinguished by their large solitary eye. Although King Balor of the Fomorii, the Wrath King Yspadden Pencawr and the Blue Hags, Cailleach Bheur and Black Annis, are all notably one-eyed they are not true Cyclopes as they actually have two eyes ; one permanently closed and useless and the other sharp and monstrous. True Cyclopes only have a single huge eye situated in the centre of their forehead; though some may also have two mock eyes situated in the normal place, but these are completely grafted shut and non-functional and have been since birth.

Cyclopes are notably smarter than most Wraths and many are talented craftsmen or skilled builders, millers or herdsmen. However they are also notoriously fierce, conniving and often extremely predatory on mankind. Though the species is far more common and virulent to the Mediterranean island of Sicily and to parts of Africa, individuals have also been reported in the British countryside.

Accounts of black-skinned Cyclopes habituating the valleys and forests of Wales are given in the Mabinogion, a fine collection of old Cambrian legends. Some of these one-eyed titans however also possess other limbs and organs in singular rather like the Fachan, or are otherwise somehow only half-formed like some Fomorian individuals.

Appearance & Attire: The most distinguishing feature is of course the massive eye situated in the middle of the forehead. Frequently though the Cyclopes' hair and beard can be reminiscent of a lion's mane. Though not known for being well-dressed, the Cyclopes' functional attire is generally more stolidly made than those of many other Giants.

Size : approx. 15 to 30 ft (4.5 - 9 m) tall.

Diet : Varied and often quite gluttonous. They are mostly carnivorous and this will often include human meat.

Habitat & Range : Woodland, caves and deserted mills mainly in Yorkshire, England.

Foawr
(Also known as ~ Stone-Throwing Giants. Fooar.)

Many Giants in Britain and Ireland displayed a propensity for throwing stones, yet the Manx Foawr were absolutely notorious for heaving boulders around. They would throw rocks at humans, at ships, at each other and they would throw rocks just for the sake of throwing rocks. It seems however that the males of the species were more inclined towards trouble-making and stone-lobbing than the females.

The masculine Foawr were despised by human farmers, not only for their rock-hurling but also for their other habit of ravishing cattle. It has been considered that the Foawr may be of the same lineage as the Fomorii and some at least were said to be the children of the haggard storm-goddess, the Cailleach Bheur.

Appearance & Attire : The Foawr are broad, uncouth and hairy. Though some of them are reputed to be adept spinners, they tend either to go naked or only wear rudimentary or shabby clothing.

Size : Between 7 - 20 ft (2 - 6 m) tall.

Diet : Usually whatever they can raid from human reserves. Whilst they were known to hurl boulders at humans and sometimes abduct them also it is not known for certain whether they ever eat people.

Habitat & Range : Across the Isle of Man, especially in hill regions. Though not known specifically by the name of Foawr, similar rock-lobbing Giants were also once known in Wales.

Garbh Ogh

Garbh Ogh was an Irish Giantess that was said to hunt deer with a pack of 70 hounds, each of which was named after a different type of bird. Unlike most Giants she seemed though to have little interest in humans, neither as objects of curiosity nor as tasty snacks. Indeed though she was apparently quite haggard to look upon, she seemed to be calm, mellow and earthy disposition. When Garbh Ogh realised that death was close at hand she carved herself a throne from a heather-laden hill, set huge stones about herself in the formation of a cairn (conical, heaped monument) and breathed her last. It is possible that Garbh Ogh was once worshipped as a Celtic Goddess.

88

Ogres
(Also known as ~ Fifel. Females known as Ogresses.)

Ogres are considerably smaller and somewhat smarter than most Wraths, but there is no debate about their character. Ogres are all dangerously blood-thirsty and they regard mankind as nothing more than meat. This is made even more unsettling by the fact that they will often attempt to lure humans (especially children) into their lair through false charm and promises.

They are generally foul both in their habits and appearance, but their numbers are thankfully sometimes maintained by their occasional tendency to eat their own offspring. Due to their potential for cannibalism, they are most often solitary. Like some spiders and mantids, their courtship could sometimes run the risk of one of the partners ending up as lunch. Some Ogres have also been accused of defiling young maidens. Whilst all Ogres and Ogresses are base and cruel, some are less primitive than others. There are frequently similarities between Ogres and other loathsome species such as the Hags, the Groac'h, Hobyahs and Necors.

Appearance & Attire: Ogres are frequently broad and muscular with thick, short necks and powerful squat limbs. Their skin is sometimes thick, blemished and occasionally garishly coloured. Their eyes are often piggy and cruel, and they frequently have protruding tusks or filth encrusted, shredding teeth. Some may be more human-like in form, but all are generally very ugly. Many Ogres will have motley other physical deformities and anomalies, such as hump backs or surplus heads (The Ogre, Red Etin [who was active in Scotland but thought to originated in Ireland] reportedly had a ruddy body and three heads). If anything, the females are often more terrible and ravenous. Their clothing can either be ragged and minimal or varied like human attire.

Size : Usually 7 to 15 ft (2 - 4.5 m) tall.

Diet : Fresh meat (sometimes also carrion), either raw or cooked (boiled in pots or roasted in ovens). They are very fond of human meat, especially children and young women. Cannibalism sometimes also occurs.

Habitat & Range : Localised in woodland, caves, ruins and deserted buildings across Britain and Ireland. A small tribe of Ogres were reputedly hunted down and eradicated close to Dundee in the early 16th Century

Anthropophagi

The Anthropophagi are a bizarre breed of Ogre for they have no heads. Their grim features are instead set apart on their muscular torsos. Their rudimentary brains are thought to lie beneath their stomachs. Whilst they certainly cannot be claimed to be amiable towards mankind, perhaps only slight relief may be found in the claim that they will only kill us if they are hungry. They frequently arm themselves with crude weaponry and use tools and artefacts often crafted from human bones. Though the Anthropophagi tend to be encountered in isolation or in small numbers, it is possible that they are closely related to very similar creatures called Blemmyae. The Blemmyae were said to live in populous and vicious tribes in Libya and Ethiopia. It is a possibility that the less numerous Anthropophagi are actually immigrant Blemmyae who sailed to Britain in primitive boats many centuries ago.

Appearance & Attire : Their bodies are squat and their skin is tough, often dark or dusky. Their mean eyes are set into their shoulders and their mouths (brimming with razor-sharp fangs) are situated in the centre of their chests. Their noses are often broad and flat or negligible (it has been suggested to enable them to eat rancid meat without retching). Their clothing consists of little more than a fur or animal-hide wrap. Details of females are uncertain.

Size : approx. 5 to 8 ft (1.65 - 2.4 m) tall.

Diet : Predominantly meat - fresh or carrion, including human flesh and on occasion cannibalisation of their own kind. Possibly supplemented with other basic foodstuffs.

Habitat & Range : Dense woodland and isolated gorges etc. localised in England.

Giant Ghosts
(Also known as ~ Thyrs.)

Whilst sightings of living, breathing Giants are perhaps becoming increasingly rare, encounters with huge Ghosts have been reported in recent times. These Giant Ghosts should not be confused with the 'Ghost-giants' or Spriggans, which are something quite different, though manifestations of both are sometimes accredited to the souls of long-dead Wraths. Such a Giant Ghost is Jack in Irons who haunts lonely roads in Yorkshire, England. Manacled and chained, it is thought that in his 'natural' life Jack was a Wrath who had been captured, incarcerated and eventually executed for crimes against humanity. Subsequent sightings have reported a motley collection of human heads hanging from Jack's belt and it has also been claimed that this ghost is well aware of the terror he inspires in people, and that he revels in the fact.
Another acclaimed Giant Ghost is the Big Grey Man of Ben Macdhui (also known as Am Fear Liath Mor or the Bodach Mor)in the Cairngorm Mountains, Scotland. also sighted at Braerich in Glen Eanich, he appears as a very large hazy male figure when actually seen, however other manifestations of his presence include the appearance of big footprints mysteriously crunching into the snow and a strange disembodied, resonant voice muttering and chanting in a vaguely Gaelic-like tongue. Some suspect that the Big Grey Man is actually the spirit of the mountain itself rather than the revenant of a dead Giant.
Wales also has its equivalent to the Big Grey Man known as the Grey King (or also as the Monarch of the Mist or Brenin Llwyd) This tall mysterious figure is said to haunt various peaks in Snowdonia and in bygone days was feared to be an abductor of children.
Another fearsome spectral Giant, black of countenance with a considerably narrow head and slender legs, but with a huge potbelly was reputedly encountered by a young lady walking her pet dog near Rhiw-newith in Wales. Perhaps the most grotesque aspect of this particular Giant Ghost's appearance though, was the extremely long jet-black tongue lolling from its formidable mouth.
Wanndlebury near Cambridge, England was said to be the site of a titanic battle between a brave mortal knight and a fierce Giant Ghost whilst several Phantom warriors of gargantuan stature are said to haunt the area around Heydon Ditch, an ancient earthwork in Cambridgeshire.

Brownies & Hobs
(Also known as Hearth Goblins. Hobgoblins. Boo-Men. Hob-Men. Hodpokers. Hobbins. Hodgepochers. Lobs. Lob-Lie-by-the-Fires. Lubber-Fiends. Broonies. Brounies. Bruinidh. Pouques.)

The Brownies (or Hobs as they are often known in England) attach themselves to households and occasionally to other industrious locations, where they prove themselves to be extremely prodigious but temperamental workers. Despite their small stature and also often some other physical impediment, their strength and stamina for work is frequently astounding and they seem to fulfil tasks with minimum effort. Many Brownies / Hobs show a great variety of skills ranging from household chores to baking, farming, milling, brewing and even on some occasions spinning, bee-keeping, cobbling and child-care. Some of their number however are well-intentioned but are too dim-witted to be of much practical use (see Dobies).

Brownies and Hobs however can be very easy to offend and they take even the most minor grievance or misunderstanding very much to heart. Should they feel exploited or if any of their traditional customs are disrespected by a human (either wilfully or accidentally), then the Brownie / Hob may storm off in an almighty huff never to assist or be seen in that precise locality again. That is if the offending party is lucky ; for the Brownie / Hob may instead stick around and become as great a nuisance as it once was an assistance (see Boggarts & Hobgoblins and also Bodachs).

Female Brownies are more rarely encountered than the males and many are strictly maternal. Brownie mothers are sometimes thought to live up chimneys and to have very long arms. A female Brownie called Hairy Meg (or Maggy) Molach was extremely industrious however and was as legendary for her hard work as she was for her harsh temper. The word Molach or Moulach was occasionally used to refer generally to female Brownies or more specifically to the hirsute creatures that mothered Brownies, Hobs, Dobies and the chimney-dwelling Bodachs.

Brownies / Hobs generally prefer a nocturnal lifestyle (cock crows are to tell them to go to bed it has been said, and not to inform us to wake up) but they are not bound by this.

Appearance & Attire : Shaggy, brown and wrinkly, their skin is often hairy and their teeth crooked. Lowland Brownies often lack noses whilst Highland Brownies and English Hobs often have conjoined digits, giving the hands and feet the appearance of mittens. Some individuals may possess both of these features and perhaps also other anomalies.

English Hobs were sometimes less hirsute than their Brownie cousins. Lobs are larger with long thin tails.They are usually naked or wear brown rags ; either way the offer of new clothing will be treated by them with scorn or disgust and cause them to cease their work.

Size : Commonly 2 to 3 ft (0.6 - 0.9 m) tall.

Diet : A small bowl of fresh, creamy milk and a cake smeared with honey was all that the Brownie required and demanded. (The brewery Brownies were also keen on the odd dram of the ale or whiskey they helped brew.)

Habitat & Range : Mainly rural homes and farms, occasionally mills and breweries across Scotland. In England (where they are known as Hobs) their range extends from the Northern counties as far south as the Midlands. The similar Pouques are native to Guernsey.

Killmoulis & Fenoderee
(Fenoderee also known as ~ Phynnodderee.

The Killmoulis and the Fenoderee are particular type of helper-spirits akin to the Brownies and Hobs. The Killmoulis is distinctive because of his huge nose , which occupies most of his face leaving no room for a mouth. They worked extremely hard in the mills but could often become quite bored. When such a mood overtook them, to entertain themselves they would set up practical jokes to befall the human workers attending the following day shift. Such a mood often befell the Killmoulis, making his presence as much a hindrance as it was a help.

The Fenoderee was thought to originally have been a member of the Manx Ferrishyn (see Trooping Faeries), however he found himself banished for attempting to woo a human young lady instead of attending the important Fay Festival at the Autumn Equinox. Either due to his exile or as a direct result of a Faerie curse the Fenoderee grew increasingly uglier , more dull-witted and quick-tempered. However his strength, stamina and willingness to work were legendary and his presence on farms was invaluable, particularly at harvest time. Some human labourers (perhaps jealous of his prowess in the field) could not resist taking advantage of his simple-mindedness however and would at times send the Fenoderee on fruitless tasks, such as collecting water in a sieve. Like other domestic-spirits and also the Ferrishyn (who were renowned for spreading secrets on the wind), the Fenordee would take great umbrage upon the realisation of ridicule and exploitation or the offer of clothing. He would either move on to another farm or become a more sinister creature known as a Buggane (see also Boggarts & Hobgoblins). It is probable that the Fenoderee is a species rather than an individual, though sightings of neither a female Fenoderee nor a female Killmoulis have been specifically reported (though it has been claimed that the Killmoulis has a wife).

Fenoderees that have become Bugganes are typically ugly and vindictive, but may also be inclined to haunt water-sources rather than homesteads. Bugganes are proficient shape-shifters and may sometimes adopt a Water-Horse type form (they are then often known as Glastyn or Glashan).

Milk and honey-cakes were also favoured foods of both species. The Killmoulis also had a fondness for pork, though in order to eat they needed to stuff the victuals into their nostrils.

The Bwca
(Also known as ~ Booka. Bwachod. Bwaganod.)

The Bwca are a similar breed to the Brownies & Hobs, though perhaps even more unpredictable in their mood-swings. The hearth and kitchen should be kept clean of dust, the fire kept alight and food should be provided for the Bwca. In return they will churn butter far better than any human could. If however the Bwca feel insulted or displeased (which they frequently do) they will instead turn all their efforts to creating as much noise, damage and disruption as possible. They also particularly dislike clergymen, teetotallers and also people with long thin noses (which is quite odd considering that many Bwca have a considerably beaky proboscis of their own). Anyone bearing one or more of these traits could find themselves a marked source of torment in a Bwca inhabited house.

Appearance and Attire : Small, shaggy and ugly, rather like Brownies but their noses and digits are often much longer.

Size : Usually 2 to 3 ft (0.6 - 0.9 m) tall.

Diet : They expect their human 'hosts' to provide them with a bowl of fresh cream on a nightly basis and also the occasional tipple of alcohol.

Habitat & Range : Mainly in rural houses and farms in Wales.

See also Bwbach & Bwciod. (Though differing but related species, these names have sometimes been used interchangeably with Bwca and the above alternate nomenclatures.)

Bean-Tighe & Tighe Fairies
(Bean-Tighe also known as ~ Our Housekeeper. Woman of the House.)

The Bean-Tighe is most happy when there is work left to be done in a house as she revels in being helpful. She will most commonly tend to the homes of single mothers (or those whose husbands are working away etc.) and elderly women ; though she is not sexist and will occasionally also assist men in similar situations. She would finish off chores and also check to see that the children and family pets were safe and sound as they slept. The Bean-Tighe is so efficient in her duties however that in the tense days of the Witch-hunts (see Witches and also Witch-finders), some old women would disrupt some of her work on a morning : they feared that a 'too tidy' house would indicate a Fay presence, who in turn may be misrepresented as an evil spirit and therefore possibly lead to the old lady being condemned for practising Witchcraft. The Bean-Tighe bears some comparison to the notion of 'Fairy Godmothers' - a character generally more familiar to Fairy-tales rather than to the folklore of Britain and Ireland.

Tighe Fairies are similar in their habits to Brownies but differ greatly in appearance and are also thought not to become quite so aggressive if offended. They will only do household chores if they want to however and not if the humans of the house grow to expect it or become used to it. The Tighe Fairies do expect to be fed in return for their efforts but are greatly disturbed by any further displays of gratitude. They normally operate in female pairs, and because of their size much of the work is completed through enchantment rather than physical labour. They dislike loud noises, spiteful gossip and will not enter a house that keeps a cat.

Appearance & Attire : Bean-Tighe - Small old women with pleasant smiles and kindly eyes. They wear traditional bucolic clothing.

Tighe Fairies - Indistinct forms either hazy or radiant, sometimes even invisible.

Perceptive humans may see them as sparks or floating spheres of light, the sharper
clairvoyants may be able to discern the Fairy's subtle feminine form.

Size: Bean-Tighe - Between 3 ft (0.9 m) tall and slight human proportions. Tighe Fairies - Usually less than 6 inches (0.15 m).

Diet: The Bean-Tighe are fond of strawberries and cream, whilst the Tighe Fairies may only consume the foyson (essence) of food, both species would be displeased if the human 'host' neglected to provide their nightly supper.

Habitat & Range : Houses and sometimes inns and hotels ~ Bean-Tighe - Ireland and sometimes Scotland. Tighe Fairies - Isle of Man

Silkies & White Ladies
(White Ladies also known as ~ Y Lady Wen.)

The Silkies are strange and solitary Fay women that finish off household chores at night when the humans are asleep in their beds. They are often contemplative and morose, the only sound usually heard from them is the gentle rustle of their elegant silk gowns. However if the Silky considers that the human servants or keepers of the house are lazily negligent in their efforts and are taking her for granted, then she will harass them at any given opportunity. The melancholic Silkies are sometimes thought not to be a Faerie breed as such, but in fact to be the Ghosts of young women who had died a tragic and untimely death - perhaps even murdered by their own lovers. They are thought to undertake the domestic tasks to distract their minds from their sorrow and pain, and to kill some time in their perhaps eternal wanderings. Occasionally Northumbrian Silkies were to be seen out of doors, especially in the locality of Black Heddon. Sometimes they were observed indulging in pursuits contradictory to their sullen, refined visage, such as felling trees, breaking large rocks or startling horses for mischief. Whether engaged in domestic chores, manual labour or lowly misbehaviour, the activities and appearance of a Silky are intriguingly converse. For when these entities were first apparently encountered, silk was still a material generally adorned only by those privileged enough to be above tasks of drudgery or vulgar pranks. Previously in Scotland, law once prohibited those of a class below aristocracy from wearing such fine attire. Other White Ladies reportedly encountered, may certainly share a visual resemblance and an equally sombre history to the Silkies but they will not assist with the errands.

Though most non-domestic White Ladies do little more than scare or alarm, a far more malevolent example was spoken of in Cornwall. The White Lady of Pendeen Vau earthworks shared traits with Korrigans and Succubi. Appearing initially as a beautiful woman bearing a single red rose between her teeth, she would entice men into the narrow Iron Age chambers whereupon she would transform suddenly into a horrific entity and bring about their demise.

A rare male equivalent (who was not known to wear silk) was the Cauld Lad of Hilton Castle, Tyne & Wear, England. Although like numerous Brownies, the Cauld Lad eventually abandoned his chores upon the offering of clothing, his origins were considered to be more in the keeping of Silkies for many believed him to be the Phantom of a servant boy beaten to death by his cruel master.

Grugach
(Also known as ~ Guagach. Grogachs. Gragon. Grogans. Gunnas. The Hairy Ones. Herders. Firesitters.)

Despite being covered in hair, the Grugach are always incredibly cold. For this reason they will on occasion, knock on the door of an isolated croft in the hope of sitting by the fire awhile. If the crofters refuse to help then the Grugach could likely cause damage to their home or steal their animals. If they were sympathetic to the Grugach's needs despite her odd, ugly and perhaps scary appearance (for most reported Grugach are female, particularly 'Firesitters') then their kindness or fearful compliance would be well repaid. She would protect their home and their animals, particularly cattle. She will feed, milk, calve, and lead the cattle to water and would also resolutely endeavour to protect the beasts from rustlers, predators, Witches and other malevolent Fay species such as the Cearb or Killing One - a Highland monster that preyed on both cattle and humans. Other Fay species that may prove to be a similar though less blood-thirsty nuisance include the Loireag - ragged female Faeries from the Outer Hebrides, who although being excellent singers and spinners were also an annoyance as they would suck cows' udders dry if left undisturbed (they could also become enraged and unpleasant should any mortal dare to join in with their music; especially so if they couldn't carry a tune) ; and also the Foawr - Manx hill-men that would hurl rocks at cow-herders and attempt to molest the cattle.

Male Grugachs do exist but are particularly rare, therefore broody females, concerned that they will never give birth themselves, have been known at times to abduct human boys. They mean no harm by this as they only want a son of their own to love and nurture and will tearfully return the child should they become aware of the real parents' distress. Male Grugachs are sometimes known as Grogachs or Grogans but the names and genders seem often to be interchangeable. The Gunna is a similar (though usually male) supernatural herder. The Gunna is described as being skinny, hairy and dressed in fox-skin.   **Appearance & Attire :** Very hairy and misshapen - their appearance can test whether a human will 'judge a book by its cover'. They often will carry a gnarled staff or shepherd's crook. Their simple clothing is coloured green , red or corn-silk gold.

Size : Commonly of human proportions though often heavily-set.

Diet : Especially fond of fresh milk.

Habitat & Range: Isolated pastures in Ireland, Isle of Man and Scotland, most prevalently in the Highlands. In Ireland the term 'Grugach' can also sometimes refer to vicious Ogre-like creatures.

Boggarts and Hobgoblins
(Also known as ~ Bogarts. Boggards. Boogies. Bugganes.
Hob-Gobs.
Tut-Guts. Tom-Tits. Tom Tit Tots.)

Certain circumstances and events may cause a Brownies and Hobs to turn 'bad'. In such cases they now often become known as Boggarts and Hobgoblins. 'Hobgoblin' though is in itself an ambiguous term, for initially it was just an alternative term for the more benevolent Hobs or Hearth Goblins but later came to represent more troublesome household and outdoor entities such as the Hob o t' Hursts.

Boggarts and Hobgoblins are generally more of a nuisance than life-threatening, however some of their pranks may verge on the dangerous. Their behaviour can range from the frustrating (hiding keys and important documents etc.) to the annoying (moving furniture at night so that people bump into them in the dark etc.) and from the destructive (smashing crockery, weakening timber-work etc.) to the downright nasty (delivering minor beatings, starting small fires etc.). In fact anything that can go wrong could be attributed (perhaps conveniently) to the activity of a Boggart or Hobgoblin. Their previous value as helpers has been replaced several-fold by their extreme and unwelcome talent for mischief.

A tale was told in Worthen, Shropshire of a home that was plagued by a pair of Bogart-like creatures; one resembling a small wizened old man, the other a similar female. The family of the house fled their home in frustration and fear of this odd couple's antics and took up residence elsewhere. However in their haste to leave, they left behind a family heirloom, a silver salt-cellar. They valued this item financially and sentimentally and were anguished by its loss, so they sent their farmhand back to the old home to retrieve it. This he did but was subsequently followed to the new abode by the Bogarts. Again the gruesome twosome made their presence grimly apparent. In response their human hosts built a roaring fire in the hearth and set nearby a comfortable bed of straw. The Bogarts soon set about making good use of these luxuries and within long became relaxed and sleepy. Suddenly the family and farmhand rushed the Bogarts and bundled the pair into the fire. Armed with pitchforks, they prevented the Bogarts from escaping the flames back into the room. Whether the Bogarts were thus cremated or whether they managed to flee to safety up the chimney is uncertain, either way the family received no more trouble from these creatures.

Hobyahs and Hob o t'Hursts
(Hob o t'Hursts also known as Hob Thursts. Hob Hursts. Hob Thrushes.

Hobyahs are extremely vicious forest Goblins whose numbers are thankfully limited due to their predilection for infanticide and cannibalism. Their range is also fairly localised but it is thought that a number of their brood stealthily accompanied early Scots pioneers to the New World , particularly to the States of New England. (though possibly a race of similar native fiends were identified as being the same homeland menace.) In their new land they preyed on both the locals and colonialists until their vulnerability to large dogs was discovered.

'Hob o t'Hurst' is a designation that along with Hob Thrust, Hob Hurst, Hob Thurst and Hob Thrush, is often interchangeable with the domestic Hob or the unruly Hobgoblin. The affix 'Hurst' is an old word meaning a 'wooded place' which refers to these particular Hob like creatures favoured abode. The Hob o t' Hursts often dwelt in small caves, burrows or deserted buildings at the heart of forests but also sometimes on moor-land or by the sea. They bear certain comparisons to both Hobyahs and Ogres, and like them can pose a great threat to human life but are not always quite as aggressive. Though they certainly shouldn't be trusted, with a sense of contrary typical of many supernatural beings the Hob o t'Hurst could be called upon to cure children infected with Whooping Cough. There is the possibility therefore that not all Hob o t'Hursts are wicked flesh-eaters, but this a risky theory to pursue.

Appearance and Attire : Concise descriptions of both the Hobyahs and Hob o t' Hursts are scarce, though it is likely that they share typical characteristics such as thick skin, long teeth, dirty hair, wild eyes and claws. Clothing if worn is likely to be coarse, ragged and stained with gore.

Size : Approx. 3½ ft (1.05 m) tall or less.

Diet : Hobyahs - Fresh, raw meat and carrion of their own kind or any other species.

Hob o t'Hursts - They are reputedly fond of stew boiled in a cauldron from a stock of children's' thumb-bones.

Habitat and Range : Both species dwell mainly in forests, though some Hob o t' Hursts also habituated sea-coves.

Hobyahs - Scotland. Hob o t'Hursts - England, particularly the Eastern Shires and the Northeast.

Bogles
(Also known as ~ Ballybogs. Boggies. Bog a Boos. Boggle-Bo.
Boggles. Bo. Bo-Men. Boggans. Mudbogs. Peat Faeries.
Swampys. Tom Loudys. Tod Lowerys. Teuz. Tuez.)
Bogles and their related species are most frequently to be found in
or around marsh-land and their weird appearance and habits seem to
well suit this environment. Because of their bizarre aspect, strange
aroma and their slobbering grunting language, many people might
find them to be repulsive and will possibly assume them to be
moronic. However though many Bogles are without doubt dim-witted,
the personal guile and intellect of individuals is often difficult to
ascertain and may well be dangerously under-estimated. The same can
often also be said of their temperament; some may actually want to
befriend humans and may attempt to help lost travellers, but how
are they to realise that as a species we are not cut out to naturally
traverse their boggy terrain ? Otherwise they may deliberately call or
guide humans unto a smelly demise, but it is claimed that they are
more prone to harm liars and murderers. Certain Bog Spirits known
as Tod Lowerys or Tom Loudys are said to be able to take the form
of foxes and have also been rumoured to enter households on
occasion.
Several theories have been suggested to account for the origins of
Bogles and other humanoid marsh species, these include -
-They have evolved from primitive swamp amphibians.
- They are the descendants (who have regressed rather than advanced
as a species) of the Firbolg race. This may be particularly relevant to
the Irish Bogles known as Ballybogs.
- As Peat Faeries they are the elemental guardians of swampy habitat.
- They are the souls of humans whose remains lie deep in the mud,
either as a result of losing their way and then their lives, tribal
sacrifice or murder (see also Will 'O' the Wisps).
Whatever their roots these creatures may be in great decline as their
habitat has diminished considerably due to over-exploitation of peat
and also to land drainage schemes. Such procedures are detrimental
both to natural and supernatural ecology, but can also be hazardous
to mankind as they can ultimately contribute to the occasional
flooding of human inhabited areas during especially rainy
weather.Most Bogles have slimy smooth skin, but some individuals
may have a rough warty complexion and / or clumps of thick matted
hair. They commonly have large bulging eyes, dribbling mouths and
no necks. Their heads frequently seem too large for their bodies and
their limbs too spindly. Their fingers and toes are often lengthy but
sometimes also palmate.

Bogies
(Also known as ~ Bogeys. Shape-shifting Bogies. Goblins. Gobelins. Gobelines. Brags. Padfoots. Boogars. Buggars. Buggers. Bugs. Frittenings. Bauchan. Boggarts. Bockles. Horse- laughs. Kows. Wirrikows. Shaggy Foals. Shug-Monkeys. Bwaganod. Bogey-Beasts. Bogey-Bests. Barguests. Bogests. Bargeists. Bogeists. Gytrash. Colt-pixys. Dunnies. Doonies. Bonelesses. Brash. Bocan. Boh. Bogan. Bugan. Buggans. Pooks. Black Goblins. Tatter-Foals. Biasd Bheulach. Its. Cutties. Bibittes.
{see also **Phookas** and **Black Dogs**})

The various forms of Shape-shifting Bogies are commonly to be found making a nuisance of themselves after dusk, along lonely roads, around farms and in other remote bucolic locations. They are generally irritating and sometimes frightening tricksters rather than deadly threats. In some regions though, certain Bogies were considered to be the Phantoms of outlaws, reivers or other scurrilous scoundrels. Probably the most basic but still unsettling of their pranks, is their habit of walking behind solitary travellers. Should the wanderer be brave or foolish enough to stop and turn there will usually be nothing to be seen or heard ; as they continue walking however, they will soon sense that they are being followed and may even hear heavy breathing or the crunch of footsteps close behind them. Again there is nothing to be seen and if alarm sets in and the human wayfarer begins to run, then the Bogey will also start to run and at times may invisibly overtake and knock the human sprinter to the ground before vanishing in a fit of laughter.

Many Bogies (though not all) can also assume a variety of natural forms including dogs, small horses and pigs, though sometimes there may be something most peculiar about them ; for instance some Barguests (or their similarly named equivalents) will assume the form of horned dogs. Other Bogey manifestations may be even more surreal such as a headless duck, a small cyclone or a dancing bag of soot. The Boneless of Oxfordshire was described as being a jellyfish-like glob of white flesh, yet it still managed to chase people. The Bibittes of Brittany resembled umbrellas that had blown away in the wind and had become tangled up in the branches of trees. Should anyone stop to rest beneath the tree, then the Bibitte would unfurl, drop down and devour them. They were apparently especially keen on preying on youths who had stopped to smoke a sly cigarette.

The Hedley Kow of the Northumberland – Durham borders was particularly known for assuming various forms for its mischief making. These include bundles of hay or sticks seemingly lost or disregarded

on the way-side and would proceed to get heavier as the discoverer struggled to get their 'lucky find' home. Upon reaching their abode the bundle would suddenly assume a humanoid form and run away laughing, leaving their victim exhausted and annoyed. It would also mimic dairy cows in order to kick over buckets full of milk and land the unfortunate dairy-maid in bother. Occasionally though some Bogey tricks went beyond humour and they would pinch, beat and bite unlucky travellers. The invisible Bocan of the Hebrides Isle of Skye and the shapeless Biasd Bheulach (also of Scotland) were the worst possible example as they were renowned for mutilating and butchering walkers of lonely paths. Equally nasty but more choosy about its victims was the Headless Trunk (also known as the Coluinn gun Cheann or Colann Gan Ceann) of the Scottish Highlands. He would not touch members of the MacDonald family of Morar, or children and women, but men travelling the lonely roads by night were fair game for his brutality.

Phookas
(Also known as Pucas. Pwcas. Phoukas. Pucks. Pooks. Pookas. Goat-Heads.)

These black Goblins share some common ground with other Shape-shifting Bogies, however they are more likely to operate in packs, particularly in Ireland (though they are highly quarrelsome amongst themselves). They are especially keen shape-shifters and will readily assume the form of goats, bulls, pigs, donkeys, horses, ponies, dogs, bats and even eagles. A common Phooka trick, executed in whatever form, is to toss weary pilgrims onto their backs and deposit them unceremoniously into a puddle, hedge or pile of dirt after first treating them to a terrifyingly wild ride. At times the Phookas will also occupy themselves by robbery, abducting children, spreading disease, blighting fruit and crops and at times sometimes causing the sudden death of farm animals. The Phookas of Ulster are reputedly more malign than those of their kind found elsewhere.

Appearance & Attire : In whatever animal form they assume, the Phookas are jet-black with blazing luminous eyes. Occasionally they may appear with a conglomeration of varied animal parts including sometimes the shadowy heads of men. They may also sometimes assume a small humanoid form.

Size : Variable depending on manifestation.

Diet : They reputedly display a fondness for blackberries and raw potatoes. (Some foragers would not pick brambles after Halloween in the belief that Phookas had spat or urinated upon them.)

Habitat & Range : Secluded tracks and rural areas most prevalently in Ireland, however solitary specimens also occur in Wales.
The Phookas are generally replaced in England and Scotland by the similar Barguests and Bogey Beasts.
(see also Bogies and Black Dogs.)

Bull Beggars
(Also known as ~ Galley Beggars.)

The Bull Beggars lie somewhere between Phantoms and Bogies, and frequently their area of activity is said to lie within the locale of an ancient burial site. They take great pleasure in scaring people. A frequent but simple trick of theirs is to lie apparently lifeless on the ground and as a human approaches to investigate and possibly assist, it will suddenly leap into the air with a blood-curdling shriek. Its other favoured pranks are more bizarre and often involve the Bull Beggar removing its own head. The Galley Beggar of the 2 Stowey Hills in Somerset, England was known to use a hurdle (woven wood fence) as a toboggan and hurtle around with its head tucked under its arm. They are also known for being proficient jumpers (see also Spring-heeled Jack).

Appearance & Attire : Either incredibly emaciated or more frequently entirely skeletal, either with or without a skull. Clothing at the very most amounts to little more than tattered rags.

Size : Of normal human proportions.

Habitat & Range : Localised around England, especially in the vicinity of discovered or suspected Celtic burial mounds or other areas of archaeological interest.

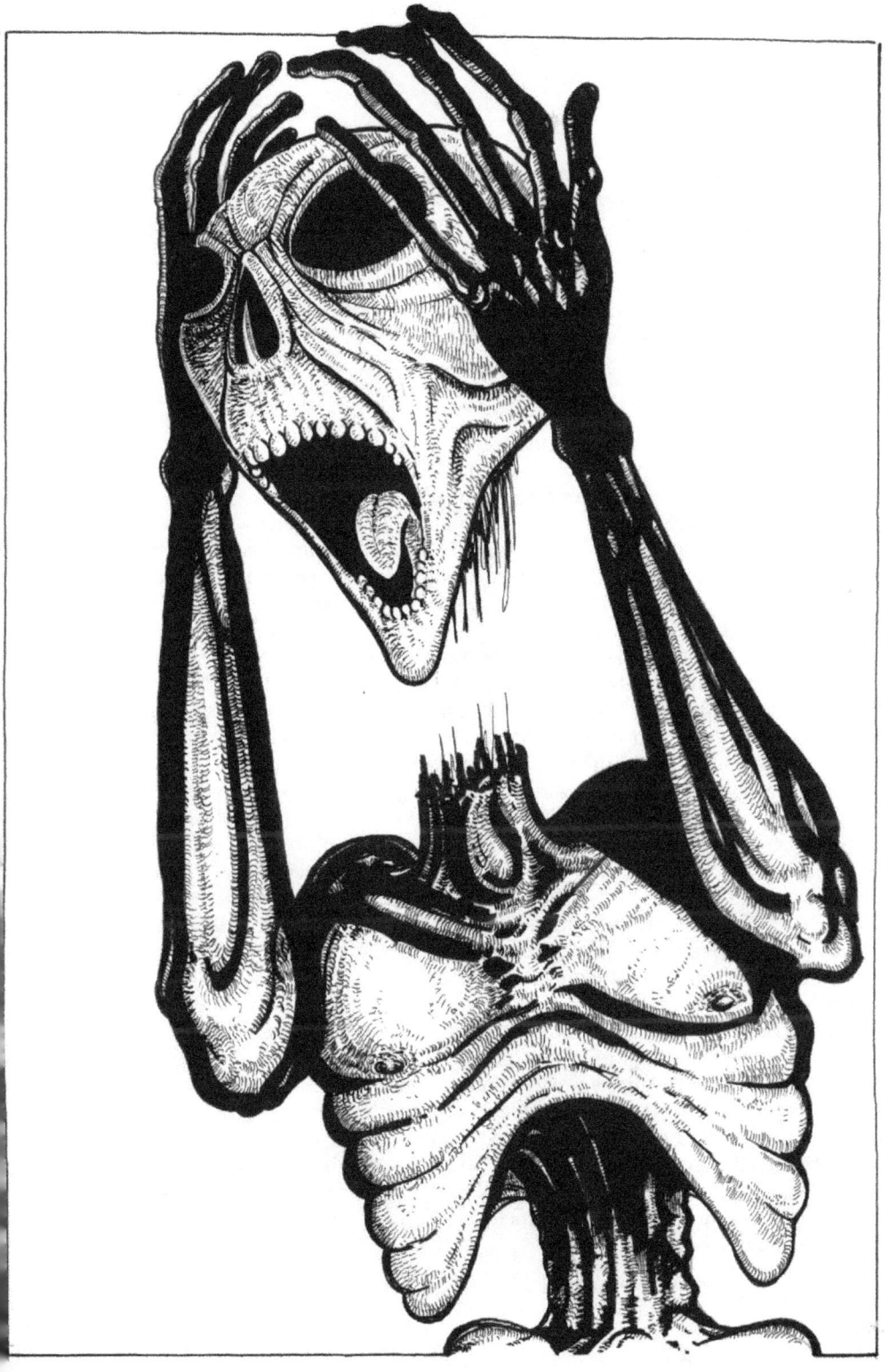

Leap-upons
(Also known as ~ Oschaert. Buckys. Dark Riders.)

In bygone times many pilgrims and wayfarers often had little choice but to travel by night and by foot. Lifts on horse-drawn carts may have been few and far between on the more remote routes, as were inns and hostels. To conserve heat energy it was better to try to catch a few winks of sleep in a field or way-side under the warming rays of sunlight , and to walk by night in an effort to fend off the chill. However night-walking could provoke other threats to health and survival, and not just originating from 'conventional' wild animals or human brigands and thieves.

The Oschaert were similar in some ways to other road Bogies, but were altogether more vile and deadly. They would suddenly leap upon the backs of nocturnal hikers and any efforts to shake them loose would only cause them to grip tighter, digging in their elbows, knees and heels ever deeper. As they forced their human beast of burden continually onwards, the Oschaert would whisper gross profanities and spiteful gossip into their ears as their fetid breath and bilious acidic, drool would scorch their necks and cause them to retch. As the journey progressed they would become increasingly heavy and force their human host into mind-numbing exhaustion and at times even death. Only the peal of church bells, the crow of a rooster or the break of dawn would cause them to release their grip and vanish.

The Buckys are an akin species that inflicts horse-riders. They would jump up behind the rider and endeavour to strangle or garrotte them.

A strange but similarly motivated entity known as Hairy Hands shows equal contempt for travellers on Dartmoor. Manifesting only as a disembodied pair of hairy hands, this aptly named fiend's activities have included slapping horses so suddenly and severely that their riders have been thrown or their carts overturned. It has also been known to wrestle with cyclists, motorcyclists and automobile drivers causing them to lose control of their vehicles and to career into ditches, trees or walls.

Appearance & Attire : Often naked or of unremarkable dress. Their skin is either bristly or slimy smooth and of varied sickly colouring. They were spindly limbed with pointy joint bones and sharp grasping digits. Their features were generally pointed with cruel eyes and malicious sneers. Commonly they were also of an odious fragrance.

Habitat & Range : Lonely roads and bridle-paths mainly in Scotland but also localised across Britain and Ireland. In Ireland the corpses of restless dead were sometimes inclined to take unwelcome rides upon the backs of the living.

Lutins
(Also known as ~ Lutins Noir. Black Lutins. Araigenees Lutins. Follet. Fions. Fouletot. Foulta. Folaton. Bon Garcon. Good Boys. House-Fairies. Cheval Bayard. Nion Nelou. Penette. Soltraits.)

It is uncertain whether the extremely capricious Lutins are a true Faerie race or are actually more closely related to Goblins as they display attributes of both. They are avid Shape-Shifters who, unlike some of the Fay breeds, do not suffer any long-term consequences of regular transformations. The Lutins use metamorphosis both as a means of transportation and disguise but also as an efficient tool for causing havoc and mischief. Though they can at times be of benefit to mankind, they also delight in causing people to feel tormented, infuriated and frustrated.

Like the Phookas of Ireland, the Lutins may adopt the forms of horses and humiliate anyone unfortunate enough to climb upon their backs. In horse-form the Lutins are known specifically as Cheval Bayard. Indeed the Lutins have a special affinity with horses and regularly feed and pet these animals. Conversely though they will sometimes bind horses manes into the matted clumps known as Hag-knots or Elf-Locks.

Sometimes Lutins may take up residence in a house and if treated well may undertake a variety of domestic chores (see also Brownies, Bean-Tighe and Tighe Fairies). In such circumstances they may be referred to as House-Fairies. They are more likely to choose a home in which there is at least one pretty young woman to gaze upon, but even so their boredom threshold is so low that they will remain in the dwelling for one year at the very most. If offended whilst in lodging, then as with Boggarts and Bwca, the Lutins will demonstrably vent their displeasure. They will pinch and scratch people, shout obscenities, unravel knitting and tangle spinning threads. They may cause greater damage in the manner of Poltergeists. Furthermore if residing on a farm, they may also decide to torment the livestock by ripping clumps of fleece from the backs of sheep, by causing cows' udders to dry-up and their bodies to break out in scabs and most extremely by even tearing the horns from the heads of cattle.

Lutins may cause other damage and inconvenience by blocking roads or damming streams and have been accused of beating-up travellers and pushing them over cliffs.

Another favourite Lutin prank is to transform either themselves, pebbles or sea-shells into irretrievable nuggets of gold in order to frustrate the intentions of would-be treasure-seekers.

Lutins are repulsed by the plant Flax and have an aversion to iron.

Appearance: The Lutins are so keen on shape-shifting that their true form is indeterminate and they may in essence be invisible or of no fixed form. Amongst their favoured assumed forms though are those of horses, wolf-headed men, levitating flickers of light or flame, fire-flies and various inanimate objects. They may also manifest as curious diminutive monks dressed in red cassocks or as little boys. They have not been known to take either a feminine form. The Follet, a sub-species of Lutin, may appear as tiny old men with long white hair and beards and may be dressed either in the multicoloured manner of a Harlequin or Court Jester or may alternatively be garbed in red coats and leggings. They may be armed with little swords. Another sub-species, the Fions who reside in Ille-et-Vilaine are said to be especially tiny.

Habitat & Range : Across France, most prevalent in Normandy and Brittany. They do not habituate any locality for any great length of time but are most likely to be encountered in rural houses, farmyards, at crossroads, near megalithic monuments, on moors, beaches, in caves, by stagnant pools or amidst the branches of trees that overhang water.

Tatty-Bogles
(Also known as ~ Scarecrows. Wurzels. Tatter-Men. Mommets. Bugbears.)

Tatty-Bogles cannot help but frighten people, as they shamble down country roads with their arms outstretched as if crucified. Yet inspiring terror may not be their prime motive as they simply want to stretch their legs after a long day of solitude standing. The fear generated in human observers may be either amusing or regrettable to them or it may even go unregistered. It is by their very name and nature to frighten for they are the Scarecrows erected in fields by farmers to protect their crops from the hungry beaks of birds (a task they frequently fail.)

The reasons for their nocturnal animation is somewhat of a mystery for perhaps not all will rise and leave their plot, but some (like certain toys of the nursery) seem more inclined to come to life at night. Perhaps this is of their own volition or maybe there is some external enchantment at work. It could be that the magic of Witches or perhaps Fay beings animate these rag-bag effigies in order to cause mischief or perform other tasks. Otherwise a Scarecrow could provide an ideal host for a wandering spirit or Demon that possesses no true form of its own. Such a strange and shapeless soul is the Brollochan. These uncanny wanderers may visibly consist of at best a mouth and pair of eyes but they can grant mobility to any inanimate object they enter. Should a Tatty-Bogle be thus possessed by a Brollochan , this would be revealed as "Thyself" and "Myself" are said to be the only words it can utter.

Animated or not, there is often something unsettling, something creepy about Scarecrows; certainly they are designed to frighten - albeit birds rather than people but there often seems something deeper , something primeval to their make-up. They often have the same vague aura reminiscent of the Corn-Dolly fertility icons, sacrificial Wicker-men, Punkies or Halloween Lanterns and the Bonfire Guys burnt on November 5th (in apparent celebration of the grisly execution of Guy Fawkes and other 17th Century dissidents) - perhaps all effigies carry an atavistic memory of Faerie Stocks or Malefactors' Corp-Creadha (the facsimiles of victims crafted from usually clay or wax and nail pairings or such-like). Should such an effigy move when theoretically it shouldn't , then any profound foreboding perhaps becomes more understandable.

Shellycoats

The Shellycoat is an odd solitary creature but is mischievous rather than malicious. His jolly japes however can be extremely annoying , but it has been claimed that if a human verbally reprimands a Shellycoat's behaviour he will go away and sulk awhile (though will subsequently soon be back up to his old tricks). A favourite Shellycoat prank preys on human compassion or conscience ; upon a person's approach the well hidden Shellycoat will shout "Lost...lost" and thinking that someone is in distress the human will more often than not follow the voice in a bid to help. Though the continuous cries of "Lost ... lost .." seem to be getting further and further away from the person's original path, they will usually proceed to search and follow for to give in now could provoke the mental torture of realising that they willingly failed to save a life. At some distant point the weary human will grasp that the deploring voice is now calling from the original source of their search and the realisation that they have been way-led and tricked will dawn. Dejected and tired the human's efforts would oft be rewarded by gurgling laughter and a round of applause from the Shellycoat.

Appearance & Attire : Shellycoats have huge 'froggy' eyes and their amphibious skin can be purple, dark-red or muddy-green in colour. Their most distinctive feature however is their attire. The Shellycoats wear a cloak and cap constructed from shells which clatter noisily as they walk, announcing their approach. Female Shellycoats are probably very similar but have not been specifically reported.

Size: Generally of slight human proportions.

Diet : Unknown.

Habitat & Range : Streams, sylvan pools, occasionally in old abandoned buildings and sometimes close to the coast, in Scotland particularly in the Border Counties.

Gremlins
(Also known as ~ Gremians. Fremlins. Vexers. Widgets. Bugs. Glitches. Spandules. Spanners in the Works.)

Whilst many Fays, Goblins and some other supernatural entities may seem to be encountered less in modern times, creatures such as Gremlins have actually prospered with the advances in technology. Whether these creatures are somehow created by machinery, have evolved with it or are simply drawn to gadgets, vehicles and industry is a matter of debate; but whatever their origins, their presence is frequently unwelcome.

The Gremlins first came to greater attention following the sightings of them sat disturbingly in the cockpits of both Ally and Axis fighter planes during World War II. Though it is possible that Gremlins have been around since at least the Industrial Revolution, many of them do seem to have a particular love-hate relationship with aircraft. One theory suggests that this is because they once had the power of flight themselves but somehow lost it and are now both intrigued and envious of mankind's aerial achievements. A particular breed of Gremlin known as Spandules are responsible for the freezing up of aeroplane engines and wings.

Gremlins however can also commonly be found in any other machinery, vehicles and electronic contraptions. They are chiefly responsible for the sudden and baffling malfunctions in normally operational machinery. They normally only cause frustration, annoyance and sometimes financial expense but some of their habits such as chewing up cables and pulling out wires could be potentially very dangerous where vehicles, heavy machinery and live power sources are concerned. Similarly the Gremlins often known as Glitches or Bugs*, who are associated to computers are very irritating when they cause (usually unsaved) work to inexplicably 'crash'. However it is a much grimmer prospect should they ever choose to inflict any software or hardware relating to sensitive functions such as medical procedures, aircraft guiding systems or nuclear weapons.

It has been suggested that the name 'Gremlin' was originally coined by a British Royal Air Force squadron based in India in the 1930's. Beset by mechanical Problems, they named their supernatural protagonist with a nomenclature derived from combining the name 'Fremlins' (the only brand of beer served in their bar) with that of the German folklorists, the Brothers Grimm.

(The term 'Bug' was initially an alternative to Bugbear but has since also come to refer both to specific arthropods and often insects / 'creepy-crawlies' in general, to viral illnesses, to surveillance devices, to general annoyances and now to technological malfunctions.)

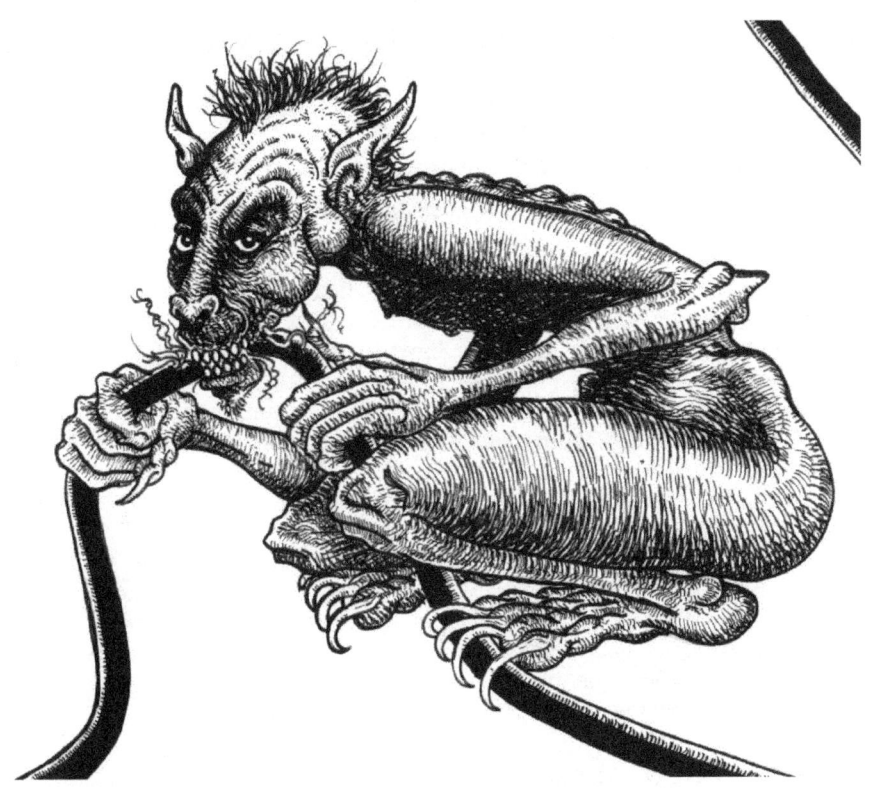

Appearance & Attire : Often invisible but otherwise may bear mischievous or wicked eyes and sharp toothed grins. Gremlin skin can be either bristly or smooth and can vary in pigmentation from greys and browns to dull yellows and greens. The females and juveniles are similar to the males and just as destructively active. Depending upon the type of machinery they infest, some Gremlins are naked or wear skin tight clothing so as not to get caught up in the workings themselves. Despite this some are said to sport impressive horns.

Size : Anywhere between 3 inches to 2 ft (0.075 - 0.6 m) tall.

Diet : Though they are said to chew electrical wires and cables, and to guzzle petrol it is unclear whether the Gremlins do this out of necessity or malice. Some Gremlins reputedly also displayed a fondness for beer, which led to the claim that virtually empty beer bottles
could be used as traps for these pests.

Habitat & Range : In factories, airports, air bases, computer centres and any other households and businesses that use vehicles, machinery or electrical items - basically everywhere in Britain and Ireland. (During the production of this Guide, there was a particularly irritating infestation of Computer Glitch Gremlins encountered!)

Red Caps
(Also known as ~ Redcaps, Bloody Caps. Fir Larrig. Red Combs.)

These malevolent Goblins get their names from their habit of butchering humans and washing their headgear in the blood-spill. They are attracted to places that have a history of war and genocide. Though the Redcaps have at times been invoked to do the foul bidding of Warlocks and Sorcerors, they are content to slaughter on their own volition and neither human nor Fay should feel safe in their company. They carry monstrous weapons ideal for hacking up nocturnal travellers, particularly those sheltering from the elements amidst the ruins of old castles.

Associated to the Redcaps are the Powries (also known as Dunters). These intangible Phantoms tend to haunt the same or similar locales as the Redcaps, and although they are not brutal themselves they may be attracted by suffering and gore. It has been suggested that Redcaps and Powries may both be the restless souls of sacrificed people or animals that were buried in the castle foundations during construction.

Appearance & Attire : The Redcap's leathery skin is pallid, aged and pock-marked whilst their eyes are wicked and bloodshot. Their teeth are long and dirty, and their fingers are like the talons of a great bird of prey. Upon their heads they wear blood-dyed hats, under which their long, gore-encrusted hair falls lank upon the shoulders of their heavy, weathered garments. Upon their feet they wear mighty iron boots (which is unusual, not only because it can alert victims of their approach but also because traditionally iron is a metal that otherworldly creatures often cannot abide). In their hands they carry sharp weapons such as halberds or pikestaffs.

Size : Approx. 3½ ft (1.05 m) tall.

Diet : Uncertain, but likely flesh and blood - human, Fay or animal.

Habitat & Range : Usually in or nearby castles, dungeons, ruins and cairns. Mainly along the Scottish / English borders, but also sometimes also in Ireland. Redcap Sly, the vile attendant of the cruel sorcerer and Lord of Lidderdale, William de Soulis, was said to reside inside an iron chest in Hermitage Castle, Roxburghshire - Borders, Scotland.

Spring-heeled Jack

Spring-heeled Jack is a strange solitary figure and may even be one of a kind, though his habit of terrifying humans simply for pleasure associates him with Bogies, Bull Beggars and Jack in Irons. His appearance and other details of his modus operandi set him apart as an entity in his own right. In addition to jumping out at unsuspecting people, Jack has been known to scale church spires and to hop from building to building, glaring in through upper storey windows. Sometimes plumes of blue fire are seen to be exhaled from his mouth and normally the extent of his attacks would be no more severe than slapping, shaking or slashing at the clothes of his victims with his metallic claws. At least one murder was accredited to Spring-heeled Jack however. That being the killing of 13 year old harlot, Maria Davis, who was thrown from a bridge in Bermondsley, London in 1845. Due to his erratic appearances over several generations it has been assumed that either Jack was particularly long-lived or that there may have been more than one character to adopt such a persona. In the 1830s, Henry de la Poer Beresford – the Marquis of Waterford was an eccentric yet entirely human individual suspected by some of being Spring-heeled Jack. The incriminations arose from the fact that he was a known practical joker, had protuberant eyes and his family crest resembled an emblem that one witness had reported seeing emblazoned on Jack's garments. No conclusive proof could be found to officially condemn Waterford however and Spring-heeled Jack reappeared after the Marquis' death in 1859. Therefore the true identity or identities of Spring-heeled Jack, as well as his essential nature still remain a curious enigma.

Appearance & Attire : His skin is pale and his nose, ears and chin are long and pointed. His eyes glow with a rum intensity and he is sometimes reported as having a tail. He wears a black hooded cloak which when thrown back reveals a pointed metal helmet and either a black or white shiny, skin-tight body-suit. Often attached to the back of his hands are metal talons and on his feet he wears high, pointy-toed, Cuban-heeled boots.

Size : Tall, but of normal human proportions.

Diet : Unknown.

Habitat & Range : Urban and rural areas of England. Most prevalent in London, the Home Counties and the Midlands, but occasionally encountered as far north as Lancashire and Cheshire. His last grand appearance was possibly at Everton, Liverpool in 1904.

Bogeymen

The most notorious of the malevolent Nursery Bogies are probably also the most enigmatic. Many generations of children across Britain and Ireland were familiar with the instructions, "Behave yourself..." or "Don't go there..." followed by "..or the Bogeyman will get you." The origins of the Bogeyman are as shadowy as his form of behaviour. The names of various supernatural creatures such as Phooka, Bwca, Bugbear, Bogey and therefore Bogeyman have been suggested to have linguistically derived from the archaic 'Bwg' or 'Bucca' which referred to a mysterious Welsh-Celtic Dark God or Spirit (possibly itself derived from the Slavic word, 'Bog' which means God). There are comparative foreign terms such as the German 'Boggellmann' or the North American-English 'Boogieman'. In Spain the term 'Coco' serves the same purpose (feminine – 'Coca') and in Italy the Bogeyman is most commonly referred to as 'l'omo nero' – the Black Man. The Child Guzzlers often portrayed on Carnival flyers and banners of the middle ages, are early representations of ravenous flesh-eating Bogeymen. On Jersey, the Bogeyman is known as Le Barboue - the Bearded One.

Definitive description of the Bogeyman can vary greatly and often are quite vague. This can also stimulate an additional fear factor, as this allows the imagination of children to go into overdrive concentrating on the attributes they personally fear most. Various experiences and elements can help to give the Bogeyman shape and character : for instance, the Bogeyman that haunted the childhood of my elder siblings was a large black man called Rahbone. He was not black in the sense of race or pigmentation, but was instead ebony stained from the dense film of soot or coal-dust that covered him. Rahbone's name very likely derived from the bewildering calls of the rag and bone men that once commonly scoured the area on their horse and carts looking for scrap. Other Bogeymen individual to particular families may also have evolved in similarly strange ways.

Whilst it is beyond dispute that the Bogeyman can be a useful parental tool to try and maintain good behaviour and safety awareness in their children, it is also apparent that there are dangers to be kept safe from. Bogeymen and Bogeywomen do exist, with or without the shroud of the supernatural, there are monsters to be feared.

Appearance & Attire : The supernatural Bogeymen often vary according to an individual child's imagination and it is possible that they employ telepathic and shape-shifting powers to do so. Occasionally they may seem nice and friendly before revealing their true colours. In non-specific form they tend to be dark and hazy, rather like shadows.

Size : Variable, often of human proportions.

Diet : They are often claimed to eat children, especially naughty ones.

Habitat & Range : Could be anywhere and everywhere across Britain and Ireland.

Bugbears
(Also known as ~ Bug-a-Boos. Bucca. Bugs. Bugans. Boggle-Boos. Boo-Baggers. Bugges.)

Bugbears are similar to the Bogeymen in their mysterious nature and their potential to be shaped into distinctive forms by the mental workings of young children. Though the term 'Bugbear' is often used to refer to any personal phobia or to anything that scares, however it can also be used to specifically refer to house monsters ; in particular those strange and sinister creatures that dwell under beds, in cupboards or behind the curtains. From these places they glare out menacingly waiting for a child to leave their bed during the hours of darkness. Night-lights have traditionally been used in some households to keep the nocturnal Bugbears at bay.

Though it has been considered that their name in part derives from the early belief that many Bugbears either wore bearskin garments or even had the faces of bears, their appearance and attire can vary greatly. The folklorist, Katherine Briggs however suggested that the name may actually derive from an old proverb, "How easy is a bush supposed a bear." The meaning of which relates to how fear or nervousness, especially in dim light can cause the eyes to play tricks on the mind (and vice versa) and the power of imagination can make the commonplace seem very extraordinary indeed.

The etymology of Bugbear as with 'Bug' in general, with its connotation to disease or creepy-crawlies (see also Gremlins) may actually derive from the ancient Welsh Bucca, a strange spirit that Welsh fishermen thought necessary to placate with offerings. Bugbears in general share several points of comparison with Trickster Spirits such as Boggarts, etc and also to the Shape-shifting Bogies. Scarecrows were also sometimes referred to as Bugbears (see also Tatty-Bogles). In recent times the term 'Bugbear' is more frequently used in reference to an object or matter of irritation or concern, rather than to indicate a malicious creature of the darkness.

Appearance, Attire & Size : They usually assume the form a particular child finds most frightening, e.g. clowns, tarantulas, wolves ...whatever. Many of them may assume the scary attributes of various different creatures.

Diet : It is feared that they will eat any child up past their bedtime.

Habitat & Range : Across Britain and Ireland. Most frequently in houses, especially in the bedrooms of young children.

Bodachs

The Bodachs have been associated with the domestic Brownies or more specifically their Boggart persona. Whether the Bodach are a specific form of Boggart or whether they are a similar species that have never bothered themselves with the initial household niceties, is uncertain. Either way they make neither a welcome visitor nor a pleasant lodger to a home. The word 'Bodach' roughly translates as 'Old Man' (their females are possibly the entities known as Moulachs) and his favourite hobbies include crawling down chimneys and poking young children with his long bony fingers. Like the Bogeyman (and also sometimes the Trows), the Bodach is said to steal away naughty children in particular ; but in the Scottish Highlands if any infant (either originally naughty or nice) was believed to be a Changeling, then the substitute child would likely be a Bodach. His strange aspect may raise some suspicion but this could be initially shrugged off as many babies look a bit odd, but due to his very mature tastes and his outspoken manner the Bodach would soon reveal his true identity.

Specifically the Bodach–Glas, or Dark Grey Man (sometimes also known as the Dovach or Mournful One) and the Bodach au Dun or Old Man of the Hill were said to be heralds of death (see also Wraiths.) The phenomenon of this gloomy harbinger extended over the borders into Northumberland. Such an abomination formerly frequented a Willow grove at Bellister near Haltwhistle. It was said to be swathed in a long grey cloak and to hover slightly above the ground. Furthermore a tremendous gash cut across his pallid face dripping gore onto his beard and long, hoary hair. Sure catastrophe followed any encounter with this entity or any of its like kind.

Appearance & Attire : The Bodach is commonly wizened and wrinkled like a raisin or sultana. His skin can be either pasty, jaundiced or brown, and may sometimes be bristly or blemished. He is generally either naked or ragged.

Size : Commonly 2 to 3 ft (0.6 - 0.9 m) tall.

Diet : Some people may attempt to humour a Bodach with offers of milk and honey, but though the bribe will likely be eaten it would probably not inspire kindness in return.

Bodachs are also notoriously fond of Whisky. The Grey Bodachs do not seem to show any especial interest in food or drink.

Habitat & Range : In and around rural dwellings in Scotland and to a lesser extent the Northern English borders.

Dobies
Also known as ~ Dobbies. Dobbs. Bobles. Cloggies. Bodachan Sabhail.)

Dobies are the Brownies and Hobs too dim-witted and clumsy to be of any practical use around the home. Instead they occupy their time befriending old people, especially those pensioners whose minds are said to be 'wandering' (as the Dobies feel that they are less likely to ridicule them). Dobies are usually jovial and mellow if not too bright, and provide good company for the old folks. In some areas such as County Durham in Northern England, they were also prone to turn up at weddings, christenings and other such celebrations.

Dobies very rarely have the inherent capacity to turn bad (see Boggarts & Hobgoblins), that is of course with the notable exception of the West Yorkshire Dobies whose mean and murderous habits are very similar to the Scots Buckies (see Leap-Upons). The White Dobbie of Furness in Scotland was a peculiar gaunt, sickly looking little fellow who always wore a dirty white coat and was constantly accompanied by a strange white Hare with bloodshot eyes.

Appearance & Attire : Either nude or shabbily dressed, the Dobies are brown, wrinkled and sometimes hairy. Their faces are somewhat ugly and gormless-looking.

Size : 2 to 3 ft (0.6 - 0.9 m) tall.

Diet : They are fond of milk and honey cakes.

Habitat & Range : Houses, barns and Rest Homes across Scotland and England, as far south as the Midlands.

Bwbach and Bwciod
(Bwbachs also known as ~ Booakers. Bottagers.
Bwbachod {may be used as a pluralism or alternative singular term})

Both of these species (like the Bwca) tend to attach themselves to Welsh houses, but unlike them they will not bother to churn butter. In fact they will not bother to help with any chores yet they still demand that the house be kept clean and cosy.

The Bwbachs are solitary Fays that affiliate themselves to houses and not the inhabitants. Though they will tolerate the residing family as long as they keep a good fire and food, any visitors to the house are instantly regarded as intruders and will be briskly and vigorously sent running. If displeased a Bwbach will likely cause a curse of bad luck to befall upon the household.

The Bwciod are strange solitary Goblins who enter homes because of the warmth they offer. Though he will commonly block the heat of the fire reaching the family, he may be rarely seen as he is an incredible fidget and can move so fast as to be beyond a blur. Any attempts to move or remove a Bwciod will likely result in chaos.

Appearance, Attire & Size : Bwbachs - Plump to the point of being almost ball shaped.

Females have not been reported, but the males commonly wear big red turbans and littlered loincloths. They also drape fur cloaks over their shoulders.

Commonly no larger than 6 inches (0.15 m) tall.

Bwciod - Very thin, with long slender fingers and big feet. Their noses are very pointed and they have milky purple eyes. Females have not been specifically reported.

They are commonly between 1 to 3 ft (0.3 - 0.9 m) tall.

Diet : Bwbachs expect humans to provide them with food, even if it is only a piece of bread.

Habitat & Range : Both species are most frequently encountered inside houses in rural Wales.

Rawhead - and - Bloodybones
(Also known as ~ Tommy Rawhead. Old Bloodybones.)

Rawhead - and - Bloodybones has been quite an industrious fiend in his time, and not a too pleasant one at that. In East Anglia, Warwickshire, Lincolnshire, Yorkshire and Lancashire under the name of Tommy Rawhead he would lure children to their doom in quarries, mires and ponds. In Cornwall, where he was known by the name of Old Bloodybones, his grisly appearance led people to think that he was the Phantom of a soldier who had suffered a brutal and bloody death in a bygone local battle.

Combining his names, Rawhead - and - Bloodybones has since moved his activities indoors as well. Hidden under the stairs he would reach out with his long arms and cruel grasping fingers and seize children up past their bedtime. A female equivalent of this Nursery Bogie is known as Nelly Longarms (see also Water Ogres and The Groac'h).

Appearance & Attire : His head and body seem devoid of skin as blood oozes over his raw, painful-looking body. At times his arms and legs appear incredibly long.

Size : Usually of normal human proportions, yet there is some suggestion that he has at least some power to alter his dimensions, if not indeed further shape-shifting ability.

Diet : He possibly eats the children he seizes, but this is uncertain and may be just a scare story. (It has even been claimed that he grabs the children only in a bid to befriend them, but this is a risky assumption.)

Habitat & Range : Potentially dangerous outdoor locations and also the dark, shadowy corners of homes (e.g. under the stairs, in the attic, in the cellar etc.) Most active in England, but occasionally reported in Ireland.

Dream-weavers
(Individuals include ~ The Sandman or Dustman. Billy Winker or Wee Willie Winkie. Old Shut-eye or Awd Luck-oiye.)

These Nursery Bogies are most active come the night, when they move from house to house checking that the children are on the road to sleep. Here they will assist the passage up the wooden hill to the land of Nod by sprinkling magic milk or more frequently golden slumber dust or sand into the sleepy-heads' eyes. This magic powder or balm opens the doors to dreams and all the strange adventures they entail. Some Dream-weavers are also concerned with setting adults away also on their somnolent excursions.

Appearance & Attire : Invisible at will, but Little Billy Winker wears an old-fashioned night-shirt and cap and carries a candle. Old Shut-eye commonly wears silks of vibrant colourful patterns and a sun / star-burst hat. (He has a brother also by the name of Old Shut-eye, but he wears a lunar hat and visits once only as the sleep he brings is never-ending. The Sandman either wears similarly colourful clothes or is otherwise shrouded in a dark cloak and hat spun from the night itself.

Size : Usually normal human proportions (though Billy Winker is below average height).

Diet : Unknown.

Habitat & Range : Nocturnally active, most commonly in bedrooms across Britain and Ireland.

Tooth Fairies

Probably our only Fay species to regularly trade with mankind on an uncomplicated basis. When a child loses one of their milk teeth it is customary for them to leave it either on their bedside table or under their pillow, then as they sleep the redundant denture will be removed by the Tooth Fairy in exchange for a coin. The Tooth Fairies therefore need to keep up to date with the current value of milk teeth and the sum paid may often vary in accordance with tooth quality and cleanliness and possibly even geographic location. Children from more affluent families may often receive a higher payment for their teeth ; this may not seem fair but it is noticeable that many members of the British aristocracy do have bigger teeth, especially the top front incisors. The Tooth Fairy may also minimise or halt payments to the enterprising children suspected of forcibly removing their teeth before their natural time.

Though the Tooth Fairies are believed to live in social groups they generally carry out this work singly and it is usually only the females who collect. What they do with the harvested teeth is uncertain but it has been suggested that they use them as building materials in their own kingdom.

An oft-forgotten superstition holds that should the Tooth Fairy fail to collect the fallen denture by midnight, then there is the risk that tiny Witches will fly into the room in egg-shell sky-boats and steal away the tooth. Not only do these witches leave no payment but they can also use the tooth to direct curses and cruel spells against the child.

An alternative belief was once held that it was actually mice rather than faerie denizens that gathered children's milk teeth from beneath their pillows, however the notion of rodents scrambling under the bed-linen has seemingly since lost its appeal.

Appearance & Attire : Tooth Fairies are generally considered to be rather pretty and kindly-looking. They usually have wings and are often dressed in radiant silk frocks.

Size : Usually no larger than 2 inches (5 cm) tall.

Diet : Uncertain.

Habitat & Range: Most commonly encountered in the bedrooms of children across Britain and Ireland.

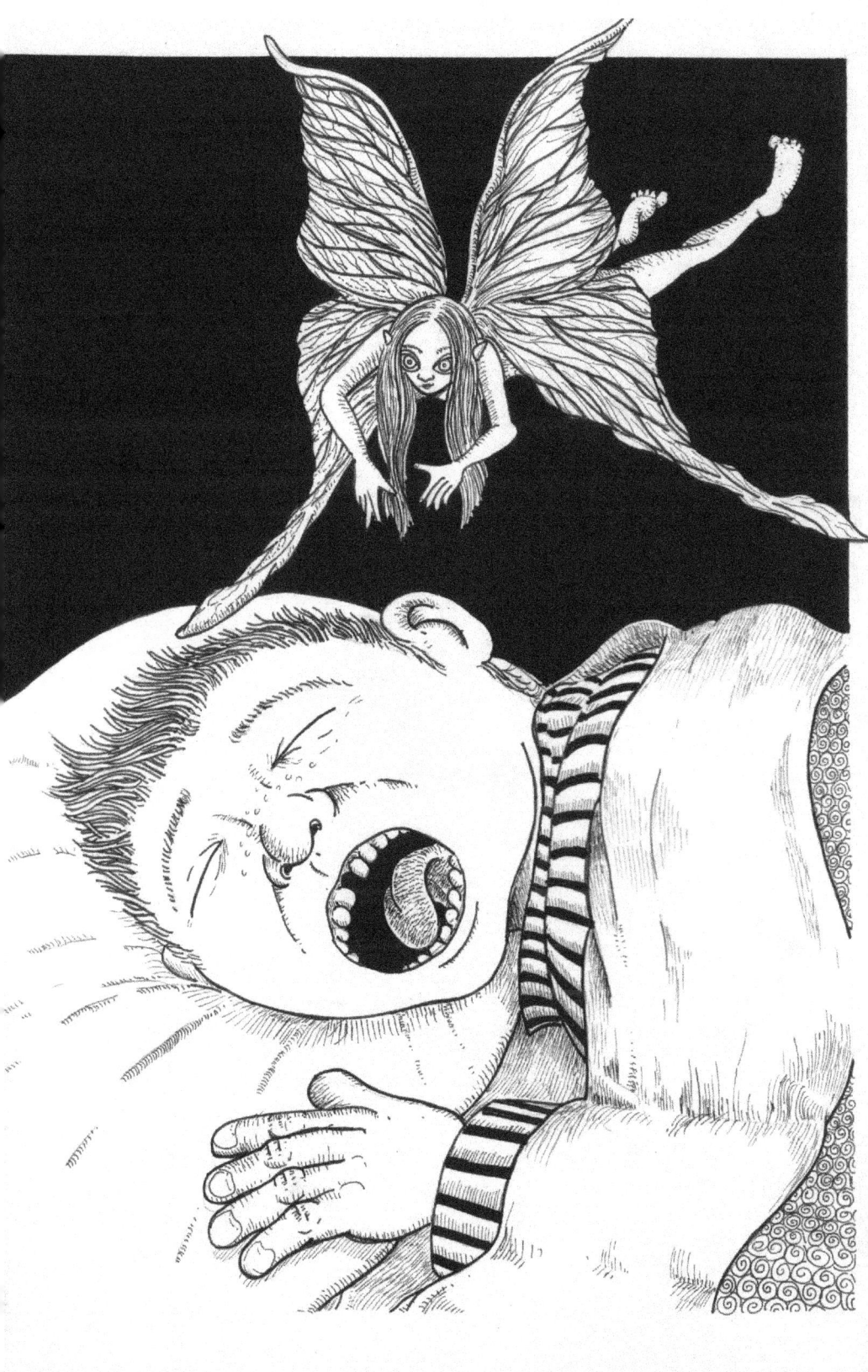

Book Bogies
(Also known as ~ Library Bogies)

Book Bogies are not true Bogies by any means and are scarcely mentioned in British / Irish folklore, yet many readers I'm sure will recognise their influence. They are the creatures responsible for attracting children to particular books and comics, gripping their attention and escorting them on many special adventures. They have transported generations of children to enchanted locations as diverse as Wonderland, Never - Never Land, Narnia, Middle Earth, the Chocolate Factory, Lilliput, Toyland and various riverbanks, desert islands, jungles, alien planets and many other strange places and times besides. They have invited children to mingle with knights, pirates, super-heroes, dinosaurs, outlaws, rascals, cowboys & Indians, Arabian Princes & Princesses and many other exciting characters and to feel part of their adventures. The Book Bogies bring the words and pages to life, though of course some of the credit must go to the authors and artists also.

Sometimes their powers wane as a child approaches adolescence and other interests ensue. Whenever an adult makes a chance discovery upon one of their special childhood books, then the Bogey's bookmark will frequently result in a wave of strange nostalgia, a rush of memories and sometimes even a passing melancholia.

The Book Bogies occasionally assist adult scholars and students by engineering those moments of 'synchronicity' or meaningful coincidence; when such things happen as a much-needed but elusive tome is suddenly discovered in a second-hand bookstore or when a book randomly plucked or even fallen from its shelf opens at a passage that will greatly assist the task at hand. Association could possibly also be drawn to the Irish superstition that upon the death of a truly great and learned person, all the books in a pertinent place would fall from their shelves.

As always with regard to all Supernatural creatures, care must be taken in the presence of Book Bogies. For whilst most are not only benign but actually beneficent, old Welsh folklore mentions that at times Demonic Imps have taken astral residence within the pages of books. Often in such cases, the books in question are of the sort that contain knowledge that if handled carelessly of selfishly, could lead to the grave corruption of the reader.

Book Bogies are generally invisible so as not to detract from the magic of the books themselves. Any visible form is probably open to the imagination.

Jack Frost and Snow Faeries

Jack Frost is the most infamous of the Snow Faeries who unlike the Cailleach Bheur, do not personify the destructive aspect of winter but instead promote the beauty and fun that can also be found in the cold season. The Snow Faeries are usually social but tend to be disinterested in humankind. Jack Frost (whom some have suggested is actually the King of the Snow Faeries) tends to be a solitary figure. He is primarily an environmental artist whose atmospheric landscapes can often be seen etched onto the glass of windows on a frosty morning. His many sculptures include the diverse attractive patterns of individual snowflakes, icicles and the ice-rings sometimes seen in rivers and lakes. Despite his appearance which may shock some, Jack Frost is not really a malevolent soul. However some of his designs such as the white windows he lays over bodies of water or the icicles he hangs from gutters and branches may be so delicate as to prove dangerous. He is also aware of the other hazards of winter and he will often alert children that they are not adequately attired for the harsh weather by touching their necks, noses, ears, hands and toes with his chilling breath and long icy fingers.

Appearance & Attire : The Snow Faeries are generally pale with dark eyes. They often wear white and sometimes have wings. At times however they may manifest as groups of children playing in the snow. Though they may sound or appear fairly close they always tend to stay the same distance away when approached.
Jack Frost's hair is frozen into impressive long white spikes and his eyes are black or icy blue. His nose and fingers are thin and pointed. His clothing tends to be sombre, either black or dark blue and he frequently wears a long heavy coat trimmed with ermine.

Size : In their Fay form the Snow Faeries are usually no larger than 6 inches (0.15 m) tall and many are much smaller.
Jack Frost can also alter his proportions at will and could stand anywhere between 6inches (0.15 m) to 6 ft (1.5 m) tall, but most commonly may be observed at approx. 3 ½ ft (1.05 m).

Diet : Unknown.

Habitat & Range : Across Britain and Ireland from late autumn to early spring. It is unknown where these beings reside in the milder months.

Santa Claus
(Also known as ~ Father Christmas. Saint Nicholas. Good Saint Nick. The Holly King. Santa. Santiclaus. Pere Noel.)

Ho Ho Ho !! Surely Santa Claus needs no introduction - He is good Saint Nicholas the jolly old guy with the big beard, big belly and booming voice. He is the one who climbs down the chimney on Christmas Eve to place toys and gifts in the hung-up stockings of well behaved kids, in celebration of the birthday of Jesus Christ. As no-one is certain of the exact birth-date of the Christ-child, the ascending Christian Church had to select a date upon which this most significant occurrence could be annually remembered. They selected December the 25th, a date considerably close to the Winter Solstice and shortest day of the year (actually 21st December which was dedicated to Saint Thomas). This was a significant choice for in the northern hemisphere this was the time of the year that the Celts held their Festival of light and the Romans their similar Sol Invictus ceremonies. Both occasions were held in respect of their respective Sun Gods (known to various factions as Sol. Helios. Belenus. Apollo, Apellon and Atepomarus amongst other names), so that in turn at the end of the season he would return with his healing, life-giving solar energy. Therefore an appropriate time, the Christian authorities considered, to remind their own followers of the birth of Jesus Christ - the Son of God and Light of the World. It was also this time of year that the ancient Romans celebrated their festival of Saturnalia, a weeklong bout of debauchery and hedonism that still echoes in the seasonal merrymaking of some folk. Furthermore December 25th was originally a day held sacred to Mithras (or Mithra or Mithris) the Persian God of Light whose worship extended to these isles via the Mystery Cults of foreign conscripts to the Roman army. On this day worshippers of Mithras would if possible participate in the sacrifice of a bull. In current times it is usually turkeys that end up providing the seasonal feast.

Prior to his own conversion to Christianity many, many years ago (an event that occurred somewhere in the east, possibly Turkey or Russia), the burgeoning figure of Santa Claus was known as the Holly King. It was his duty to oversee the land during autumn and winter - to see that the deciduous trees and hibernating beasts got off to sleep , that the migrating birds had set off for warmer climes and that the evergreens and seasonally active animals fared well when the Cailleach Bheur came calling. Even then though he was still a pleasant hoary-haired man who loved to make merry, especially at the Teutonic winter festival of Yule when the spirits of Holly, Ivy and Mistletoe were invited into a home to share the warmth of a good log fire.

Due to the increase in his workload in the 19th Century, having also assumed Christmas duties, Santa the Holly King uses enchantment but also employs many assistants to help him with his tasks. Elves, a species known for their craftsmanship are employed in Santa's workshop designing, constructing, testing and wrapping toys. In some areas these assistant Elves and perhaps also Gnomes were known as the Julnissen. Ranked highly amongst his motley little helpers was an odd character by the name of Knecht Ruprecht (or Black Peter). Whilst Father Christmas was of course laden with gifts of toys and sweet foods destined for well-behaved children, in bygone times Ruprecht, his stunted companion carried a Birch twig ready to infect a stinging present of his own upon less pleasantly-mannered boys and girls.

Ruprecht is associated with the strange entities known as Krampus.

Sometimes an infant boy known as Kris Kringle, believed to be the Christ-child himself may accompany Santa on his mission.

To transport himself and the abundance of gifts great distances over the sky from home to home Santa harnesses his sled to a small herd of fast flying Reindeer. The delivery of presents is assisted across Europe by other benevolent Xmas spirits such as Befana, Babushka, Bertha, Kalyda and other Christmas Aunties. Naughty children may receive a single piece of coal rather than a nice present, but sadly it sometimes occurs that a well-behaved child may also be unintentionally overlooked on Christmas morning - unfortunately errors are inevitable in such a large enterprise as Xmas.

The Easter Bunny

The Easter Bunny is not actually a 'bunny' rabbit at all, but is actually a hare. The hare was the sacred animal of Eostre (or Oestra or Ostera) the ancient Teutonic Goddess of the Spring Moon. At the time of the vernal equinox (March or April) the hares are famed for going 'mad' and it was at this time of the year that out of character for its species, one of Eostre's hares laid an egg. Not just any old egg but the Egg of New Life - the Easter Egg.

But surely Easter is a Christian festival marking Jesus Christ's resurrection after dying on the cross and not ceremonial to a Pagan hare-headed goddess? Well, actually it's both. Following debate at the Synod of Whitby in the 5th Century, the 'Christian Easter' is destined to fall roughly around the same time as the 'Pagan Easter' due to its association to the Judaic Passover which is also fixed by the lunar cycle. Both festivals could also be said to reflect new life, either Christ's return from the dead or the blossom and birth of Spring. So it was not much of a stretch for the ascending Christian Church to merge both festivals. This is known as 'assimilation' and was a habit frequently employed in those times and these isles to ease and encourage rather than force the conversion of heathens. Perhaps it is a little surprising that the pagan name was retained however.

But where does chocolate come into it ? Well, Easter Sunday also marks the end of Lent, the Christian time of abstinence which remembers the 40 days of fast and temptation Jesus endured in the desert. In this time Christians are expected not so much to fast now , but to do without luxury. In the past staple food such as butter and eggs were luxury items. These would be used up on Shrove Tuesday (Pancake Day) and then done without until Easter Sunday. Games such as egg-rolling and searching for eggs hidden by the Easter Bunny were played on this day to celebrate the end of the time of self-restraint. After the voyages to the Americas, chocolate became *the* luxury food hence the chocolate eggs hidden, delivered or laid by the Easter Bunny. Conversely in some areas in medieval times, it has been suggested that it was as customary to eat rabbit or hare at Easter as it was to eat roast beef or goose (and now commonly turkey) at Xmas. The consumption of hare-meat was thought to possibly have been taboo to at least some of the Celtic clans in earlier times however. The concept of the Easter Bunny as it is known today derives a lot from the American custom of taking old European folk-habits, adapting them to their own tastes and then exporting them back into Europe.

Care should be taken however in pursuing a suspected Easter Bunny as hares were a form frequently assumed by shape-shifting Witches and white hares are sometimes thought to be the Phantoms of murdered girls.

Appearance, Attire & Size : Traditionally a regular enough looking hare, the Easter Bunny has oft since somehow come to be represented by a man-size anthropomorphic rabbit.

Diet : Probably the vegetation common to regular hares.

Habitat & Range : Most active around Britain and Ireland around the time of Easter Sunday and the nearest full moon

Other Notable Bogies, Fiends and their ilk.

Captain Moonlight : Captain Moonlight was a shadowy figure most prevalent in Ireland, where come the night he would perform all manner of misdeeds such as setting fires, injuring animals and sometimes even murder.

Clap Cans : Clap Cans is rarely seen but more frequently felt and heard by children. As they try to sleep he will pull away their bed-sheets and strike the wall loudly. He may also give them the odd shake or slap and may be the Bogey who actually does break the things for which they get wrongly blamed.

Wry-neck : Originally a haunter of streams and becks, especially in Lancashire and Yorkshire, Wry-neck moved into homes where he now lectures on both the dangers and delights of water. Though this may seem conscientious, some people consider that Wry-neck should not be trusted and could even prove deadly.

Tom Dockin : This Nursery Bogey is fond of giving advice, sometimes wise - sometimes not so clever. However any child that disregards his opinions off-hand will likely have their ears chewed off by his formidable metal teeth.

Old Scarf : Though generally invisible this entity certainly makes his presence felt by holiday-makers in Norfolk, England. He will indiscriminately poke, prod and even push people to the ground. He is also known to violently rock caravans.

Tom and Mum Poker : These related spirits are most active in the Isle of Wight and East Anglia where Tom likes to cause shivers to run down children's' spines by touching their necks with his icy cold fingers whilst they are listening intently to spooky stories. Mum Poker is satisfied to just poke children roughly with her bony fingers, particularly if they are trying to concentrate or sleep.

The Night-Man : (Also known as Dooinney-Oie. Howlaa.) This misty formed spirit from the Isle of Man and will alert people to the approach of storms by suddenly appearing and wailing loudly. A similar creature is known in Cornwall as the Hoope

Robin Goodfellow : (also known as Puck.) This celebrated Hobgoblin is notorious for pulling the linen from beds as people try to sleep (particularly lazy servant girls) and pinching them black and blue. He is also known to play tricks on solitary wayfarers.

Tankerabogus : (also known as Tanterabobus.) This West-Country Bogeyman became renowned for its habit of dragging off badly behaved children to its deep, dark hole in the ground.

Long Lankin : (also known as Lammikin. Long Lonkin.) This Scottish / Northumbrian fiend was noted for its habit of nipping the flesh of children with its pincer-like fingers, and should the fancy take him, for brutally stabbing them with his razor-sharp blade. Should the terrified child call for its mother, then this could prove a devastating folly however, as Long Lankin would threaten to slash the parents' throat and catch their blood in a bowl.

Crum'ell (also known as Black Old Noll) : Following the English Civil War and the restoration of the monarchy, another Bogey figure made the rounds as a mother's threat to an errant child. The Bogey, Crum'ell was almost certainly originally inspired and based upon Oliver Cromwell, the fervent republican leader. His lifetime crusade involving ransacking as many monasteries and destroying as many religious icons and paintings as possible, inclined many of his opponents to think him in league with the Devil. After death Cromwell was destined to rest in pieces, as his head was removed and put on public display. However after a while, this grisly artefact was to go missing so perhaps this fiend would stop on occasion to nourish himself on naughty children, a convenient sustenance for his eternal trek in search of his head. (Similarly in later times, Napoleon Boneaparte - the French adversary of the British, was also demonised in England as a Bogey figure named Boney.)

Mother Bunch : Considered to have originally been the landlady of a London tavern and house of ill-repute, Mother Bunch lived on to become a source of cautionary fables, pub wisdom, rural advice and vulgar jokes, as well as being the 'Nursery Bogie' of hard drinking, boisterous adults.

Beither : In the Scottish Highlands, Beither was a useful tool for parents warning their children off from playing in caverns and caves. For this mysterious spirit was said to lurk in such locations and was prone to maltreating anyone who dared to disturb his solitude.

Le Beu : This Guernsey Bogie delights in very quietly sneaking up behind unwary people and without warning suddenly shouting in their ear.

The Amadans (Fools) : Children and adults alike are both ill-advised to disturb Faerie Hills or prehistoric barrow graves especially at night, for not only may they wreak the wrath of various Trooping Faeries or the spirits of the dead known as Barrow-Wights, but in Ireland they also risk attracting the attention of an Amadan. The Amadans are Faerie Jesters but possess a rather cruel and bleak sense of humour, at least as far as humankind is concerned. The touch of their fingers can cause partial paralysis or blood-clots to form on the brains of their victims. There are various forms of Amadan including the Amadan Dubh (the Dark Fool) whose music can induce madness, the Amadan-na-Breena (or Stroke Lad or the White Fool) who walks last in the Faerie Troop and the Amadan-Na- Briona , the shape-shifting fool who favoured manifesting either as a bearded sheep or a little, fat man with a tall hat and a long red scarf. Amadans are most active and dangerous during the month of June.

Boag : The wheels of old water-mills and the underside of bridges can obviously prove to be hazardous places and this is especially true in the South-West of England; for the Boag may be found lurking in such locations. A favourite trick of this cider-guzzling, bulbous-nosed Dwarf is to mimic the calls and pleas of a distressed human female in order to lure men to his domain. Instead of finding a damsel in distress these would-be heroes would instead find themselves facing this repulsive, leering drunk. Before they could react the Boag would pounce.

Eachrais Urlair : This Scottish Fay habituates the palaces and mansion-houses of Scotland, where she incites young children to misbehave or otherwise causes havoc for which they will be blamed. Known also as the Mischief of the Floor, the Eachrais Urlair also gains great satisfaction and pleasure in using magic to transform human beings into varied types of animal.

Flibbertigibbet : Any young maidens venturing out between the hours of dusk and dawn in East Anglia and the Midlands may find themselves the victims of a gruesome Goblin by the name of Flibbertigibbet. Though William Shakespeare considered Flibbertigibbet to be a Demon, it seems that this nocturnal nuisance is content merely to cause distress and fear rather than do any real physical harm. The sound of a cockerel crowing would usually send him fleeing.

Samanach : This formless, shadowy fiend usually resides in Scottish sea-coves, but come Halloween night he will roam rural and urban areas in search of children to abduct.

Nature Spirits

In the very distant past the majority of Britain and Ireland was covered with dense forest and people could not help but live closer to the land. It was a matter of survival - hunt and be hunted, mankind was equally prey and predator. The land could also provide a variety of food and other useful products and with the advance of civilisation humans learned how to influence nature through agriculture and farming. However, even though they recognised that they could help to sway some matters, they realised that they were a part of the environment and not its masters. This developed as a religious or sacred sensibility and a sense of Animism arose - this is the belief that like humans, animals, plants and even some inanimate objects such as rocks also had souls. This is an opinion evident in many world religions such as Buddhism and Jainism for example and is akin to the Totems of locations as far apart as the Americas, Siberia and Australia and the Fetishism of Africa. In Britain and Ireland (and numerous other nations) these notions developed into the Fertility Gods (see Green Man / Foliate Heads and also The Horned God) and into more defined Elemental and Nature spirits. These deities and the elements they controlled could be extremely generous but at times they could also be very cruel. Therefore in order to show gratitude and to keep the deities appeased, certain rituals and ceremonies were exercised. It is believed that sometimes this may have involved human sacrifice.

Plants and in particular trees were extremely sacred to the Celtic priest class known as the Druids. Though their name linguistically has been suggested to derive from 'dru' = Oak and 'id' = knowledge, the Oaks (*Quercus* species) though regarded with great esteem, were not the only trees considered divine by the Celts. Indeed all trees were considered holy, though some more than others and there were varying serious degrees of punishment depending on species, issued for the unlawful damage or destruction of trees. Ash, Yew, Hawthorn, Hazel, Willow and Birch are just a sample of some of the other trees and plants sacred to the Druids. The precise concept of photosynthesis - the biological process by which leaves convert sunlight into energy (which makes its way up the food chain thereby sustaining every living thing) and produces oxygen as a by-product (thereby ensuring our air is breathable) must surely have been beyond their scientific understanding. Yet even through superstition, the distant ancestors of these isles displayed a better sense of the true value of trees and nature in general than do very many people living today (that said we must not romanticise our predecessors into being environmental angels, for then as now there were undoubtedly individuals who sought to overexploit the treasures of the Earth, those who casually destroyed and many who killed not for survival or environmental benefit but simply for sport).

Truly though there are many benefits that the trees bring to the world both to mankind and to many, many other different species, both through their processes and their many nutritious, medicinal or functional products and it must not be forgotten that they are imperative to our existence. Though they are beneficial, that does not mean they are solely here for our benefit and they should not be taken for granted. Considerate use makes far more common sense than systematic abuse. If the world was really as rational now as it likes to think, then at the very least as many trees should be planted as are felled. When it comes down to the basics of survival versus transitory financial gain or convenience, or the simple matter of ensuring that whatever is used is replaced (something that surely makes conventional and economic sense also), then it could easily be questioned who are the truly primitive society ? Historically speaking , our society is not the first to ruefully exploit the landscape as the ancient Romans had over farmed the soil of Britain before they finally left the country in order to defend their homeland. Luckily though, the Vikings did not critically diminish the tree population in Britain and Ireland as they did in Iceland. That is not to say that nature is a feeble victim, far from it as any forest fire, active volcano or tidal-wave for instance can obviously demonstrate, but its time-scale and powers of adaptation do not compare to ours. By this I mean that by seemingly destroying nature we are actually working to destroy ourselves and though it may take many years, nature has the capacity to adapt and recover whilst the ultimate survival of the human species is more fragile. Basically we need nature more than nature needs us and our downfall could likely be of our own doing. The ancients reminded themselves of this through the personification of the Elemental beings and Fertility Gods and through their customs and rituals aimed to placate nature and achieve a vital sense of symbiosis.

Though ecologically speaking, many of the ancient arboreal customs (especially those of the Celts) were sagacious, they were influenced more by supernatural rather than scientific thought. Many of the archaic tree, plant, water and animal beliefs have existed into the modern day as superstitions, though many people may be unaware of their original significance. For instance the habit to 'touch wood' when expressing a hope originates from the seeking of a blessing from the tree spirits who may overhear the ambition and to show humility so that the powerful forces do not take the statement as an arrogant boast and work to prevent its fulfilment. To kiss under the mistletoe at Christmas reflects the creeper's past use as a fertility charm. The use of Holly and Ivy as Christmas decoration stems from the invitation of evergreens into the house during the winter festival of Yule, so that the humans' generosity will be repaid by these plants sharing their stamina and skills in surviving the hard cold season . Early Christianity also extended sacred symbolism to plants and trees, for instance Holly wreaths were representative of Christ's crown of thorns and the red berries signified beads of blood.

Other trees were considered to have the power to invoke or protect from supernatural beings. The Rowan (*Sorbus aucuparia*) also known as Mountain Ash, Witchen, Quick-beam, Quicken and Witch-tree, is a good example of this. It has been said that the Druids would sprinkle its vibrant red berries onto the flayed hides of bulls in order to call upon wise spirits. Another enduring belief about Rowan is that crosses made from its branches or twigs and bound with red thread would ward off the attention of malevolent Witches and bad Faeries.

In addition also to being nurturing and generous with its beneficiary produce, nature is also fascinatingly beautiful but in its ambivalence it can also seem notoriously cruel. For instance a walk in the woods can be a pleasant and inviting experience, yet at times the human presence can begin to feel most unwanted. The trees can sometimes seem to congregate closer together as if in a bid to block the reassuring rays of the sun. The gentle rustle of the leaves in the breeze may turn to coarse, unintelligible whispers and the gaze of many unseen eyes may be felt to prick the skin. A projectile of stones may be hurled from a hidden source (see Elves) and brambles and branches may suddenly bar a well-trodden path. The human will often feel inexplicably threatened and panic may cause them to suddenly flee (a sensation accredited to the work of Pan - the half goat / half-human deity of Greco-Roman belief and associated to the Horned God). Should such a feeling of panic suddenly occur it may often be wise to take the hint for their may be more severe consequences for infringing upon the privacy of a supernatural forest-denizen.

And let us not forget the plants and flowers of the under-storey and other habitats. Though of a less imposing stature than the trees they still have a massive impact on both life and lore. Likewise they too should not be dismissed offhand as even the smallest flower or toadstool could be the guardian of a strange supernatural secret

Monants, Sleepers and Old Head

Certain trees or combinations of trees (such as three thorns growing entwined, particularly on a hill side or the association of Oak, Ash and Thorn) may mark an entrance to the Otherworld. Sometimes they may appear rather unremarkable or otherwise quite magnificent with their long gnarled limbs, huge distended boles sometimes splitting open to reveal dark canyons and a labyrinth of twisted writhing roots. These portals to the Hidden Kingdom and also the trees that provide a home to a considerable brood of Tree Sprites or other sylvan Fays are known as Faerie Trees, Monants, Bile, Sceach or Skiough. Whatever their nomenclature, it is oft considered very unwise or unfortunate for a mortal to fall asleep under one of these trees. To do so would be to risk abduction or enthralment into the Otherworld, insanity or a sudden and mysterious death. Such a tree of sinister repute was the ancient Yew that stood in the dead centre of Ffrid yr Ywen (the Forest of the Yew) in Matharven, Wales. This particular evergreen was believed to yield a long and deep association with the Tylwyth Teg, the most capricious of Cambrian Faeries.

Some Trees though are reputed to link to realms more sinister still than Faerie, perhaps even providing a doorway to Hell (though many once would have argued that the Devil's Underworld and the Fay Otherworld are actually one and the same). An example of the sylvan-Hell connection is embodied by the King Billy (also known as the Big Belly Oak), an impressive tree that still stands in Savernake Forest in Wiltshire, England. It has been claimed that anyone who dances naked, twelve times anticlockwise (withershins) around this tree's gargantuan bole will be greeted by the presence of the Devil himself.

However some trees go beyond being doorways or dwelling places and display a sublime sentience of their own. Some of these trees bare their soul more visibly than others and some of them profoundly so. Many trees seem to display anthropomorphic features but this is frequently written off as coincidental simulacra, tricks of the light or the human brain's habit of constructing recognisable patterns in places they shouldn't really exist. Indeed some of the eternally fixed faces on trees may not be true faces but carvings by Fay or Elven artists, but at times others seem to move. Perhaps not dramatically so, maybe just the inaudible murmur or blink, though on occasion the movement may be far more pronounced.

The faces of trees may sometimes be seen to fade or even vanish seasonally, particularly in winter - the time of hibernation and natural defoliation for deciduous trees, only to reawaken when spring has sprung. The two main forms of commonly stationary faces to be seen upon the bark of trees are the Sleepers and the Old Heads. Some trees may show signs of both these species within a single sample but frequently a Sleeper may be seen in isolation within the tree's natural form. The Sleepers manifest as a single large face that often occupies a considerable portion of the bole and some may be bearded by a growth of Ivy or a tangle of unearthed roots. They have a mellow aged ambience about them and though many display a wise and kindly expression, others seem somewhat melancholic, weary and senescent. Perhaps understandably so for many occupy trees that have lived far longer than any human possibly could, and so may have witnessed many strange events and changes in their long silent vigil.

The Old Heads however manifest as a collection of numerous faces of considerably varying size and demeanour within the trunk, crown or roots of trees. Some appear mirthful and comical whilst others seem sinister and brooding. Their individual features may mingle with those of others to produce other curious conjoined faces. Further faces may also become apparent through the formation of bracket fungi or pronounced insect galls.

Sleepers and Old heads may be encountered in trees of different species and of varying age across Britain and Ireland. Though they are often most well defined in mature specimens, with close observation they may also sometimes be sighted in young saplings, coppice bases and the apparently dead trees which on closer inspection may still be seen to be teeming with life. Though they may be manifestations of the tree's own soul, there is suggestion that some trees may at times harbour the souls of dead humans particularly those who breathed their last hanging from their branches either through execution, accident or suicide (see Herne the Hunter).

Celtic Dryads
(Also known as ~ Sidhe Draoi, Faerie Druids, Tree Nymphs)

Though, like the Celtic priests known as Druids , the Dryads' name has been linguistically connected to the Oak , they are not particular only to these trees. Indeed many Dryads are said to have a stronger association to Willow trees (*Salix* species). Willows have traditionally been associated to the moon and the Dryads may be observed or heard singing harmoniously on moonlit nights, for these nature spirits are said to be devotees of the lunar goddess Tana (also known as Diana or Selene). Dryads may be observed also during daylight, though often only fleetingly moving through the greenery. Unlike the Greek Hamadryads, the Dryads are not bonded to a single tree and though they may have an individual favourite, they are free to move about between them. Whilst the Greco-Roman Dryads have a male counterpart (known as a Drus), the Celtic Dryads are generally regarded as being female. Also unlike the various Nymphs (nature spirits most specifically recorded in Greek and Roman myth, but likely related and associated to some British / Irish nature and water spirits also), the Celtic Dryads are not particularly sociable towards humans, though they are infinitely more likely to try and avoid us rather than do us harm. However it has been suggested that they may have communed with Druids in the distant past.

The Green Ladies are a similar species to the Dryads, though they are more inclined to Ivy (and sometimes other creepers or vines), either snaking their way up trees and brickwork or blanketing the woodland floor. Like the White Ladies and the Grey Ladies, Green Ladies are sometimes thought to be the Phantoms of young women who met a tragic mortal demise, rather than being inherent Elemental spirits.

Appearance & Attire : Frequently the Dryads will mingle within the foliage of trees and may only be vaguely observed. However they may sometimes also be seen in a beautiful feminine form, either naked or clothed in natural finery. Their long hair alters seasonally to match the changing colours of deciduous leaves and they are naturally pleasantly perfumed.

Size : Often of normal human proportions, but likely alterable at will.

Diet : It has been suggested that the Dryads eat fruit and berries and drink nectar, dew or spring-water, but it may only be the essences they consume.

Habitat & Range : Across Britain and Ireland, mainly within Willow or Oak, but possibly also in Ash, Birch, Thorn and Rowan trees, especially in groves or in the vicinity of a sacred site.

Lesidhe

The Lesidhe appoint themselves as woodland guardians, a position whose duties they seemingly regard as largely consisting of making life difficult for human ramblers and forestry workers. The local Lesidhe generally seem content to frighten and bewilder mankind by causing them to lose their way in the heart of the woods. This of course can be quite distressing, but we should perhaps be grateful as many of their East European relatives are said to include serious assault and battery amongst their activities. By name and by nature, comparisons can be drawn between the Lesidhe and the Slavic arboreal god, Leshy. This red-cloaked, clog-footed, shape-shifting deity would also way-lead travellers amongst the leaves and boughs and like the Lesidhe was also thought to hibernate throughout winter.

Appearance & Size : The Lesidhe may bear a varying degree of anthropomorphic features but tend to resemble small trees or shrubs more than anything, so gender is hard to determine. Several Lesidhe may be observed in close proximity but they do not tend to be noticeably sociable towards each other.

Diet : Unknown.

Habitat & Range : Mainly in the oldest and densest forests in Ireland.

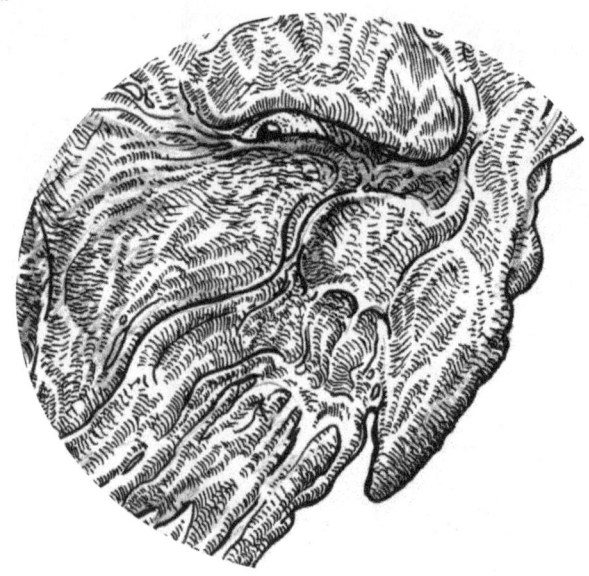

Tree Sprites
(Known in Northwest England as Poldies. In South England as Pottons. In Ireland as Skeagh-Shee.)
Some Fay breeds choose to live within the trees of our world rather than in the Fairy Hills, Sunken Isles or Otherworldly domains. Possibly these particular Faerie Trees or Monants exist both in the material and astral realms or may even be bridges between both worlds. These sylvan Fays can be generically classified as 'Tree Sprites' and many may resemble Elves but there can be an array of differences between species. Some Tree Sprites are specific to particular species of trees, (such as the Oak-men and the Lunatishee who are looked at in more specific detail within this Guide) but others are seemingly less partial and may even be nomadic between trees. Though they may at times be defensively territorial against humans and nip them if they wander too close, they are willing to share their arboreal homes with other creatures such as birds, arthropods and some mammals as well as sometimes with other supernatural entities such as Dryads , Old Heads and Ghillie Due. Whilst all Tree Sprites and Spirits obviously begrudge losing their homes as a result of human need or greed, many will grimly accept the fate of the axe or saw and may be pacified against taking revenge by a simple, polite verbal request before commencement of the work (see also Elder Mothers). The Pottons of Southern England were more malevolent than a lot of Tree Sprite species and it was claimed that they were in the habit of abducting and enslaving human children.

Appearance, Attire & Size : This can vary considerably but often they will be very small, sometimes only standing a couple of inches high and rarely larger than 1 ft (0.3m) tall. Their clothing could either be baggy or very tight fitting but will frequently be constructed from natural products of their environment such as leaves and acorn cups etc.This obviously makes for good camouflage, as does many of the Sprites' natural colouring.
The Pottons were said to have blazing red eyes and disproportionately large hands and feet.
Diet : Frequently fruit, berries and fungi or the essences thereof whilst others may hunt or steal other foodstuff. Pottons were fond of squirrel, rabbit and wild-bird meat.
Habitat & Range : Potentially in any tree across Britain and Ireland. The Pottons of Buckinghamshire and Northamptonshire were said to reside in the hollows between and beneath the tree-roots rather than in the branches or crown.

Tree Sprites - Lunatishee
(Also known as ~ Moon Faeries. Lunatisidhe. Blackthorn Sprites.)

The Lunatishee are the guardians of Blackthorn trees (*Prunus spinosa*) and they rarely leave their host plant. They are mainly nocturnal and as their name suggests are moon-worshippers. Humans will harvest the Blackthorn berries (Sloes) to make preserves and will cut its wood to make the Irish-style walking sticks known as shillelaghs, and for this reason the Lunatishee hate mankind with a passion. Given the opportunity they will pinch a human's skin between their long fingers until the resulting bruise is as black and blue as the fruit of their tree.
The Sprites of the Hawthorn (*Crataegus* species - also known as May Tree, May Flower, White Thorn and Moon Flower) may also likely be lunar devotees as it is sometimes claimed that the flowers of this tree will first blossom under moonlight and it has been considered very unlucky to take Hawthorn flowers into a home. In Ireland the Hawthorn Sprites are known as Sidheog (or alternatively as Sheogues, Sigh Oges, Sheoques or Shoges). The Hawthorn is very significant to the traditional May-Day / Beltain festivities and the Glastonbury Thorn which blooms instead at Christmas time was said to have grown from the staff of Joseph of Arimathea, (the Biblical figure who is credited as bringing the Holy Grail of Arthurian legend into Britain.)

Appearance & Attire : The Lunatishee have bald heads with pointed ears , keen glinting eyes and long teeth. They have long slender digits and limbs ideal for climbing and also for nipping. They are either naked or wear skin-tight clothing the exact same colour as their silvery-white skin. Females have either not been specifically reported or may not be instantly distinguishable from the males. Hawthorn Sprites may vary greatly in appearance and dress.
Size : Usually approx. 6 inches (0.15 m) tall and generally less than 1 ft (0.3 m) tall.
Diet : Possibly Sloes or perhaps only the natural essence of their host trees.
Habitat and Range : The Lunatishee live in small groups in Blackthorn trees across Britain but especially in Ireland. They are said to be most active on the night of 11th November (Old Samhain). The Hawthorn Sprites may be found in woods and hedgerows across Britain and Ireland, but may not be exclusively bonded to this tree species.

Tree Sprites - Oak-men
(Also known as ~ Inifri Duir. Bodachan na Croibhe Moire. Oak-Shee.)

Like the Lunatishee the Oak-men are very protective of their host tree and though they far prefer to live in the most ancient and imposing Oaks, they will begrudgingly settle in pollards and coppices should their mature tree be lopped or chopped. However should this occur the Oak-men would sometimes seek revenge, not necessarily upon the 'guilty' lumberjack or tree-surgeon but upon any passing human. A typical means of vengeance was to assume the form of bucolic human traders and in apparently generous spirit offer appetising looking cakes to hungry and weary passers-by. However these succulent treats would actually be poisonous fungi glamorised to look good and wholesome. Though their opinion and treatment of humankind is generally low, the Oak-men are reputedly very protective and nurturing towards the various other natural creatures that share their woodland habitat.

Appearance & Attire: Despite the name Oak-men, females and children have also been encountered. They all seem to possess some shape-shifting ability, but normally appear with squat bodies and bulbous features. Their complexion can vary but is frequently of a queasy hue and their noses and cheeks can be considerably ruddy. Their proportions may often appear somewhat peculiar, and those thought to be of Germanic lineage have disproportionately large heads.
They are often quite coarsely attired and their caps often seem to be made from fungus (or sometimes in their smaller stature from acorn cups).

Size : They can alter their proportions from a few inches to possibly larger than human proportions, however they have commonly been documented at a height approx. 3 ft (0.9 m) for an adult male.

Diet : Uncertain, but probably either the essences of or the actual produce of their environment, acorns, fungi etc.

Habitat & Range : Usually in family colonies or small Troops in any part of Oak trees. Especially in old forests and groves, but sometimes in isolated specimens in parks etc.across Britain and Ireland. The presence of Bluebells in the vicinity of Oak, may also be indicative of an Oak-Men residence.

Orchard Guardians

Some supernatural creatures become most protective of fruit trees even when they are growing in human plantations and their presence could either be a bonus or a bother to the orchard owners. The Orchard Guardians, particularly the Apple Tree Men will chase away fruit-raiders but may also take umbrage with genuine harvesters. Though they will begrudgingly accept fruit-picking they may demand certain conditions. In the traditional Cider counties such as Somerset, apple-pickers could only harvest fruit at particular times of the day. Other customs such as 'Wassailing' and 'Apple Howling' involved unusual rites such as beating the tree with a stick wrapped in a cider-soaked rag and making lots of noise. Festivities involving the trees were habitually employed both at harvest time and often also at Xmas and New Year, in order to placate the spirits and hopefully guarantee a good fruit crop for the following year. It was also customary to leave a single apple on the tree for the Apple Tree Man at the end of the season likewise to ensure that the next yield would be bountiful.

Orchard Guardians were often known by individual names according to their locality and children would often try their luck by taunting these figures and attempting to steal their fruit. In Yorkshire Awd Goggie would chase after the young rascals. Although he could run very fast he rarely, if ever, would catch the kiddies and it would seem therefore that he intends only to scare rather than do actual harm. Lazy Lawrence of the English West Country is, as his name suggests, far more laconic and instead of pursuing fruit-thieves he would instead inflict them with painful cramps. He was also said to possess a ring with the power to send anyone to sleep and was therefore a convenient scapegoat when bosses discovered their workers sleeping on the job.

Rumour had it that all Orchard Guardians nestled a horde of treasure beneath the roots of their favourite tree. However it is said that the treasure hunters seeking these spoils would end up uprooting every tree in the garden with the result of not only finding no riches but also destroying the natural source of nourishment and income in the process. Being alarmed both by the destruction and avarice the Orchard Guardian would long since have departed in search of another plantation with whatever treasure they possessed in tow.

The power of causing cramps and bloating were also attributed to the spirits known as Melch Dick and Churn-milk Peg. They were the male and female guardians of nut trees, particularly Hazel. They may be sporadically encountered as they check on trees at random and not just those in a certain location. Both Melch Dick and Churn-milk Peg at times will give chase, but tend not to like to exert themselves too much so will often instead give a warning nip to potential fruit and nut thieves. Similarly the Acorn Lady punishes the pilferers of Oak fruit with pinching, cramps and bloating. The Gooseberry Wife of the Isle of Wight protects fruit bushes from the attentions of naughty or greedy children by the novel defence of transforming herself into a giant fearsome looking caterpillar.

Appearance, Attire & Size : The Apple Tree Men frequently seem aged with a pale, possibly greenish -white skin. Their garb sometimes resemble either Druidic-style gowns or alternatively 'long-john' style underwear. Apple Tree Men may appear very small as they recline in cobweb hammocks between branches, it soon becomes apparent as they give chase, that they are of tall human proportions with long slender limbs. At times they may blend so closely with their host tree as not to be instantly discernible. Churn-milk Peg, Melch Dick and the Gooseberry Wife are all of small stature - generally no taller than 3 ft (0.9 m) and dress in old-fashioned rustic attire. The Gooseberry Wife has noted shape-shifting ability. The fruit of an undisclosed Irish orchard was said to be guarded by a strange sentinel in the form of a headless fox that stood upright to the height of a man and emitted an aura of palpable menace.

Diet : Milk, fruit and nuts or the essences thereof. Also libations of the first Cider brew of the year to the Apple Tree Men (generally poured down to the roots of its favoured tree).

Habitat & Range : Apple Tree Men - commonly in planted orchards, but sometimes also in wild fruit trees localised across Britain and Ireland (though due to a decline in traditional orchards may now be more prevalent in Kent and South-Western England). Churn-milk Peg and Melch Dick - either together or separately, in random fruit or nut trees (mainly Hazel), across Britain and Ireland.
The Gooseberry Wife - in smaller fruit bushes on the Isle of Wight.

Willows

As well as being a favoured haunt of Dryads, Willow trees (*Salix* species) often display a distinctive character of their own. Whilst many of the inherent tree spirits such as the Sleepers display little or no animation, the Willows have a reputation for uprooting themselves at night and going wandering in their entirety. Should they observe a human taking a nocturnal stroll in front of them, then the Willow will likely follow them muttering and grumbling to themselves all the while. Should the walker stop and turn, then the Willow will itself stop and when they carry on the Willow will also resume walking and whispering. Unlike 'Old Man Willow' from J.R.R. Tolkien's epic Lord of the Rings, (and also the African Baobabs and the Ya-te-veo of Malagasy and South American lore) the Willows are not renowned for eating humans, animals or Fays.

The drooping branches of Willow trees often give them a melancholic countenance and traditionally a person who was grieving the death of a loved one or a disappointment in love sometimes would affix a sprig of Willow to their lapel to alert others of their sorrowful mood. The wood of some species of Willow (particularly Osier) is excellent for weaving with and along with Hazel was widely utilised in the construction of hurdle fencing and reputedly also the colossal Wicker Men, giant effigies filled with livestock and people and ceremoniously burnt by the Celts (though some researchers question whether these structures actually ever existed). Therein exists a lingual connection between Willow, wicker-work and Wiccan - a term originally linked to Wizards and in modern times to Neo-pagans.

In the days when children were commonly caned as punishment, it was considered risky to chastise them with a Willow rod because it was feared that they would no longer grow as a result. The wandering Willows look like conventional trees, though some may display pronounced Sleeper -like faces.

181

The Elder Mothers

(Also known as ~ Old Mothers. Elder Witches. Burtree Witches.

Old Women of the Elder Tree. Old Gals.)

The Elder tree (*Sambucus nigra*) divides human opinion as some see it as a large and intrusive weed with a foul odour, whilst others prize it for the cordial, wine and preserves that can be made from its berries and flowers, the medicinal quality of its natural produce and the rudimentary whistles that can easily be made from its twigs to entertain children for a short while. However to the minds of many people the Elder meant much more. Whilst it is advisable to show respect to all trees, many lumber-men would verbally ask permission of the Elder before cutting its wood. Even then it would not be taken into a home as there was the risk that burning its wood on a house fire would invite evil spirits or death into a home, and that a baby laid in an Elder-wood cradle would at best be nipped by unseen fingers or at worst be damned to an early grave. It was thought that live Witches would sometimes transform themselves into Elder trees in order to spy on or to escape capture from their enemies. An old tale from Syresham near the Northamptonshire / Buckinghamshire boundaries, describes how a man was startled to see blood flow upon the cutting of an Elder twig, doubly so when he soon encountered an old woman (who was locally suspected as being a Witch), with a fresh oozing wound on her hand. The man dutifully and fearfully related the occurrence to the parish authorities. They considered the events to be beyond mere coincidence and the old woman was subsequently tried and executed. Other Elders were reputed to harbour the soul of a dead Witch or their own feminine spirit. Not all of these Elder mothers were sinister, some may even be caring and compassionate and allowed their twigs to be carried as charms to ward off other malevolent entities and likewise an Elder tree left unmolested on someone's premises would protect the abode from evil. Their perceived temperament may have often simply depended upon the region they were growing in, but few doubted their power. The most wicked however would cause death to any human that had the mere audacity to sleep in their shadow.

Elder trees which are not fruit-bearing may instead possess male spirits known as Owd Lads.

Menacing yet silent is another Tree-Witch known as The One with the White Hand . This haunter of Birch trees, would at times gently caress passers-by with her twig-like fingers. Should she touch the vicinity of their heart they would instantly fall dead, yet if she touched their head then either insanity or Stroke would occur.

Woodwose
(Also known as Wild Men. Wode-wose. Wood Men. Woses. Wuda -Wasa. Wodwo. Wyllt. Woosers. Green Men. Bachlach.)

The Woodwose were greatly feared but often provoked figures, especially in the Middle Ages. These rough human-like beings made the forests their homes and despite many of them being of clumsy stature they could navigate their way through the trees as efficiently as any woodland creature. Suggestions of their possible origins include -
- That they are coarse Fays or the embodiment of the forest itself.
- That they were babies born out of scandal or into abject poverty, and were therefore abandoned in the woods. (This procedure was sometimes referred to as 'being left for the Faeries'.) However rather than die as expected they grew to be hardy and feral.
- That they were a form of anthropoid or ape-man, perhaps unknown to science.
- That they were once from a conventional human community, but instead opted for a hermetic lifestyle in sylvan surroundings. (Possibly as ascetics or outlaws, or simply to seek solace from society.) The years of solitude then taking their toll on appearance and sanity.
- That they are the descendants of primitive tribes that took to the trees when faced with slavery or genocide by more advanced invaders.
Therein exists the possibility that the Woodwose lived in clans or at least in family units, but they have more often been encountered in isolation. Wild Women are far more seldom encountered in these isles, yet they are more commonly and distinctively recorded in the lore of several mainland European nations. The Wild Woman Of Bronsgrove, Worcestershire is one however whose reputation has lingered. This feral female was believed to have originally been a Witch or Enchantress, but being set upon by a fervent mob had decided to shun mankind and instead live deep in the woods. Her only constant company was a wild boar that many local people believed to be her own transformed son. The Woodwose may often try to avoid human contact but if cornered or made to feel threatened then they can be considerably aggressive. Others though would gain a reputation for being a menace as they would attack men with heavy clubs, ravish women and sometimes seize children to eat. For these reasons and simply for sport it is claimed that the knights of medieval courts would frequently seek out Woodwoses to test their mettle in combat. The Irish Suibne and the Scots Lailoken would be sought for other reasons however as both of these feral forest-dwellers were regarded also as being gifted prophets. A strange creature encountered at Bolam Lake, Northumberland in 2003 perhaps displays more kinship to Wild-Men of

the Himalayan Yeti or North American Sasquatch description, than
to the traditional European Woodwose. Described as being about 8
feet tall, covered in hair and having blazing red eyes, the local
press gave the creature several names including the Bolam Lake
Bigfoot and the Geordie Yeti . Similar creatures known collectively as
Big Hairy Monsters (BHMs) have also been reported in the English
Midlands at Sherwood Forest and Cannock Chase.
 It is possible that the Woodwose have been hunted into extinction
or near-extinction in these isles. Though they habitually inhabit
forests the name Woodwose may in fact refer to the old Anglo-
Saxon word 'Wood' or 'Wode' meaning 'mad'. It is uncertain
whether there is also any connection to the God Wode (also known
as Wotan or Woten and comparable to the Norse Odin).

The Green Man / Foliate Heads
(Also known as ~ Jack in the Green. Jack in the Bush. Burry-Man. Green George. The Hidden One. The Wild Herdsman. The Garland. The May King. The Green Knight.)

'Green Man' is a name that has commonly been used in modern times to refer to the varied but essentially similar vegetation icons that are evident in old art and traditional festivities. To many, his image represents the spirit of rain and vegetation or an archaic agricultural and fertility deity, perhaps even an aspect of The Horned God. This is perhaps most evident in the Green George spring rites of the Gypsies, however many of the Green Men costumes seen in other traditional May-day or Beltain processions are actually representations of Woodwose. The Jack in the Green was a figure common to the May-day processions of 18th Century southern and central England, most commonly represented as tall heavily leafed form frequently accompanied by several chimney-sweeps. Though such celebrations rarely occur anymore or have often been made more commercially viable for tourists, genuine traditional ceremonies do survive in some areas.

The carved images of the Green Man to be found in some Norman and Gothic style churches (and also conversely painted on the signs of some public drinking houses) were formerly known as Foliate Heads. These are either sculpted from wood or stone and appear as disembodied heads wearing leaf masks or surrounded by a garland of leaves (most frequently Oak, Ivy or Hawthorn) that has generally spewed forth from their mouth. Their expressions can vary considerably from being serene or morose to lecherous or sinister.

To the early converted Christians they likely reflected their earlier pagan beliefs as above, but to the stonemasons who crafted these icons they may have been an artistic reference to very similar images that appeared earlier in Roman decorative arts. The Roman Foliate Heads most probably represented their own Fertility Gods such as Bacchus , his attendant Silensus and the Greco-Roman Pan or Faunus. They may also have depicted Satyrs and Fauns, lusty goat-men hybrids that were neither human nor Gods (see also Urisk). Within these isles there may have existed an association to Cernunnos the Horned God, for in Celtic depictions this deity was sometimes shown as a source of vegetation and some later church carvings do indeed show a noticeable resemblance to him. It may seem strange to some then that the Christian ministers would feature icons suggestive of paganism within their churches, yet other pagan notions were also assimilated into

Christianity (see also Celtic Saints, The Easter Bunny and Santa Claus). There is the possibility that the Foliate Heads also alluded to some Christian symbolism which may have varied according to their expressions, though if that is the case the explanatory meanings often seem to have since been lost and subsequently guessed at. They may have also have had the hoped purpose of scaring evil spirits away from the hallowed ground. This is suggested also for other church carvings such as Gargoyles - demonic sculptures often utilised as water-spouts and the Sheela -na-Gigs - representations of surprisingly lewd females, which are suggestive of fertility icons and possibly even of the Earth Goddess or Mother Nature. The true relevance of Sheela-na-Gigs is as speculative as that of the Green Men and some commentators have suggested that they are female counterparts to these figures, thus being Green Women or May Queens. They have also been tenuously associated to the Morigann, the Celtic War-goddess.

Though sometimes fearsome or morose, as pieces of artwork Green men and their ilk are often strangely beautiful as well as being enigmatic and inspiring. Furthermore they could also have been intended as being a symbolic representation of inspiration itself, whether that be divine, artistic, spiritual, practical or ecological. Foliate Heads can be found in numerous churches and cathedrals (as can Gagoyles and less frequently Sheela-na-Gigs) in Britain and Ireland, however should a fleshy lascivious face be seen glaring out from real shrubbery then it is probably better to run away quickly!

Brown Men
(Also known as ~ Moor Men. Brown Men o' the Muirs.)

As the Woodwose are to the forests, so are the Brown Men to the moors. They are the guardians of the wildlife that inhabit the heath, scrub and moor-land, however they are extremely shy and wary of human presence. Whilst the Woodwose have been demonstrably dangerous the temperament of a confronted Brown Man is generally uncertain (though they are considered sly and troublesome in Northern England). Therefore should a Brown Man actually be encountered in close quarters it is advisable not to let them feel threatened. If the wiles or wrath of a Brown Man is incurred, then if possible it is recommended that the offending human should cross a river or brook, for it is said that this creature is extremely reluctant to pass over running water in pursuit. The Brown Men are more commonly thought to be a Fay species rather than feral humans and it is possible that they possess the ability to transform themselves into the form of hares or other moor-land creatures in order to avoid being observed or captured. Whilst females have not been distinctly reported and Brown Men are usually sighted in isolation, it is not impossible that there may be more than one Brown Man per moor and they may even live in mated pairs or in small social groups, perhaps in dens below ground or under shrubs, bracken or heather.

Appearance & Attire : The Brown Men have an earthy complexion and often have a bodily covering of brown hair. Their head hair is often ginger or black, wiry and straggly. Their arms sometimes seem peculiarly long and they may either be slender or squat . Clothing, if worn, is crafted from rough moor-land foliage and possibly any remnants of fur, feathers and fleece that they might find.

Size : Often of slight human proportions, but sometimes a lot smaller.

Diet : Nuts, berries, roots, mushrooms and crab apples. Brown Men reputedly abhor the concept of eating meat.

Habitat & Range : Moor-land across Britain and possibly Ireland, especially in the Scottish Borders, Northern England and on Bodmin Moor, Cornwall. An encounter with a rather unconventionally brown-clad Pixie on Dartmoor (related in 'The Middle Kingdom' by D.A. McManus) describes an entity more akin to the 'Brown Man' type.

Flower Faeries - Pillywiggins / Shefro
(Pillywiggin Troops include ~ Vairies. Farisees. Hotties.
Feerins. Greenies.)

In modern times the Pillywiggins have come to represent *the* picture of Faeries in many peoples' minds and indeed they probably are the Fay species most commonly encountered by children at the bottom of the garden. The Pillywiggins display a strong relationship to flowers and small plants and certain Pillywiggin Troops may be linked only to a specific location or species of plant, whilst others are more general. Pillywiggins are well represented in art by the paintings of Cicily Mary Barker (1895 -1973), though she used the general term 'Flower Fairies' and developed her work through a thorough knowledge and deep understanding of plants and flowers rather than Faerie-lore. Indeed it was reported that she said that she had never personally seen a Fay and it was hinted that she never actually believed in them (a claim also made about Arthur Rackham (1867 - 1939), another celebrated and talented illustrator of enchanted and enchanting scenes). Though the paintings of both of the above artists have an accomplished beauty and Rackham's work in particular often displayed a strange undercurrent; however due to the sanitised and saccharine work of some other Edwardian writers and illustrators, many people have developed a mawkish opinion of Flower Faeries. It is never a wise move to underestimate or trust any Fay species too deeply however. Granted, the Pillywiggins are often very pretty and jovial but that does not necessarily equate with overtly sweet. Usually they only seem mildly curious of humans and the Pillywiggins that inhabit churchyards may be seen to mimic the ceremonies that they have observed. They are not human though and their morals and behaviour could be as unpredictable as those of any other Fay species. Pillywiggins are deeply protective of their floral environment, and as many of them often display insect attributes such as wings or even antennae it is also possible that they would adopt other features such as swarming tendencies, chitin armour and painful bites or stings if they felt exceptionally threatened. It must also be remembered that amongst the plants they frequent are poisonous specimens such as Foxglove, Henbane, Bittersweet and Ragwort.

Whilst some commentators have suggested that miniscule Fairies are merely a creation of Shakespeare popularised by the Victorian and Edwardian Fairy artists and writers , and that any 'true' Fays were likely to bear the dimensions of the Tuatha de Danaan or the Heroic Otherworlders of Celtic myth : there have been many tiny humanoid

creatures noted in the folklore. These diminutive creatures range from the nature-loving Pillywiggins to the jovial Portunes, from the dusty Thrummy-caps to the unfriendly Nanny Diamonds. This last pocket-sized species hail from the English county of Dorset, where they reside within the chinks of dry-stone walls. Though certain flowers including Bluebells, Primroses, Wild Thyme and Cowslips hold special appeal for Pillywiggins, they may also be observed in flower gardens, parks, cemeteries, meadows and hedgerows across Britain and Ireland, but only in spring and summer. There are many Pillywiggin troops known by individual group names according to specific national region. In some areas there seems to be a stronger association between the Pillywiggins and Trooping Fairies. In Ireland, Pillywiggins are known as Shefro.

Flower Faeries - Floriales and Devas

Unlike the various Pillywiggins who congregate in Troops, other Flower Faeries such as Floriales and Devas tend either to be solitary or observed in small numbers.

The Floriales may be the servants of the Green Man or Iolanus the Meadow God, as they endeavour to bring life and a splash of colour to even the most desolate of locations such as building sites and quarry edges by applying a liberal sprinkling of wild flowers. The Floriales are active in assisting propagation and they have an inherent knowledge of which plants are best suited to particular conditions. They will generally be far more interested in a person's garden than in people themselves, whom they usually try to avoid.

Whereas the Floriales may possibly be native to these isles or to Europe anyway, the Devas are thought to have originated in Persia (now known as Iran) and made their way here via Greece. The Devas are a peaceful race renowned for their compassion and potent healing abilities. These powers are most often applied to rare or delicate plants. The word 'Deva' means 'Shining One' and around dusk their aura may be seen extended around a particular plant that are nurturing. There are several different forms of Deva recognised in the Persian heartland with the species becoming established here being known more specifically as Golden Devas and Green Devas. Respectively the Golden Devas are concerned with the transmission of solar energy whilst the Green Devas nurture growing plants. They are often curious about humanity but may be very shy. (It is possible that White Devas {also known as Sylphs} who are spirits of the air and Violet Devas who are connected with the spiritual aspect of nature are also present in these isles but because of their ethereal quality have not been widely recognised as such.)

The extremely controversial photographs taken at Cottingley beck in West Yorkshire, by two young girls, Frances Griffiths and Elsie Wright between 1917 and 1921, apparently show Flower Faeries that are comparative to these types. At the time these pictures captured great national attention as well as alternately attracting both derision and support. Probably the most famous individual to champion the Cottingley photos as being genuine was the author Arthur Conan Doyle (most famed as being the creator of Sherlock Homes). Conan Doyle's interest in Faeries was deep-rooted for his father , Charles Altamont Doyle, and especially his uncle, Richard Doyle, were renowned Victorian Fairy Painters. However alcoholism and epilepsy tragically saw his father consigned to the Montrose Royal Lunatic Asylum.

Following Conan Doyle's enthusiastic support of the girls' claims and his subsequent publishing of a book on the matter, some saw fit to question his gullibility if not indeed his sanity also. The Cottingley photographs continued to stir debate throughout the 20th Century, though it is said that in 1981 the girls (by then old women) finally admitted that at least four of the five photographs were faked (though not maliciously hoaxed). They remained rather ambiguous about the fifth and possibly most convincing looking photo. Though the Cottingley Fairy photos may very well have been faked, the girls hinted that they were based on creatures they had actually seen and indeed they represent a form that many people would commonly imagine Fairies to possess.

The Groac'h
(Also known as ~ Water Ogresses. Water Witches. Water Trolls. Drowning Faeries. River-Women. Fuath. Fuathan. Bean Fionn. Cuachag. Cailleach Uisge {Water-Hags})
(Notable individuals include ~ **Peg O' Nell. Peg Powler. Nanny Powler. Jenny Greenteeth. Nelly Longarms. The Fideal. Grindylow. Groac'h Lanascol.)**
Groac'h is a little-used collective term for the malevolent female spirits that inhabit ponds and more commonly rivers. These entities are an exceptional threat to human life and especially to children. Indeed one of these fiends Peg Powler, (who inhabits the River Tees in County Durham and Cleveland in England) is said to place eye-catching trinkets on the riverbanks in order to lure more children closer to the edge. As they wandered within her reach, she would then grasp their ankles and drag them under the surface of the water. (The River Skerne, a tributary of the Tees in Darlington also harboured a Groac'h by the name of Nanny Powler.) Similar modus operandi and appetites are shared by other Groac'h - Jenny (or Ginny) Greenteeth for instance would frequent stagnant ponds as well as the different rivers running through the English counties of Cumbria, Yorkshire, Lancashire, Cheshire and Shropshire. In order to further assist and conceal her heinous activities, she would make good use of the thick blanket of algae and pond-weeds that tend to gather on still or slow running water. The Fideal of Scotland is more attractive looking by human standards than many of her aquatic sisterhood, yet the end intention remains the same. She prefers to feed on young adult males rather than children and will use seduction as her means to the hunt, but her appetite is equally voracious and grim. The Groac'h Lanascol of Brittany may venture quite far from water.
Suggestions regarding possible origins of the Groac'h include -
- That they are solitary specimens of Elemental water spirits akin to breeds such as the Rusalkai , Potamids and Undine. Elemental species such as these tend to be more frequently recorded in the lore of continental European nations, however the Bean Fionn of Ireland do display uniformity as such a breed.
- That they are the personified spirits of the rivers themselves or are the evolution of archaic and redundant water goddesses such as Sabrean of the English Severn, Minerva of the Ribble, Sully of Bath, Abnoba of the Avon and Boann of the Irish Boyne.
- That they are hauntings by suspected Witches who perished during 'Tests by Swimming' or 'Dunking'. These tests and punishments were

not officially sanctioned by the British authorities as Witch - trial methods but occurred nonetheless. Basically the accused were submerged under water upon a specially constructed stool, if they drowned they were deemed innocent, if they floated or survived then it was considered proof of guilt and they were otherwise executed. (Dunking Stools were also once used to punish malicious gossips and other minor offenders, however in these latter cases the intention was to provoke transitory humiliation rather than death by drowning or proof of guilt.)

-That they are hauntings by women who drowned there as a result of accident, suicide, murder or ritual sacrifice, or who died elsewhere but whose bodies were deposited in the water. This theory is oft applied to Peg O' Nell, the bane of the River Ribble in Lancashire. Legend states that following her death whilst collecting water from a well in Clitheroe, her panic-stricken employer dumped her remains in the river. The restless spirit of this hapless servant girl has since assumed fiendish magnitude and will claim a human victim at least once every seven years. In times past concerned locals would make an annual animal sacrifice in a bid to satiate her wrath and hunger.

Water Ogres
(Also known as ~ Necors. Nykers. Water Wolves. Fuath. Fifel. Afanc. Nekkers. Nikkisen. River-Men. Water Trolls. Orc-Thyrs.)

Some of the waterways of these isles are the territory of fearsome male entities. Whilst more specific lore regarding masculine aquatic fiends may be found on the continent, the Water Ogres of these isles tend to share their more barbarous features and less of any of the few favourable qualities they may possess (such as musical skill). The Water Ogre species known as Nekkers have a female counterpart called a Nix, and whilst their women may be more pleasant to our eyes they still should be considered potentially dangerous. The Nix of mainland Europe however are more likely to seduce men-folk into deadly situations than the localised British Isle equivalents though.

There seems to be several different breeds of Water Ogre, some of which are entirely habitual to water and others who are amphibious and may trek the land also in search of victims. Nicky, Nicky Nye of the River Usk in Gwent, Wales (and possibly also encountered in Somerset, England) has also been rumoured to either snatch victims from small boats or to cause strong undercurrents in order to upturn the vessels. Cuttie Dyer was a shark-toothed, boggle-eyed Water Ogre with dreadlocked, snake-like hair that haunted the river Yeo (Ashburn) on Dartmoor.

The spring tide of the English River Trent was once widely known as

the Aegir, especially in the region of Gainsborough in Lincolnshire, where it is potentially very dangerous. As such the Aegir was considered to be an Old God degenerated into a Water Ogre. Bitter at its fall from grace and in the absence of dutifully paid sacrifice, the Aegir is said to greedily claim at least three human lives each year. Other Water Ogres may likewise be dimly recalled or corrupted folk-memories of erstwhile Water Gods such as Mourie, Manawyddan, Manaan Mac Lir, Neptune and Teron. The Old English word 'Nicor' is an archaic generic term that applied to varied forms of water fiend, both to the semi-humanoid creatures such as Water Ogres, but also to large monsters such as Nessy (see Long Necks) and Knuckers. The Scots term 'Fuath', the Irish 'Abhac' and 'Abac', and the Welsh 'Afanc' and 'Addanc' also have a similar generic meaning.

The Muilerteach
(Also known as ~ Muileratach. Muireartach. The Sea-Hag.
Mother Carey. Old Woman of the Seas. The Cailleach Uisge.)
The Muilerteach is the Goddess of the Sea and is actually the sea itself personified. Sometimes calm and beguiling, at other times tempestuous and cruel, she was once extremely feared and revered by Scottish mariners and fishermen. Even today some might return their first catch of the day to the waters in order to keep the 'Old Woman' placated (as their Welsh counterparts once gave the same tribute to the mysterious spirit known as Bucca). It was always feared that she would demand a more valued tribute than fish. So profound was the terror inspired in the sea-trawling men, that should one of their comrades find themselves drowning, they would show reluctance in mounting a rescue. It is also said that upon finding themselves on the wrong end of such a dire predicament , some sea-men would fight off any attempts of being rescued. The reason being the belief that if deprived of her own choice of victim, the wrath and hunger of the Sea-Hag would grow to such a level that she may instead claim the lives of more, possibly all of the crew instead. For the same reasons those that worked upon the seas may refuse to assist in the retrieval of human bodies washed ashore, perhaps even refusing to look at them. They would also often insist that such casualties of the waves be buried below sea-level and as close to the shore as possible should the Muilerteach wish to again take claim of her prize. Fishermen and sailors were well known for holding true a vast array of superstitions, but faced with such an unpredictable and often treacherous mistress it was probably wise to err on the side of any caution and not tempt fate.
The euphemistic term 'Mother Carey' could possibly have been equally used in reference to the Cailleach Bheur by 'land-lubbers' as to the Muilerteach by the mariners, for the name has survived down to us mainly through the phrase 'Mother Carey's Chickens'. The Chickens in question refer to snowflakes or alternatively to Storm Petrels. Either way, be they frozen water crystals or sea-birds, the sighting of Mother Carey's Chickens (especially if seen suddenly and in great number) is a clear indication that bad weather is on the way and that a callous Storm-Goddess is possibly close at hand.
Though a Celtic legend claims that the hero Finn MacCumhal destroyed the Muilerteach in combat, the essential wrath and influence of the sea remains unconquered. The benevolent aspect of the sea was also given anthropomorphic identity in the Orkneys, in the form of the Sea Mithir or Sea Mother.

Water Elven and Nixies
(Water Elven also known as ~ Gwragedd Annwn. Gwagedd
Annwfr. Gwraig. Ladies of the Lake. Lake Maidens. Water
Maidens.
Water Faeries. Be-Find. Morgans. Morgens.
Nixies also known as ~ Water Nymphs. Potamids. Limnads)

It is considered that the Welsh Otherworld of Annwn (sometimes
known as Annwfn or Annwvyn) can be reached beneath the surface
of certain lakes. Here in their submerged towns and villages dwell
the Gwragedd Annwn, stunning golden-haired Faerie maidens. They
are not restricted to this watery abode however and there are several
tales that tell of love affairs and marriages between these Water Elven
and mortal men. Indeed they are said to make superb wives and
mothers but certain conditions will be placed upon such a union. If
the human husband breaks any of these instructions for whatever
reason, be it through anger or arrogance, jest or mishap then his
Faerie bride will disappear never to return to his side.
Though Water Elven are often regarded in purely feminine terms and
indeed the Ladies of the Lake from Arthurian tradition very likely
belong to their kind, there are males of the species though they are
far less frequently encountered. The Gwragedd Annwn may be seen
walking upon the surface, floating beneath the water or otherwise
sailing in small golden boats.
Delicate pale-skinned , green-haired maidens known as Nixies were
believed to inhabit some if not all British rivers. Whilst their
temperament of these Water Nymphs is capricious, in essence they
are not usually as dangerous as the Groac'h, though besotted mortal
males risk drowning as a consequence of their enraptured pursuit of
Nixie love.
Habitat & Range : Water Elven - localised in lakes across Britain,
Ireland and Brittany, but most prevalent in Wales (especially around
the Black Mountains in Dyfed). Hidden gateways between the
everyday world and the sunken gardens of the Gwragedd Annwn
were once said to become apparent on certain lakeside boulders
every New Year's morning. However due to the misdemeanours of
some human visitors it has been claimed that for many years now
these portals have remained firmly locked. It was believed that
entire submarine kingdoms such as Tir fo Thoinn (The Land Beneath
the Waves) lay submerged off British and Irish coasts.
Nixies (Potamids) - particular to rivers and deep streams across
Britain and possibly Ireland.
Pool and Lake Nymphs are known as Limnads.

Asrai, Ellyons and Water Guardians
(Asrai also known as ~ Ashrays. Scarille. Dancers on the Mist.
Ellyons also known as ~ Water Sprites. Water Fairies.
Water Guardians also known as ~ Sea Sprites. Sea Guardians.
Fees des Houles. Nikkisen.)

The Asrai are a Fay species confined to water. During the day they remain at the depths but may be sighted below the surface on moonlit nights. They seem to be exclusively female and exhibit a strange beauty. Some human men have been so filled with longing at the sight of an Asrai it has been said, that they have attempted to capture the being. However if caught or even if exposed to sunlight the Asrai will melt away into a pool of colour-reflective water. The Asrai may also sometimes be seen as they flit and dance upon the surface of the water as vague nocturnal maidens comprised of mist. The touch of an Asrai may be cold enough to burn or wither human skin.

The Ellyons and the Water Guardians are similar species though the former are associated to fresh water and the latter to salt-water. The Ellyons are thought by some to be the attendants of the Water Elven and Ladies of the Lake, though they do not appear confined to an aquatic habitat. The Water Guardians are thought to be the servants of the Celtic Sea-God, Manannan Mac Lir (known in Wales as Manawydan fab Llyr) and also to be the protectors of marine wildlife. An associated water species is the Nokkes of the Orkney and Shetland Islands. However whilst the Nokkes may be heard as strange but harmonious music moving across the waters, they are very rarely if ever seen. The Manx Nikkisen (a name also used in reference to Water-Ogres) were said to lead the souls of drowned people in procession over the water.

Appearance, Attire & Size : The Asrai have a delicate, almost translucent beauty and may be witnessed as mist dancing above the surface of the water. Though individuals may be several hundred years old, they retain the appearance of young ladies. Their skin is pale and sometimes has a silvery sheen. They are generally naked or clothed in ethereal robes. Their size generally seems to be of slight human proportions but they can also be tiny. The Asrai seem unable to speak human languages.

Both the Ellyons and Water Guardians are of both genders and are so small that they can use eggshells as boats. The Manx Water Guardians often have an aura of green-blue light that shimmers and dances about their being.

Habitat & Range : The Asrai are most prevalent in rivers and pools in Shropshire and Cheshire - England, and may also be encountered in Scotland.

The Ellyons are most prevalent in the lakes of Cornwall and Wales.

Sea-sprites and Water Guardians occupy the waters surrounding Britain and Ireland, but are most intense around the coast of the Isle of Man. The Fees des Houles may be encountered in sea-caves in Brittany

Swan Maidens
(Also known as Swan-Spirits. Whoopers.)

At first glance these creatures may appear to be extremely elegant but nonetheless familiar enough breeds. Yet not all swans may be what they first seem. Some may shed their feathery coats at night and reveal themselves to be beautiful female Fays. If these coats are stolen then the maidens will become trapped in humanoid form. If the thief is a human male, he may then take the maiden as a possibly unwilling bride. Should this occur, then raises the possibility that when the man least expects it, a whole flight of swans will come to liberate their sister and her swanskin. Despite their usual serene demeanour, swans should not be underestimated for should they become displeased they can prove themselves to be considerably powerful and aggressive creatures. Therefore any brigand and boor meddling in the life of a Swan Maiden could very likely come to sorely regret their actions.
Other Swan Maidens though may be trapped in avian form as a result of a curse bestowed upon them. In Celtic myth it was customary for someone to embark upon and complete a series of heroic tasks on behalf of the Swan Maidens (and occasionally Swan Men), in order that their human form may again be resumed. The Celtic Goddess / Saint Bridget was also worshipped in some localities as being a Swan-Goddess.

Appearance, Attire & Size : Shape-shifting Swan Maidens appear as naked, pale but pretty young women when they shed their feathered coat. Beguiled Swans may find their human bodies extremely aged and decrepit if the quest or the lifting of the spell has taken a considerable number of years to be achieved. In swan form both of these types are of normal appearance and proportions, however may be distinguishable at times from conventional birds by the chains of either silver or rose-gold that are draped around their slender necks.

Diet : In swan form probably water-vegetation. In humanoid form possibly the usual fare of Faerie beings.

Habitat & Range : In the air or on bodies of water across Britain, Brittany and especially in Ireland.

Water Horses and Water Bulls
(Also known as ~ Kelpies. Each Uisge. Ceffyl Dwr. Aughisky. Glashans. Glashtin. Glastyn. Goberchinu. Tangies. Nuggies. Noggles. Nygels. Neugles. Nuggles. Neagles. Nyaggles. Nennir. Cheva. Shopiltees. Shoneys. Sponies. Shags. Beistes. Peistes. Muirdris. Croath Mara. Cabyll Ushtey. Tarbh Uisge. Taroo Ushty.)

Water Horses can vary in temperament from shy to mischievous to downright nasty. Like the Scottish Kelpie, many will suddenly appear at bank-sides and encourage or force weary travellers onto their backs. Then they will suddenly charge at alarming pace into the nearby body of water and dump the startled human there. Normally an embarrassing soaking is the worst that will befall the hapless human, though some Water Horses will drown their victims also. The Irish Aughisky in particular will do this in order to feed upon their victims, eating humans entire except for their livers. The Welsh Ceffyl Dwr tend to buck the trend and often will themselves jump onto the backs of the weary human travellers. Some Water Horses are also thought able to assume humanoid forms, usually either as small hairy men or as youths who initially seem very handsome, but on closer inspection have weed-encrusted hair, a musty smell about them and hooves instead of feet. Water Horses can vary in their habits and appearance somewhat depending on specific breed and location. Some Irish Water-~Horses may bear a single Unicorn-like horn.
Some of these amphibious beasts have more bovine attributes and as such are known as Water Bulls. Water Bulls are notorious for attempting to breed with conventional cattle or leading domestic stock into the watery depths, whilst the Manx Water Horses known as Glashans have gained a reputation for attempting to abduct or molest women. Sometimes Glashans would adopt the form of dapple foals or lambs or a more humanoid appearance and on occasions would assist farmers with manual labour in exchange for food. An unusual tale from the Scottish Isle of Islay describes of a ferocious battle between a Water Horse and a Water Bull.

Mentioned also in Irish folklore is the creature known as the Dobhar-Chu (or the Anchu, Water-Hound, Master Otter or King Otter). Resembling a common otter though much bigger and sometimes almost albino in pigmentation, the Dobhar-Chu was thought ready and capable to kill humans and horses. However it was believed that the pelt of such a beast would protect ships from wrecking, horses from drowning and heal humans of gunshot wounds.

Selkies
(Also known as ~ Selchies. Roane. Seal People. Seal Folk. Sea Faeries. Haaf-Fish. Finn-folk.)

Whilst wearing their sleek fur coats the Selkies are indistinguishable from seals, yet at times they will shed these skins and appear as strangely beautiful humanoid creatures. Several love affairs between humans and Selkies have been rumoured. At least one of these relationships occurred as a result of a human man finding and hiding a shed seal skin, for deprived of this hide a Selkie cannot return to the sea. Upon the eventual retrieval of the enchanted garment this Selkie returned beneath the waves. Other Selkie / human romances appear to have been built on genuine and mutual affection however. At times the Selkie may adapt to a terrestrial life but at others the mortal lover may have opted instead for life below the brine. These trysts could involve either a mortal woman falling for a Selkie male, or a male human and a Selkie maiden. Crossbreed offspring were sometimes born out of such unions. Whilst these mixed-race children that were delivered into our world do not seem to have inherited their Selkie parent's acute amphibious ability, they are often regarded as having a deep respect, sympathy and understanding of the sea. In addition they may also be of an unusual though attractive appearance and may also exhibit some supernatural abilities such as healing or Second Sight (clairvoyance). Some mariners thought that the Selkies were the souls of drowned sailors.

Appearance & Attire : Frequently no different from seals or sea lions, but upon shedding their skin they appear as beautiful men and women. Their bodies are lean and toned, and their skin is smooth and hairless, often with a pale silvery sheen. Their head-hair is commonly sleek black or blue-green and tends to be long and luxurious, though the beautiful Roane maidens of Western Ireland had long golden tresses. Their eyes are large, black and soulful. Having shed their sealskin the Selkies are generally observed naked. The offspring of intimate human / Seal Person liaisons would sometimes have webbed fingers or toes.

Diet: Like regular seals,Selkies love fresh fish. Conversely however some Irish Roane taken as brides by humans would sternly refuse to consume fish.

Habitat & Range : around the coasts of Scotland (particularly the Hebrides, Shetland and Orkney isles), the Faeroe Islands and Ireland (especially Northern Ireland). Selkies have displayed a great aversion to Christian Churches and in some places it is believed that should a priest so much as touch a Selkie's seal-skin cape then the creature would no longer be able to return to its aquatic domain.

Sea Trows
(Also known as ~ Sea Lions. Sea Kelpies. Blue Men. Haaf-Fish.
Whistling Seals.)

Despite their given names, these marine entities are possibly more closely related to the Selkies if anything, than to the Kelpies and land Trows. Some Sea Trows are said at times to appear to assume the form of strange horse-like creatures or seals, but it is uncertain whether their metamorphosis involves the Selkie practice of the shedding and redressing of an outer layer. Sea Trows however are more notorious in their humanoid form as they are feared to stir up tempests in order to cause great mischief. However if they were challenged to a game of riddles, they would not be able to resist participating in such mind-play. Should the human mariner manage to outwit the Sea Trow in the art of conundrums, then on this occasion the entity would leave the vessel without causing further damage or harm. In earlier times fishermen believed that the spirits of the sea demanded a sacrifice and would relent some of their catch and it has even been proposed that they would be reluctant to save people from a death by drowning in case the spirits would claim more lives in spite. Following the advent of Christianity, many then considered that the Sea Trows were Fallen Angels - the banished usurpers who following the Biblical war in Heaven plummeted, not into the bowels of Hell or to the earth, but instead directly into the seas .

Appearance & Attire : The Sea Trows are most frequently encountered as masculine humanoids with either grey or blue skin (however it has been suggested that they may be ruled by a Queen). Sometimes it is reported that their faces are peculiarly long and that their hands and feet are palmate. Some of them are bearded. The only clothing that they're noted as wearing is a wide belt contrived of emerald scales.

Size : Usually of normal human proportions.

Diet : Fish, though it is sometimes feared that they may devour human flesh.

Habitat & Range : In the seas around the coasts of the Scottish Highlands and Ireland.

The channel between Lewis and the Shiant Islands in the Outer Hebrides is said to accommodate a large clan of dreadful Sea Trows known as the Blue Men of the Minch or Blue Men of the Shiants. In Orcadian lore, a mythical isle known as Heather-Bleather said to lie close to the Orkneys, was thought to be the domain of Sea-Trows and Selkies.

Mermaids and Tritons
(Also known as ~ Merpeople. Mer-Men / Mer-Wives. Fish Folk. Sea Gardeners. The Lady's Own. Tritonids.
Individual Species / Local names include ~ **Seirenes. Ceasg. Daoine Mara. Maighdean Mara. Ben Varrey. Mari-Morgans. Sea-Morganzed. Marie Morgans. Merrows. Maighdean na Tuinne. Merucha. Muardhuacha. Meer-folk. Fin-Folk.**)

Perhaps the most celebrated of aquatic entities are the Merpeople, especially the females known as Mermaids or sometimes as Sirens (males are known as Tritons or Mermen). These creatures have been reported in virtually every sea across the globe and the waters surrounding Britain and Ireland are certainly no exception. At times the Mermaids may appear stunningly beautiful as they recline on coastal reefs, combing their long tresses. So exquisite are their visage and sometimes also their song, that they could inspire sailors into such yearning distraction that their ships could often be caused to disastrously run aground on rocks. Indeed some seafarers considered that the merest sighting of a Mermaid was a grim portent of doom. Other Mermaids would take a much deeper interest in human males and would lure beguiled men beneath the waves. Frequently the enamoured mortal would drown, either due to the Mermaid not appreciating fundamental differences between species or as a deliberate sequence of cause and effect. The fatalities would perhaps be engineered simply for sadistic, morbid humour or in the case of the Seirenes of the Channel Islands, as a means of obtaining a source of food. Other Mermaids however display a more genuine attraction and kinder interest towards mankind (see Merrows).
In 1830, a small but physically developed Mermaid was reportedly seen close to the coastline of Benbecula island in the Outer Hebrides. After failed efforts to capture the creature a young lad hurled a rock at her in frustration. The missile struck the Mermaid squarely on the back and she vanished beneath the surf. Sadly though after a few days had passed, her delicate lifeless body washed up on the sands a few miles down the coast. The Benbecula folk were and are familiar with the animals of the sea, yet they regarded the carcass before them to be so different and so special to warrant it being given a dignified ceremonial burial.
Mermen or Tritons have been reported less frequently as it is believed that they tend to prefer to spend more time at marine depths. Non-marine 'Mermaids ' have been reported at Hayfield in Derbyshire and also in fresh water sources along the Welsh- English border.

Merrows and Muardachas
(Also known as ~ Mara-Warra. Moruadh. Murrughach. Sea-Cows.
Walrus-People)

The Merrows are a distinct breed of Merpeople whose genders also differentiate greatly. Whilst the males are friendly enough characters, in appearance though they are generally considered to be gruesome. This opinion often seems to extend to their comparatively gorgeous females as they have been known prone to fall in love instead with human males.

The name 'Muardacha' is sometimes used as an alternative to Merrow, however it has also been specifically used to refer to other weird marine creatures that bear a fishes' tail but not the upper parts of humans but those of cattle, goats or horses. Whilst it has been suggested that some alleged encounters with Muardachas (and other Merpeople species also) may have been mistaken sightings of natural creatures such as dolphins or other marine mammals, the hybridisation of piscine and animal parts is perhaps also reminiscent of the ancient Fomorii.

Appearance & Attire : The Merrow Tritons tend to have more fishy attributes, webbed claws and spiny fins. However their ominous visage is rarely indicative of their character as they are often of a friendly enough disposition. The Merrow maidens are of a gentle beauty and demeanour. Both genders have fish-like tails and both wear red feathered caps. This headgear enables the Merrows to transport themselves great distances throughout the water and is also likely the source of their limited shape-shifting abilities (to go upon the land they either assume legs or instead may adopt the form of small cattle). Should their hats be lost or stolen then it is said that the Merrows will be unable to return to their homes. Muardachas have fish tails but the upper parts of goats, horses or cattle.

Size : The humanoid or animal parts are of normal proportions but their tails may be of considerable length.

Diet : Mainly fish and /or marine vegetation. Male Merrows also have a penchant for alcohol.

Habitat & Range: Coastal waters around Ireland. A strange river creature comparable to a Muardacha has also been reported in the River Tamar in Cornwall and Devon.

Black Dogs
(Also known as ~ Shock, Old Shuck, Black Shuck, Black
Angus. Gwyllgi. Moddey Dhoo. Mauthe Dogs. Strikers.
Skrikers. Shrikers. Trash. Tchi-Co. Spectre-hounds.
Glassensykes. Gytrash. Gurt Dogs. Barguests. Padfoots. Thost
Dogs. Hairy Jacks. Cappels.Capelthwaites. Le Tchan de
Bouole. Cu Sith. Dogs of Darkness. Hooters. Muckle Black
Tykes. Farvan.)

Numerous locations across the British Isles have long been reputed to be haunted by large phantom dogs. Depending on location and individual, these weird hounds can either be savage and deadly or otherwise protective or disinterested. Either way their apparitions seem unnatural and alarming. Though some may indeed be closely associated with Shape-shifting Bogies, Barguests and Phookas, other possible suggestions regarding the supernatural roots of Phantom Black Dogs include ~
- They are either supernatural Wraiths sent as a herald of doom, or strange but natural dogs that can somehow sense and are attracted to the shadow of death.
- They are guardians elected by an unknown authority but assigned to particular locations uch as certain paths, streams, burial-sites and churches (see also Church-Grims). Some also are suspected to watch over hoards of buried treasure.
- They are manifestations of the Devil himself or perhaps lesser Demons who traverse this world on their missions of malice and mischief. Otherwise they may be the lap dogs or strays of Hell.
- They are temporarily adapted guises of Shape-shifting Bogies, Wizards or Witches.
- They are the Ghosts of ordinary dogs who died in absence of their master (or alternatively it was the owner who died) and are observed searching eternally in vain for their former mortal keeper.
- They are the Ghosts of either suicides, murder victims or murderers condemned and executed for their crimes.
The last theory was applied to the Black Dog of Newgate Gaol, who was reportedly observed sat beside condemned felons on the waggons transporting them to the gallows. It was thought that this particular Black Dog was the phantom of a Wizard who had been imprisoned and then killed and eaten by other starving inmates. A Phantom Grey Dog reported haunting a man named William Sutor in 18th Century Scotland revealed itself to be his brother, David, damned to roam after death in canine form for having murdered a man by setting his dog upon him.
Regardless of their true origins those who survive an encounter with a

Phantom Black Dog may find themselves profoundly changed. Indeed the term 'Black Dog' has also become associated with either a succession of misfortune or bouts of deep depression. A church in Blythburg, East Anglia has deep, seemingly burnt grooves upon its door that are attributed to the claws of a monstrous Black Dog.

The Wild Hunt
(Also known as ~ Gabriel Hounds. Gabble Ratchets. Hell Hounds. Heath Hounds. Yell Hounds. Yeth Hounds. Wish Hounds. Wist Hounds. Wisht Hounds. Wight Hounds. Herlething. Dando Dogs. Devil's Dandy Dogs. Hounds of the Hill. Hounds of Odin. Hounds of Annwn. Cwn Annw. Sky Yelpers. Cheney's Hounds. Dewer's Hounds. Lyme Hounds. Gaze Hounds. Cwn y Wybr. Sky Dogs. Hergest's Dogs. The Furious Horde.)

Many local legends proclaim the sightings of a spectral hunt embarking across ground and sky. As it careers across the air, like the Host of the Unseelie Court in Scotland, the Wild Hunt may at times sweep up an unlucky mortal into their unholy throng. Should they actually survive the ordeal then they would likely be tainted so deeply by their heinous activity that they would be caused immense mental and spiritual, if not also bodily damage. The procession of the Hunt is comprised of many hellish dogs, some of which may even breathe fire and should such a cavalcade pass directly over a house then it was often thought that death or misfortune would soon call within (see Wraiths).
The Wild Hunt is commonly presided over by a single Wild Huntsman or Midnight Hunter. Often this figure is cloaked and wears a wide-brimmed hat that casts his features in shadow. This makes his true identity all the more enigmatic but suggestions include ~
- The Devil himself.
- Odin or Wotan (Woten, Wodan Grim, Grimnir or Wode) the Norse-Teutonic God, whose lore spread into parts of these isles with the coming of the Anglo-Saxons and Vikings.
- King Arthur.
- Herla, a mysterious King of Ancient Britain who was said to have spent several centuries as a *guest* in a Faerie or Gnomic kingdom.
- Varied local landowners, hunters or brigands whose practices in life continued after their death, such as Dando and Cheney both of the English West Country.
- Herne the Hunter, or possibly Cernunnos or other aspects of the Horned God, or Lord of the Hunt.
- Arawn or Gwynn ap Nudd , Kings of the Welsh Faerie domain of Annwn.
- Diana, the Romano-Celtic Goddess of the Hunt and her Witch devotees.

There is speculation what the actual quarry of the Wild Hunt may be also, but it is often considered that the desired prey are lost souls.

One grisly encounter with the Wild Hunt is related in Devonshire lore. A man was walking the lonely expanse of Dartmoor when he saw the Hunt charging past at ground level in the direction of Wistman's Wood. The man was either brave or a fool, for he called brazenly to the Midnight Hunter requesting a share of their catch. Silently the Hunter threw the man a tied bundle before charging away. Upon arriving home the man eagerly opened the bloody package and to his horror he was faced not with a prime cut of boar or venison or other such tasty meat but instead he gazed upon the body of his own infant child.

Alien Big Cats

The reported sightings of these strange felines which have increased in modern times indicate natural corporeal creatures rather than supernatural beings. However their inclusion in this guide is warranted by the fact that their actual and unquestionable presence in these isles has not at the time of writing, been proved beyond doubt. Despite considerable study and tracking, the Alien Big Cats (ABCs) remain enigmatic. The word 'Alien' in their given name relates not to an extra-terrestrial origin but rather to being 'out of place'. These creatures seem to show considerable similarity to feline species native to Africa, Asia or the Americas. Although many such cats have been introduced to these isles within the confines of zoos, circuses or even as exotic pets of the aristocracy, they have not been officially introduced into the wild and most are not thought to have ever been native here. Though escapees from any of the former could account for some sightings, the range and number of alleged encounters seems too large to be explained simply by this theory. Their considerable presence would seem to indicate breeding colonies or as some have suggested a more supernatural explanation. Hoaxes, mis-identifications and ambiguous evidence aside, the Alien Big Cats remain a shadowy but comparatively frequently reported phenomenon. Unlike many of the other creatures featured within this guide, more tangible proof has been forthcoming regarding the presence of ABCs in these isles. Droppings, hair and tracks have at times been found but more dramatically, over the years bodies of several large felids have also been discovered in various counties. Some of theses creatures had been shot and killed, whilst the bodies of others had been unexpectedly chanced upon. The corpses uncovered have included those of Jungle Cats, Lynx, Caracals, Puma and even a Lioness in Lancashire. In the Scottish highlands the bodies of several melanistic large cats have also been recovered, these animals are different from the previously known Scottish Wildcats and have been named Kellas Cats after the area they were first discovered. In the past the Highland Scots knew these beasts as the Cait Sith and believed that they were transformed Malefactors. The large Demon-Cats of Ireland sometimes bore the ability to speak and were frequently considered to be the guardians of hidden treasure.

Alien Big Cats have found their place also within Arthurian legend with the battle between Arthur and the Demon Cat of Losanne and the tale of Sir Cai (or alternatively King Arthur himself) versus Palug's Cat (also known as the Anglesey Cat , the Chapul or Cath Palug).

An old Irish tale also speaks of a ferocious conflict between a hero named Ceatach and the large, aggressive Great Cat of the Cave and a 15th Century legend from Barnburgh in Yorkshire relates how a man named Percival Cresacre battled with a giant Wood Cat till their mutual destruction.

Church-Grims
(Also known as Grims. Kegrims.)

Grims are animal spirits that most frequently inhabit churches and burial grounds. Though their appearance may alarm the unwary, their presence may be there by device as it is their intention to protect the hallowed ground and not to defile it. It has been commented, that as the oldest churches were being built or before the first body was consigned to a necropolis, an animal was sacrificed and buried in the foundations. It was thus believed that its spirit would rise and protect the grounds from evil and wrongdoers. Alternatively it was believed that the first body to be interred in a graveyard would be claimed by the Devil. Therefore to spare a human whatever torment or servitude lay in store, the carcass of an animal would instead be buried first.

Some church spirits however were not invited and not welcome. Such entities were often assumed not to be the actual spirits of animals but instead were Demons or the souls of dead Malefactors that had assumed the guise of a natural creature. Some of these evil spirits proved very difficult to exorcise or remove. In Wales such devilish spirits were most prone to take the form of horrendous black-skinned pigs, but there has been considerable variety. In England, two churches in Lancashire (one in Burnley, the other in Winwick) were said to have had their construction irritatingly hampered by the mischief of great Demonic Pigs. Lydford in Devon was also said to be haunted by a Phantom Black-Pig that was believed to have been a man in its natural lifetime. This particular porcine horror (which generally seemed to avoid entering churches) was specifically considered to have once been the notorious Judge Jeffreys transformed after death as a result of a despicably callous nature. Like Jan Tregeagle (see the Damned), Jeffreys was another West-Country magistrate familiar enough with greed and cruelty but a stranger to kindness and likewise the recipient of a bizarre eternal penance.

The guardian Grims could be a lamb, black dog, dove or other creature that may be momentarily glimpsed but have little other interaction with benign humans.

The malign church spirits most frequently appear as Black Pigs but at other times may also assume the form of a black goat, fierce dog, monstrous fly or a murder of crows.

The Worcester Cathedral Grim is described as most resembling a Bear. Humanoid shapes are also not unknown.

The Yorkshire Grims apparently prefer dwelling in the bell-towers, where they would discordantly peel the bells at inappropriate times. Evil church spirits are most prevalent in Wales.

Tash
(Also known as ~ Thevshi. Thivishes. Animal-Ghosts.)

These Ghosts may manifest in human form also but frequently will assume an animal form. The particular species of creature can vary greatly and it is not known whether the selection is achieved randomly, by choice or is somehow reflective of the deceased person's character in life. Though they are sometimes astral, the Tash may frequently display a more fleshy form and therefore it is also uncertain whether the Tash's animal manifestation is a spirit-form or physical, suggesting reincarnation or a transmigration of souls. Many Tash however can be differentiated from regular animals by their ability to speak in a human tongue. A celebrated specimen of this type was reported on the Isle of Man in the 1930s. Lodging at a farmhouse called Doarlish Cashan belonging to a family named Irving, this Tash had assumed the form of a mongoose but identified itself verbally as 'Gef' and it apparently claimed that it had once been human. Tash are commonly thought to be the souls of those who had died a violent death either as a result of suicide, murder or accidental folly. Their presence at the scene of their demise is thought to either bring attention to the area or to mark a cautionary warning to those still living.

Tash frequently assume the forms of various animals including birds, rabbits, rodents, dogs, cats and butterflies. At times they may display some abnormality even to the extent of being headless, though normally they are conventional in appearance if not in behaviour.Animal ghosts occur randomly across the British Isles, though the Tash are more prevalent in Ireland.

A similar creature described in Ireland is the Dobhar-Chu or King Otter. Described as being like an amphibious hound with strange markings or aquatic features, this creature was deemed responsible for the deaths of humans and was said to emit an eerie whistling sound when it itself expires.

Galley Trots
(Also known as Wulvers.)

The Galley Trots are a peculiar hybrid of canine and human parts and are associated mainly with old burial grounds and ancient buildings. Their presence was once thought to indicate that valuable items or money was hidden somewhere in the nearby vicinity. There was also again the suspicion that to see a Galley Trot is an omen of approaching death (see Wraiths). In parts of Wales, tales are told about the Dog of Death. This strange white hound was rumoured to suddenly appear when serious disease or injury was in the air and to then sit mournfully outside the home of the terminally ill person.

Appearance & Attire : The Galley Trots frequently have the bodies of large Black Dogs but the heads of men. Some, such as Mrs Dog of Lincolnshire, England have the heads of human females but these are encountered less frequently. Other Galley Trots are reversed in having the bodies of humans (often attired in conventional clothing of a particular era or sometimes monastic habits) and the heads of ferocious dogs.
Galley Trots may also sometimes appear as entirely canine, shaggy white dogs about the size of a calf.

Diet : Uncertain. The Wulvers of Shetland however show a great interest in fishing and sometimes leave their excess catch on window-sills as gifts for humans.

Habitat & Range : Graveyards and lonely country roads localised across the Midlands and Southern England, especially in the Home Counties.

Glashtin
(Also known as ~ Howlers. Howlies. Glastyn. Cow-lug Sprites.)

The Glashtin are a strange Fay species which at times may assume an odd humanoid form but more frequently will appear as a strange blend of equine and bovine parts. Glashtin may often be heard rather than seen however, hence their alternative name of 'Howlers'. Their eerie cries may have the benefit of warning humans about approaching storms, however the Glashtins' wailing is likely to arise out of joy not fear and some people suspect that these creatures may actually cause harsh weather. The Glashtin have at times been associated with Water Horses, Bugganes and the Fenordee, whilst there may be deeper connections as yet unknown between these creatures, there is also the possibility that confusion has simply occurred as it tends to do over the years.

Appearance & Size : The Glashtin most frequently will appear as either cows with horses' heads or alternatively as horses with cows' heads. The bovine headed Glashtin are considered to be quite excitable and moronic whilst the equine headed Glashtin are thought to be of a more astute intellect. They are generally of regular farmyard proportions, though may sometimes be smaller.

In humanoid form the Glashtin either appear as a handsome young man with curly dark hair and sparkling eyes or as a strange child-like being. Either way their ears will be pointed or like those of a cow or horse.

Diet : Uncertain.

Habitat & Range : The Glashtin are most active prior to and during storms, especially in coastal areas on the Isle of Man and the Scottish Outer Hebrides.

Grants

Grants resemble small horses but walk only on their hind legs. They were most active during World War II when they would alert people of the blitz by inspiring dogs to bark and horses to whinny in advance of incoming air-raids. In earlier times they would alert people of the outbreak of fire or other potential catastrophes. Their diet is unknown and they were most commonly reported in certain villages in the Midlands, East Coast and Home Counties of England In Warwickshire and the West Midlands demonic Horses known as Knops have also been reported

Boobries

The Boobrie is a weird, unpleasant water-bird that is generally only encountered by sailors and passengers at sea. These grotesque birds tend to prey on ships carrying livestock. The Boobrie's hunting strategy usually consists of mimicking the call of a lamb or calf (or whatever animal the vessel is carrying). Should an adult animal then stray over to investigate, the Boobrie would grasp it in its horrid talons, drag it overboard and drown it. Obviously the human mariners would attempt to thwart the Boobrie's bizarre rustling, however other Boobries may attempt to distract the sailors by assuming the form of a horse and running across the surface of the water. Should the Boobrie be denied its quarry it is said to bellow like an angry bull.

Appearance & Size : At times the Boobrie may assume the size and form of a horse (see also Water Horses), though habitually it appears as a black sea-bird standing about 1 ft (0.3 m) tall. They are however phenomenally strong for their size. The Boobries' feet look like deformed human hands with sharp claws and they have a large vicious-looking beak.

Diet : Though it favours the meat of sheep and cattle, the Boobrie will likely also eat fish and other marine animals.

Habitat & Range : The Boobrie may be seen either flying over or swimming in the seas and channels around Scotland, especially off Argyll. It has been suggested that the Boobrie is intrinsically water-bound and for one to venture on-land would be to destroy itself.

The Baiste-na-Scoghaigh

The Unicorn , a beautiful white horse with a single spiralled horn growing from the centre of its head continues to be one of the most famous and enduring mythical creatures ever described yet despite being common in British heraldry, Unicorns have always seemed to have been considered as exotic creatures of the eastern world and were never believed to have either been native or introduced here. (Though the tusks of Narwhals [an odd-looking species of Whale] pandered as Unicorn horns, may likely have been exhibited or even sold in Britain and Ireland.) However the Isle of Skye at least was said to have nurtured a creature that may have bore some relationship to the Unicorn. Despite its hooves and the single great horn growing from its forehead, the Baiste-na-Scoghaigh, however was a shambling, unkempt quadruped of dubious pedigree. Some Water-Horses have also been reported bearing single Unicorn-like horns.

Griffins

Griffins, (Gryphons or Griffons) are fearsome creatures that have the head, wings, plumage and talons of an eagle but the body, legs and tail of a lion. They can either be bland or vibrantly coloured and they often stand taller than horses. Though Griffins are far more common to the lore of Russia, India and the Middle East, they are mentioned in the British tale of 'Jack the Giant -Killer' and are a familiar motif of heraldry. The terrible Griffins encountered by Jack (either in Wales or Cornwall) guarded a magnificent hoard of treasure shared by a Wrath and a Wizard. Griffins were also employed as guardians of the enchanted apple orchard of Hesperides as related by an old Irish tale. A Griffin was also said to guard an old well in Griffydam, Leicestershire.

Gittos

Gittos (also known as Gryphons) have the bodies of goats and the heads of horses, and though they have no wings they can fly for limited distances. Like the Phookas, the Gittos seem keen to blight or gorge on crops ready for harvest. Gittos are most active in Wales from dusk till dawn, between the Celtic festivals of Samhain and Beltain.

The Glatisaunt

The Glatisaunt or Questing Beast was another weird hybrid creature. This foe of King Arthur's Round Table had the head of a great lizard, the legs of a deer and the combined body of a lion and leopard. This strange beast was regarded as the embodiment of anarchy and deviant lust. The cry of the Glatisaunt was said to have sounded like a pack of dogs howling in unison.

Werewolves
(Also known as ~ Lycanthropes. Wolf-Men. Wer-Wolves.
Conriocht. Le Varou. Conoels. Sirites.)

Most celebrated amongst the Theriomorphs (humans that assume
animal form either mentally or through complete physical
transformation) are the Lycanthropes or Werewolves. Though the
lore of Lycanthropy (from the Greek Luk Anthropia meaning Wolf
Man) is far richer in France and across the European mainland
where the causes and cures (generally fatal) of such conditions are
discussed in great detail, the older sources inform us that
Werewolves were also present in these isles but unfortunately the
details are sketchy. Some tales relate episodes of cannibalism or of
individuals with a truly bestial nature and although there are no
shortage of shape-shifters in British lore, tales of specific Werewolves
are vague (though there was apparently a Werewolf epidemic in
Devon in 1195 and again in 1700). In Irish lore, there are more
Werewolf tales to be found as well as vague allusions to Conoels -
She-Wolves, and to Celtic outsiders called Sirites who were feared
able to assume the form of both wolf and bat at will. One such tale
originating in Ireland however relates the case of a man called
Connor who, whilst searching for strayed cattle, sought to seek
shelter from a breaking storm, in an isolated cottage in the middle
of a moor. He was bid to sit by the fire by a strange and silent
elderly couple. Their reluctance or inability to talk and the constant
glare of their beady eyes disturbed him a little, but he deemed it far
preferable to weathering the storm. After a while came a rap on the
door and into the cottage entered a large grey wolf, which settled
itself by the fire and proceeded to also stare intently at the man.
The old couple did not seem concerned about the wolf in their
midst, but the man despite his own silent alarm kept his place for
the storm now raged outside. Then came another knock on the door
and a second large grey wolf entered the room and took its place
by the fire. Now the man was greatly disturbed yet he felt rooted to
the spot both by fear and the fixed glare of human and animal eyes.
Still they stared and stared as the storm raged on outside. Then
came a third rap at the door and again another wolf came in out of
the grim weather and sat by the others next to the fire. The man's
heart and mind did well to take the strain he now felt, as the five
pairs of eyes set upon his person seemed to grow ever hungrier. Yet
within the eyes of the last wolf there was something else, a spark of
contemplation now glinted into recognition. Suddenly this wolf cast
off his hide to reveal the form of a naked young man and
proceeded to explain to his elderly

parents and wolfen kin that he recognised their guest and potential meal as a man who had once protected him from being trapped by hunters whilst he was in wolf -form. For this previous act of kindness, the wolf pack now decided to spare the man's life.

More recently in the Yorkshire Wolds and around the area of Barmston Drain there have been numerous reported sightings of a red-eyed Werewolf dubbed locally as Old Stinker because of his rancid breath. On one occasion this beast was said to have effortlessly leaped an 8 foot fence whilst carrying a German Shepherd dog in its mouth. Another apparent Werewolf sighting was reported at Croom Court near Pershore, Worcestshire in 2016

Faerie Deer

At times certain deer may also be transformed Fays, Enchantresses or Celtic Goddesses. In this guise they often appear as snow-white does with golden hooves and sometimes antlers (which even without the regalia, is itself an indication of a supernatural presence as out of our native and natural deer species, only the males are antlered). Occasionally the Faerie Deer may be restricted by certain conditions and may only assume a humanoid form for limited periods of time, whilst others may change shape at will. The brisk form of a deer could at times help a Fay escape capture, but likewise make it a potential prey either for human hunters or for the Wild Hunt. Faerie Deer may be encountered in certain woodland across Britain and Ireland but often only at either dusk or dawn.

Faerie Cattle: (Also known as Dun Cows. Glasgavlens. Fuwch Gyfeiliorm)

Though Faerie Cattle often look small and fairly unremarkable, (frequently they were white with red ears like the semi-feral Chillingham Cattle of Northumberland - a breed reputedly still protected by Faerie-folk) they are such prized animals that the ancestral courts of Irish legend were even prepared to go to war over possession of a single specimen. Another celebrated example was the Dun Cow of Dunsmore Heath, in Warwickshire, England. This cow which once belonged to a Wrath, was renowned for always filling a container to the brim with her delicious milk. However one day, out of sheer spite an old Witch milked the cow into a sieve until blood passed from its udders. This act transformed the Dun Cow from a marvel into a monster, and her subsequent rampage was only ended with her slaughter at the hands of Guy, Earl of Warwick. Some Faerie Cattle (known sometimes as Crodh Mara or Gwartheg Y Llyn) would mingle amidst herds of conventional cattle before leading the beasts either into deep water or inside a Faerie-Hill. Elf-Bulls would sometimes mate with conventional heifers and for the most part the calves borne of such unions were generally considered favourably.

Brawn

Before they were hunted into extinction Wild Boar provided many humans with a hardy meal and challenging sport. However certain boar (known as Brawn) grew to such proportions and power that if anything were to be doing any hunting or eating, it would be they. Some Brawn were such monstrous creatures that caused a great trail of destruction and claimed many human lives. These animals would often become the quarry of distinguished hunters and aspiring heroes. County Durham in northern England has several tales relating to giant boar ravaging the region. The oldest dates back to Roman times in the region of Bollihope Common in Weardale, but more well known are the Medieval monsters that terrorised the localities of Brandon and Brancepeth and another in Bishop Auckland. Both these creatures were finally slaughtered under the patronage of the ruling Prince Bishops, the first by a valiant knight named Roger de Ferie and the latter by a brave young man by the name of Pollard, but not before both had caused great destruction and misery on their way. The Boar of Ben Bulben and the Twrch Trwth were other extremely powerful wild pigs that are to be found in Irish and Welsh legend respectively, though these were both said to have once been human. Whilst there are many Wild Boar still bred in captivity, there is currently a program established in the New Forest, Hampshire regarding the possible reintroduction of Wild Boar back into the wilds of England. Boars were considered sacred animals by the Celtic peoples.

Ravens & Crows

Seen in such quantity that they blacken the sky, crows and ravens may be interpreted as a portent of great disaster or possibly even war (see Corpse Birds). However individual crows and ravens may also be more than mere birds, as this was a favoured manifestation of the Badb - the war persona of the Morigann, the Celtic tripartite Dark Goddess. Hooded Crows are also a form commonly assumed by the deadly Baobhan Sith. Celtic legend reveals that other crows or ravens may have been humans or Fays transformed as a result of a curse (see also Swan Maidens) whilst others still may be the hosts of evil spirits. Even as a purely avian life-form, crow breeds may be seen to hold a court or parliament. When such a Crow-court occurs, a circle of crows may surround an individual bird and its wings may even be held in their beaks. Individuals will take it in turn to caw as if laying out charges and evidence. Then the most dominant crow that has been silent throughout will croak the judgement and the captive will either be released or the others will rush in and peck it to death. The Raven's call was once considered to be an ominous chorus of the words "Corpse. Corpse."

Horses

(See also ~ **Water Horses, Grants, Glashtin.)**
Horse-Whisperers.)
Horses are swift, strong and often beautiful creatures both sides of the Supernatural border. They are the sacred animals of the Celtic Goddess Epona , who was herself sometimes represented as either being a horse or at least having a horses' head (most frequently though she is represented as a maiden sitting side-saddle upon a horse). Epona was

known by various other names including Eponina, Potia, Ipona, Atanta, Catona, Epotia, Vovesia, Dibonia and Rhiannon, depending upon particular Celtic tribes. A number of large and impressive representations of horses are to be found amongst ancient English sacred land-art. The Uffington White Horse on the Berkshire Downs in England is probably the most celebrated example of equine chalk-down carving. Whilst a number of British horse carvings are of no great antiquity or have had their ancient borders re-cut into more acceptably 'horse-like' shapes, the Uffington Horse has retained its original design, a motif that has been discovered replicated on unearthed Celtic coins. A White Horse was also used as an emblem of the Jutes, the Germanic race that invaded South-east England in the mid 5th Century. Costumes and effigies of horses known generically as Hobby Horses, continued to be a notable facet of British folk-ceremonies for very many years, though their true association to the primal horse-cults is uncertain. Varied superstitions also arose concerning items such as horse-shoes and horse-brasses as well as the bones of actual horses. They were generally considered efficient wards against evil or as having the power to attract good luck or improve the harmonics of a building.

It is without doubt that the ancient Britons and Gaels regarded horses as being both valuable and sacred. This does not mean that these creatures were beyond being ceremoniously sacrificed however as tales of Celtic nobles relate how on certain significant occasions they would feast upon and bathe in a broth stewed of horse flesh and bones.

The Faerie Courts would often ride magnificent horses whilst out on cavalcade. These Faerie Horses shared their riders' ability to alter their proportions and the imperial horses would often have manes of gold and hooves of silver. On May-Day it is said that the Irish hero, O' Donoghue may be seen riding over the lakes of Killarney upon his sturdy white steed. He is preceded and succeeded by Fays strewing flower petals in his path and passing.

Mortals such as Oisin, True Thomas and Tam-Lin who were enchanted into the Faerie realm as recounted in legendary ballads, were said to have been transported by milk-white steeds. This draws further comparison between the Otherworld and the after-life kingdoms of religious belief (Heaven, Hell, Hades etc.), as biblical tradition holds that 'death' also rides a pale horse (see also Ankou). Monstrous black horses carrying sinister riders such as the Devil and the Midnight Hunter, or strange phantoms such as Headless Horsemen have also been reported in the lore of Britain and Ireland.

Horses were also often considered to be the unfortunate targets of mischief and malice caused by Witches, Lutins, Hags and Elves. Varied superstitious practices were often employed to counter such advances. Some people believe that horses are more acutely sensitive to the Supernatural world and are more likely than humans to see or sense Phantoms. Also by their very nature some horses can be wild and troublesome. Mortals with specific though seemingly mysterious abilities were (and sometimes still are) called in to becalm these boisterous beasts (see Horse Whisperers & Toad-Men).

Toads
As well as professedly providing a daylight safe body for some photosensitive Dwarf breeds, toads are traditionally in their own right both a reviled and valued species. To discover that a toad had entered a human abode on its own volition was considered a most unfortunate omen, for these warty creatures were thought to be a favoured form both for shape-shifting Witches and also their Familiar spirits. Any misfortune that happened to befall the household around that time would thus be attributed to the presence of the toad and the amphibian would likely be killed as a result (being thrown alive onto an open fire was deemed an efficient method of disposal and countering the bad luck). However sometimes toads would be actively sought out and deliberately taken into a home. Despite the concern that toads secreted toxic oils that were feared to cause warts at best or at worst kill painfully, that they were feared able to spit venom and that their body parts were thought to be a potent ingredient in Witch's Brews (Toad saliva mixed with sow-thistle sap, applied ceremonially to the body was said to render Witches invisible), they were also considered to be an effective component in medicinal folk-remedies. Dead toads would be used either whole or in part to try to combat a variety of diseases. Live toads were either rubbed on infected areas or even placed in a patient's mouth before being released in the hope that they would take the illness away with them. Some people were reluctant to kill a toad lest the action raise a terrible thunder-storm.
Toads were also thought to contain a precious stone within their heads which if removed could protect a person against poisons and infections as well as easing child-birth. Dubious gems and fossils purported to be Toad-stones were often set into jewellery and sold as amulets.
Live Toads, as well as Frogs, have at times also been found inside of apparently sealed stones, some of which were discovered considerably deep below the ground.

Cats

In addition to the Alien Big Cats and the Wag by the Way, common or domestic Cats have a strange reputation of their own. Numerous superstitions surround cats within these isles ; for instance that they have nine lives (a belief that is sometimes also extended to the Faeries), that a black cat crossing your path is either lucky or unlucky (depending upon locality) or that incoming weather can be forecast by their habits. Many parents are dubious about leaving cats with their infant children due to an old fear that the creature will leap into the cot , sit upon the infants chest and attempt to steal the child's breath (see also Night Hags). Likewise if a cat leapt upon or over a corpse lying in state, it was also deemed an omen of grave consequence.Occasionally odd-looking cats are born amongst otherwise conventional litters. Some may have unnaturally coloured fur (fluorescent green for example) whilst others have been reported with wing-like growths. In Oxford in the 1930s, one such Winged Cat was allegedly able to fly, though more frequently the wings do not seem to function. Freaky felines such as these are usually considered to be mutations rather than a significant supernatural breed.

However some other cats seem to betray a more Otherworldly status. The relationship between cats and Witches has been traditionally well noted , though some shape-shifting Witches were said to adopt a feline form, this is only one amongst varied animal disguises they'd assume (Hares generally being the most common). Again in the company of other animal forms, cats were also highly suspect as being a common form of the Witches' demonic aides known as Familiars. Sometime possibly around the 1840s a man by the name of Johnny Reed was said to have been walking in Staindrop, County Durham when a cat approached him. This moggy suddenly proclaimed "Johnny Reed. Johnny Reed. Tell Madam Momfort that Mally Dixon is dead!"

Not knowing either of the folk mentioned and more than a tad astounded he related the happenings to his wife upon his return home. His own cat, which was sitting nearby and who hadn't been known to utter a single word before that day, suddenly leaped up exclaiming "Is she? Then I'm the Queen of the Cats!" and bolting out of the door was never seen again. The God of the Cats however was said to be a large fierce Moggy by the name of Big Ears (Iruscan in Ireland). He was said to appear at the end of the Taghairm, a grisly ceremony involving cat sacrifice and grant the wishes of Malefactors (though it is sometimes suggested that they would also receive a curse which they had not bargained on).

Dragons, Demi-Dragons and Water Monsters

Though the image of the Dragon (from the Greek Draco or Drakon meaning both a large serpent and as a verb to watch) probably needs little introduction, many of the weird creatures perceived to be Dragons actually aren't ... well not in the purest crypto-zoological sense of the word anyway. Indeed out of the many Dragon-like species reportedly encountered across the globe, some researchers hold that only five species can be classified as 'True Dragons', the other terrible species (that vary greatly in their level of similarity to the True Dragons) may be generically classed as 'Demi-Dragons'. The five species of True Dragon are the European, Indian, Near Eastern, Middle Eastern and Oriental. Four of these species are quite similar with only the True Oriental Dragon or Lung showing a marked difference in both appearance and character. In legend these sinuous, bearded creatures are said to live in the sky and are noted as fortunate omens and delivers of rain. The image of the Oriental Dragon is familiar now in Britain and Ireland due to the Dragon-dance ceremony (sometimes known as Lion-dance) held in celebration of the Chinese New Year as performed by the Eastern population resident in many of our cities. However no living Dragon of this type has been reported within these shores. The more terrestrial and unpleasant True Dragon familiar to the British and Irish of yore, belongs to the True European or Heraldic variety. In addition to these gruesome beasts, several types of equally dangerous Demi-dragons have been apparently encountered within these isles. Although not as eloquent as the Oriental, the True European or Heraldic Dragon and also the various Demi-Dragon breeds seem to possess a far deeper alertness and intellect than their bestial nature suggests (and they are generally very savage and bloodthirsty indeed). However due to the decline of viable habitat in which such large and monstrous creatures could hide, it would suggest that the land Dragons are already extinct within these isles. The decrease in reported sightings in modern times would tend to indicate that this is so, however perhaps the same cannot be said about their aquatic relatives. Whilst encounters with large marine or freshwater monsters cannot be described as an everyday occurrence, sometimes when someone looks out across deep, dark waters they see something strange, something primal stirring beneath or even breaking the surface.

Note : Some mythologists have used a simpler classification of Dragons labelling those capable of flight as Drakes and those bound to the surface levels as Wyrms, this categorisation is especially pertinent to Anglo-Saxon beliefs (evident in some old accounts where a variety of legged yet wingless beasts have been named as Wyrms)

Heraldic Dragons
(Also known as ~ True European Dragons. Classical Dragons.)

The Heraldic Dragon is an extremely recognisable creature of British lore due in part to England's patron, Saint George being an acclaimed Dragon-slayer. There is however much speculation as to whether he rid Oxfordshire and Berkshire or actually Syria, Palestine or Libya of such a beast. Some claim however that the tale is merely an allegory of good triumphing over evil or even symbolic propaganda referring to the conversion of pagans and later to the medieval Crusades in the Middle-East. Though Dragons were generally considered evil in western nations, their use in heraldry tends to instead denote strength and resilience as exemplified by the Red Dragon on the Welsh national flag. The symbolism of the battle between the Welsh Red Dragon and a White Dragon is thought to allude to the ancient Britons' struggle against the invading Anglo-Saxon forces. It would seem though that many Dragons were aggressively territorial as another tale from Little Cornard in Suffolk also relates, for here was said to provide the battleground between a Black Dragon and a Red Dragon. Again the Red dragon was to prove the victor. A host of fiery dragons reputedly seen in the air over Northumbria in 793 AD was deemed symbolic of the advance of the Viking invasion.

Dragons display a natural arsenal of terrible weapons such as vicious talons, large sharp teeth, a thick almost impenetrable hide, and often a devastating fiery breath. In addition to this it would appear that their cunning is far sharper than may be at first apparent. Many Dragons though could be betrayed by a single, relatively small *soft spot* on their underbelly. Into this weakness, a fortunate Dragon-slayer could sink their sword blade, thus bringing relief to society and glory upon themselves. Often though, Dragon-slayers would need to resort to thoughtful guile rather than sheer brute force, should they have any chance of vanquishing these dreadful reptilian foes.

A grim pedigree is granted to Dragons in the legend of Piers Shonks from Pelham, Hertfordshire. Having just slain such a formidable beast, Shonks himself lay dying from the poisoned wounds he'd gained in the conflict, the Devil apparently appeared in person to the fading hero and berated him for destroying his very own beast.

True European Dragons always have four legs that culminate in long sharp claws. They also tend to have large bat-like wings that stem from the ribs. These wings are sometimes marked with intimidating *eye-spots* (rather like the patterns of some moths and butterflies). Despite the Dragons' immense bulk the wings are functional and

capable of sustained and skilful flight if desired. A long sinuous tail often culminating in a vicious barb could assist both balance and be used as an additional deadly weapon. Their hides are compromised of thick scales, which though commonly green could show great variance in colour and shade to the extent of being black, white, yellow or red. Their long snouts would sometimes be horned. Smaller Heraldic Dragons were sometimes known as Dragonettes or Fire-Drakes. (The Drakes notably would sometimes also manifest either as small boys dressed in red or as streaks of fire resembling shooting stars.) Dragon lairs (commonly in caves) were often said to be littered with gold, silver and gems. Occasionally they will venture into urban areas also, as in the late autumn of 1222 when a brood of Dragons were reported flying over the city of London.

Wyverns
(Also known as ~ Gwiber. Vermine. Penmaenmawr.)

Despite being smaller and less dextrous than the Heraldic Dragons, the Wyverns were still a notorious bane to life and an engaging challenge to Dragon-slayers. Indeed the symbolism attributed to Wyverns is equally as potent as that of the True Dragons. Though used on heraldic emblems, the Wyvern was commonly thought to embody pestilence, war and sin. The creature was itself considered to be a plague-carrier. In the symbolism of the esoteric scientists known as Alchemists, the Wyvern represented base matter and the battle between a Wyvern and Knight symbolically represented the quest to transform lead into gold.

Though comparatively placid when young, Wyverns increase in aggression and appetite with age. Perhaps luckily then their estimated longevity is far less than that attributed to the True Dragons and actually unremarkable even on a human scale. Female Wyverns, especially those with young, are sometimes considered to be the most vicious. Like Dragons the Wyverns are also known to hoard treasure and some also breathe fire.

Appearance : Wyverns only have a single pair of legs which are equipped with savage claws. Their wings are fore-limbs, ribbed and membranous rather like those of bats. Their tiny infants (which mature quickly and considerably) have leathery, bright green scales but by adulthood these scales develop into hard, razor-sharp plates of varied colour (though often deep green). Their tails are tipped with a barbed sting.

Size : Between 6 to 18 ft (1.8 - 5.4 m) long.

Diet : The fresh meat of cows, sheep, goats and humans. The juveniles can be sustained with milk.

Habitat & Range : Localised across Britain especially in or around forests in upland areas. A notable specimen was recorded in Mordiford, Herefordshire - England. The Wyvern was possibly introduced into British folklore by the Normans.

Knuckers
(Also known as ~ Peisht. Swamp Dragons. Draigs.)

The linguistic similarity between the word *Knucker* (meaning swamp or water dragon) and *Nicor* (meaning unspecified Water monster - see Water Ogres) is significant as numerous pools and mires across Britain were held in the Anglo-Saxon tongue to be *Nicorhusa* - the home of a water monster. Whilst some of the older tales regarding these water-holes are quite vague regarding the nature of the specific fiends housed within, some distinguish between human-shaped monsters and others that can only be regarded as a form of Dragon. The Dunna Knucker of Lyminster, West Sussex was certainly a large reptilian creature but was a rare example of a Dragon or rather a Demi-Dragon, having the ability or inclination to speak with a human tongue. (Some Oriental Dragons were said to be rather eloquent, but their relatives in these isles as a rule could not or chose not to speak.) The majority of Dragons reported in Ireland belonged to the Knucker or aquatic / swamp variety and are known in this land as Peisht, Piast or Peist. Though in appearance they can sometimes bear strong resemblance to the True or Heraldic Dragon, their natural habitat and their adaptation to such mark them as a related but different Demi-Dragon breed. Despite spending much of their existence in an aquatic or at least very damp location, some Knuckers also had a breath that could scorch skin from bone. They would often leave their watery abode in order to ravage towns and villages in search of food.

Appearance : Often very similar to Heraldic Dragons in having 4 limbs and spiked tails, however not all Knuckers would necessarily be winged. It is likely that they have gills as well as lungs.

Size : Up to 45 ft (14 m) long.

Diet : Livestock, human-flesh, milk and possibly also fish, though some Knuckers were quite opportunist in their diet.

Habitat & Range : Caves and dens in or near to quagmires and deep, still pools mainly in Wales, Southern England and Ireland. Generally replaced in other areas by other forms of aquatic Demi-Dragons.

One theory suggested that all Dragons were eradicated from Ireland in the 5th Century, alongside all regular serpents at the bidding of Saint Patrick. However, the Christianised Arthurian Legend of Sir Tristran (or Tristram) of Lyonesse & Cornwall and his Dragon slaying exploits in Ireland, would seemingly have occurred in post-Patrick times.

Wyrms
(Also known as ~ Serpents. Serpent-Dragons. Worms. Wermes.
Wyrrms. Wurms. Orms. Askes. Stoorworms. Vurms. Carrogs.
Paiste.)

Wyrms are a fairly commonly reported Demi-Dragon form within these isles. Despite being less mobile than some other breeds they were just as capable of causing great devastation. Wyrms could also prove to be a perplexing quandary for potential slayers as many had the ability to congeal their body parts together again should they be hacked apart. Though a single slicing blow from a woodman's axe was enough to end the suffering caused by the Great Worm of Shervage Wood in Somerset. The Linton Worm of the Scottish Borders was dispatched by a burning lance being thrust down its throat.

The Lambton Worm of the River Wear in County Durham possibly one of the most well-known of the numerous Wyrms that scourged medieval Britain, was such a beast that displayed this curious ability. However upon the instructions (and weird conditions) of a local Witch known as the Lumley Sybil, a young nobleman by the name of John Henshaw, the future Lord Lambton, garbed himself in a suit of armour studded with many sharp blades and confronted the monster in the fastest flow of the river. The Wyrm coiled itself around the young knight and was promptly severed into many parts that were carried off by the current before they had time to fuse together again. Thus the Wyrm was slain, however the tale does not have a happy ending : the Witch gave guidance on the condition that Lambton also slaughter the first living creature that he saw after vanquishing the beast. Thinking that he was most likely to witness his own hound first, Lambton mournfully agreed, such was the abhorrent reign of the Wyrm. However the first living creature to greet the triumphant slayer was not his dog but his own father. Lambton could not bring himself to kill him and ignored the mandate placed upon him. As a result the Witch laid a curse upon successive generations of the Lambton family.

Occurring after Saint Patrick had supposedly banished all serpents from Ireland, Saint Murrough was said to have rid Derry of a colossal Wyrm known as the Lig-na-Baste (or Lig-na-Paiste) meaning the Last Great Reptile.

Wyrms are commonly semi-aquatic; they generally develop in water, mainly rivers but upon maturity they may often coil themselves around hills after gorging on a hefty meal. Scottish Stoorworms often preferred brine rather than fresh-water. The Laidley Worm, which terrorised Bamburgh in Northumberland was according to legend, actually a Saxon Princess transformed by a spell cast by her jealous step-mother.

Basilisk and Cockatrice

The Basilisk and the cockatrice are two similar, small but equally reviled Demi-Dragon species. In spite of its peculiar and perhaps considerably unassuming appearance, the Basilisk was an extremely powerful and feared beast. Its intense gaze could halt a man or much larger beast dead in its tracks and even cause rock to crumble to dust. Its rank breath and caustic saliva carried many strains of disease and lethal bacteria, and would cause plant-life to wither and die. Any waterhole from which the Basilisk supped would instantly be rendered poisonous for other creatures. Even its body odour was fatally toxic to inhale. Though just a diminutive beast, a single Basilisk could turn a lush paradise into a barren wasteland.

The methods of disposing of this monster were equally bizarre, for its only weaknesses were :
~ The crow of a cockerel.
~ the bite of a weasel.
~ Leaves of the plant, Rue (which could reputedly also heal a weasel or cockerel bitten by a Basilisk/Cockatrice).
~ The sight of its own reflection in a mirror. (Sometimes this was not considered fatal to the beast in itself, but would render the creature entranced thus simplifying the slayer's job.) Sometimes it was claimed that the Basilisk / Cockatrice would attack their own reflection with such violent enthusiasm that they would succumb to fatal exhaustion. The Cockatrices of Horndon-on-the-Hill and of Saffron Walden (both in the English county of Essex) were both vanquished by the sight of their own reflections.

The Cockatrice of Renwick in Cumbria, England (which was said to have emerged from the foundations of a church) was however apparently battered to death, with a Rowan branch.

The term Cockatrice is often interchangeable with Basilisk, but can also specifically refer to the later evolutionary appearance of the Basilisk. The Cockatrice was as strange a creature as the Basilisk, yet its birth process was far weirder. Whilst Basilisks were thought just to hatch from eggs laid by others of the species, the Cockatrice hatched from an egg laid in a compost heap by a seven year old cockerel whilst Sirius the Dog Star was in the ascendant. Not only that but the spherical, leathery egg would need to be incubated by a toad. Who made this discovery and how is an extremely uncertain matter. The Cockatrice of Wherwhell Hill, Hampshire was unique in that it was said to have hatched from a duck's egg.

The earliest Basilisks were beaked, crested, khaki or yellow and black snakes that carried their head high as they slithered. Intermediary evolutionary stages developed legs (sometimes as many as four pairs) and scaled wings. The later Basilisks/ Cockatrices developed a cockerel's head, a snake's forked tongue, feathered wings, bird-like legs and a reptilian body and tail. Its colouring by this stage showed greater variance. In all its stages its crest resembled a crown and the word 'Basilisk' has been said to translate as 'Little King' or 'Serpent King'. The monstrous Basilisk should not be confused with the exotic lizard of the same name (though this creature is remarkable in its own right due to its perceived habit of running across water on its hind legs).

In Wales, the sudden deaths of working miners due to the effects of firedamp and toxic gas, were once accredited to the noxious breath of tunnel-dwelling Basilisks.

Amphipteres and Winged Serpents

Amphipteres are similar to early adolescent Wyrms, though they can be easily distinguished by their small but functional wings. Commonly Amphipteres are about 9 ft (3m) long with a chunky girth and are covered in large thick scales. Their colouring and patterns may vary somewhat. Amphiptere eyes are often large and set back in ridged sockets. In their sharply toothed mouths sit two black tongues, one normal and the other spear-shaped. Despite their visage they are generally timid rather than aggressive. The last recorded encounter with an Amphiptere occurred in Henham in Essex, England in 1669.

Winged Serpents also probably inspired deeper fear than deserved, however as many people display a phobia towards conventional snakes, it is totally understandable therefore that serpents flying down out of the trees could cause great alarm. It was partly for this reason that concerned folk would try to kill these beasts on sight, however it is not known whether they were actually venomous and it seems that they were more inclined to attack poultry rather than people. The past tense is used as these creatures have not been reported for quite some time, but if not already hunted into extinction it is possible that dwindling batches of Winged Serpents may remain in more remote locations. Described as being the typical dimensions of a grass-snake or adder, these creatures were brightly coloured and sported magnificent, patterned wings and crests which were both feathered and scaled. Historically they were said to have been witnessed in various areas of Wales including the Brecon Beacons, Plinlimmon, Cader Idris and the Berwyns. Indeed, up until the late 19th Century Winged Serpent encounters were reported near woodlands in Penmark, Porthkerry, Penllyne and Ederynion in Glamorgan.

Salanderees

Salanderees are weird Fay beings rather like anthropomorphic lizards. They are about the size of a sand lizard or newt and are just as nimble, though they may often be seen to walk upright on their hind legs. They wear no clothing but are covered in scales that may vary somewhat in colouring but do not tend to be particularly vibrant. Always cold, the Salanderees will seek out fire and will enter homes in order to sit by the hearth. Though some people may find their presence unnerving, Salanderees have not been reported to be especially aggressive towards or even that interested in humankind. They are most commonly reported in Wales, though a colony of similar creatures were apparently encountered by the Glaswegian psychic, Ian Shanes on the Scottish isle of Eilan Ban.

Water Leapers
(Also known as Water Jumpers. White Duikers. Llamhigyn Y Dwr.)

These bizarre creatures are the bane of the Welsh fishermen unfortunate enough to encounter them. Looking like a hybrid between a bat and a frog, the Water Leapers have been seen to bounce along the surface of water especially in coastal areas. They could prove to be an alarming sight due to their fat slimy bodies, trailing tails, membranous wings, wide mouths and big bulbous eyes. More alarming still is the claims that Water Leapers will readily swoop at and bite people, and may even endeavour to drown them. Farmers as well as fisherman also had grounds to loathe and fear these creatures also as it was rumoured that they would also drag lambs down beneath the water in order to feast. Some apparent Water Leaper sightings could possibly be observations of either Daubenton's Bats (Myotis daubentoni) or Natterer's Bats (Myotis natteri) as both of these species have been known to flit close to water in search of insect prey.

Marool

The Marool is another strange marine beast. In Form it was like a large fish though covered with many eyes and a fiery crest. The water around its body was said to bubble and glow. The Marool enjoys stormy weather and should it witness a sea-vessel being wrecked amidst a tempest, it would loudly gurgle with delight

Sea Lizards

Sea Lizards are often described as being rather like crocodiles, but of colossal proportions (up to 60 ft (18 m) long including their long pointed tails). They either have powerful flippers or four hefty limbs culminating in webbed feet. The Sea Lizards bear considerable resemblance to prehistoric and considered extinct creatures such as the Thlattosuchian, the Mosasaur and the Pliosaur. Sea Lizards may have scaled, plated or smooth hides and their jaws are particularly formidable. They have been reported off the Irish coast.

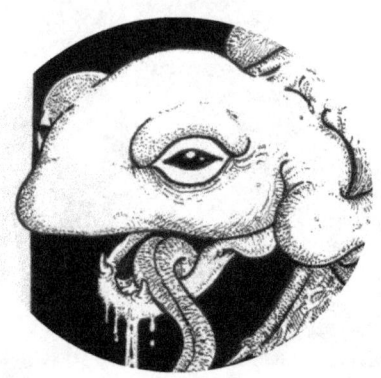

Long-Necks
(Also known as ~ Lake Monsters. Beasties. Living Fossils.
Saint Columba Dragons.)

The Long Necks are a notorious form of water monster despite
attacks by them upon human beings being rarely reported. Sightings
of them do however continue to this day in many lakes world-wide.
The most infamous Long Neck of all is most probably the Loch Ness
Monster (also known as Nessy). This elusive beast of Inverness,
Scotland has captured imaginations across the globe and across the
ages. Indeed the first recorded encounter with this creature involved
the Celtic Saint, Columba in the year 565 A.D (hence the alternative
name St. Columba Dragons). Seemingly Nessy was more aggressive in
those days as Columba, the founder of Iona Monastery, resorted to
banishing the beast to the depths of the Loch for attacking a local
man. (It has also been claimed that Columba also dealt with a
particularly nasty Kelpie (see also Water Horses) in the River Ness.)
However as the Loch Ness Monster has apparently been seen and
perhaps even photographed many times since that first report, it
would seem that this creature either has an incredibly long life-span
or that a breeding colony has been sustained by the loch. Many
expeditions have been established to uncover the secrets of Loch Ness
and these activities continue still in the 21st Century, however the
existence of Nessy still remains an enigmatic puzzle. Those sceptical
of Nessy's existence have argued that the loch simply could not
provide enough food for a single creature of this nature, never mind
a long-term breeding colony. Others have argued back with the claim
that Loch Ness is actually connected to the sea, thus solving the food
source dilemma.
Ness however is far from being the only large inland pool in these
lands or certainly across the world that is rumoured to harbour such
a creature. Long Necks have also been reported at sea, but the
freshwater variety often claims the most attention. The similarity
between the given descriptions of Long Necks and aquatic dinosaur
species such as the Plesiosaur are apparent, however as these
dinosaurs are regarded as generally being marine habitual and more
significantly as being extinct for millions of years, then proof of a
direct connection would be a major scientific discovery. The
supposition alone though gives rise to another alternative name of
Living Fossil. This however is a wider ranging term that can cover a
variety of creatures, that once thought to have been long since extinct
have since been re-discovered alive.
The theory that Nessy is such a Living Fossil seems to find
contradiction in a local legend regarding the origins of the loch.
Rather

than being a watercourse of primal antiquity, it has been told that Ness was originally a freshwater spring of no great size. It was remarkable however in the sense that when exposed this spring would flow freely but would cease whenever a cover was placed upon its source. One day though as a local woman was drawing water, her chore was interrupted and her attention diverted by the distressed calling of her child. In her anxiety she rushed to her child's aid, forgetting to return the cover in the process. Unrestrained the spring continued to flow and to flow, and within a surprisingly short time a lush Scottish valley was instead replaced by the majestic, enigmatic loch familiar to us today. However as lakes were often considered 'Thin' places, others have suggested that Long Necks emerge from the Otherworld or other times, or are observed as if through a pin-hole in the time-space continuum.

Sea Serpents
(Sea Serpent species include ~ Serpent Whales. Serpent Dragons.
Marine Long Necks. Horse-Eels.)
Sea Serpents can reach up to 200 ft (61 m) long and 20 ft (6 m) thick. Some maintain a similar thickness from tip to tail rather like a marine equivalent of a Wyrm or like an over-sized sea-snake or eel. Others though may be more bulbous at the front and tapering to the tail, rather like a gigantic tadpole. This variety may or may not have a separate head and their neck can either be lengthy or squat and they may show varied flipper development. Some show considerable similarity to the Long Necks and it is possible that they are a brine-water relative to these creatures. Others of the large-bodied variants are comparable to the primitive Serpent Whale species such as the Zeuglodonts, though these beasts are thought to be long-since extinct they have seemingly since been reported at sea as well as smaller equivalents (Horse-Eels) in Irish freshwater.

The celebrated Cornish sea -monster Morgawr, (Sea Giant) could possibly belong to either the Long Neck or Serpent Whale strain, but despite their immense size these creatures remain extremely elusive to further study. Apparent sightings of Morgawr have been reported at least as early as 1882 and as recently as 2000, though there are claims that this case is a hoax. Sea Serpents may sometimes display such features as ridges or humps along their spines, hairy manes, intense sparkling eyes and their bellies are often lighter in colour than their backs. Their hide is generally described as being smooth like that of a frog or sleek and hairy like an otter. Sea Serpents have been reported off the coasts of Britain and Ireland. A minor wave of sightings were reported off Cardigan Bay on the Welsh coast as recently as the mid 1970s. The partially decomposed carcasses of Basking Sharks have sometimes been misidentified as being the dead bodies of Sea Serpents.

Uilebheist (Also known as ~ **Draygan.)**
Though some terrestrial Dragons have been described as having more than one head, within these isles this is so rare that it must be considered that such specimens are possibly mutations. However the marine Demi-Dragons known as Uilebheists are renowned for having many fearsome heads. Yet despite their frightful appearance it has been considered that these creatures aim to protect the inlets and coasts of the Shetland and Orkney Islands, rather than savage native or peaceful ships and sailors. Uilebheists' numerous heads rest upon long necks that stem from a large squat body that may sometimes be quite vibrantly coloured.

Kraken

Extremely feared by the Vikings and other mariners of old was the dreaded Kraken, though the exact likeness of this terror of the seas could not be agreed on by the ancient sources. Some took it to be a ferocious whale or perhaps a Serpent, whilst others still likened it to a colossal crustacean or mollusc. Whatever, they all regarded the Kraken to be of a magnitude great enough to devour whole ships if it so chose. Some said that it was so large that even when it was only half-visible above the sea's surface, it was still as large as a small island. If all sailors have the same regard of scope as fishermen when it comes to describing the 'one that got away' then we can perhaps assume that the Kraken was not quite so large. Indeed, in modern times it has been suggested that the Giant Squid , a creature that exists in the depths of reality may account for the legendary Kraken's true identity. Scientists have examined the remains of Giant Squids measuring almost 60 feet (20 metres) long and suspect that these may merely be tiddlers. This is based on the premise that 4 inch long scars found on the bodies of Sperm Whales corresponded to the suckers on the tentacles of a 50 foot long squid, however scars measuring 18 inches across have also been discovered, indicating far more massive creatures may be lurking in the deep. In the early 19th Century a monstrous Kraken was said to have entered Scalloway Bay in the Shetland Islands, unfortunately however nobody present dared linger around long enough to identify the creature as being a Giant Squid or otherwise.

The Grampus

The Grampus was another strange marine creature, superficially akin to a dolphin or porpoise. Perhaps the oddest of their kind dwelled not in the sea but in the rather unconventional habitation of an old Yew tree sited in Highclere churchyard in Hampshire. This creature's custom of chasing terrified Villagers and emitting a chilling cacophony of noises resulted in a local clergyman successfully ridding the area of the Grampus, through the means of exorcism.

Nuckelavee
(Also known as ~ Nuchlavis.)

It has been suggested that these malodorous sea-monsters could be either a grotesque Fay species or the corrupted souls of cruel pirates who died at sea. Whatever their origin the Nuckelavee is possibly the strangest entity to be encountered within the waters surrounding these isles. Sometimes though this weird beast will haul itself onto the shores of Northern Scotland especially the Hebrides. The Nuckelavee reeks like a mixture of dead fish, mildew and rotten eggs, but just as offensive as its odour is its appearance. From the upper centre of its horse-like body sprouts a human torso with extremely long arms and a huge head that lolls limply on a scrawny neck. The equine legs that project from its body culminate not in feet or hooves, but instead with flippers or fins. Its mouth is wide and lolls open dripping foul saliva beneath a porcine snout whilst its single large eye glares cruel and fiery. The Nuckelavee has no outer layer of skin and its thick black blood can be seen coursing through a twisted mass of white gristle, yellow veins and raw, red muscle. The Nuckelavee will chase humans but it cannot cross fresh running water, so if pursued by such a beast it is advisable if possible to head for the nearest tributary. Whilst like most Sea-monsters, the Nuckelavee may sustain itself on krill, plankton, fish and marine mammals, it is likewise feared that they may appreciate the taste of human flesh and blood. The Nuckelavee was also feared to be a carrier of Plague.

Mal-de-Mer
(Also known as ~ The Evil of the Sea. Sea Sickness.)

It is difficult to describe to describe the Mal-de-Mer of Brittany and Cornwall for it is generally considered either to be invisible or seen only as a strange disorientating light, yet its influence is greatly apparent. The Mal-de-Mer stirs up a calm sea initially inducing feelings of nausea in sea-farers, but as it gains in momentum causing a tempest to rise, feelings turn to disorientation and then to terror as ships are torn apart.

Some mariners may consider the Mal-de-Mer to be a powerful Spirit or Sea-Monster, whilst others may regard it as a throng of lost souls - the ghosts of pirates or wreckers or simply those that died by drowning. To some it may be considered punishment from God or the fruit of malice invoked by spiteful Water-Faeries or Sea-Witches (see Malefactors). Many possibilities occur, both natural and supernatural, yet the victims of the Mal-de-Mer have neither time nor luxury to formulate any theories as they suffer the Evil of the Sea.

The Horned God
(Also known as Cernunnos. Cerne, and associated with Esus, Belatucadrus. Arawn. Gwynn ap Nudd. Hermes-Mercury. Pan. Faunus. Silvanus. Tarvos Trigaranos.)

Out of all the Old Gods that preceded Christianity, perhaps the oldest is the Horned God. However though as many of the other Gods and Goddesses of the varied ancient pantheons have now been consigned to the pages of history books, the image of the Horned God still lingers, albeit often in a somewhat altered form.

Initially he was probably among a number of Totemic or sacred animals of Animist Belief, in this case represented as a ram, bull, goat or stag but later given anthropomorphic features. International equivalents of this Stag God and various other animal deities can be found amongst the relics of prehistoric cultures and within the beliefs of tribal folk today. To some peoples' faith or philosophy, the eating of an animal deemed sacred may seem strange or even taboo. Yet some creatures such as deer were readily hunted and eaten by the very societies that worshipped their image. Indeed they were considered holy because their meat was often integral to the tribe's very survival. They killed and consumed these beasts but they maintained their honour and worship of them so that their numbers would remain enough to keep them fed. To consume certain flesh may however have been considered taboo by particular Celtic tribes though, or at least by individual members placed under a Geis (plural - Geisa). Geisa were personal obligations or restrictions that were bestowed upon some Celts. Though they could vary greatly in nature, one of the hero Cuchulainn's own Geisa was the abstinence of eating dog-flesh.

To the Celts the Horned God was known as Cernunnos, a humanoid figure who was more commonly depicted as having stag-like antlers rather than true horns. One of Cernunnos' titles was Lord of the Hunt, but by this time agriculture could sustain alongside hunting and the Horned God became the god also of a broader fertility. Worship of this deity was hoped not only to maintain plentiful meat, but also a bountiful crop harvest and even the successful procreation of mankind. In such we find the concept of life, death and rebirth ; a motif oft to be found within Celtic myth. As death is integral to the continuous circle of life, Cernunnos has also been associated to the Underworld, the realm of the dead (though perhaps not forged as closely as the Morigann or Donn – see also Celtic Hags and Ankou). Indeed Cernunnos himself was symbolically slaughtered and boiled in a cauldron before being reborn. Cernunnos was depicted as a humanoid figure with impressive antlers and sometimes hooves, generally sat cross-legged and either wearing or holding a Torc (a thick open-ended precious metal necklace).

Occasionally depictions of Cernunnos are double or triple-aspect, but little is truly known about his specific lore and possible other manifestations. There has been association suggested between Cernunnos and Esus, another self-sacrificed Celtic God also associated with life, death and rebirth. When the Romans invaded Britain, they too could perhaps have associated the Celtic Horned God with the Greco-Roman deity Pan, as well as the half-goat, half-human creatures called Fauns and Satyrs. Association was possibly also drawn with the god Mercury-Hermes, the guide to the Underworld and master of wild beasts (and according to some versions of Greek myth, the father of Pan).

The early Christian church seem to have had difficulty converting the notion of the Horned God into their own structure, possibly due to his relationship with fruit fermentation and fornication as glorification of fertility. There is the possibility that the fertility status was identified with the Roman God of Wine and Fruitfulness, Bacchus (Greek – Dionysus) and that both were assimilated into the image of the Green Man. This was perhaps not an icon to worship as such, but instead to maintain vigilance of sin and hedonism. However by medieval times, the church had grown far less tolerant of people who clung to the worship of the Old Gods, and in a bid to get people to give up their homage to the Horned God they 'demonised' this deity, associating him directly with the biblical Devil. Hence the stock or cartoon image common today representing the Devil with horns and cloven hooves. The older view of this Old God however retains more relevance with both researchers and modern pagans.

The Earth Goddess
(Also known as ~ Danaan. Dana. Danu. Anu. Don.
Madron. Modron verch Avallach. Maeve. Ogma. Gaia. Enu.
Erce. Eriu. Brigid. Bridget. Brid. Bride. Brig. Briganti.
Bree. Brud. De Develski. Matrona. Marian. Goda.
Arianrhod. Frigg. Aradia. Mother Nature. Mother Earth.
Earth Mother.
Triple-Aspect~ **The Matres. The Matronae. The Matronas.**
Dea Mattes.The Suleviae. Terra Maters. Tellus.)

The aspect of an Earth or Mother Goddess was extremely important to the Celts and Anglo-Saxons as she represented the land itself (which they considered sacred) and was seen as the source of life. For this reason many springs and rivers were consecrated to her, as were hills that resembled womanly curves. Generally in humanised form the Earth Goddess is represented as a naked (sometimes heavily pregnant and wode-tattooed) beautiful woman however she could also represent the 'Triple-Aspect' common in some readings of Celtic Lore and as such could be the mother who nurtures, the sister who befriends or the lover who puts the knife in the back and twists. Therefore terms such as the Matres, Matronas. Matronae, Suleviae and Dea Mattes refer to triads of Goddesses or a Goddess shown in Triple-Aspect. The given individual names of the Matres, as with all Celtic deities varied according to tribe and locality, but these Goddesses were generally associated with birth, life and death as well as sometimes more specifically with fertility, healing and regeneration. In the persona of Dana, the Earth Goddess was the mother of the Tuatha de Danaan ; the race of people that evolved into the Daoine Sidhe or Faeries. However as with other Celtic Deities there existed a less comforting and more threatening aspect to the Mother Goddess, as she could be a ferocious warrior should the need arise. A combination of beauty and force which may also be noticed in nature. Some mythologists have suggested that the association between the Earth Mother and the War Goddess (see Celtic Hags) is especially close and that the representative notions of birth and death, creation and destruction are but flipsides of the same coin.
It is rather apt now then at a time when nature faces various threats as a result of human activities, that some groups concerned with ecology and conservation have again looked to the Earth Goddess (particularly in her Ancient Greek persona of Gaia or Gaea) as a symbol of hope and inspiration as well as a figurehead for their battle against those who show disrespect to the planet and its varied inhabitants.

The Celtic Goddesses are known by various names often depending upon locality, yet sometimes the names seem interchangeable. This can lead to modern confusion as to whether separate Goddesses are referred to or whether they are different aspects of the same figure.   For instance the Welsh Goddess Arianrhod is sometimes referred to as an Earth Mother, or by others as a Moon Goddess.

This even extends to early Christianity with strong associations being drawn between the Celtic Saint Bridgit (or Bride) and the Goddess Brigid (or any of her other given designations). The Cults of Saints (which was later strongly discouraged by the Medieval Church) possibly eased the conversion of heathens (used to the worship of numerous male and female deities) into a religion that recognises a single and masculine God. By venerating particular Saints and remembering the miracles and wonders accredited to them, the spirit of the Old Gods and Goddesses was possibly also kept alive for some people.

Proto-Druids (Also known as Shamans.)

Prior to the coming of the Celts, little is known about the religious beliefs and practices of the people of the British Isles and Ireland . It is known that the earlier Bronze Age people buried their dead with some indication of ceremony and the inclusion of drinking utensils found within graves led to them also becoming known as the Beaker People. Their interments indicate respect for the dead and hint at belief in a life after death, both of which suggest at least a rudimentary religious awareness. Above ground the many megalithic monuments that litter these isles also are a mysterious testament to archaic times. Whilst it is known that many of these structures serve as agricultural clocks tombs and landmarks, it seems likely that they provided a wider ceremonial purpose also. Many mysteries and theories surround megalithic sites, including evidence of animal and human sacrifice. It has been suggested also that the earthen ramparts commonly erected around ancient villages, were reversed around megalithic circles, as if it to contain some unknown force.

The earliest religions of Britain were likely Animist in character, the attribution of spirit and even personification to natural forces and objects, the sun, moon, trees, water etc. basically thanksgiving to the essential factors of human existence. This probably extended also to the animals they hunted and ate, by showing grace and gratitude one day, the faith held that they would not hunger tomorrow. From this a belief in the survival of the soul beyond death may develop and worship of ancestors arise. Very similar (but landscape / culturally altered) concepts have been witnessed world-wide existing within societies past and present in all continents, so it is likely that the early Britons prescribed to these ideas also. In these cultures there would usually be a man or woman naturally inclined to act as a conduit between the material and spiritual worlds. Though these magician-priests and priestesses are known by various local terms (the early examples of these isles sometimes being known as Proto-Druids) the Siberian word Shaman has now generally been accepted universally with reference to these tribal figures. Either naked and marked with body-paint or tattoos or clad in the fur or feathers of the Totem, the Proto-Druid would use meditation, musical mantras and psycho-active plants and compounds to attain an altered state of being. In such a condition they would behold visions or travel to the Spirit-realm in astral form (some were said to be able to transform fully into animal form or perform other astounding feats also). Upon their return to the everyday world, they often related important messages regarding matters essential to earthly wellbeing, from Ancestors or Totem Spirits.

Druids (Feminine - Druidesses or Drui-ban)

The Druids were the Celtic priest-class but it is still uncertain whether they originally developed within Celtic society, preceded it or arrived in these isles separately (a romantic theory places their origins in the lost island of Atlantis). The Druids however were not merely preachers, but like the Celtic Gods were respected for being able to perform a number of different functions and abilities. Therefore they needed to learn a lot of skills preferably from an early age. Indeed Britain was said to host an exceptional ancient school of Druidry, to which students were sent to attend from Ireland, the Isles and also the French-Celtic regions of Gaul and Brittany. As well as augury, magic and ritual, they would need to learn also to be efficient judges, councillors and teachers. They could later concentrate on certain areas and assume specific roles such as Ovates (Shamanic bards and poets), Uatis (scholars of sacrifice and nature) or Brehons (diviners and judges). Everyday matters provided just as an important a role for the Druids as did the divine and spiritual.

The Druids and Celts kept very few written records, which is not to suggest that they were illiterate. Indeed they were thought to have a good grasp of various scripts and in Ireland they debatably developed their own tree alphabet, Ogham, for ceremonial or political reasons. Whilst the Celts were certainly not pacifists and held great glory and thrill in battle, they would not always spill blood lightly and sometimes Druids were sent out as ambassadors to other tribes and foreign adversaries in order to negotiate and ascertain situations. Druids held considerable power within their societies and the Celtic Chieftains and Queens paid great heed to Druidic advice and council. One ancient Irish King, Ollav Fola was actually a Druid himself (Ollav being a Druidic rank roughly meaning a Master of Science). Furthermore, amongst the Irish Celtic clans, upon the death of a tribal leader it is believed that the Druids were responsible for electing their successor, for ascension to this position was not necessarily a hereditary right. The decision was not defined by debate alone but also by divination in the form of the Bull Feast. A bull would be ceremonially slaughtered and the Druid would eat of its flesh and drink the broth boiled from its bones. He would then retire to slumber on the bull's hide and whomever he then dreamt of would subsequently be elected the new leader. Within time many Druids themselves grew to accept and even convert to Christianity. Legend holds that many Druids foresaw the advent of Christianity long before the faith reached these lands and one Irish tale relates how the Druid, Conchobar spoke of Christ's crucifixion at the very moment it occurred. His knowledge of which was said to stem

from augury and the observance of planetary motions. The concept of Druidism existing alongside Christianity in a non-aggressive manner is well represented in the character of Merlin from Arthurian tradition. Merlin bears all the hallmarks of the Druids of Celtic legend, but is the trusted confidante and council to a Christian court and king.

The perception of Druids as natural mystics seems to have then passed down and evolved into the likes of the Seers, Wise-folk and other magicians of the Middle Ages and later. The Druids who are to be seen in modern times, descending upon Stonehenge at Midsummer are actually Neo-Druids. The Neo-Druids origins actually lie with an 18th Century Welsh sect called Eisteddfodau.

Celtic Saints

To become a Christian Saint requires devout faith and performance of miracles, yet some of the tales and deeds attributed to the Celtic Saints may have actually predated their actual existence. Likewise some of the sacred sites such as certain Holy Wells that were said to have sprung from where their blood was spilled, possibly had an older lore and history (see also Grey Ladies). However the fact that such tales were readily accredited to the Saints says something in itself. Indeed some of the Celtic Saints such as Columba (see also Long Necks) were said to have studied originally as Druids, before embracing Christianity. Columba (circa 521 – 597 A.D. and also known as Colum or Colmcille) was certainly not alone in being accredited with wondrous deeds for other Celto-Saxon Saints such as Cuthbert, Ia, Bridget, and Winifride were amongst numerous other Saints of these isles who were said to have been blessed with visions and miracles. Indeed either the working of miracles or a martyr's death was the main distinguishing point between a true Saint and other venerable Christians. Abilities attributed to them included conversing intelligibly with wild animals, healing sickness and vanquishing evil spirits. They were however keener to attribute the unusual events in their lives (and sometimes also deaths) to divine intervention or the will of God, rather than to Magic or the supernatural as such.

Certainly the most celebrated of the Celtic Saints is Patrick - the patron saint of Ireland. Patrick is remembered mainly for explaining the Holy Trinity (Father, Son and Holy Spirit as one) using a shamrock plant and also for apparently ridding Ireland of snakes. There is though a school of scientific thought that suggests that these reptiles were never actually ever present in Ireland ; however if we take snakes to mean serpents or specifically one certain serpent then the tale can take on a different meaning. Cromm Cruach (also known as the Bloody Idol, Bloody Crescent or the Oilliepheist) was a terrible Celtic Serpent God (perhaps akin to a Wyrm) that demanded human sacrifice and was therefore a difficult deity to assimilate into the Christian Church (though comparison could perhaps be drawn to the monstrous Leviathan of the Old Testament). Therefore if Patrick at least banished the Irish people's homage to this fiendish creature, then symbolically he can be said to have rid Ireland of serpents.

Various Celtic Saints such as Collen of Glastonbury reportedly thwarted Faerie caprice, yet others seeking a hermitic, austere existence found themselves tormented by goblin and demonic forces. The Church occassionally performs rites of Exorcism of Evil Spirits still, though with less fervour and regularity than in days past.

Magicians - **Wise-folk**
(**Also known as ~ Cunning-folk. Conjurors. Repellers. Pellars. Conjurors. Filidh {Poet-Seers}.White Witches. Healers. Hedge Witches. Charmers. Slieveens. Whisperers. Witch-Doctors. Fairy-Doctors. Sages. Witchy-folk. Spae-folk. Knowing-Folk. Mediciners. Healers. Sages.**
Males -**Wizards. Tabhaisvers. Taibhsears. Seers. Skeely-Men. Seoltaiches. Dremidydds. Carles. Lyblaecas. Thyles.**
Females - **Sibyls. Hen-wives. Spae-wives. Good-wives. Seeresses. Carlines. Lybestresses.)**

Within the communities of Britain and Ireland there was a tradition of people outside of an organised religious discipline that could be called upon to administer to supernatural needs : (though it must be noted that some had strong Pagan or Christian faith . In fact individuals such as the author and Otherworld observer , Robert Kirk and John Morrison - the Petty Seer were actually men of the cloth). Known as Wise-men or women (or by a variety of other names, some pertaining to particular abilities), these people were likely sought to cure ailments or dispel evil spirits that had proved too difficult for conventional physicians and priests. Other tasks they may be approached to undertake could also include countering the effects of Malefactors' curses, locating lost or stolen property, preparing herbal remedies and protective talismans, predicting or advising on future events and possibly even delivering babies. Those living by the coast were also said able to assist maritime voyagers with fair winds and currents to assist the progress of their vessels. This was sometimes achieved by the use of knotted ropes or bound bags. Some Wise-folk would sometimes assist people without taking any payment in return, but others expected money or other gratuity for their services. Whilst there is nothing wrong with making a living from talents or abilities, then as now some individuals would fake paranormal prowess and exploit people's needs and beliefs in order to turn a profit and perhaps gain a powerful profile within society. This led to the word 'cunning' as in Cunning-folk, being taken to mean 'sly' or 'crafty'.
Whether genuine or not these Cunning Folk displayed a knowledge of strange matters and enough charisma and spark to attain the trust and belief of many people. Some however did seem to display powers that went far beyond the norm though. Whilst some feats were contrived illusions (hence the designations of Magician and Conjuror being adopted by show-business illusionists in modern times), other professed abilities may have been genuine. The ability to see the hidden events of past, present and future and also into the Faerie / Spirit realms is

often known as Second Sight. Notable prophets of this ilk included Ursula Southeil - Mother Shipton of Knaresborough, Yorkshire and Coinneach Odhar Fiosaiche of Mackenzie - the Brahan Seer of the Scottish Highlands. Clairvoyant abilities of this kind was often said to be inborn rather than learned but certain practices could hone the abilities. Second Sight was considered also to be hereditary, though not every member of a family would necessarily inherit the capability (traditionally and especially amongst the Romany / Gypsy people, a seventh son of a seventh son was considered to hold especially potent psychic prowess). Others thought very likely to inherit the gift were those born on Good Friday, Christmas Day or between the hour of twelve midnight and one a.m. It is said that a family history of Second Sight has continued in the bloodlines of some individuals living today. Whilst Wise-folk would certainly have stirred the attention of church and state in Medieval times, many of the celebrated examples seem to have escaped the fervour of the Witch-Finders though it is likely that others were brought to trial. The aforementioned Brahan Seer (circa 1600 – 1660s) made many sound prophecies, some extending far beyond his lifetime and a number remaining that may yet see realisation. However he made an accurate yet unfavourable forecast for Countess Isabella Mackenzie of Seaforth and as a result was burned to death in a barrel of tar.

Magicians - **Malefactors**
(Also known as ~ Witches. Black Magicians. Overlookers. Ill-Wishers. Tempestarii. Carlines. Males ~ . Warlocks. Wizards. Sorcerers. Nicknevins. Enchanters. Females ~ Sorceresses. Pishogues. Gwracho. Beldames. Cailleachs. Enchantresses.

The word 'Witch' means ' one who casts a spell' in Old English and can apply to both males and females either of a good or wicked disposition. It is however most commonly applied to those people who live on the fringes of society who use magic for malign and devilish purposes (Maleficia). Such individuals are believed to have been resident in Britain and Ireland long before the coming of either the Anglo-Saxons or Christianity. Malefactors have consistently used their powers to steal or extort the property of others, exact feats of spite or revenge and generally to heighten domination over others. Such capabilities attributed to them were Overlooking also known as casting the Evil Eye or Ill-Wishing (causing misfortune, disease and disaster to befall people) and causing crop blights and the Murrain (disease in livestock). They were also said to possess the ability to transform their bodily size and shape into that of animals or other weird forms . Witches were also often blamed for provoking trouble and consternation at dairy farms by magically redirecting milk from cows' udders to a tap in their residence, for causing their victims to vomit pins or other unsavoury foreign bodies, become infertile or impotent (Ligature) as well as being the procurers of sudden devastating storms at sea. Experts in the latter were known as Sea-Witches and could also be paid to ensure good sailing weather.

Even the suggestion of possession of such abilities was often enough to gain someone, who may otherwise have been disregarded by society because of age, appearance or other reasons, a sense of status within community. Although such individuals would still be reviled and avoided whenever possible, they could still use their uncanny reputation to manipulate others into providing their needs. Whilst fear and threat were well utilised, if anything did go wrong (e.g. The death of a child or a spoiled harvest etc.) then suspicion and perhaps revenge would fall upon the person insinuating uncanny ability, but if actually empowered then they could actually have been to blame and possibly capable of further malediction.

It was thought that the powers of the Malefactors stemmed from both inherent aptitude and intense study of many varied disciplines. Also as the clairvoyant ability known as Second Sight can sometimes provide an effective communication channel with Otherworldly creatures, then some of these beings could bestow arcane knowledge upon the Witch if they so wished. Although the Fays can be either foul or fair depending upon mood and individual breed, they were all considered agents of the Devil in the eyes of the Medieval church. As such a potentially dangerous public nuisance developed into a heavily punishable offence . In Scotland especially, communication with Faeries was considered an aspect of Witchcraft. Indeed many tried Witches admitted to dealing with the denizens of Hell, or at least holding the company of fiendish minions known as Familiars, however it must be remembered that many of these admissions were made under serious duress. (Though others such as Isobel Gowdie, a 17th Century Scots-woman, made surreal confessions without any apparent provocation.)

Another accusation made against many suspected Witches was that they indulged in Image Magic. It is so claimed that the Malefactor would construct a small effigy of a person crafted from wax or clay or another such malleable material, to which would be added some personal artefact of the target such as a shred of clothing or lock of hair. Any abuse then inflicted upon the effigy (known as a Poppet or Corp Creadha), would be equivalently transferred upon the intended victim. Alternatively Candle Magic could be employed ; whereby a specially prepared candle would be lit and as it burnt down so the required hex would reputedly unfold.

Some Witches claimed that they could attain the power of flight (Transvection) by anointing their bodies with a curious balm. In order to help steer their flight they claimed to ride on such unusual transportation as pitchforks, spinning rods, hurdle fences and , broomsticks. Not all Witches claimed to fly on weird vehicles however. It has been suggested though that broomsticks and the act of sweeping also may have carried symbolic meaning. It has been questioned whether the Witches' flight occurred physically, mentally or on an astral level. It has been suggested that the flying concoction they ingested, absorbed or smeared over their bodies contained psychoactive and potentially fatal plants such as Henbane, Belladonna or Wormwood. Whilst many of the alleged Malefactors brought to trial were indeed elderly women, this was not exclusively so and males and younger people also fell under suspicion too.

Suspected Witches and Wizards were not always simple country -folk clinging to a Pagan Past as some were figures of quite high standing whose positions of power, some believed, were attained through the use of strange rites of invocation, Sorcery and transactions with Demonic entities. Amongst those accused of such behaviour were the Scottish Lord Alexander Stewart (the Wolf of Badenoch, near Kingussie) and Gerald Fitzgerald (the Wizard Earl of Desmond and Kildare, Ireland).

280

Familiars
(Also known as ~ Imps. Puckrels. Familiar Spirits.)
Familiars are minor Demons resident in this world and under the servitude of Malefactors. Either appearing in human form, as varied but recognisable animals or as weird indefinable beasts, Familiars would assist malevolent Witches in the spread of their wickedness. Their service had a cost however as their human employers were required to feed their Familiar on warm blood direct from their own veins. Such suckling would leave a distinguishable blemish upon the body (the so-called Witch-Marks), or so the Witch-Finders claimed as they stripped Witchcraft suspects in search of physical evidence. Additionally further proof of guilt could be asserted should any creature approach a prisoner incarcerated under suspicion of crimes of magic. However as the medieval dungeons were particularly low on hygiene, it would likely be inevitable that some vermin would be seen in the vicinity. Even a single beetle or such-like would sometimes be enough to merit a guilty verdict. Some folk suspecting a visit from the Witch-hunt are said to have resorted to turning out or giving away their cherished pets (though if the Witch-Finders became aware of this, accusations of 'passing the guilt' would also be levelled against the suspect) or sometimes even killing the animals before they could incriminate further. The official slaughter of animals deemed to be Familiars did not occur within these nations to the level it did in mainland Europe (though the concept of keeping familiars was less common on the continent). A 17th Century engraving shows a Witch surrounded by a host of attendant Familiars ; with names such as Vinegar Tom, Griezzdl Greedigutt and Pecke in the Crowne , some of these Imps are recognisable animals whilst others are curious beasts.

Witch-Finders
(Also known as ~ Witch-Hunters. Prickers.)

Though it is highly probable that the Celtic Brehon Druids and the law enforcers of other early cultures in Britain and Ireland, dealt rough justice to the Malefactors that proved threatening to society it was not until 1563 that Witchcraft became an official capital offence in Britain. Between 1450 and 1750 much of Europe was to fall under the shadow of the Witch-Hunts. Although the number and harshness of British /Irish procedure fell far short of the quantity of suspects condemned on the European mainland (particularly Germany) that of course would have been of little consolation to the many people (innocent or otherwise) that did suffer as a result of the Witch-trials in these lands.

The first official documented local Witch-Trial (as opposed to earlier cases against Sorcery - the laws and terms were specific as well as strange) occurred in Ireland in 1324. However, perhaps rather surprisingly, in spite of the combination of deep Christian belief as well as Old Religion superstition that pervades Ireland, the next known trial here did not occur until 1578. (Both of these cases occurred in Kilkenny and the later incident is notable in that it is the only reported instance of a black-skinned person having been executed on Witchcraft charges in Ireland and Britain.) In fact, large-scale Witch-Trials as ordained by the authorities did not occur in Ireland and only six cases were recorded between 1324 and 1711. Across the British Isles, it was Scotland and the Channel Islands that took the hardest line against alleged Witches and it was also in these places that excessive torture and also burning as a means of execution were most commonly applied. Hanging was the more favoured retribution in England and Wales (with sleep deprivation, starvation and constant walking being the favoured means of achieving a confession). Some Witch-Hunters, such as the notorious Witch-finder General - Matthew Hopkins (c 1621 - 1647) and his associates John Stearne and Mary Phillips maintained that their work was for the good of society and undertaken as a holy duty, though some onlookers were not so certain. There was money to be made from such work and when being paid per each head hunted, corruption and fraud also ultimately resulted in murder. Therefore in some instances rather than evil being vanquished it was instead spread. This often applied to the work of the Witch-hunters known as Prickers. Their name derives from their method of stripping the accused of their clothing and searching their body for Witch-Marks (Familiar's suckling teats) and / or Devil-Marks (Satan's brand denoting the Witch's servitude to him) and then pricking these marks with a needle to see if pain was registered or blood was drawn. However they would often target natural blemishes such as warts, moles, flea-bites and scar tissue and apply the needles in such a manner that sensation was minimal and blood would not flow, thus apparently proving guilt. To ensure that they got the results they desired, numerous unscrupulous Prickers would utilise devices with retractable needles. Whilst most Witch-Finders admitted that there was the possibility that not all of the condemned were guilty they stuck by the retort "that it was better to suffer an innocent to die, than to suffer a Witch to live." Some responsible authoritarians including a number who genuinely feared Witches disagreed though and strived to ensure that whilst Witchcraft be crushed no innocents should suffer as a consequence. Unfortunately though the Witch-trials were rarely fair; a Guilty verdict often being delivered without recourse to legal defence and based upon hearsay, frequently fraudulent accusations and the flimsiest of evidence. Should a suspect pause or flounder upon being caused to recite the Lord's Prayer, then this too was considered proof of guilt. The Witch-Trials however also provided a convenient means for members of the public to point the finger and rid themselves of rivals or nuisance neighbours, or as a means of settling feuds or claiming property. The laws concerning Witchcraft were repealed in 1736, however it was still a crime to claim or insinuate the possession of supernatural or diabolical ability (therefore profiteering Cunning-folk and fortune-tellers were liable to prosecution.) It was not until 1951 that the anti-Witchcraft laws saw a full repeal in Britain.

Alchemists

Rather than being a truly esoteric art, Alchemy also had strong bonds to the earthly sciences and has been considered the precursor of modern chemistry. However as it was not generally understood by the uneducated masses of the Middle Ages, its practitioners often fell under suspicion. To be truly efficient the Alchemists believed in the importance of being spiritually pure and generally imposed a mystic discipline upon themselves. Though Alchemy developed and was spread by non-Christian races, certain monasteries took a keen interest in it.

Whilst the Alchemists are generally best remembered for attempting to transform lead into gold, their work and study went far beyond this. Their main cogitation went into discovering a mysterious fluid known as the Elixir of Life and its solid counterpart the Philosopher's Stone, which could transmute metals into gold but could also reputedly prolong life and restore youth. Notable Alchemists active in Britain included Roger Bacon, Sir Kenelm Digby and allegedly Sir Isaac Newton and King Charles II.

Necromancers

Necromancy is a form of Magic in which the practitioner seeks to foretell the future or discover secret knowledge through the summoning of the spirits of the dead. Such rites would often require the actual presence of the corpse and would therefore either be performed in a cemetery or perhaps require some clandestine body-snatching. Obviously such procedures would be undertaken under clandestine conditions and due to the taboos that surround the dead, Necromancy was often considered one of the vilest forms of Sorcery. Dr. John Dee (1527 -

1608) an English philosopher, mathematician and astrologer of great renown, was subjected to scandal and scorn, as well as mob justice, following allegations of Sorcery. The accusations of Black Arts levelled against Dee included the claim that he and a nefarious associate called Edward Kelly, had raised or attempted to raise the dead in a Necromancy ritual performed at a graveyard in Walton-le-Dale, Lancashire and possibly also in his native Surrey. (It has however also been suggested that Dee was not in fact present at the Walton-le-Dale incident and that Kelly's accomplice on that day was a man named Paul Waring.)

Horse-Whisperers, Toad-Men and Horse-Charmers

Horse-Whisperers (also known as Horse-Men) were far more common in the times when horses were more widely utilised for transportation, agriculture and industry. Some horses, more than others are loath to be ridden and strongly resist being tamed. It is in these circumstances that a Horse-Whisperer would come into their own. They were so named because they were believed able to calm and train wild horses by whispering into the animals' ears (the Horseman's Word). There has been suggestion that concoctions of certain aromatic herbs may also have been utilised in the soothing of equine temper and nervousness. Whatever their true methods it however could not be disputed that the Horse-Whisperers generally had an excellent and impressive record of breaking beasts. Onlookers and clients would often conclude that supernatural powers were afoot, a supposition that Horse Whisperers did little to dispel and may even have encouraged. Not just anyone could become a Horse-Whisperer however for they guarded their prowess with the utmost secrecy. Elaborate Masonic-style initiation was the only way into the ranks in Scotland and women were never made privy to the Horseman's Word. Rumours spread that the introductory rites and the deliverance of knowledge involved the presence of the Devil. The form of Horse -Whisperers known as Toad-Men heightened this sinister notion further. Their name was derived from their habit of carrying the skeleton of a Toad (preferably that of the Natterjack species) around in a pouch. Long reputed to be an element of Witchcraft and a fairly common guise assumed by shape-shifting Witches and their Imp Familiars, the involvement of Toads may have caused some pious or superstitious folk some consternation. However as the majority of Horse-Whisperers and Toad-Men seemed benign and helpful people to have around (if not always entirely seemingly trustworthy), they were normally shown great tolerance yet people would often be fearful not to cross them. The amphibian bones utilised by Toad-Men, were said to have been collected by bizarre means and prepared by complicated ritual and were widely held to be the source of their horse-taming ability. Some folk also regarded the Toad-Men as possessing the power to forecast future events and in exchange of some payment would sometimes also consult them on such matters. Horse-Men were once widespread across Britain and Ireland, but were perhaps most prevalent in East Anglia and Scotland where they were believed to have formed the most complex and enduring secret societies. In Ireland, Cow-Doctors were similar people of knowledge who could instead be called upon to treat and soothe sick or troubled
cattle.

Similar to Horse-Whisperers but of less benefit to the public were the Horse-Charmers. These individuals were more likely to cause rather than cure equine problems. Women could and were frequently counted amongst Horse-Charmers ; two 19th Century examples being named as Priss Morris of Shropshire who could make horses stand transfixed to a spot until a word from her released them, and Anne Blackmore of Somerset who could cause horses to buck or fall beneath their riders.

Celtic Hags and Enchantresses
(Hags also known as ~ Crones. Cailleachs. Bone Goddesses. Beldams. Beldames. Crone Goddesses)

The Gaelic word 'Cailleach' means 'Old Woman' but it has more frequently been applied to refer both to Witches and to the Celtic Dark Goddesses. Some Hags however seem to exist somewhere on the line between earthly Enchantress and malignant Deity.

Old, ugly and bestowed with strange powers, the Celtic Hags tend either to be solitary or to congregate in groups of three or multiples of three. To the ancient Celts the number three is of great sacred significance and a number of their Gods and Goddesses displayed what is known as the Triple-Aspect . This is most significant in relation to the War Goddess, the Morrigan. Somewhat confusingly perhaps, the name Morrigan can refer to the War-Goddess as a single personification, but the three separate entities comprising her can collectively be known as the Morrigna. The individual aspects of the Morrigan are usually named as Nemain, Badb and Macha. However each of these individuals could appear as a beautiful young woman, a hideous old crone or as a Crow. The names of the sisters as well as that of the Morigann also appear to be interchangeable and vary considerably according to region and clan. Therefore the Goddesses or Queens, Maeve, Medb, Badb-Catha, Eriu, Fodla, Andrasta, Etain, Echraide, Eire, Erin, Flaitheas, Banba and even the Horse Goddess Epona / Rhiannon have all been associated with the Morrigna in varied mythological accounts. Some of those just mentioned are more commonly regarded as being tutelary, maternal, domestic or fertility deities rather being associated specifically with war and bloodshed, but therein lies the Celtic ambivalence and more tellingly the speculation rather than hard and set facts that surround the ancient Keltoi-Pagan faith. Appropriate then for the Goddess of War, who would obviously take a great interest in confounding the human mind, beguiling both sides in a conflict to ensure an abundance of carrion on the battlefield , upon which she would dine whilst in crow persona. Such is the treachery of War and its avatar, in her varied forms she may seduce the warrior, peck out his dead eyeballs and laugh or even lament at his passing. Her loyalty in the end lay with the spilling of blood, not with either army or with any individual warrior no matter how many of his own enemies he had delivered to her. (There were also several War Gods recognised by the Celts in addition.)

Other Hags of Celtic lore whilst being less divine perhaps, were no less malignant and sly. The mutilated Daughters of Calatin were three such treacherous termagants ; huddled round a fire spit-roasting a

hound, these daughters of a Fomorian bloodline Druid, brought about the subsequent downfall of the hero Cuchulainn by trapping him between two of his own Geisa (personal taboos). He was not allowed to turn down an offer of food but could not consume dog-flesh, which is of course the very meat that the Hags offered.

Again the company of three can be seen ; as well as being suggestive of the Morigann, it is also reminiscent of characters to be found in the tales of other ancient cultures. The Norse-Teutonic myths spoke of the Norns (also known as the Wyrd Sisters or Daughters of the Night) whilst the Greco-Roman tales told of the very similar Fatae (also known as the Fates, the Parcae or the Moerae), all of whom were haggard old maidens that could also assume a more favourable form. In either shape though they were commonly bent over their spindles weaving the threads of time. Also of comparison were the Gratae or Grey Sisters of Greek myth ; these three twisted sisters lived in a rank cave and all being blind shared a single crystal ball that functioned as an eye and though crazed they also possessed great knowledge and clairvoyant ability. In literature the motif is most apparent in the form of the Weird Sisters of the heath from William Shakespeare's 'Macbeth'. The 'Bard of Avon' possibly also drew inspiration for these characters from the account of the three witches discovered burning an effigy of Duff, the 10th Century Scottish King, on the heath of Forres in Moray. In Arthurian legend the Courtly Knights also encountered the Nine Hags of Gloucester (3 x 3 = 9 ; a triple triplicate). Most formidable of the Gloucester Hags was the Kundry, whose cunning was matched by her fearsome martial prowess.

As a single persona the Celtic Hags were still a potent and deadly force, either as homicidal she-demons such as the Luideag or Rag of Skye who loved nothing more than to spill the blood of men-folk; or otherwise, as shrewd magicians as can be seen in the grim form of Ceridwen, the Welsh Crone who boiled up a brew of profound knowledge in her cauldron.

To conquer a male enemy, being hideously ugly was not of great benefit when hatching such a plot. This brings us to those associated Femme Fatales known as Enchantresses or Sorceresses. Enchantresses were often exquisitely beautiful and frequently used seduction to achieve their grim desires, as the Hags used fear and revulsion. Such differences were only skin deep however, as below the surface both types were infinitely wicked and ugly to the bone. Furthermore, like the Morrigan, there were also those who could metamorphose between being foul or fair to the eye depending upon whim or intention .

In Arthurian legend, the seductive yet sly aspect was well exemplified by Morgan le Fay (or Morganna or Morgause). This enchantress caused the downfall of King and country when she seduced her brother, the monarch Arthur, (albeit in glamorised form) and caused him to father his own usurper, Modred. Some researchers identify Morgan le Fay as a later incarnation or avatar of the Morrigan, whist some versions maintain that Morgan and Morgause were separate though related individuals. In these accounts it was Morgause rather than Morgan who enchanted Arthur and gave birth to their treacherous son.

Other Femme Fatales of Britain and Ireland have drawn association or comparisons with Celtic Dark Goddesses, mainly the Cailleach Bheur, Black Annis and the Muilerteach and other Groac'h but also the Banshees, Baobhan Sith, Leanan Sidhe and various other Bad Faeries and powerful Witches. The Grached Coz are a race of Hag-Faeries native to Brittany.

Many places scattered across the Celtic lands are reputed to host their own terrible supernatural Hags. They may be said to dwell in woodlands or waterfalls, sea-coves or cellars, towers or cemeteries. Though their habitat may vary, these creatures known by grim names such as Burn the Ladle, Jenny Gallows and Old Harrow-Tooth for example, are almost always rumoured to have a great fondness for the taste of young human flesh. Canrig Bwt, the brain-eating Hag of Llanberis in North Wales was said to sleep under a great stone monolith. The strength and combat skills of the Celtic Hags often also far surpass the preconceptions suggested by their paltry frames. Not all of Britain's flesh-eating crones may have an antiquity dating back to the Celtic age. Some are likely derived from the memories of certain individuals caught up in the Witch Trials whilst others were inspired by accounts of real-life murderesses. Such is the case of Jenny Cut-Throat of Wolsingham, County Durham, for in her natural lifetime she was a wife and mother by the name of Jane Garthwaite. Her new name and reputation flowered on that fateful day of 25th May 1718, when Jane cut the throats of three of her own children before turning the blade upon herself. The family home turned murder-site was known for some years afterwards known as Cut-Throat Cottage and even into current times the belief persists amongst local schoolchildren, that upon running a specific number of times around a certain grave in the town cemetery the grotesque presence of Jenny Cut-Throat will be invoked.

But whether they be Witches, child-killers or indeed degenerate Goddesses, the Hags all share a loathsome kindred spirit.

The Cailleach Bheur
(Also known as Cailleach Bheara. The Blue Hag of the
Highlands. Beira. Beire. Gyre-Carline. Gentle Annie. Cally
Berry. Caillagh ny Groamagh. The Old Lady of Gloominess.
The Storm Hag. The Storm Goddess. Stone Woman. Mountain
Mother. Verah. Dera. Dhera. Clooth-na-Bare.)

According to Celtic lore, some of the Nature Goddesses would be of a
youthful and cheerful countenance at Spring-time, but as the year
progressed and with the turn of the seasons they would gradually age
until come the winter they were gnarled and harsh. Such was the case
of the Cailleach Bheur, however following a natural disaster caused by
her own unfortunate folly, it is said that her blood froze and her visage
grew grimmer. The advent of Christianity eventually resulted in the
redundancy of many of the Old Gods and Goddesses and it was as
such with the Cailleach Bheur. Time denied her healing , her dreadful
countenance became permanent and the Cailleach Bheur lingered on
earth as a seasonally active monster.
As the embodiment of Winter she is merciless, leaving any positive
aspects of the season to the likes of Jack Frost and the Snow Faeries.
Instead the Cailleach Bheur drifts through the lands leaving death and
hardship in her wake, her touch and breath turning all to ice. The
only company that she will tolerate is a large Crow that sits upon her
shoulder but sometimes it is said that on occasion Dark Elves may also
assist her in misery making. With tremendous force the Cailleach
Bheur hurls rocks, hailstones and Elf-bolts to the earth. other accounts
of her wonder-tale however claim that she was tended by eight hideous
hag-maidens and furthermore that she had wed several times and gave
birth to Fomorii, Wraths and Foawr.
Though immense, her power is not eternal for once the time has come
for the land to warm and bloom again the Cailleach Bheur hides her
stave under a bush and turns into a stone until the seasons once again
turn in her favour (though at certain times she may stir and survey
the land in the form of a large bird).
It has also been said that to herald in the winter, the Cailleach Bheur
will wash a tartan cloth in the whirlpool of Corryvreckan, Scotland
until it is virgin-white (see also Bean Nighe).
Though the Cailleach Bheur was the most potent and consistent, she
was not the only crone to wreak environmental hardship upon man
and beast. A strange, winged Hag known as the Muime was held to
blame for the decimation of the Great Caledonian Forest that once
swept across most of Northern Scotland.

(Cailleach Bheur Image overleaf top)

Black Annis
(Also known as ~ Cat Anna.)

Although there are inclinations towards a Crone Goddess origin as suggested by the recumbent hill figure of *Black Combe* near the former site of the *Annaside* Stone Circle in Cumbria, several snippets of local Leicestershire history have seemingly contributed to the mystery of Black Annis.

Allusions to a local Witch who prophesied the death of King Richard in the Battle of Bosworth have been made, but also to Agnes Scott, an anchorite nun who lived in a cave and also ran a Leper colony in the area. A local mayor also had the name 'Annis' but both this nomenclature and the alternative Cat Anna have been considered both as corruption of Dana, Danu or Anu - all names of the Earth Goddess or as a reference to activities of the Easter Monday Drag Hunt. This hunt proceeded from the Dane Hills (Black Annis' own locality) and commonly utilised the odd habit of dousing a dead *cat* in *aniseed* and dragging it behind a horse. Possibly this was done to rouse the hounds, but traditionally the intended quarry would have been Hares, which considering the timing of the event also draws acknowledgement to Eostre - another ancient Goddess.

Essentially though, Black Annis is the Hag of the hills ; a foul wretch who lurked in the branches of an old Oak tree, surveying the land around for young children playing out after dark to seize or if need be even attempting to snatch them from their own homes. Claiming her prey, she would drag her victim back to her cave, a dark fetid grotto carved out of the rock of the hills by her own monstrous talons and given the name Black Annis' Bower. In this foreboding hole she would feast upon her victims' flesh after first carefully flaying their skin. These pelts would be used either to drape the walls of her cavern and the branches of the old Oak as grotesque decoration or as cloth for her garments. It was claimed that Black Annis' horrifying screeching would carry for miles but at other times Black Annis cared for a lower profile. On such occasions, to assist stealth and to avoid possible capture she was said to assume the form of a cat. Association may also be possibly drawn to the legend of Lady Ann Smith from nearby Edmondthorpe. One night this lady's butler confronted a cat that he feared to be uncanny. Furthermore he caused great injury to the beast's paw with a meat-cleaver. The moggy naturally took itself away from the scene rapidly. Upon his next meeting with Lady Ann (whom others already suspected as being a Witch) the servant noticed that his mistress's hand carried a wound correspondent to the damage he'd inflicted upon the cat.

Night-Hags
(Also known as ~ Night-Mares. Mara. Mera. Mares. Crushers. Drudes. Mare-Demons. Hagges. Haints. Entities. Mallt y Nos. Night-Fiends. Cauchemar. Night-Elves.)

Sometimes people who suffered from wasting diseases such as Tuberculosis Consumption were said to look 'Haggard' or 'Hag-Ridden'. This refers to the belief that as they slept, a Night-Hag had entered their bedchambers and either sat upon their chests crushing them (but not to the point of fatality) and perhaps sucked away at their breath or their vitality. Or alternatively had actually ridden their victims entirely into the air and sometimes over distance. Either way, their human victims were left exhausted and often diseased. The alternative name of Mara and its similar derivatives, is said to have meant Crusher in Old-English, and it is from this word that the term Night-Mare originated - initially meaning not a bad dream but an actual external terror.
Whether these creatures are of Demonic, Fay or Human Descent is uncertain and it is perhaps the case that all three may equally apply. It has been claimed that at the age of 40 years old a Witch could qualify for the title of Drude and with it the power to torment the sleep and sanity of whosoever they wished. Some people thought that these fiends would enter an abode through key-holes or cracks in the wall, perhaps in the form of mist (a theory also applied to Demon-Lovers). In excess of Crushing it was feared that these miscreants would also suckle the milk from new mothers as they slept and either abduct, kill or infect the new-born infants with disease.
The term Hag-Riding has also been applied when horses who had been left resting, have been found to be exhausted and covered in sweat in the morning. Again it was considered that the Night-Hags had been riding the horses around in circles to the point of collapse during the hours of darkness. In some locations it was thought that these fiends on horseback delivered bad dreams to households, thus giving an additional meaning to Night-Mare. (Henri Fuseli displayed both variations of the meaning of the word in his different versions of the painting 'The Nightmare'.) An alternatively used term to Hag-Riding is to be Owl-Blasted, which refers to the belief that Night-hags would sometimes take the form of these nocturnal birds.
To combat and deter the Night-Hags riding either people or horses, charms were hung above beds and stable-doors. Such charms could be iron horseshoes wrapped in red flannel or frequently self-bored stones known as Hag-Stones, Witch-Stones, Fairy Cups or Adder-Stones . In the 19th Century Hag-Riding was such a commonly feared experience

in Somerset, that one man claimed to sleep with a board studded with sharp nails pointing outwards in order to thwart any Mares intent on sitting upon his chest. From this county and also from Dorset came some court reports of the same era detailing beatings executed upon several old ladies , whom local vigilantes had suspected guilty of Hag-Riding. This was not merely a 19th Century phenomena however as Night-Hag visitations had been feared for many centuries previously and also still occur today. Whilst sleep-researchers have suggested convincing reasons for the physical and mental mechanics of such a phenomena, the persistence of the very similar and disturbing archetypal imagery experienced by different people at different times remains somewhat mysterious and eerie.

Shadow Men
(Also known as - Black-Men. Dark Men. Dark Men of Dreams. Shadows. Fear Dorcha. Fear Dubh.)

An ancient Irish tale recounts the hero Finn Mac Cumhail's encounter with a strange dark figure known as The Shadow Man or Aillen Mac Midhna. This wretch would leave the Otherworld each year at Samhain. Wandering through the land he would play a small golden harp (or tambourine in some versions of the tale) and the strange melody it issued would cause mortals to fall into a sleep as deep as death. As this unwelcome minstrel progressed, buildings would fall and people would burn in the flames of his devastating hot breath. No one seemed able to halt his advance and Aillen maintained his destructive visit annually for 23 years until the young warrior Finn Mac Cumhail decided to test his mettle by attacking the creature. Armed with his shield and a spear that prohibited sleep because of the prurient odour of its venomous tip. Though protected from the strains of slumber and guarded by his shield from the Shadow Man's incendiary exhalations Finn initially made little headway in conquering the fiend and looked as if he himself might falter and fall. He dug deep however and strove harder upon Aileen and his persistence paid dividends when he finally managed to wrench the enchanted musical instrument from the Shadow Man's hand. Deprived of this device, Aillen was also deprived of his power and Finn thrust his spear into the Shadow Man's heart. He then severed its head, which he brandished awhile as a trophy. Thus the Shadow Man's corporeal reign was ended and subsequent Samhain eves were spared one less wandering fiend, however other dim figures continued to lurk in the half-light, in the shadows and in dreams. This was not the only dark Man that Finn was to encounter upon his adventures however. Another Irish legend gives account of his encounter with Ri na bh Fear n Gorm (the King of the Black Men). As this figure and his entourage were stated as originating from foreign shores, it is possible that they were simply people of a darker pigmentation than the Gaels. People that may have sailed to Irish shores from Africa, India or the Middle East. However further description seems to indicate that these strangers were of Ogre-like proportions and great magical learning. The term 'Black-Men' has been used throughout the history of British /Irish folklore and legend to refer to all manner of enigmatic beings ranging from swarthy Dwarves and Goblins to the black giant Cyclopes of Welsh Romance and more besides. Whilst on some occasions the description may refer to their colouring, it could equally apply to their Cimmerian nature instead or in addition.

The Dark Men of Dreams tend to prey on the sleeping psyche of women. The details of individual dreams will differ but the fundamental aspect of the Dark Man varies little. He is the figure on the edge - the lurker, the stalker, the intruder. Shrouded in darkness and shadow, always just out of reach for identifiable details to be distinguished but always close enough to threaten. Emitting a palpable atmosphere of mystery and danger the presence of the Dark Man lingers after the sleeper wakes.

Incubi and Succubi
(Also known as ~ Demon-Lovers. Entities.
Male singular ~ Incubus. Female singular ~ Succubus.)

An Incubus is a male spirit that seeks to indulge a mortal woman in carnal activity whilst a Succubus is a female spirit that likewise preys on the passions of mortal men. However it has been suggested that both spirits are one and the same, and that the Incubi / Succubi adopts only a specific gender in relationship to its particular victim. The nature of these nocturnal paramours preyed heavily upon the minds of the Medieval Church, possibly because many of the alleged victims were members of their own ministry who had prescribed to a life of chastity. (Merlin, the great sage of Arthurian legend was thought to be the offspring of an Incubus and a Nun.) The Church scholars deliberated on whether the phenomena was mere hallucination borne out of celibate frustration or sinful fantasies made flesh ; but this held their own people to blame almost as much as the other considered option that such claims were in fact a cover-up for actual corporeal liaisons with human partners. Frequently though, those who claimed an encounter with an Incubus / Succubus seemed not to have been pleasured by such a visit but to have been genuinely shocked and frightened. Therefore further attention was concentrated on seeking out an external, supernatural culprit. They questioned whether these night-visitors were perhaps a salacious breed of Faerie or maybe vengeful Ghosts, but as all were considered agents of the Devil anyway then it was simple enough to label them Demon-Lovers - a notion that was echoed independently in ancient Hebrew lore as well as other faiths and cultures.
Regardless of their specific origins the Incubi and Succubi continued to enter the beds of people both within and outside of the clergy. Whilst they may not have had to deal with the same level of guilt and shame that some of the more pietistic victims may have felt over their sacred vows being broken, the non-ecclesiastic victims rarely enjoyed such visitations either. (It must be noted however that following the enforcement of celibacy upon ministers by Papal law ordained at the Synod of Rome in 1047, many of the pious were very capable of breaking their own vows.) Sometimes but rarely would the Incubi / Succubi experiences be especially violent but they were sudden invasions of privacy, usually commencing whilst the victim was still asleep. The touch of the Demon -Lovers was often said to be as cold as ice and their caresses devoid of any pretence of affection. People greatly feared that they could be accused of inviting such dalliances as to do so would be to condemn themselves to the charge and to the

punishment of practising Witchcraft. There was also concern that the result of such lewd unions would be the birth of hellish creatures that would further plague mankind.

Folk-remedies traditionally used to ward off Incubi assaults included placing a Peony flower or a cauldron in the bedchamber and to deter Succubi assaults Bluebells and phallic symbols were utilised. A 'Goblin-Salve' concocted of various ingredients was said able to dispel either, whilst some Demon-Lovers seemed powerless to act when confronted by the prayers of the genuinely faithful and devout. Frequently though devotion alone was seemingly not enough to stem the Demonic ardour or bolster the victim's spirits enough to resist the seduction or violation imposed upon them. In modern times there have been a few claims of the masculine Incubi attacking male humans, but it is uncertain whether this occurred in earlier times but may not have been mentioned by the victim to avoid the further shame that would likely have arisen in those outwardly intolerant days

Korrigans
(Also known as ~ Corrigans. Loathly Ladies.)

The Korrigans are most prevalent in the lore of the French-Celtic Bretons, who believed that they were originally female Druids or Heathen Princesses who had been cursed by early Saints for refusing to give up the Old Religion. Though not as frequently as in Brittany, the Korrigans do sometimes appear in British lore, including within Arthurian legend and also Chaucer's Canterbury Tales , where they tend to be known as Loathly Ladies.

Tales of the Korrigans tend to take a similar slant - by night or in private company she would appear as a woman so beautiful that she could turn the head and heart of any mortal man ; by day or in public view however, she appears as a hideous Hag. This would likely prove a troublesome quandary for any man who had fallen in love with only the beautiful aspect or for those who had not perhaps even glimpsed on the horrid alter-ego until the morning after their wedding. Often this dilemma could test true love against lust or prestige.

In the case of the Arthurian Knight (named in some versions of the tale as Sir Gawain) the courtly hero would find himself bound in marriage to the Hag in course of an agreement, for she had provided the answer to a riddle bearing dire consequences. Not until the Wedding night was the Korrigan's alluring visage revealed to him and then the new wife posed another predicament. Giving her husband the choice, she asked whether he would prefer her to be beautiful by day and ugly by night or ugly by day and beautiful by night. The wrong answer could result in her maintaining an unpleasant countenance both night and day. Thus if he were to answer that he preferred her to be beautiful by night, she would scold him for his selfishness in maintaining a beautiful wife for his own pleasure and not caring that other eyes would look upon her ugly frame and possibly mock and jeer. If instead he stated a preference for her being beautiful by day, then she would again condemn him for his selfishness in maintaining a trophy wife that others may compliment him on, but who when sharing a bed at night he could not bear to look upon never mind touch. Therefore the only wise choice was to leave the decision entirely up to the Korrigan to choose for herself. In response to this answer and granting of freedom of choice, the Korrigan could now rid herself entirely of her Hag aspect and would remain a beautiful though unusual wife both day and night. The particular Loathly Lady of this tale is sometimes named as Lady Ragnall.

A reversal of transformation however occurred in other tales of Loathly Ladies, as the ballad of Thomas of Ercledoune recounts. In this

medieval romance it is revealed how a beautiful Faerie-Queen instantly metamorphoses into a discoloured, hideous old crone instantly after laying down with the eponymous hero. In this instance, the lessons that Thomas may have been intended to learn were not to trust unquestionably in the superficial or first impressions, not to take anything for granted and to also be wary of the consequences of his own pride and desires. Some Korrigans, such as the one encountered by Niall the destined King of Tara, near a Sylvan well in Ireland also displayed sublime prophetic power.

*Note: The name 'Korrigan' is also sometimes used to refer to a race of Breton Sea-Fairies or dwarfish Mer-Folk, rather like the Mari-Morgans (see also Mermaids and Tritons).

301

Celtic Vampires

(Also known as ~ Vampyres. Revenants. Sanguisuga. Guidmannies.
Biasd Bheulach. Mairtchenn. Neamh-Mhairbh {the Undead}.
Dreach-Fhoula {Bad Blood}. Cadaver Sanguisugas. {Blood-sucking
Corpses}. Marbh Bheo {Night-walking Dead}. Dearg-Due. Dearg-
Diulai {Red Bloodsuckers}.)

The Slavic word 'Vampyre' only entered English vocabulary in 1745, but
tales of revenant and living blood-drinkers existed in the Celtic isles long
before that.
In England the dead thought most likely to rise again were suicides
and executed criminals. For this reason in the past, the cadavers of
such deaths were not permitted a burial within hallowed ground but
were instead interred at crossroads. The logic behind the grave location
was that if the body were to rise, either through the power of its own
corrupt soul or perhaps reanimated by a wandering spirit that lacked a
corporeal form of its own, then caught between roads it would become
confused and unable to make its way back to the area where it once
lived and breathed. To maintain a further level of security it was
prescribed that the body should be buried face down and staked to
the ground. Yet despite such precautions some carcasses rose from
their pit all the same. In Tarrant Gunville, in Dorset, tales of Vampirism
blossomed after the exhumed body of suicide, William Doggett was
found to be incorrupted after many years in the soil. Though his legs
were discovered to show signs of being bound with yellow thread, his
rosy complexion was taken as indication that he had not been
prevented from post-mortem wandering.
In 1196 a Vampire plagued Alnwick in Northumberland on a nightly
basis, its fetid breath causing outbreaks of plague and in nearby
Berwick-on-Tweed another foul corpse trod its path pursued by a pack
of baying dogs (on another occasion in the same town, a tramp was
reputedly beaten to death and burned by a local mob who were
convinced that the vagrant was also a Vampire). Other walking dead
swollen with blood not their own , were on occasion reported from
Scotland down to the south of England especially in the 12th Century.
In most cases they were destroyed by gangs (or sometimes single
individuals) hacking it asunder and burning the parts. Their sudden
alarming reappearance finally being laid to rest in pieces.
Much later in the 1870's, similar dire measures were allegedly
employed in dealing with a repugnant Vampire that was said to have
terrorised Croglin Grange, a country-house in Cumbria. This particular
Revenant was described as having very wrinkled brown skin and
blazing eyes. A century later, rumours abounded that London's
Highgate Cemetery was frequented by a Vampire. Investigations in

1970 failed to unearth the Undead, but concluded that alongside rather grisly shenanigans, the necropolis may have indeed witnessed the rites of Devil-Worshippers.

In Ireland however not only did the people at one time know when the dead would rise but would also welcome their coming. The Failte na Marbh (Festival of the Dead) was held annually on the 31st October (Halloween, the Celtic Samhain and the Christian All Hallows' or All Souls' Eve, known in Wales as Nos Cyn Gauf - the Night before Winter). At this time the dead would pay a short visit to their living relatives and after a year in the grave they were obviously thirsty and famished. It was the duty of the living kin then to provide them with food and drink. Rather than being horrific this was initially considered a cause of celebration, but as hard times hit Ireland for some families the feast became a time to fear. Some people had little enough food to sustain themselves and their living relations, never-mind having to provide nourishment for the dead also. But still the hungry came on that dark eve and still they expected to be fed. With little else to spare, in desperation the living offered the dead their own veins to sup. The little that could be safely offered was perhaps not enough or perhaps the dead developed a keen taste for warm blood in their bellies, but either way the Church, keen to stamp out the old ways, encouraged the people to abandon giving succour to the dead. Dejected and ravenous some dead still rose to take what they felt was theirs by right, and if not offered willingly then they would take it by force. Their victims often being the very ones who had loved and grieved for them. These creatures were known as Marbh Bheo - the Night-walking Dead. If it was habit or desperation that caused the Marbh Bheo to rise, then on the Scottish Isle of Skye pure vengeance was often thought to be the prime mover for the Biasd Bheulach. These Vampire-like creatures would not only spare their revenge for the specific individuals who had done them wrong in life or had sent them to the grave, but would exact grim penance upon any living soul that fell within their grasp.

Some Vampires may not have even reached death by the time their tastes had turned to blood. The Irish Dreach-Fhoula (Bad Blood) could be living or dead. Those amongst them who had not yet reached the grave were said to have derived their appetite and sometimes also their shape-shifting ability as a result of a curse bestowed upon them.

Prevalent also in both Irish and Scottish lore were Vampires that had no discernible human heritage and instead seemed to be of a malevolent Fay stock. Such a shadowy creature was the Irish Dearg-Due or Dearg-Diulai - the Red Bloodsucker. Frequently the Dearg-Diulai

appeared as a beautiful, pale female cloaked in a sanguine-red cape, yet there is some suggestion that there may also have been males of their kind. The female Dearg-Diulai were said to haunt lonely roads and derelict buildings as well as graveyards. They would use their feminine appeal to attract passing mortal men. Whilst going through the early motions of seduction, they would sink their teeth into his jugular vein and drain him of his blood and life. It has been claimed that should she instead find an attractive young female to feast upon, she could then either pass or spread the blood lust to her following the attack.

Though many Vampires seem to favour drinking human blood warm and fresh directly from the vein, a Revenant from County Cork was said to slit the throats of his victims whilst they slept and to have mixed their blood with oatmeal to make cakes. Be they Fay or Revenant, the Vampires of Britain and Ireland would generally avoid the presence of Rowan-wood or cold iron. Either out of necessity or choice they would generally shun the daylight in favour of feeding by night. The power of prayer uttered with belief and conviction rather than out of desperation or fear, was sometimes considered effective in warding off their frenzied assaults and also in some rare cases of actually lifting the Vampire of their curse. In the middle ages a priest was burned alive at Melrose in the Scottish Borders under the suspicion of being a nefarious blood-guzzler. His means of feasting were to apparently pierce his victims' necks with a pointed blade and to drain the blood through a funnel. Sometimes he would consume the blood whilst it was warm and fresh but would also bottle some up for later. The areas around the Scottish / English borders also spawned some tales of Cannibals, the Vampires' equally loathsome mortal cousins. Whilst cannibalism sometimes arises through dire need or in some areas of the world through cultural or religious concerns, the Cannibals of Berwick, seemed to eat people for pleasure. Led by a hoary, bedraggled old lunatic by the name of Sawney Bean, this group of cave-dwelling, incestuous flesh-eaters were the bane of travellers over the borders.

Baobhan Sith
(Also known as ~ Spirit Women.)

There is a story of a man named McPhee who went hunting with three friends near Ross, in the Highlands of Scotland. Having strayed further from home than they had intended and it already being dark , they decided to take refuge for the night in an empty sheep-shelter. They lit a fire, roasted the rabbits that they had caught and passed around a hip-flask full of whisky. Warmed and relaxed, McPhee began to hum a tune to which his companions light-headed and light-heartedly danced. Joking the while, McPhee complimented his comrades on their movements to which one of his friends replied that they'd be all the better should they have some pretty maids by their sides. At that moment sounds of disquiet arose outside of their shielding, as the wind suddenly roared, a dog barked and their tethered horses became uneasy. The door of their hut suddenly blew asunder and in entered four cloaked women, fair of face but somehow quiet and strange. One came to the side of McPhee and he felt peculiarly compelled to continue singing. The other three maidens partnered his associates and the dancing continued as the lilt took on an intense mesmerising tone. How long the singing and dancing continued, McPhee could not tell but in time his mind suddenly snapped to attention and alarm. Before him he saw the women descend upon his friends, the flirtatious caresses had turned into a brutal feeding frenzy. In horror, McPhee ran out of the hovel quickly pursued by the other hooded figure. No longer did she appear so pretty as she hissed and bared her teeth to the gums. Most shocking however was the revelation that her feet were not those of a human, but instead the hooves of a Deer could be seen below the hem of her verdant gown. McPhee hid amongst the horses , which were now whinnying, and kicking in panic but his pursuer seemed wary to approach, perhaps repulsed by the iron of the horseshoes. Instead alone she paced and grumbled, trying to coax him close. Come the eventual light of dawn, the strange woman was nowhere to be seen and all was quiet inside the hut. The horses and dogs had all calmed down considerably as well, but it was a while before McPhee plucked up enough courage to leave his hiding place and go back into the shielding. Inside he beheld the bodies of his companions lying on the floor, their throats ripped out and their bodies drained dry of blood. The hunters of rabbits had been visited by hunters of men, the Baobhan Sith ; Faerie-Vampires that hunted in packs by night and spent the days in the form of Hooded Crows.

Image of Baobhan Sith. Opposite Right.

Glaistigs

Akin perhaps to the Baobhan Sith, the Glaistigs however are solitary creatures. They also tend to be quite contrary in character, if she chances upon an old person or child that needs assistance she will generously help however she can. At times also she would help farmers by herding their cattle and particularly by preventing calves from suckling at night and causing a shortage for people when it came to morning milking. This work had its price however and it was customary in some regions for the dairymaids to leave a daily propitiation of milk for the Glaistig, otherwise she would disrupt the herding. Glaistig-Stones - rocks with a hollow basin into which the milk could be poured, were known to be utilised in at least Iona and Argyll. (Similar libations were also utilised to appease mysterious subterranean creatures known as Frids, Fridean or in the Orkneys as Wilkie). There is however a more sinister side to the Glaistig. If she sees a lone human male at night, perhaps a shepherd tending his flock or a wayfarer covering distance, then she will encourage them to dance with her. Usually they need little encouragement as the Glaistigs are considerably attractive, unless one investigates too closely. Her dancing partners however have little chance to discover her physical peculiarities as seduction soon turns to savagery, as the Glaistig bites into the man's veins to drink his blood. Sometimes it is said that if there is suitable water nearby, she will drown her victim first. The term Green Glaistigs has sometimes been used to generically refer to a variety of Green-clad supernatural Scottish females.

The Leanan-Sidhe and the Sceurettes
(Also known as Lhiannan-Shee. The Spirit-Lover. The Dark Muse.
The Faerie Sweetheart. The Faerie Mistress. The Dark Seductress.)

The Leanan-Sidhe sits beside old secluded wells and springs and waits. She bides her time until a mortal man wanders into the vicinity. If he meets her approval then the Leanan- Sidhe will then accompany him back to his home and remain there as his lover. In his eyes she is faultless but more than this she inspires great creativity within him. Enlightened by this beautiful muse who suddenly appeared to him the man will develop into a great poet brimming with bittersweet joy and sublime melancholy. Yet there is darkness to the tale, for those who accept the Leanan-Sidhe as a lover are destined to burn bright but fast. Gradually she will drain him of his spirit until he is only a hollow shell, and then death will follow like a blessing. Before leaving her dead lover to find another victim it has been said that a Leanan-Sidhe will first pour the blood and vitality of the man into a great cauldron. From this melting pot it is assumed that the Leanan-Sidhe derives her nourishment, longevity and youthful allure, but that it also the source of the artistic inspiration that she temporarily imparts to her lover-victims. The Sceurettes or Little Sisters of Brittany are another deadly feminine race. However unlike the Leanan-Sidhe they do not have the time or patience for the wiles of seduction and slow, subtle murder, instead they rampage through the countryside ravishing and butchering men as if there were no tomorrow. In this sense they are reminiscent of the Greek Maenads or Roman Bacchantes - Nymphs who revelled in debauchery, drunkenness, animal slaughter, murder and cannibalism in honour of the God Dionysus / Bacchus.

The Ganconers
(Also known as ~ Gancanaghs. Gean-Cannahs. Glanconers. The Love-Talkers. Dark Seducers.)

The Ganconer appears only to solitary women and preferably young and pretty ones at that. Engaging them to sit with him and talk awhile, so pleasant was his appearance and manner that the females instantly forget any reservations they may have had about talking to strange men in lonely places. Such is the Ganconer's charm and charisma that events soon transcend talk. So attractive does he seem that even the purest and most conservative of maidens would succumb to his seductive wiles. Perhaps such conquests are of most pleasure to him, but either way as the women snuggle up in his arms and begin to daydream of their life together, with a leery grin the Ganconer will vanish never to be seen by the paramour again. When they realise that he is long gone it is not shame or humiliation that the ladies feel but total and utter despair. So deep does their longing and despondency instantly become that their hearts feel fit to burst. The lovelorn maidens then cannot bring themselves to eat and they cannot sleep for their mind always returns to their mysterious lover. Within too long they pine to death over the encounter, which some consider is the Ganconer's main objective. Any pleasure that the Ganconer gains from the lovemaking is perhaps eclipsed by the joy he feels at knowing that he has ruined another woman's life. It could be that this Fay seducer is not fuelled by love of mortal women but actually his hatred of mankind, or it could be that the Ganconer is either not aware or simply does not care about the heart-break he leaves in his wake.

Night-Prowlers
(Also known as ~ Night-Walkers. Haunters.)
At night when most people are sleeping, silently keeping to the shadows the Night-Prowler moves about her business. Her own wizened child hung limply in her arms like a bundle of rags. Instinctively she would know in which house a human baby could be found sleeping and biding her time she would linger in the darkness outside until she was certain that the parents too had retired for the night. Careful not to awaken anyone she would lift the latch and enter the household. Once inside she would lay down her progeny by the hearth, then soundlessly leaning over the human infant's crib she would proceed with her grim task. Returning to her own child she would bathe it by the glow of the fire embers. It was not water that she washed her foul offspring with though, but the still-warm blood of the human baby. When she had finished anointing her kin with the sanguine balm, the Night-Prowler would leave as quietly and as suddenly as she had arrived. Come the morning, the human parents would turn to the cot only to find their own baby cold and lifeless.
This green-clad waif and her hideous progeny were the bane of croft houses and fishing cottages in the Scottish Highlands, particularly in Cromarty, on the Black Isle peninsula.

The Living Dead and Golems

Although the corporeal dead may have walked through Britain and Ireland either of their own accord or through the influence of evil spirits (see Vampires) most of the dead in these isles return only in spirit (see Phantoms & Hauntings). Necromancers would at times attempt to raise the dead in order to gain specific information, but usually they would try to activate only the soul or at most the mouth rather than the whole body and part of their rites endeavoured to maintain that the dead would permanently leave the land of the living once they had provided the required answers.

There is however little indication of Sorcerers within Britain or Ireland reanimating corpses for prolonged use. Though the word Revenant is more apt, resurrected corpses of this kind would likely today be known as Zombies but specifically this word refers to an element of the Afro-Caribbean religion known as Voodoo (or Voudou). Basically a hybrid of Roman Catholicism and traditional African Fon religion beliefs, Voodoo is practised quite widely (though not necessarily sinisterly) in various countries but most notoriously on the island of Haiti. Here, the dark side of Voodoo, as utilised by nefarious sects such as the Petra, is also known and feared. Voodoo Malefactors known as Boku profess the ability to reanimate the bodies of the dead and use them as slaves called Zombies (possibly named after the Congolese Snake God, Zombi). The dead person's soul may also be enslaved as a separate entity known as a Duppy. Anyway, whilst Voodoo may very likely be practised in Britain today (and not necessarily exclusively amongst Afro-Caribbean immigrants), there seems to be no evidence of true Zombie activity in these isles in modern times. The Northumbrian fiend known as the Alnwick Zombie seems from the description given to have been a Vampire rather than a Zombie. To find the nearest local comparison we have to look back to the Living Dead of Celtic Legend.

In the tale of Bran the Blessed, this chivalrous Welsh Giant was said to have owned a Cauldron of Healing, that originally belonged to the Dagda (the Celtic father-god and original chief of the Tuatha de Danaan). If the bodies of slain warriors were placed into this enchanted vessel, then they would return to life, fit for battle but now for some reason entirely mute. Following the brutal mutilation of some prize horses by one of his subjects at a wedding feast, Bran felt compelled to relent the cauldron to Matholwch, King of Ireland. This was done in a bid to prevent war as the horses were the King's own. Despite this gesture, war did eventually break out between the two countries and in the ensuing turmoil the Cauldron of Healing was rent

asunder. Without the means to regenerate the dead, the loss of life on both sides was extreme.

Much later in 13th Century England, there was rumour that the Franciscan Monk and esoteric scholar Roger Bacon had created false life (i.e. that not ordained by God). It was suggested that by following the ancient Jewish rites of the Cabbala, Friar Bacon had created a Golem and granted it life. A Golem was a sturdy effigy of a man usually moulded from clay (but it has been suggested sometimes as being from the body parts of dead men). These archaic robots were said to be activated by a charm called a Shem, either hung around its neck or placed in its mouth. Apparently inscribed with the true name of God, the removal of the Shem was said to deactivate the Golem. This was perhaps for the best as Golems were incredibly powerful and whilst they could prove to be valuable servants, they were also prone to go on sudden and devastating rampages.

Ankou
(Also known as ~ Death. The Grim Reaper. Old Father Time.
Azrael. The Dark Angel. The Angel of Death. Sammael. Mortis.
Mort-Head. Mors. Death's-Head. Harvester of Sorrow. The
Graveyard Watcher. The Graveyard Guardian. Donn. Da Derga.
Aed. Aericura. The Great Leveller. Jack O' The Shadows.)

Though the most specific tales of Ankou are common to French Celtic-Breton lore, it is perhaps unavoidable that the influence of this figure should have spread to Britain, Ireland and also further afield. For the Ankou is the personification of Death and for most of us death is unavoidable. Death can come in a vast array of guises, sometimes sudden and invisible, sometimes bizarre and almost comedic and at other times long, lingering and all too painfully evident. Likewise the Ankou is not restricted to a single form either.

Perhaps in these times and these isles, the image of the embodiment of death that most readily springs to mind is that of the Grim Reaper ; a skeleton garbed in a billowing hoodand cloak, armed with a mighty scythe with which he harvests the souls of those whose time has come. This face of Death, often represented in the fortune-telling Tarot decks and also in modern fantasy film and literature, has been prevalent in art and the psyche since at least the early Middle Ages. Yet it is not the only personification of Death to be found globally or even within these nations.The Breton aspect of Ankou spread most significantly to Ireland and Cornwall (though more-so in form rather than name) but has also been dispersed elsewhere across Britain.

To the Celtic tribes this Lord of the Dead was most commonly known as Donn. Whilst in this lore he would still sometimes manifest as the Grim Reaper, he would also frequently appear as a tall, gaunt old man befitted in mourning attire. It is claimed that his head can turn entirely upon his shoulders and that his eyes are empty black chasms. Apparently cast sightless by Saint Peter himself who wrenched the orbs from their sockets, the Ankou may be blind or simply indifferent to the suffering and grieving of those left behind but he does not fail to find his quarry. Many people have attempted to cheat Death and perhaps have succeeded, but most often they only manage to temporarily delay the inevitable. Scottish Sorcerers maintained that whilst it was impossible to halt Death once it had made its advance, through certain ritual it was possible to make him claim another soul rather than the one originally intended. There would still be a death , albeit of an unfortunate scapegoat and eventually the cunning survivor would also be claimed.

The Ankou was known to come calling at the dead of night, driving an old-fashioned hearse or body-cart usually hauled either by horses or oxen. (sometimes though the beasts of burden are more Demonic or cadaverous and may consist of pigs, dogs or even giant beetles.) Sometimes he would walk alongside his vehicle (known as Ankou's Chariot, the Karrig an Ankou, the Hell-Wain , or in Wales as the Ceffyl Heb un Pen - though this often refers literally instead to a Headless Horseman), smelling the air for lives that were ripe to claim. Alternatively, the Hellwain's coachman is sometimes claimed to be the Devil.

It has been suggested that the Ankou was originally Cain, the son of the biblical Adam and Eve. According to the Book of Genesis, Cain became the world's first murderer after he fatally struck down his brother Abel. Islamic lore however holds that Death is the Angel Azrael (known to Hebrews as Sammael). Others believe that the Ankou was the last person to die each year and annually could find peace as a replacement took up the role on New Year's Eve.

The term Ankou has also occasionally been applied to the Phantoms more commonly known as the Graveyard Guardians or Watchers . There was once held the belief that the first person to be interred into a burial ground was destined to rise and become its protector (see also Church-Grims). Indeed some thought that this inhumation should not be a cadaver but a body still living and breathing at the time of burial. Nobody of any great considered value to a society would likely be used for such a grim task, therefore convicted criminals, imprisoned enemies, retards and anyone else that may be assumed to be of little worth or to have outlived their usefulness would be at greater risk of sacrifice. Whilst it is uncertain whether this form of deliberate entombment actually occurred or if so how frequently, quite a disturbing number of accidental live burials seem to have occurred over the centuries. The testing of breath on a mirror or a pinprick was not a very efficient way of defining true death from a deep catatonic state and some people may have had a brief last grasp at life from within a casket covered with earth. Even today at times reports occur of morticians getting the shock of their lives as the dead specimen lying on their slab suddenly sits up and looks around.

An old Irish tale recounts an ominous meeting between the Fianna (a formidable troop of warriors) and the personification of Death. To their amazement, Death presented itself as a withered decrepit white-haired old man. Yet still it proved its strength and power to be unconquerable.

The Ankou is represented as a masculine figure within Britain and Ireland though in some other cultures Death is regarded as feminine.

However some of the heralds that precede Death's progression are female. At the time of the Great Bubonic Plague that sporadically devastated Europe in Medieval times (in Britain most notably in the 13th, 14th and 17th Centuries); so heavy was the Ankou's workload (25 million people across Europe following 1347) that some people thought that feminine wretches known as the Plague Maidens assisted him with the reaping of souls. Also prevalent in the art of these grim times was the figure of King Death usually shown as a skeleton clothed in fine regalia meeting a living mortal dressed in similar apparel. These images served to remind all that death showed no prejudice and would welcome both prince or pauper with open arms.

The involuntary shiver down the spine claimed to be "someone walking over your grave" is sometimes attributed to the movements of the Ankou (but it could just as well be attributable to the Lob or other Phantoms, as well as to natural causes).

314

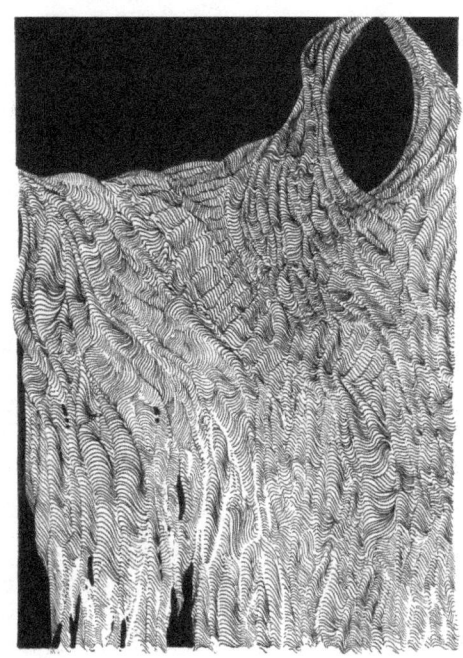

Hooded Entities.
(Also known as ~ Genii Cucallati. Hooded Spirits. Black Monks.)

Across the centuries mysterious Hooded figures have at times suddenly appeared in various locations across Europe (including Britain and Ireland). Due to their semblance many observers have taken these Phantoms to be the Ghosts of dead Christian Monks and indeed many of them could be exactly that, for some British and Irish Monasteries carry a heavy history. Some of these abbeys lie now only in ruins due to the looting, destruction and bloodshed that occurred mainly at the hands either of the Viking invaders or centuries later, Oliver Cromwell's Roundhead forces. Therein arises a curious enigma, for these Hooded Spirits were known within these isles long before the coming of Christianity. A Romano-British relic contained within the archives of Cirencester Museum depicts three of these cloaked figures known as Genii Cucullati. It is thought that the Romans adopted or represented these icons from the beliefs of earlier civilisations (mainly in Celtic-Gaul but also in Britain). Rather than representing priests as such, they were thought to be Supernatural Fertility Spirits. The visual similarity to the first Christian Monks probably didn't escape the Celts and Britons either, however there is little known about the Genii Cucullati, and the Hooded Spirits that are reported today are likewise shrouded in mystery. Sometimes these spirits are to be seen as if in funerary procession. Though Hooded Entities are usually eerily silent, the Phantom Monks of St. Alban's Abbey in Hertfordshire are said to have been heard singing or chanting. The Hooded Spirit that haunts the old gibbet near Potsford Wood in Letheringham, Suffolk has been reported by startled observers, as having a grisly, skeletal face. Traditionally the Genii Cucullati each have three faces (triple-aspect). Genii Cucullati worship was most prevalent in England in the Cotswolds, Gloucestershire and along Hadrian's Wall in Northumberland.

315

Screaming Skulls and Talking Heads

The Ancient Celts considered the head to be the vessel of the human soul and it therefore held a sacred significance to them. Whilst carvings and representations of heads featured prominently in their iconic art (as it does in many other religions and cultures globally), the actual skulls and heads of human beings were of especial regard. As reported by classical observers the Celtic Head Cult could be considered as being peculiarly grisly as warriors would sever the heads of their enemies and display them as potent trophies. The skulls of esteemed ancestors would also be put on prominent display at Samhain. As this festival is a precursor of Halloween, it is possible that these skull displays also form a basis for Punkies or Jack 'o' Lanterns; these are the hollowed-out and candle-lit pumpkins, turnips and mangle-wurzels of 'Trick or Treat' festivities. ('Jack 'O' Lantern is also an alternative name for the Ignis Faatus.)

Some heads however continued to function despite being separated from the body. Numerous tales of severed heads displaying an independence from their body and maintaining the ability to speak or perhaps even sing jovially, wisely or prophetically can be found within Celtic / Anglo-Saxon Paganism and Christianity. In Celtic myth this most notably included the epic journey of the head of the gigantic Bran the Blessed (also known as Urien and Bendigreid Vran). During the Welsh - Irish War, a poisoned spear wound to the foot fatally injured Bran. He instructed his vassals to remove his head before the toxin reached it and to take it for burial within the White Mount (now the site of the Tower of London). This they did, however the journey there took an astounding 87 years in which time the head of Bran not only remained incorruptible but also continued to eat, drink and commune in considerably high spirits. One tale claims that King Arthur Pendragon (who was believed to be a bloodline descendant of Bran) later removed the head from the White Mount. Another disconnected head reputed to speak was that of the Anglo-Saxon King and Saint, Edmund. After being hacked off and discarded by his Danish murderers, Edmund's head was said to have called to his followers and alerted them to where it lay hidden and guarded by a grey wolf. Talking Heads are also known as Vital Heads. Also, in addition to his alleged creation of a Golem, the 13th Century Monk Roger Bacon was rumoured to have constructed from brass, an articulate and intelligent Talking Head.

Bereft of flesh or metal, the Screaming Skulls however have proved to be a tormenting nuisance even into modern times. Mainly to be found in certain English Country Manors and Farmhouses, the Screaming Skulls normally tend to actually be very quiet and resemble any other human remains of this kind. However this expectable good behaviour would be due to the begrudged and hard-learnt respect of the dwelling's living occupants and owners.

Should anyone try to remove the skulls, even to transfer them to more acceptably appropriate places of rest, then the Screaming Skulls would live up to their name. Guttural blood-chilling shrieks would vent from their cold, lip-less mouths. Some skulls were nevertheless removed despite their hollering, but were reputed to have mysteriously returned to the abode under their own volition. The original shoulders that such skulls were thought to have rested upon during life, varies considerably from case to case. For instance the Screaming Skull of Bettiscombe Manor in Dorset (where it has resided for over 200 years), was said to have been that of an Afro-Caribbean slave. Sensing death approaching, this servile apparently requested that his remains be shipped home to the West Indies. When his dying wishes were reneged upon, the accursed skull was said to emit a terrible howl if placed anywhere except its current position (where it could serve as a reminder of the consequences of broken promises). However there has also been suggestion that not only is the Bettiscombe Manor skull actually of a much greater antiquity but it is also female. The Screaming Skull of Burton Agnes Hall in Yorkshire is thought to have been that of Anne Griffith a well-bred Elizabethan lady whose dying request was to be laid to rest within the hall. She died young and her wishes were taken as mere folly and ignored. However as she laid within her designated sepulchre, Poltergeist type disturbances wracked the hall and did not cease until her surviving sisters honoured their last promise to her and placed her skull behind a blocked up wall within the hall. Anne's Skull was later given the nickname of Awd Nance. Other English buildings that harbour or harboured Screaming Skulls include Timberbottom Farm near Bolton, Calgarth Hall near Lake Windermere, Cumbria, Tunstead Farm in Derbyshire, Higher Farm in Chilton Contelo in Somerset, Wardley Hall near Manchester and Warbleton Priory in Sussex. The last example is said to house Two Screaming Skulls ; one apparently a brutally murdered Catholic and the other his killer.

Headless Ghosts
(Also known as Dullohan. Dallahan.)

Though the Screaming Skulls could be said to be Phantoms without bodies, so too have many Ghosts without heads been reported throughout Britain and Ireland (though the two do not seem to be connected). Perhaps the most infamous, but certainly the most regal of Britain's Headless Ghosts is that of Anne Boleyn, one of the most ill-fated wives of King Henry VIII. Executed by decapitation her splendidly attired body is said to wander the precincts of the Tower of London. Her stately elegance is however marred by her head being tucked under her arm. (The Phantom of Anne Boleyn is also thought to haunt other locations notably Blickling Hall and Hampton Court, though generally in a more bodily complete form.)
Simon Lovat was a Scottish Anti-Royalist plotter also executed by means of the chopping block in London in 1747. His restless spirit is also rumoured to carry his decapitated head under his arm as he leaps amongst the rooftops of England's capital.
An unnamed Headless Ghost (that could actually have to have been a Shape-Shifting Bogey) was said to haunt a quiet road near Longridge in Lancashire. She was a fair enough maiden when first encountered by a man named Gabriel Fisher, on his way back from a night at the local tavern. To his inebriated eyes anyway she was comely enough to embark upon a bout of flirting. When he offered to carry her basket for her, she handed it to him without a care. Suddenly a jeering laugh burst forth from the basket and as Fisher flung the wickerwork in terror, out rolled a woman's head. With little time to question his eyes, sanity or just how much he had drunk he turned in alarmed bewilderment to the lady by his side. He could not fail to notice now that beneath her bonnet was nothing but a gaping hollow - her own head was missing. Horrified, Fisher fled down the road turning only to see the Headless Woman throwing her maniacally- laughing head after him. As it landed at his feet the disembodied, giggling head rolled around biting at his ankles. Again he ran and again the roaming body hurled the imbecile head after him. Only when he crossed a stream did this hellish pursuit desist, with neither the body nor head seemingly willing or able to pass over the brook.
A more placid, mournful ghost carrying its own severed head is reputed to haunt Judith Hill Lane in Halstock, Dorset. This despondent spectre is usually identified as being that of Saint Judith (or Juthware) who was decapitated by her own brother in the 7th Century. Also in Dorset on the Poole to Upton Road the Headless Ghosts of four men have been seen carrying a coffin before disappearing into a hedge.
Walking without a head could theoretically pose some obvious difficulties yet Phantoms are not necessarily affected by the shortcomings of the living, however some Headless Ghosts do indeed seek other forms of locomotion.

Amongst the strangest Headless Ghosts reported are the Headless Nun and a blood-drenched woman (also minus a head) cradling a small child in her arms both of Walton Abbey In Yorkshire and the Ghost of the Duchess of Queensbury, who despite her aristocracy was said to have been seen pushing her separated head around the grounds of Drumlanrick Castle in a wheelbarrow.

Headless Horsemen were sometimes considered to be outcasts of the Wild Hunt, but are more frequently thought to be the ghosts of warriors who had been beheaded in battle or criminals such as Highwaymen , who had been executed by similar means. Headless Horsemen and their steeds may travel either on or above the ground and often both are as black as the night. Such an example of this is the Headless Rider of Castle Sheela in Ireland. At times the drivers or horses leading Phantom Coaches are often also reported as being devoid of heads (see also Phantom Vehicles). A Headless Ghost was once said to have driven a mourning-coach (known as the Coiste-Bodhar) through the streets of Doneraile in Ireland every Saturday night. It was said furthermore that this phantom known locally as a Dallahan, had the unusual and unpleasant habit of throwing a bowl of blood into the faces of any who dared to gaze upon him. Another Phantom Coach containing coachmen, footmen and four maidens all lacking heads was said to rise from a pond near Great Melton in Norfolk every day at noon and midnight. After a hasty sprint around an adjoining field this grisly vehicle was said to again return to the waters from whence it rose.

Poltergeists
(Also known as ~ Noisy Spirits. Racketing Spirits. Stone Throwing Ghosts. Polter- Ghosts. Polter-Sprites.)

From the German 'Polter' - to make a racketing noise and 'Geist' - Spirit ; Poltergeists are known across Europe and across the world. As far as Hauntings go, Poltergeist activity is especially common and often incredibly distressing for those people inflicted with such a presence. Though generally associated with buildings or perhaps more significantly with the people living within, Poltergeist activity can just suddenly occur rather than manifesting as course of a long, haunted history. Poltergeists sometimes seem the most modern of Ghosts, however they have been reported for at least 1500 years.

Due to their propensity for causing damage and chaos, they have at times drawn comparison with other Supernatural creatures such as Boggarts and Bogeys. Such is the case with Knocky-Boh, a supernatural pest that frightens children and disturbs sleep by knocking on walls and doors for it is uncertain whether this creature is Phantom, Fay or something else. They have been known to move objects and even people through the air and from one location to another, to cause domestic fires and floods, to smash glass and ceramics, to scrawl cryptic messages upon walls and various other nuisance activities. Frequently a Poltergeist will begin merely with a few disembodied knocks and rattles, but over time it will build up to more considerable violence and destruction. Their actions may either diminish over time or otherwise suddenly stop. To adequately define what a Poltergeist actually is can be problematic as they are actually invisible (though the mess they can cause certainly is not). Therefore it is often assumed that they are actually an energy force, though there does seem to be sentient guidance involved rather than a random spurge. The source of this energy however has raised considerable speculation. For many years, Poltergeists were thought to have been either created or guided by Malefactors.

Many Poltergeist cases find a focus in a certain inhabitant of the afflicted house. Even though such individuals may often bear the harshest brunt of the paranormal assaults, it has been considered that these people may not merely be an especially targeted victim but may actually be the cause of the disturbances. Frequently the focus will often turn out to be a young girl in or on the verge of adolescence. Therein lies the suggestion that Poltergeists are manifestations of Telekinesis (the ability to move or affect objects by the power of thought alone). Such Telekinetic powers are triggered possibly by hormonal and mental changes occurring within the youth and may be released not only unintentionally but perhaps also unconsciously.

There also exists the alternative suggestion that humans who are under considerable emotional and / or physical stress may attract the attentions of disembodied spirits (see also Demons). Such targets could include adolescents but also younger children and adults with mental disorders or who are straining under other pressures. The focal point of the celebrated case of the Enfield Poltergeist that tormented the lives of the Harper family in their home in Middlesex between 1977 and 1979, was seemingly their pre-teen daughter. 11 year old Janet was the objective of much of the most intense activity and was actually photographed apparently being forcibly ejected from her bed by an unseen force. Possibly more disturbing still was a tape-recording made at the house by the investigator, Maurice Grosse. From the mouth of the young girl (who appeared to be in a trance-like state) growled a deep, adult male voice claiming to be a previous occupant who died in that house. Though the voice cannot be proved beyond all reasonable doubt to have been either genuine or hoaxed, many Poltergeists choose to remain anonymous nonetheless.

Whether they are manifestations of Demons, the restless dead or the work of the human mind in solitude, Poltergeist activity has been noted across Britain and Ireland for centuries. Some other notable examples of Poltergeists include the Stone-Throwing Ghost that plagued five houses in Thornton Road, Birmingham (between 1979 and 1982), the Electric Horror of Berkeley Square, London (active 1850s), the Stone-Throwing Ghost of Truro, Cornwall (1821), Old Jeffrey or the Epworth Rectory Poltergeist , Lincolnshire (that tormented the Wesley's, the founding family of Methodism from about 1716), the Demon Drummer of Tedworth (now North Tidworth), Wiltshire (1661 to 1663), the Glenluce Devil near Newton Stewart, Galloway (1654 to 1656) and the Royalist Ghost that pestered Oliver Cromwell's envoys at the Palace of Woodstock (now Blenheim Palace, Oxfordshire) in 1649 following the felling and burning of a King's Oak. Tales of Stone-Throwing Ghosts also abounded in Wales.

Spunkies and Invisibles
(Spunkies also known as ~ Sad Ghosts. Tarans. Spunks. Pisgies. Souls. Soullh. Sowlth.
Invisibles also known as ~ Imaginary {or Invisible} Playmates.)

Spunkies are believed to be the wandering souls of children who had died before being baptised. As they have not formally been given a name in the eyes of God and as they did not have chance to be rid of Original Sin (the sin committed by Adam and Eve, said by the Catholic Church to be inherited by everybody at birth and only rid through the sacrament of Baptism); these dead children do not appear in Saint Peter's ledger and cannot gain entry into Heaven. Instead they are doomed to wander the earth until Judgement Day.

Spunkies do not seem to intend any harm to living human beings and may only approach them out of loneliness or the hope that they may be given a name. At sea however, where the Spunkies can also appear, they have been blamed for the loss of lives and boats. Mistaking their luminescence for landing lights, sea-faring vessels were said to have headed towards the lonesome Spunkies, only to be torn apart upon the reefs. (The Mal-de-Mer of Cornwall and Brittany were other strange sea-spirits that were also blamed for causing shipwrecks, though it is uncertain whether there is any connection between them and the Spunkies.) Even on land Spunkies may also cause death by the same means as the Ignis Faatus (with which they are often closely associated). Some would suggest that such deaths are deliberate and that the Spunkies are inherently evil, yet others suppose the fatalities to be tragic accidents that only serve to make the Spunkies more melancholy. Spunkies are said to gather in churches either on Midsummer's Eve or Halloween in order to greet the recently dead. Some folk also considered sightings of Spunkies (and also night-flying Butterflies) to be an omen of death , though this does not seem to be a uniform opinion.

Whilst the deceased, un-baptised child theory has also been applied to Pillywiggins and some other Fay species, there may also be a connection between Spunkies and Invisibles. Invisibles are more commonly referred to as the Imaginary Playmates of children. Though the vast majority of these playmates are nothing more than healthy imagination and creativity on the part of the child, there has also been occasions when these invisible companions have apparently been sensed by psychics or have even been said to have been caught on camera. Their image or at least the sensation of it, is usually childlike. Imagination and photographic process anomalies aside, perhaps some Invisible Playmates are the Spunkies or other supernatural creatures attracted by life and especially youthful vitality. Such creatures probably mean no harm and if they are indeed Ghosts of the dead, they may not even be aware of their own demise.

Unlike the Spunkies however, Imaginary Friends often seem to know their own name or are soon given one. They are not always human in form. The Invisibles should not be confused with Invisible Assailants such as Poltergeists and Bocan.

Ignis Faatus and Corpse-Lights
(Also known as ~ **Ignis Fatui. Fool's Fire. Faery Fire. Fox Fire. Funeral Fire. Elf-Fire. Walking Fire. Shell-Fire. Rolling Fire. Will 'O' The Wisp. Will With The Wisps. Willow Wisps. Willy Wisps. Will 'O' The Wykes. Weize. Seize. Billy With The Wisp. Kitty Wi' The Wisp. Kitty With The Candlestick. Kitty Candlestick. Kit 'O' The Canstick. Friar Rush. Friar's Lanthorn. Peg a Lantern. Jack a Lantern. Jack 'O' Lantern. Jacky Lantern. Lantern Men. Hobby Lantern. Hobbledy's Lantern. Jenny Wi' T' Lantern. Jenny Burnt-tails. Gyl Burnt-Tale. Joan In The Wad. John In The Wad. Moon Dancers. Hunky-Punks. Hinky-Punks. Pinkets. Punkies. Puck Lights. Pwca Lights. Ghost Lights. Tanwedd. Ellylldan. Canhywallan Cyrth. Gaelghan. Teine Sith. Canwyll Corph. Canwyll Corff. Corpse Lights. Corpse Candles. Corp Candles. Dead-Candles. Sylham Lamps. Fair Maids of Ireland. Weird-Lights. Bob-a-Longs. Blobs. Globs. Globsters. Death of the Druid. Dr'eud. Water-Sheeries. Le Faeu Boulanger. Fioles. Sand-Yan-Y-Tad.**)**

As can be seen above, the Ignis Faatus (Fool's Fire) is known across Britain, Brittany and Ireland by many names (and these are only some of the local names for it is a global phenomenon). Will 'O' The Wisp is possibly the most widely recognised British name for these weird dancing lights that have been claimed to lure people to their deaths. Nocturnal travellers lost in unfamiliar surroundings may see these lights glowing in the apparent distance and take them to be the glow of a homestead or the lanterns of fellow wayfarers. However rather than leading mortals to safety they would instead lead them to their doom. Their bodies often disappearing without trace, perhaps over a steep crag into a quarry or the sea but most frequently at the bottom of a stinking quagmire. Whether these deaths are due to deliberate malice on the part of the Ignis Faatus or occur as an unfortunate consequence of their being is uncertain. Several theories have however been suggested concerning the actual essence of the Ignis Faatus. These include -
In Wales, especially as the Canwyll Corff, Canhywallan Cyrth (Corpse Candles) or Tanwedd (Ghost-Lights) and elsewhere in Britain as Funeral Fire they are considered to be heralds of death. The lights are often assumed to be the glow of candles carried by invisible Ghosts or markers for the path of a funerary procession. Observations of the colour, size, quantity and intensity of these lights can be read to indicate precisely who is destined to die. Corpse Lights may differ from other Ignis Faatus in that they may be seen to rise from a dying person's mouth or to be seemingly carried by a Co-Walker or a Phantom. Ignis Faatus is however often blamed for actually causing death rather than merely ushering it .

Like the Spunkies, Ignis Faatus are either the souls of dead, un-baptised children or the souls of others who lost their own lives traversing the same hazardous surroundings.

~ They are hot coals carried by Will the Smith, a Giant too wicked even for Hell and doomed to walk a lonely and eternal earthly path (see also the Damned and Wanderers). Tales of a similar vein are told regionally pertaining to other localised legendary individuals.

~ They are weird Elemental Spirits that entice humans to their death so that they may feed upon their souls.

~ They are Earth-Lights often attributed to speculated trails of energy that flow under the earth's surface. These trails are generally considered to be spiritually charged and are known as Ley-Lines. Ley-Lines and Earth-Lights have also been associated to significant natural land-marks as well as megalithic monuments and other sacred sites, as well as sometimes to the formations of Crop-Circles and sightings of UFOs.

~ They are lanterns carried by Pixies, Pwcas or various other Fay species, either to simply illuminate their own path or to purposely draw mortals into danger and dismay.

~ They are misidentifications of Glow-worms or Fire-flies. These luminescent insects were once more common in the British countryside but are now increasingly rare

~ That they are the combustion of natural gasses igniting upon contact with air. Vapours escaping from the stagnating vegetation of swamps or even dead bodies (either in the mire or in cemeteries - both of which are Ignis Faatus haunts) could cause such a chemical reaction and explain some encounters. This theory may not always apply so well to the forests, beaches, moors, hills and cliff-tops that have also been said to harbour Ignis Faatus.

Phantom Armies

Throughout history and the motions of war, gallons of blood have been spilled onto the landscapes of Britain and Ireland. Strange and sinister brews of violence, fear, hate, sorrow, mental and physical pain have seeped into the soil, plants and rocks of the ancient battlegrounds charging them with a potent emotional vitality. Little wonder then that the echoes of carnage and bloodshed have been said to resonate across the centuries

At times only the sounds of trooping or battle may be heard but sometimes an unsuspecting person may suddenly find him or herself amidst a scene of unbridled fury. Though the spectator generally endures no physical injury to their own person, the full horror and brutality they witness between the opposing forces of a long-past conflict can have a deep psychological effect.

At the beginning of the 20th Century, an English woman on a bicycle suddenly found herself amidst a bloody war near Blair Castle in the Pass of Killiecrankie in Perthshire, Scotland. Men in scarlet coats fired their cannons in vain as a horde of tartan-clad warriors descended upon them with swords and shields. (Historically speaking however, it is claimed that although they continued to brandish and use daggers and broadswords in battle, the Highlanders did also utilise firearms.) The astonished woman reported seeing the redcoats fall to the cutting blades of their opponents and as the last soldier descended into the mass of dead and dying bodies, the scene shifted as a mist of passing time seemed to fall in an instant. She gazed on transfixed, as a beautiful woman with thick, dark hair and a shawl cast around her shoulders, picked her way amongst the moribund and the deceased. Armed with a dagger, the stranger cut valuables from the dead soldiers' personage and cast them into the wicker-basket that she carried. At times, her blade was utilised to sever a stubborn ring-bearing finger or to finish off a warrior that desperately clung to the last remnants of life. Seeing the grim scenes of looting following so soon in the wake of unexpected and savage butchery, caused the out of time and out of place English woman to release an involuntary moan. In an event unusual to Phantom Army Hauntings, the Ghost woman not only heard the living but also actually advanced upon her in a threatening manner with knife in hand. This was finally all too much for the cycling tourist and she thus passed out in fright. She awoke safely in the location of her faint the next morning, but she was still disturbed by the events she had seen and believed them to be more than merely a dream or hallucination. Having been inspired to research the history of the location of her experience, she discovered that centuries earlier the locality was indeed the scene of a ferocious battle. In 1689, Scottish Highlanders loyal to their deposed monarch James II, had taken a victory in battle over the red-coated British soldiers sent by William of Orange.

She also discovered that in the centuries that had since passed, she was not alone in reporting having seen the long-dead soldiers battling and the grisly aftermath re-enacted again in all its gory detail. Due to the lack of modern landmarks in the locality and to the experience being perceived in solitude, it is not possible to say definitively whether this battle was visually re-played in modern times. Whether the observer was somehow transported back or otherwise gazed into the past. Or whether the profound history of the landscape provoked a befitting hallucination or psychic vision in the mind of the relaxed and unsuspecting observer. However the Pass Of Killiecrankie is not the only reputedly Haunted Battlefield in Britain.

Other places that are said to on occasion display the battles of their antiquity include Edgehill in Warwickshire (where the first battle of the English Civil War occurred in 1642), Otterburn in Northumberland (1388) and Neville's Cross in Durham (1348). Sometimes though the Phantoms that are seen or heard preparing for or engaging in battle greatly pre-date these and the other Haunted battlefields of the Civil War, the War of the Roses and other border wars. In Glastonbury, Somerset the ghosts of Medieval Knights have been reported. Glastonbury has strong associations to Arthurian Legend and from which stems the tale of the Sleeping Warriors. Somewhere in Britain within a dark remote cave are said to lie the Knights of the Round Table, their weapons and horns fastened to the cavern walls. Here they sleep deeply as they have done for centuries and if left undisturbed, will continue to do so until Britain's greatest hour of need, when it is believed that they will leap to the defence of the nation . Off the Isle of Iona in Scotland, a fleet of Viking Long-ships dating to approximately 986 AD were seen at sea in the 20th Century. Also in Scotland, a troop of Picts from the War of Nechtanesmere (685 AD) were witnessed in the 1950s, and on several occasions Ancient Britons and Romans have been seen to continue their battles in Woodmanton in Wiltshire.

The Lob
(Also known as Psychic Ghouls. Psychic Vampires.)

The term 'Lob' has at times been applied to creatures such as Hobs and Brownies, but may also apply to a weird creature that is somewhat between a Ghost and a Goblin. Although they could also be referred to as 'Ghouls', this word of Arabic descent means 'leech', but also refers to Asian / North African creatures (human or supernatural) that feed on the cold flesh of human cadavers. In modern usage the word Ghoul may also often be applied to *ambulance chasers* or other people who take pleasure in morbid pursuits. The Lob however may perhaps more correctly be referred to as a parasite. Their victuals however are not flesh or blood as the Lobs feed instead upon raw emotions and the more negative the better. The alternative name of Psychic Vampire can also equally apply to human individuals who either unconsciously or purposely display the ability to drain others of their mental and spiritual energy (which consequently can often provoke a depletion in physical energy also).

Appearance : Lobs are commonly invisible though their presence can often be sensed rather than seen. At times their visible form may be glimpsed and those with second sight may observe the Lobs as a black or dark purple amorphous shape, rather like a storm cloud though sometimes their limbs and features may be distinguished. It is uncertain whether the 'red mist of rage' is attributable to a Lob presence. Possibly also of association is the Welsh phenomenon known as the Yellow Spot of Death. This amorphous shape that sometimes appeared close to someone whose death was at hand has defied conclusive explanation. Whilst it could be a Psychic Vampire, Demon or similar foul creature come to devour the released soul or drain the last ebb of life-flow, it could otherwise be an Angel or a previously deceased person come to collect the newly expired. The vague shape seen by others may be more crisply defined to the eyes of the dying. Alternatively the Yellow Spot may actually emanate from the body of the failing person and could be part of the aura or spirit departing its former vessel (various cultures developed the belief that the human soul was not singular but comprised of numerous separate elements that could pass on separately at the time of death – see also Co-Walker and Ignis Faatus).

Size : They can range from very small to the size of a cow or larger. This all depends on how much nourishment there is available to them.

Diet : The energy of negative emotions such as anger, hate, grief, sorrow, pain, regret etc. etc. They are not however to be regarded as beneficial cleaners, for rather than abolish any maudlin or violent emotions it is thought that as they eat, a strange chain-reaction occurs in which more bad feeling is actually created.

Habitat & Range : Across Britain, Brittany and Ireland (possibly originating from Wales). Lobs are attracted by arguments, fights and other acts of violence, tension and hurt. They may also linger awhile at scenes of war, murder, gruesome accidents and lingering sickness. At such places they may be responsible for the unsettling atmosphere that gives some people the 'creeps'.

The Damned

It could be claimed that all the Ghosts of the Dead are damned as they seemingly cannot rest in peace. They may eternally trek this mortal coil because their physical body lies undiscovered or bereft of a proper burial. They may linger to alert the living of where their remains lie, or to act as a warning to others of the consequences of their own folly. Others may remain to wreak a torturous revenge upon their murderers or others that may have been responsible for their death or for making their life a misery. Some others may be consigned to earth due to specifics of their demise or even simply because they do not truly realise or refuse to accept that they are dead. However some folk were so wicked in life that an adequate penance or recompense would require far more time than their natural life span to fulfil. Instead of being consigned directly to the pits of Hell some twisted souls were said to have instead been damned to earth and given monumental tasks to complete. (The notion of Purgatory - a limbo plane where the deceased souls too good for Hell but not good enough for Heaven are said to reside until the Second Coming of Christ, was not accepted as a tenet of Catholic faith until the 13th Century.)

Two such doomed individuals' eternal punishment resulted due to the sins they committed during the Black Death or the great Bubonic Plague of 1665 - 66. The first of these wretches was the Pastor of Vernham Dean in Hampshire. This priest had instructed his congregation to leave their homes in the village and instead take to the top of a nearby hill, in order to try and avoid the pestilence that had already devastated London and now threatened to ravage the rest of the land. He informed them that he would administer to their needs and keep them well provided with food and clean water. So the villagers took his advice and headed upland, however unbeknown to them there were already some amongst their number that already harboured the vile disease within their bodies. As the malady took root and swiftly spread from person to person, wiping out life after life, the Pastor remained healthy in the village below. Fearing for his own health and mortality, and considering them to be beyond help, he neglected the needs of his Parishioners. Though it is true that he could have done nothing to save their lives and certainly it would have been putting his own life at risk, the holy-man could have displayed some truth to his vocation by delivering some compassion and provisions. Such charity could have perhaps brought at least a little comfort to his peoples' final days. Instead the lack of food and especially water caused further suffering as each and every one of them died there upon the hill. For abandoning his flock, the Pastor of Vernham Dean was condemned to carry an extremely heavy load of provisions upon his back on an endless hike around the hill.

The second of those condemned for Plague-crimes was a man called Robinson, who was the Squire of Swinsty Hall near Washburn, in Wharfdale, Yorkshire. His crimes however took place further south in the sickness-ridden streets of London. Whilst others around him fell ill and died, fled for their lives or tried to comfort and protect themselves and their loved ones, Robinson instead plundered the homes and pockets of disease victims. Not even the coins holding corpses' eyes closed were safe from his greedy clutches. The outbreak of the Great Fire of London that added to the capital's woes in 1666, forced Robinson to leave the city and head northwards. When he first reached Yorkshire however, he was shunned by the locals who feared that he would bring the Black Death into their midst, so he took refuge awhile in a barn that lay on the outskirts of Washburn. To pass the time, Robinson repeatedly scrubbed the coins he had gathered in a nearby stream. After some time the onslaught of the epidemic abated and the peoples' fears diminished somewhat and Robinson made his way into the community free to spend his ill-gotten gains. He founded the fine manor of Swinsty Hall and spent the rest of his days there living in comfort. However following his death the Squire of Swinsty Hall was doomed to forever wash the pestilence and shame from his plunder in the very same stream.

Another Phantom that received punishment for his crimes in both life and death was the infamous Highwayman, Dick Turpin. Executed for his wanton ways in York, his Ghost have been reported in many places across England. It is in Loughton, Essex however that his damnation seems most surreal and mordant. Amongst the many sins he committed in his lifetime, it was here that he was said to have slowly toasted an old woman over an open fire until she revealed where she had hidden her life-savings. It is also here at Trapp's hill that Turpin's Phantom has been reported riding his ghostly steed. However on this occasion he also has the unusual passenger of an old woman clinging onto his back, digging in her nails and hissing abuse into his ear.

Another example of the Damned was John (or Jan) Tregeagle (or Tregagle), of Treorder near Bodmin Moor in Cornwall. In his lifetime Tregeagle was a harsh, corrupt magistrate who had condemned many to death or imprisonment, more so on a lack of a decent enough bribe rather than true evidence of guilt. Rumours abounded in the locality however that his own crimes extended to extortion, torture, deviancy, murder and despite his pious condemnation of many accused Malefactors, it was also feared that he himself was involved in Black Magic and Communication with Evil Spirits. When he died in 1655, few if any were sad to see him go. However, a few months after he was laid to rest in consecrated ground (either due to the authorities failing to investigate the rumours or due to a pay-off to the church), it seemed that Tregeagle's presence might actually be beneficial. A lawsuit concerning a moneylender and a debtor was brought to court and it transpired that Tregeagle had held some information that could have solved a particular quandary of the case. The solution of course had died with Tregeagle, but either by deliberate Necromancy or as an unforeseen consequence of sarcastic jest, the dead man was called upon in court to state his piece and much to local horror that is in indeed what he did. The now decayed and demonic looking magistrate did not swear on the bible but condemned the debtor all the same. He then turned to the gallery and informed all present that it would now prove far more difficult to rid him than it was to call him.

And so it proved as Tregeagle and an entourage of sinister black shadows tormented the land and people with a fervent passion and pleasure. Those who had managed to avoid Tregeagle's perverse justice and wrath whilst he lived were now exposed to it after his death.

Local priests and Wise-folk were called upon to try and lay his troublesome spirit, yet it remained such a fruitless task that in the end they had to join forces. It appeared that together they could muster enough power to rid themselves of this fiend, yet the priest felt a pang of conscience. He felt that he could not knowingly condemn a soul to the trials of Hell, regardless of what they had done, so the clergy and the conjurors deliberated on an alternative means to counter the fiend.

By their powers and prayers they bound John Tregeagle to an earthly penance. He was compelled to empty a deep, vast expanse of water called Domarzy (or Dromarzy) Pool using only a tiny, cracked limpet shell. This he persisted at for years but for whatever reason, the hold of the spellbinding was relinquished and Tregeagle once again returned to torment the living. (Domarzy Pool, which has also been associated as a possible contender for the abode of the Lady of the Lake from Arthurian legend, was considered by many locals to be bottomless but it has been said that in 1859, the pool was indeed drained dry.) Perhaps then Tregeagle did indeed somehow manage to fulfil his epic, seemingly impossible task. Yet either way, he was not yet to find solace in eternal rest or even to wreak hell on earth for that much longer. Priests and Wizards were again called in to try and combat the menace and eventually Tregeagle was again damned to perform other prodigious chores.

He was ordered to weave rope from the grains of sand in Gwenvor Cove, and to sweep sand from Porthcurno Cove to Nanjisal Cove or Land's End; all the while being tormented by the strange black shadows as he himself had once tormented others. It is said that on the calmer days the sobbing of Tregeagle may be heard on the surf, whilst on stormy days the roars of the wind are amplified by his anguished wailing as the gale and sea wash away his work once more.

Similar tales to Tregeagle's post-mortem penance are told elsewhere in Britain's West Country. For instance, Cranmere Pool is only one of Devon's lagoons supposed to harbour a phantom dredge-man. Cranmere's ghost worker was a certain Mayor Benjamin Gayer, known ever after as Binjy. Executed as a sheep-rustler, Binjy also was damned after death to drain the pool using a sieve. This cunning spectre however remedied this seemingly fruitless task by stealing and slaying another sheep, then using its pelt to line the sieve. No merciful release was forthcoming however as Binjy was also therefore condemned to weave rope from grains of sand. (In another version of the tale it is claimed that the restless soul of Binjy refused all exorcising by the clergy until it was addressed in Arabic. The spirit then reputedly took the form of a colt that was subsequently driven to its demise into Cranmere Pool.)

Herne the Hunter

According to legend, in the 14th or 15th Century or perhaps earlier, a gamekeeper / huntsman in the employ of Windsor Park in Southern England was to undergo a weird metamorphosis and to gain a mournful yet notorious immortality. His name was Herne and he was such a loyal subject of the king that one day he put himself between the monarch and a rampaging stag. Such was the force of the collision that both Herne and the beast were grievously wounded. Grateful for his own rescue and wanting to help save his minion's life in return, the monarch summoned a Wise Man to the scene. However in order to gain Herne's salvation, the Wizard deemed it necessary to combine the forms of the wounded through the powers of magic and thus did Herne gain antlers. He continued to loyally serve his master in life, but other vassals of the king were to grow scornful of Herne. Perhaps they feared his peculiar visage or perhaps they merely resented the favour he carried with the king, but whether through spite or fright or a combination of both, they plotted the downfall of Herne. Rumours of ill repute concerning Herne's character were to purposively reach the ears of the sovereign. Either believing the lies or sensing the turmoil amongst his other staff, the king decided to dismiss Herne. So grieved by his master's action and so consumed by shame and despair was Herne, that from the bough of a majestic Oak standing in the royal grounds he sought to take his own life. However at the exact moment of Herne's suicide, a terrible bolt of lightning struck the tree. In his death throes Herne the Hunter was eternally changed.

Armed with a bow and a quill full of invisible yet devestating arrows that could instantly still a man's beating heart. As Herne coursed by night, the mournful blast of his hunting-horn has been said to wither foliage, kill livestock and even cause distant cows' milk to run with blood. At times he may be seen to travel on horseback accompanied by a pack of hounds and sometimes also by a screech owl. Such observations have drawn association to the Midnight Hunter and the Wild Hunt, but Herne's range of activity is generally considered to be more localised and specific.

His general appearance has also drawn comparison to that of Cernunnos (see the Horned God), but whilst there could be more abstruse links between the two figures, they are difficult to verify. It could be that the circumstances of Herne's death released some ancient primeval energy that animated the keeper's body for its own ends. It could also be possible that the misdemeanour that so mortified him into committing self-murder, involved the practice of Witchcraft or the worship of Ancestral or Animist Gods, though all is mere supposition for the mysteries of Herne's transgressions and state of being run deep. Any answer is also unlikely to be forthcoming, especially as some consider Herne the Hunter to be a Wraith, and that an encounter with him may not only herald the death of the self but possibly also mark disaster for the Royal Family and possibly also Britain as a whole.

Lham-Dearg
(Also known as ~ Ly Erg. Spectre of the Bloody Hand. Red Right Hand.)

The image of a Red Hand has a potent history in Britain and Ireland, and is generally symbolic of either bloodshed or strength. In England, the Red Hand of Stoke D'Abernon in Surrey observes the memory of a senseless murder committed upon a wager or dare. Whilst in Cranbrook, Kent - the Red Hand of Bloody Baker marks either the severed hand of a victim or the gore-encrusted gauntlets of the legendary murderer Sir Richard 'Bloody' Baker.In Ireland however, the sanguine mitt is most significant as the Red Hand of Ulster. In modern times this has been used as an emblem by Ulster Loyalist groups, but in the 14th Century it was the symbol of the Ui Neill dynasty - whose soldiers would charge into battle with the war-cry "Leamh-Dearg Abu !" ~ "The Red Hand Forever !" However the Irish tradition of the Red Hand dates back much further to the Milesian Invasion of ancient times. In one account of the invasion legend, the warrior-brothers, Eremon and Eber sons of Mil (or Miled), raced their boats to the shores of Ireland under the wager that whoever reached the coast first could claim the rule of the nation. When Eremon realised that his brother's boat would land first, in a bid not to be out-done he hacked off his own hand and threw it ahead onto the beach. Before either of the siblings could lay claim to the land however there was the matter of dealing with the existing ruling race. The inhabiting Tuatha de Danaan were defeated and driven underground (where they became the Daoine Sith or Faerie race) and the Milesians claimed the country and became the first Gael race. As to who would be king, the brothers consulted their Druid on the matter and as technically Eremon was the first to touch the land with a part of his body (albeit not attached to the rest of it), he was crowned the first High King of Ireland (Eber was however given control over a sizeable territory in consolation).

Cardiganshire in Wales also has its own potent Red Hand legend. Here, Red Hand was another name for Owen Lawgoch , a revered Ancient Briton king. It is said that this long-departed monarch lies sleeping deep beneath an isolated Hazel tree on a stretch of lonely moor-land, but should the dire need ever arise Red Hand and his formidable army would again rise to defend the land (see also Phantom Armies).

In Scotland the Supernatural connotations of the Red Hand or Lham-Dearg are likely the strongest and most strange. Here it refers to an ill-tempered Phantom that will stop men-folk in their stead and thenchallenge them to fight by cussing and shaking his red fist. It is considered better to just run away rather than indulge the fiend in rough and tumble. For although proud, sturdy men may consider this slight phantasm to look like not much of an opponent, they would likely be proven woefully wrong. Those who accepted the Lham-Dearg's challenge were thought certain to be facing death within fourteen nights. In 1669 the Lham-Dearg was said to have brawled with three brothers, all of whom were killed almost instantly. The presence of this fiend was even more dire for members of the Kinchardine family, for if any of their number were merely even to see the Lham-Dearg it was considered enough to mortally seal their fate.

Road Ghosts

Roads have always had weird connotations due to the many reported apparitions of strange Black Dogs, Shape-shifting Bogies and other weird and eerie beings. In the past, wayfarers on horseback or even on foot, may have found themselves the recipient of an uninvited Leap-Upon passengers. Even now though, in the days of the automobile when there are more roads than ever and not all of them so lonely, all may not be as it initially seems. Whilst some Phantom figures such as the Genii Cucullati seem oblivious to mechanised progress as they wander their paths of old and other mobile dead supply their own form of locomotion (see Phantom Vehicles), others still may be in need of a ride.

Of all the myriad Road Ghosts it is perhaps these Phantom Hitchhikers that attain most prominence, especially within the scope of modern or urban folklore. Tales of these entities are told across the world and often follow a similar basic pattern. It is usually said that a lone driver was travelling down a remote, quiet byway usually at night, when ahead of them they see a solitary person by the wayside, thumbing a ride. The driver stops and lets the hitchhiker into the vehicle. There may a little or no conversation as the journey progresses , but once the required destination is reached upon turning to face their passenger, the driver discovers that he or she is entirely alone in the car. No matter how much they rack their brain they cannot put themselves at ease by adequately explaining how their passenger suddenly came to vanish. Sometimes the tale ends there but it often continues. Intrigued and often disturbed by the inexplicable disappearance of their travelling companion. The driver proceeds to an address either mentioned by the mysterious passenger or as stated within an address-book, purse or other personal item they may have left in the car. Either way, upon reaching the residence the inhabitants there inform the driver that their son / daughter certainly fits the description of the hitch-hiker. Upon being shown a photograph, the driver may also confirm that the shown person was indeed their passenger. However it usually transpires that the person under discussion has already been dead for some time. Not only that but the place upon the road where they were picked up was actually the scene of the road accident in which they lost their life. Sometimes the driver is informed that they were not the first person to come to the door claiming to have given a lift to the dead person. In variants of the tale, sometimes the driver actually collides with a person who has suddenly appeared in front of their car, but when they pull over and get out to check there is no one around to be seen. Whilst stories like these pass from person to person, either as spooky 'campfire tales' or otherwise as *true* accounts of events that apparently happened to a 'friend of a friend', and accounts of Phantom Hitchhikers may fit this bill, occasionally these tales may differ from other Urban Legends in that specific dates, names and locations are sometimes given.

Various roads in Britain and Ireland have been claimed to host Phantom Hitchhikers, but perhaps the most notorious of these is Bluebell Hill near Maidstone in Kent, England. Since at least the early 1970s, a number of drivers have claimed seeing, picking up or even knocking down a strange disappearing girl. Generally described as having fair hair and being in her late teens or early twenties, her face was often said to cast a sombre expression. However not all those claiming to have witnessed the Bluebell Hill Ghost have reported seeing such a demure waif, as encounters with a vile old Hag have also been reported on the stretch. Rather than being two separate Ghosts, it has been suggested that the girl and crone are actually different aspects of the same being. Whilst Bluebell Hill is not the only English road to claim such a haunting, it is notable that places bearing an association to Bluebells often have a Supernatural reputation, for these attractive wild-flowers have long been pertinent to Fay beings. Furthermore the Girl / Crone dualism of the Bluebell Hill Ghost is reminiscent of the tales told of Shape-shifting Celtic Goddesses, whom some consider to be the original Faeries anyway. Whether they be Goddess, Fay, Ghost, Psychopath or genuine damsel in distress, there may be more to a hitchhiker than first impressions reveal.

Phantom Vehicles

Phantom Ships : In addition to the ghostly Viking Vessels seen off Iona , several other Phantom Ships have been reported off the coasts of Britain. In 19th Century Cornwall, such spectral boats were thought to be the heralds of heavy storms and were imagined to be piloted either by Dead sailors (possibly the Ghosts of Pirates and Wreckers) or by the Devil, out harvesting the souls of sailors. Such ships as these were said to travel over land as well as sea.

Two Phantom Ships said to sail off the Goodwin Sands in Kent are known by name and detail. The warship, Northumberland was destroyed as it ran aground onto rocks in a devestating storm in November 1703 ; whilst the Lady Lovibund was said to have been deliberately sunk by the ship's own first-mate in 1748 (after discovering that his wife was indulging in a love-affair with the ship's captain). Both ships are said to reappear, complete with ghastly crew, at fifty-year intervals.

On a smaller scale, a Phantom Barge has been reported floating down the Little Ouse River near Ely in Cambridgeshire. Upon it lies an open coffin containing a woman's body and surrounding this, congregating in hymn are a crew of Monks (see also Hooded Entities). The woman is believed to be Saint Withburga, who founded East Dereham Convent in 654 AD. In 974 AD however , upon the orders of the Abbot of Ely a troop of Monks exhumed and stole her body from the convent grounds. Then by navigating the river they took the dead Saint to the isle of Ely, in the hope that the Abbey there would subsequently become a Pilgrimage centre and thus bring in cash.

Phantom Planes : Phantom war-planes have been reportedly seen flying over several British counties and cities including Dyfed and London. One encountered over the Derbyshire moors was identified as being a Douglas DC3- Dakota, further research revealed that a plane of this type had indeed crashed in the vicinity in 1945. Whilst not all Ghost-Planes are observed with the eye a great number continue to appear as unaccountable 'blips' upon flight-control radar screens.

Phantom Coaches and Waggons : There are numerous roads in Britain and Ireland that are said to be haunted by horse-drawn vehicles. Amongst these, probably the most prevalent are the Spectral Carriages. These are sometimes associated to the Hell-Wain or Death-Waggon , the cart driven either by the Ankou or the Devil (depending on local tradition) but either way, used for the harvesting of souls. Otherwise the passengers, drivers or owners of such Spectral Carriages may either be anonymous or associated to local history and characters. The black Phantom Coach that sweeps across the raw Dartmoor landscape in Devon, followed by a pack of baying hounds is thought to be that of Sir Francis Drake. Whilst another strange carriage that runs from Tavistock to Okehampton (also in Devon), is thought to be the vehicle of Lady Howard who reputedly died in 1671. This rig is not thought to have been her normal mode of conveyance in life however as it is entirely constructed from human bones and is elaborately adorned upon each corner-post by a skull. These remains are thought to be those of each of her husbands, all of whom were rumoured to have been murdered by the lady herself.

A succession of Phantom Coaches are reputed to convoy down a lane that leads to the appropriately named Waggoner's Wells, three large ponds near the village of Bramshott in Hampshire. Sometimes like the Turberville Coach of Dorset, sightings of Spectral Carriages are thought to be omens of death, but more often they are thought to contain those who are already dead. These waggons are most frequently black and the horses that pull them are often monstrous. Sometimes these beasts are skeletal or rotting, sometimes they are sturdy and as black as the night whilst others may be ethereal, headless, luminous or may even breathe fire. In addition to the Phantom Coaches already mentioned they have been reported in many other areas of Britain, most notably in East Anglia, Gloucestershire, the West Country and Wales.

Other Ghostly vehicles have been reported within these isles and some of a more modern tradition. St Mark's Road in Kensington London was said to be haunted by a Spectral Double-Decker Bus. The Cockenzie to Prestopans road in East Lothian, likewise is said to be haunted by a bus. Thankfully perhaps, the next Haunted Vehicle remains stationary for it is a Tiger Tank. Housed at Bovington Camp Military Museum in Dorset, this particular war machine is said to be haunted by a Nazi Officer, affectionately nicknamed 'Herman the German'. A Phantom Gypsy Caravan and a Vanishing Car (as well as a Phantom Black Dog) have been reported by different people on separate occasions in the vicinity of the Rollright Stones, a mysterious megalithic circle in the district of Oxfordshire / Warwickshire. Dartmouth in Devon and also the A6024 road running through the bleak Holme Moss moorland are both reputed to be haunted by pristine Black Cars of a 1920s model, possibly Daimler. Other Phantom cars, vans, motorcycles and trucks have been reported on the

roads across Britain and Ireland as well as across the wider world ;
perhaps this is unsurprising, as many lives are lost annually in
terrible motor-accidents. It may be appreciated then why the roads
are haunted but the apparitions of apparently soulless machinery
may seem odd to some peoples' understanding of ghosts. Perhaps
being an integral part of the death is enough to hold their
connection to this world: or perhaps the sightings of Phantom
Vehicles (like Phantom Armies and perhaps other Ghosts) are
psychic visions of the past or mysterious re-enactments of poignant
events that have somehow been recorded upon the landscape itself
(this is known as Stone Tape theory). It is worth noting however that
the ancient Celts and Vikings would sometimes bury chariots with
their dead. This could've been intended as a symbolic tribute to
esteemed and valued charioteers, nobles or warriors or could have
been a means of appropriating lifetime property to their owners, so
that others may not claim it without right. However due to the
complex spiritual beliefs of both races the interment of vehicles
were possibly intended either for transportation to the after-life or
perhaps for further use either in this or the Other-world.

Wraiths and Omens

To encounter any of the Supernatural entities listed within this Guide is a potentially dangerous – perhaps even fatal business ; to encounter a Wraith is perhaps the most unfortunate. For whilst the term Wraith can specifically be applied to creatures of the Co-Walker variety, it is also used to generically refer to any Death Visitant – that is a Supernatural creature whose main function seems to be to inform mortals of their mortality. Therefore any experience with such a being is especially likely to be an indication of a forthcoming tragedy, if not the observer's own demise then that of a friend or family member. Some of the other Supernatural creatures covered in other sections of this Guide may be perceived in some localities or by particular individuals, to be Wraiths but that may not be the general opinion. Those covered within this specific section however are widely considered to be portents of subsequent grieving.

It is thought that some Wraiths attain their position through the specific details of their own mortal death, whilst others may have a more ancient attachment to the Supernatural realm. It has been considered that some other Wraiths, however are actually emitted by the human mind, body or spirit prior to death. If the latter theory has credence, it must be noted that it frequently would seem to be an automatic or unconscious process, for the doomed often seem entirely oblivious to their fate or fatality up until this point. Mystery and supposition surround the Wraiths (as indeed it does virtually all other Supernatural denizens), but it would be ill advised to seek out such a creature merely to satisfy curiosity.

The motley gathering of death-portents apparent in Wales, according to one theory were all initially invoked by the country's patron, Saint David (or Sant Dewi). The reason why this holy man (who was also reputed to be of Gigantic stature, exquisite beauty and to have achieved considerable longevity), would summon forth such grisly, strange and distressing signs and omens was not an act of malice however. In his opinion too many people were too wrapped up in the hedonism and material pursuits of this world to pay proper heed to their spiritual wellbeing and preparation for the Afterlife. Therefore he intended that such weird sights and sounds would act as a reminder that one day, perhaps all too soon, this existence would loosen its hold on each and every person, so due consideration should be given to whatever may follow.

Banshees and Death Sounds

(Also known as ~ Beansidhe. Bean-Si. Benshee. Fairy Woman. Woman of the Hills. Bachuntas. Badbh-Chaointes. Cointeach. Wailers. The Keener. The One Who Keens. Mna-Sige. Mna-Sidhe. Cyhiraeth. Cyraeth. Cyoerrath. Cyhyraeth. The White Lady of Sorrows. The Weeper. The Skree. Caoineag. Caointeach. Fear-Sidh. Seinn-Bais. Death Music. Tolaeth. Ghost Sounds. Bocanachs. Bowa.)

Though possibly the most infamous of all the Wraiths, mystery surrounds the Banshee and several theories are suggested regarding her true origins. It remains uncertain whether they are the Phantoms of dead human women or are actually of a Fay lineage. Indeed the word 'Banshee' is the Anglicised version of the Gaelic 'Bean-Si / Beansidhe' which loosely means 'Fairy Woman'. If she is indeed of Fay stock, she still maintains a deep and mournful interest and association to human mortality (though there have long existed theories linking the Faerie Otherworld and the human Afterlife). There are also some points of comparison that may be drawn between these harbingers of death and the Celtic Goddesses. Upon a human's death it was once considered that the Moon or Mother Goddess reabsorbed the soul into her being until the time for rebirth was ripe. Celtic myth also claimed that a hundred warriors fell dead upon the spot upon hearing the doleful shrieking of Nemain, an aspect of the Morrigan /Badb War-Goddess. It is certainly the sound of a Banshee that proclaims her presence rather than her appearance, which can vary somewhat and may not even be seen at all.

The wail of the Banshee (known as the Keening) is said to be heard either by the person whose death is imminent or by someone closely associated to them. People with a strong Celtic bloodline are considered more likely to encounter a Banshee and some old families may hold a peculiarly strong bond with one of these creatures. This is sometimes thought to indicate a distant Fay strain within their genes but others have suggested an earthier, more sinister reasons for the connection. The finger points at certain reputedly Banshee-ridden families with the accusation that one of their ancestors murdered a young lady, possibly a pregnant mistress or other similar unfortunate and so it is believed that their descendants must carry a reminder of this shame for evermore. The shadow of this sin falls at the approach of their darkest hours and may be specifically regarded as being a Hateful Banshee. To those who have not heard the Banshee's cries (and count themselves lucky for this), it is often imagined that this must be a loud, dreadful noise and sometimes it has been reported as such (usually in the cases of Hateful Banshees) but not always. Sometimes her Keening was described as being oddly melodic and strangely comforting (especially if heard by someone who was old and failing , had endured a long, discomforting illness or was of a family favoured by the Faeries). It has been suggested that some traditional Irish Funereal tunes were based upon the Banshees' lament and perhaps also there is some association between these heralds and the professional Keeners – women who were paid to outwardly grieve and sing at some vigils, burials and wakes.

The Welsh Cyraeth and the Scottish Caointeach and Caoineag (creatures very similar to Banshees though more often heard only rather than seen) do not generally predict death in such a harmonious manner. The call of the Cyraeth was said to have three distinguishable stages : beginning with distant yelps of pain, it rises to a guttural groaning before finally descending into sighing and sobbing (and sometimes a death rattle). The Cyraeth may also be associated to a particular old family but they have also been claimed to prophesise deaths on a mass scale through the outbreak of disease or disaster. When mariners out at sea heard the Cyraeth, within a few days at least one human carcass would wash ashore on the nearest Welsh sands. The cries of the Caointeach are said to extremely harrowing and its loud scream-like hollers may be heard lasting for several nights. Whether melodic or monstrous, the death calls of these Wraiths invoke a deep resonance and feeling of foreboding in their mortal beholders that earthly sounds can very rarely if ever produce. It has been said that the sound of several Banshees Keening in unison, is said to mark the passing of an especially noble or holy person.

The Welsh Tolaeth (Ghost Sounds) are always invisible and differ from the Keening species in that the sounds they make extend beyond that of the voice. Strange disembodied rattles, knocks, whistles, footsteps and rumbles like the wheels of an old cart.

Bean-Nighe
(Also known as ~ Night Women. Washer Women. Caoineag. Ban Nighechain. Nigheag-Na-H'ath. Washing Women. Little Washers by the Ford. Washers by the Banks. Washers of the Shroud. Washers of the Night. Night Washers. Cannerd Noz. Konnerez Noz.)

The Bean-Nighe are generally encountered either sitting beside or sometimes paddling in remote streams and the shallows of rivers. Here they attend to their laundry, yet they are not conventional mortal women tending bucolic washing chores. A single glance at their hideous visage and the grim cloth they wring betwixt their fingers is more than enough to determine her anomalous character. The clothing that the Bean-Nighe is seen to wash is either the blood-drenched clothing of the observer or the burial shroud that will consequently wrap their lifeless body. Like the Banshee, there is some association drawn between the activities of the Bean-Nighe and those of certain Celtic Goddesses. Badb, an aspect of the War Goddess, was said to have sat by the banks of a ford and laundered the uniforms of every soldier due to die in a subsequent battle. In another Celtic tale the Cailleach Bheur, a notorious storm hag, was said to have scrubbed the Tartan of old Scotland in a maelstrom until it gleamed white. Her actions, like those of the Bean-Nighe have been claimed to be symbolic either of grief or a grievance.

Rather than scrubbing shrouds, in Ireland it has been said that the Washers have been observed cleaning corpses in the water. A shocking sight to chance upon perhaps, yet more horrifying still would be the observer's realisation that the face of the cleansed cadaver was a mirror-image of their very own.

The Bean-Nighe is often however accredited with mortal origins, albeit those of a tragic poignancy. These creatures are said to be the souls of women who died whilst giving birth. Doomed to remain on this earth either until Judgement Day or, as it is more frequently thought, until the day that they would otherwise have died. As a grim consequence of their fate, they are also aware of all the other people that will soon be visited by death and are sometimes reported as crooning a mournful dirge to themselves that recounts the names of all the ill fated. The destiny of the Bean-Nighe may seem extremely harsh as it is not imposed by the leading of a wicked life but by a very sorrowful demise. However, as is reflected in the ancient beliefs of very varied cultures worldwide, to die whilst giving birth held a great and grave significance. The combination of birth and death, both times when gateways to other worlds would temporarily open, was thought a grim omen even though unfortunately the death either of the mother or child (sometimes both) was a more considerable and common risk in earlier times and less technologically advanced cultures. Those who died in such circumstances were frequently considered damned though through no fault of their own. The particular details of such a damnation varies globally, according to culture and location.

The doom foretold by the Bean-Nighe's wringing may however be averted if one has the specific know-how. This however involves the difficult and unsavoury task of sneaking up on the Bean-Nighe and taking suckle of one of her drooping, wrinkled breasts. If this is managed, the Washer Woman will then consider the mortal to be her foster-child and protect them from their impending fate on this instance.

Otherwise, should the observer manage to get past the Bean-Nighe and stand in the stream before they themselves are observed, then she will grant them three wishes or inform them of the details of their predestined death (the information may possibly help them avert that particular, dire situation). Such ventures were not always guaranteed to attain the required success and were not always without other risk. The Caoineag of the Scottish Western Isles is a Wraith that can assume either the habits of the Banshee or the Bean-Nighe. However, should an opportunistic human skulk into a brook in front of her as she laundered, they would certainly not be rewarded with wisdom or wishes. Instead the Caoineag would violently flick at the mortal's legs with the wet cloth, causing paralysis in those limbs. Such a predicament could theoretically and subsequently lead to drowning.

The Cannerd Noz or Konnerez Noz of Brittany are probably the most malevolent of all the Supernatural Washer Women. They may sometimes congregate in pairs or in small groups but even on their own they are still very intimidating. They will compel any human observer to assist her in wringing the garment before her. If the person then turns the cloth in the wrong direction then their arms may very well be wrenched from the sockets. A refusal to assist a Cannerd Noz with her grisly chores will likely result in the person having their body wrung like a wet rag instead.

Water Wraiths and the Gwrach-y-Rhibyn

The habits of the Water Wraiths lie somewhere between those of the Groac'h and the Bean Nighe, though they are not known to consume human flesh or concern themselves with laundry duties. They do however inhabit watery abodes and can either predict or perhaps even be the cause of human fatality. Generally the Water Wraiths will leap or rise from their conduit and silently but menacingly scowl and point at passers-by. Often this encounter alone would cause the observer to flee in terror, but they may feel that this meeting was intended to proclaim their death. The mere suggestion of which could perhaps help to hasten his or her demise. However should the onlooker become frozen in their tracks by fear and lie within the Water Wraith's grasp or even respond to her beckoning gestures, then the wretch may well bid to fulfil their own perceived prophecy. Any foolish or star-crossed soul caught within the clutches of a Water Wraith may find their death by drowning incredibly imminent.

The Gwrach-y-Rhibyn (also known as the Hag of the Dribble, Hag of the Mist and also sometimes as y Cyhiraeth – the latter term being an equivalent of Banshee) shares some characteristics with both the Water Wraiths and Banshees. Though like the Cailleach Bheur and the Muilerteach or possibly also Black Annis, the Gwrach-y-Rhibyn may be a twisted corruption of a neglected Celtic Goddess, there seems to be some indication that there may be more than one of her kind. Like some of the Irish / Scottish Banshees, the Gwrach-y-Rhibyn is said to favour the old Welsh families with her dire attention, yet others with no known blood-ties may occasionally fall foul of her presence also. Like the Scottish Water Wraiths, the Gwrach-y-Rhibyn may also suddenly leap out of a water channel, but otherwise she will invisibly stalk her victim until they pass a crossroads or stream. Here she will become all too visible and audible, for in both instances her cries like those of the Banshees and Cyraeths, are harrowing. If the person thus doomed to die (either the observer or someone close to them but not present) is a man the Gwrach-y-Rhibyn will holler "Fy ngwr! Fy ngwr!" ("My Husband! My Husband!") but if a youth is to succumb, then she will cry "Fy mlentyn! Fy mlentyn bach!" ("My child! My little child!") and so forth. The Scottish Water Wraiths seem to be a strictly female species, though occasionally in Wales tales are also told of prophetic male water-spirits. Their manner and visage usually differ somewhat however. The Water Wraiths as such, are most commonly described as being tall and ugly with matted hair and long bony fingers. Their countenance is grim and their eyes are said to glint with malice. They sometimes wear green, occasionally black hooded gowns.

Co-Walkers and Fetches
(Also known as ~ Wraiths. Waffs. Swarths. Ghosts of the Living. Mawkins. Living Pictures. Doubles. Double-Men. Doppelgangers. Echoes. Reflections. Reflex-Men. Reflexions. Copies. Autoscopies. Finis. Death Visitants. Tokens.Tasks. Lledrith. Freits. Waiths. Thrumpins.)

The concept of the Co-Walker is known by various names across Britain, Ireland and indeed the world. Known sometimes as Ghosts of the Living, their origins have been oft debated. Appearing as an exact likeness or Double of someone still living, to see one's own Co-Walker is most frequently regarded to be an omen of the arrival of death within the near future. However there often seems to be enough time remaining to at least document or inform others of the encounter. Frequently the beholder of such an unexpected sight will sadly resign themselves to their fate, but in the Northeast of England (where the spectacle was known as a Waff) it was believed that by talking harshly to the apparition may allay the approach of fatality on that occasion..

The term Fetch is sometimes used as one of the motley alternatives for Co-Walker, but it can also be used specifically to refer to a variant of the phenomenon. When the ghostly likeness of a living person is seen by someone else, usually a close friend or relative, this apparition is often referred to as a Fetch. Often the timing of the Fetch's appearance coincided near to exact with the moment that their mortal semblance ceased to live. Sometimes the Fetch will wither to the form of a small flickering flame before vanishing. Such a guise may further be known as a Fetch-Light or a Fetch-Candle and may be associated to some perceptions of the Ignis Faatus. Tales of Fetch activity are often common during sustained periods of war. These accounts frequently follow the line that whilst a woman at home anxiously pondered the wellbeing of their active soldier son or husband, the likeness of the absent loved one would suddenly appear. Sometimes these visitants would speak but sometimes they would remain silent. Either way, within too long news would arrive, alerting the woman of their beloved's subsequent death. Again the actual time of the death and of the visitation coincide very closely. A very strange example of this phenomenon describes how upon the moment of King William Rufus' death at New Forest, many miles away the Earl Of Cornwall witnessed his body being carried across Bodmin moor on the back of a black Goat.

Accounts like these compare also to the appearance of Crisis Apparitions ; here the materialising figure is generally familiar to the viewer, but is also often known to be dead already. Sometimes these apparitions may be thought to deliver comfort or to bring an end to prolonged grieving, but at other instances they may be thought to act as a warning of forthcoming trouble or disaster.

Other tales pertain to a pact, such as those attributed to Lord Brougham (1778 – 1868), Lord Chancellor of England and an unnamed associate, or to the Reverend Theodore Abis Buckley, Chaplain of Christ's College, Cambridge and his friend R.H Mackenzie in the 1850s. In both instances, following discussions on the survival of the human soul after death, a covenant was made agreeing that the first of the pair to die would send their Wraith to visit the other upon their demise. Both Brougham and Mackenzie were reported shocked by the sudden appearance of their friends respectively in their bathroom and bedroom. They both subsequently learnt that their friends had indeed died around the time of their appearances. Local legends that follow the track of the afterlife pact sometimes have the returning dead grabbing the wrist of the living person, leaving a permanent bracelet of burnt scar tissue as reminding proof of both the encounter and life after death.

Corpse Birds

The association between birds and death is both ancient and enduring, and can take varied forms. In Shamanic societies the form of a flying bird was often considered the ideal means of travelling via a trance state to the world of the Ancestral Spirits. Within the reckoning of conventional nature, birds could be said to thrive in more than one of the ancient elements (i.e. in the air as well as on earth or water). Therefore it was also conceived that they might also travel at ease across the boundaries of our world into the Faerie Domain or Otherworld. Several associations have been drawn between these supernatural realms and the land of the dead and numerous Celtic myths relate tales of Shape-shifters (human, godly or Fay) assuming varied avian forms. Within these narratives, certain individuals are reported as taking the form and feathers of birds as diverse as swans and ravens, owls and eagles. Throughout the myths of many nations, birds are thought to represent the soul and either its ascent into paradise or as a vessel of transmigration. Sometimes this sentiment is intended symbolically but often it has a literal belief. For instance, an old Cornish superstition regards choughs as sacred birds due to the belief that the soul of King Arthur alighted in this form.

Many beliefs and superstitions however regard birds as notorious harbingers of death, though they may often be considered as melancholic messengers rather than sinister agents. Crows and Ravens, especially when seen in great numbers, were often thought to be an omen of disaster and war. This belief is perhaps associated with the tales of the Celtic War-Goddess, the Morrigan (especially in the aspect of Badb) taking the appearance of these dark birds. Conversely it is believed that should the ravens ever leave the Tower of London, then disaster will befall Britain.

In ancient times on the night of Samhain, when summer paved way for winter and the dead wandered the earth, it was said that 3-headed vultures and other strange birds with feathers the colour of fresh blood, would flock above the Mound of Cruachan in Connacht, Ireland.

For any wild bird (i.e. not a caged pet or domestic fowl) to enter a house or to tap against the glass of a window is often considered bad luck. In some areas it signifies nothing less than the approach of death. To take feathers into a home often has mixed meaning, especially concerning the tail feathers of a peacock. Whilst some people believe that they will invite the Evil Eye or death into the dwelling, others believe the opposite in that these feathers will ward off negative influences.

Owls are often considered to be especially ominous birds. To observe one flying through the day or to hear one screech suddenly may be taken to indicate that death is at hand. Despite their striking and unusual beauty, traditionally the reputation of owls is often rather sinister. Due to their nocturnal habits and individual appearance it is claimed that other birds will repeatedly mob and harass owls, therefore for company they will ally themselves to the supernatural creatures of the night. The form of owls was thought to be favoured by Shape-shifting Night-hags, nocturnal Witches and their ilk. Indeed in parts of Scotland the Owl was known as Cailleach Oidhche (Hag of the Night) or Cailleach Oidhche Gheal (Hag of the Night Moon) - names which in themselves associate these birds to dark and magical forces.

The Derwyn Corff (or Corph) or Corpse Bird is especially dreaded by the Welsh, who tend to regard it as a Supernatural rather than conventional species. This is due to its reputed habit of perching itself on the sill of a room where a sick person lies within or where a death will soon otherwise occur and tapping on the window with its beak. If the Corpse Bird specifically resembled an Owl or called at night, here it was known as Adern y Corff. On some occasions though the Corpse Bird has been described as having neither feathers nor wings. In Herefordshire it is the Robin who performs the duties of the Derwyn Corff. In some areas of Britain it was also considered very unlucky to kill or capture Robins due to the tenet that whenever a human died or was murdered in the woods, these birds would attempt to bury the body.

The Caladrius was a bird that caught the attention of Medieval Bestiary compilers, not because it was aggressive, for it was a notably gentle creature, but because its presence could determine whether an ill person would live or die. Similar in form to a raven though much larger (approximate height 1 – 2 ft (0.3 – 0.6 m), approximate wingspan 4 – 7 ft (1.2 – 2.1 m)), the Caladrius bore a plumage of the most brilliant white feathers. As it gazed down upon the ailing individual the turn of its head would mark a turn of events. If the Caladrius turned its head to the side then the person would surely die, yet if it kept its head fixed to the front then recovery from the affliction could be expected. For as the bird maintained eye contact, it absorbed the malady into itself. When the strange osmosis was complete, rather than die, the disease-ridden bird would soar high into the sky. Every molecule of sickness that entered the body of the Caladrius would then be dispersed and destroyed by the healing rays of the sun leaving the bird completely unharmed.

White Birds in particular have been thought to inform certain English families of an impending death in the lineage. These bearers of bad tidings may be expected to visit successive generations at their time of reckoning and reports of their calling continued into the 20th Century. The Pearce family of Cranbrook, Kent, the Oxenham family of South Zeal and Tawton, Devon and the line of the Bishops of Salisbury were all said to have subsequent fatalities heralded by the appearance of strange white birds. One may assume that any living descendants or the current holder of that particular religious post avert their gaze from the skies whenever possible. In appearance these pale omens are often comparable to the Caladrius, but unlike the medieval accounts these feathered wraiths merely alert but never cure.

The Tamhusg of Skye and the Highlands' T-eun Bais were also strange white birds that were said to screech violently as death approached members of old Scottish families. In the Outer Hebrides if a Cockerel was felt to have cold legs then this too was often regarded as an omen of human demise. The Curlew also had a grim reputation in Scotland, known colloquially as a Whaup, this bird was said to carry off the souls of wicked folk come nightfall.

Chagrin
(Also known as ~ Cogrino. Harginn.)
This bizarre wraith that appeared in a form not unlike a hedgehog, was
once well known to the Travelling People of Romany descent.
Often silent and brooding, the Chagrin was believed able to speak
in human tongues if it so wished but merely to see the creature
was unfortunate enough never mind conversing with it. The origins
of the Chagrin are either unknown or considered best not to
mention, though it is generally considered evil rather than merely
being a harbinger of sorrow. Its appearance was often feared above
that of any other Death Visitant, for it may not mark an isolated
fatality but could instead predict a disaster set to befall the convoy
in its entirety. On the Scottish Borderlands, the sudden appearance
of a strange Hedgehog was also considered a sign than a member
of the Herries' family was soon to die.

Wanderers

For many people the prospect of dying is possibly the greatest mystery and fear that they can grasp. Yet it has been claimed that there are others for whom death is a mystery or even a luxury that is not available to them. Such an individual became known as the Wandering Jew. Various other names have been attributed to this enigmatic figure however, including Cartaphilus, Ahasturus, Salanthiel-ben-Sadi, Joseph the Repentant, Isaac Lakedion and John Buttadeus. Even greater still are the number of lands across the world that he has reputedly visited, though it is postulated that his true origins lie a long time past in the Holy Land. Whatever his true name or profession (he has alternatively been claimed to have been a cobbler, a rabbi or Pontius Pilate's gatekeeper – Pilate was the Roman governor of Jerusalem at the time of Christ), his prolonged destiny is said to have been as a result of his lack of compassion and spiteful tongue. As Jesus Christ struggled to Calvary bearing the weight of the cross, it is said that a man jeered in his face telling him to make haste. To this Jesus replied , "I am going, but you will tarry until I come again". This man was thus ordained by Jesus Christ himself, to become the Wandering Jew and from that moment nearly two thousand years ago he was doomed to trek the earth until Judgement Day. Or so goes the basis of a tale that was popular across Medieval Europe , but the tales were far from over. Numerous people reported having come into contact with the Wandering Jew and some of these witnesses were figures of respect not known for their gullibility, mischief making or sense of sensationalism. Some claimed that he was already aged at the time his penance was issued and so he remained in this decrepit state, never degrading never improving. Others held that at the end of each hundred-year period, the Wandering Jew would enter a state of trance and upon awakening, would find himself again at the age of about thirty years. Some accounts stated that the Wandering Jew felt genuine remorse at his foolish and heartless sneering, and had as a result finally embraced Christianity. Otherwise it has been considered that in his stubbornness the Wandering Jew has refused to find any fault in his own actions and considers his punishment to be unjust and excessive. Thus it was thought that with each passing century, he grew more bitter and miserable. The accounts of the Wandering Jew's history and temperament are as diverse as the lands he is thought to have roamed through. In Britain he is recorded to have at least visited St. Albans in 1288, Ipstones in Staffordshire around 1650 and Stamford, Lincolnshire in 1658. At the latter it is claimed that people would seek his aid in the brewing of herbal remedies, an art that he apparently excelled in. There were other alleged appearances of the Wandering Jew in Britain in the 18th and 19th Centuries, though by this time anyone claiming this identity was regarded with scorn, scepticism and suspicion, likely being branded as charlatans or madmen. Remembrance of the ancient Semite's infinite meandering is captured by the flower *Saxifrage tricolour*, whose common name is 'Wandering Jew'.

Another evidently eternal Wanderer is the Count St. Germain (or the Comte de Saint Germain). However his strategy of playing the game of life without death, differs considerably to that of the Wandering Jew. Possibly because it is oft suspected that the Count attained his longevity through choice and not as a result of an imprecation. Accounts of actual encounters with the Count St. Germain date back to around 1740, yet he himself claimed to have been present at the wedding feast in Cana where Jesus Christ was said to have turned water into wine. Such claims obviously were nigh impossible to prove but St. Germain was reputed to have a habit of expressing accurate details about other peoples' youth (or even that of their parents). This was generally information that should really not have been known to him. His knowledge would also seem to betray his age, for superficially the Count appeared to be relatively young. Many of course suspected that the man who called himself the Count St. Germain was nothing more than a conniving confidence-trickster or possibly even a hypnotist. There were however those that embraced all of the Count's claims without the merest glimmer of doubt. As a number of the faithful were affluent ladies, this could be of great advantage to the Count. An alluring sense of mystique surrounded St. Germain but pondering upon the origins of his apparent immortality could stir a sense of unease. Some proposed that Count St. Germain had studied as an Alchemist and had succeeded in discovering an elixir of life. If this was so, then it seems that this was a secret that he was unwilling to share, for Count St Germain, for all his boasts and bravado remained extremely guarded on some issues. Others feared that St. Germain was actually some kind of Demon or Sorcerer, or that he had made a pact with the Devil. Upon the mention of such hellish forces, it was said that St. Germain would appear to be gravely disturbed. Whether this was genuine terror or another piece of mind-play is a matter of speculation.

Whatever the truth surrounding Count St. Germain actually is, in the 18th Century in particular he revelled in his notoriety and apparent immortality. Like the Wandering Jew, Count St. Germain was reputed

357

to have visited numerous European countries (though his own nationality was uncertain). Britain was also amongst his points of call, notably so in 1745 as he was arrested in London on suspicion of being a Jacobite spy. He wasn't prosecuted and left the land. However upon his return in the 1760's he had managed to stir up trouble in France, following accusations that he was unofficially negotiating with the English concerning the Hundred Years War. Indeed it seems that St. Germain acted as a diplomat in various nations, elected or otherwise, and often using odd pseudonyms such as_General Welldone and Prince Rakoczy. His detractors however would_accuse him of using his alleged esoteric knowledge to mint his own coinage. Certainly he was accredited with amassing a considerable fortune, the source of which was questionable. The Count often seemed to court controversy on his travels and gathered both friends and foes intent either to acclaim him or shame him. However on February 27th 1784, the Count's allusions to immortality floundered and the only travels left available to him would be beyond the grave. A gravestone marked his passing, though rumours persisted that it wasn't the body of the Count St. Germain that lay beneath and reports of international encounters with him alive and well continued until at least 1820.

There are varied reasons why the seemingly undying would persist in the continual roaming of the earth. Travel in itself can be an interesting and entertaining pastime and an eternity is a lot of time to fill. To remain in one place for centuries could possibly prove boring, even in a region of regular flux and change but there were other more important reasons for not setting down roots in a particular area for too long. After centuries of life, perpetual drifters such as the Wandering Jew and Count St. Germain would certainly be familiar with death though not actually tasting it for themselves. Familiarity however does not necessarily mean that it would be any less painful to watch those around you grow old and die whilst you yourself have remained unaltered for aeons. Perhaps better then not to settle and grow attached to people, but instead to keep on moving. Whilst the Wandering Jew may have maintained an aloof, brooding nature, the Count St. Germain seems to have intermingled and enjoyed himself more but still kept mobile nonetheless. Another reason for being nomadic would be concerns over personal safety. Though reputedly unable to die, there is nothing to suggest that these wanderers were immune from bodily pain. The risk of potential attacks would be considerable if people recognised that an individual member of the community remained unaltered as ageing and death claimed successive generations around them. The prospect of such a figure would likely inspire suspicion, speculation

and fear which in Medieval times could provoke a dramatic response from the fervent and paranoid Witch-Hunting authorities or incite mob violence in any age. Not realising that in many ways it could be a curse rather than a blessing, some people could otherwise be jealous of another's apparent immortality. This in turn could result in acts of spite and aggression and therefore another good reason to keep moving would be to avoid the possibility of such confrontation.

Though encounters with both the Wandering Jew and the Count St. Germain have not been reported for some time, that does not necessarily indicate that their roaming days are over and that they have finally laid down to rest. As the lore surrounding them subsided, they could have assumed numerous identities to shield their true history and thus continued their roving. Modern transportation and technology can offer access to the more far-flung corners of the world quicker and easier than ever before (though why rush a journey when time is no issue?) Also, sometimes sadly, the most populated modern cities can offer the leanest social contact and therefore more scope to hide out awhile if so desired. If they ever existed as such, then these two named wanderers may still travel the world, as may have other eternal drifters who possibly achieved anonymity rather than notoriety.

UFOs and Aliens
(UFOs also known as ~ Unidentified Flying Objects. Flying Saucers.
Aliens also known as ~ Spacemen. Little Green Men [L.G.M.s]. Extraterrestrial Biological Entities [E.T.s or E.B.E.s].
Types include Nordics and Greys.)

UFOs are possibly the most significant *paranormal* enigma of the current age. This is because they continue to be reported on a fairly regular basis and seem to a phenomena still in a state of evolution or development. In this often technologically minded age, to some people, UFOs may also suggest a glimpse of the future rather than a remnant of the past. 'UFO' is an acronym of 'Unidentified Flying Objects' and refers to aerial anomalies most commonly seen but sometimes also caught on film or recorded on radar screens. Many UFOs remain unidentified simply because they are not reported to the correct authorities or if they are, are not given sufficient investigation. Many of those that have been given ample study have produced an explanation (therefore becoming known as IFOs - Identified Flying Objects). Frequently they are accounted for as being a misidentification of a conventional event or object, perhaps seen from an unusual perspective or under particular conditions. These have been said to include conventional aircraft, stars, planets, flares, fireworks, car headlights, flocks of birds, weather balloons and even floaters (eye-debris). Sometimes the witnesses accept the given explanation, sometimes they do not. Though the vast majority of reported UFOs may instead offer a more mundane explanation, there remains a percentage that do not offer a ready conclusion. These aberrations remain unidentified and as such unexplained and are considered by some to be craft carrying visitors from other planets or possibly other dimensions.

Observed UFOs generally prescribe to two main types, either strange lights or solid-looking objects. The lights may manifest in varied sizes and colours, sometimes in isolation or otherwise in formations consisting of several numbers. Those appearing in quantity may appear independent of each other or else they may appear in a rigid formation, perhaps suggestive of aircraft guiding lights. Frequently they are seen to move erratically or at seemingly impossible speed. The British Dragon Project is an organisation that has devoted time and study particularly to anomalous lights. They suggest that much of this curious luminous activity may be attributable to Earthlights. Earthlights are thought to be the by-product of the earth's own geophysical and tectonic activity. Laboratory experiments have supported their findings as certain types or particular combinations of rock have been found to discharge unusual light emissions when put under certain pressure.

Such conditions may be comparable to natural occurrences such as plate movement and earthquakes, yet the specifics of the visual firing are not as yet fully understood. It has however been suggested that this activity may operate at wavelengths that could invoke hallucination in humans and interference in electronics and machinery. Disorientation and vehicle / appliance failure have been reported as part of many UFO encounters. Earthlights have often notably been associated with the sites of Standing Stones, Megalithic structures and venerated natural land formations, both of which have many roots spreading through the folklore and myth of these lands. Low-level Earthlights could also be suggestive of some Ignis Faatus encounters. Some have questioned whether Earthlights are in any way connected to the creation of Crop Circles and other cereal crop formations. These large and often strikingly beautiful configurations of flattened and bent cereal stalks have been reported in fields on occasion for centuries. The earlier examples were simply circular in design and some people considered them to be evidence that the Devil had been mowing. Crop Formations came to prominence and significantly increased in both number and complexity of design, mainly in southern England in the late 20th/ early 21st Centuries. Theories abounded around them, some suggesting that they were the work of either inter-planetary UFOs or Earthlights. Others questioned whether they were formed as a result of freak windstorms or electromagnetic activity. Others of a more New-Age persuasion claimed that they were a direct message from the Mother Goddess instructing us to stop abusing the planet. The sentiment of this is worthy in itself, but it may be argued that would such an important message be delivered in so cryptic a manner? It is now known however that many Crop Formations were actually created by clandestine human craftsmen. Though the work of these situationalist land-artists is technically illegal and prosecution is possible should they confess or get caught in action, few have been charged. Many of the farmers whose land was thus graced with a design did not seem to mind so much as they could make up any losses and possibly even turn a profit by charging a fee to curious spectators. Some Cerealologists (as Crop Formation researchers are known) may feel cheated when a design they have investigated turns out to be the creation of Doug 'n' Dave or some other Circle-maker. There exists a rather odd notion that formations created by humans are not genuine. If they exist they are genuine - regardless of their origin, for Crop Formations do not come supplied with a list of rules. Even if all Crop Formations turn out to have been created by people, that is no reason to consider them a disappointment . It does not detract from their scope, beauty and the great skill and speed needed for their construction.

The solid-looking UFOs (which may or may not be seen in association with strange lights) often bear a greater credence to the Extraterrestrial Hypothesis or the Nuts 'n' Bolts Theory. This is the suggestion that UFOs are constructed flying craft usually considered to have originated from worlds other than our own or otherwise experimental and top-secret military craft built to an extraterrestrial design. Proponents of the latter view have claimed that the constructing authorities (usually claimed to be the USA) gained the technological know-how either from the alleged retrieval of crashed alien spacecraft or through deals drawn up between earth authorities and other interplanetary cultures. The UFO and Alien phenomenon has given rise to several such Conspiracy Theories which tend to concern the world governments lying, covering up information and confusing the issue further through programmes of disinformation (deliberately putting out false information to undermine a mode of thought or to conceal another issue).

The exact planetary or even dimensional origin of these purported craft is another oft-debated topic. The early claims that they came from Mars and Venus or from another planet within our solar system, have since been opposed by scientists and astronomers who state that apart from earth, no other body orbiting our sun is capable of sustaining advanced life. Some argue the point but others instead have turned their eyes towards other stars, constellations and perhaps even other galaxies. Because these points are so distant from our earth, often distances so vast that it takes many, many years for even light to cross, some people feel that it would be impossible for spacecraft and living entities to endure such journeys. Others may argue that the ways and means are not impossible but merely beyond mankind's current knowledge and ability. These *Nuts 'n' Bolts* UFOs seemingly come in all shapes and sizes, but the term 'Flying Saucer' (first used in reference to an American Sighting in 1947), has survived as a frequently used colloquial alternative, regardless of actual shape reported.

A major factor pertaining to the Extraterrestrial Hypothesis are the numerous reported sightings of, or encounters with the occupants of such craft. The visual appearance of the Extraterrestrial astronauts (or Aliens as they are more generally known) can vary incredibly. Some types are more frequently reported than others are however. The term 'Little Green Men', though once commonly used, generally belongs more to the realm of early science-fiction tales. Though green-skinned Aliens have been reported, they tend to be a minority.

Reports of human encounters with Alien species have seen some quite dramatic changes since the 1950s and 60s when such experiences first began to gain greater attention. Even in these seemingly early days, a strange variety of Alien creatures were apparently witnessed in destinations across the world. Most prevalent amongst these at the time were the sort often referred to since as the 'Nordic' type. These beings are so-called, because of a superficial resemblance to people of Scandinavian descent, yet they bear little likeness to the stereotypical burly Viking types of yore. Indeed the general profile of the Nordics as being tall and slim with long angular features, almond-shaped blue eyes and long straight blonde hair bear some similarity to descriptions of the Light Elves of Norse myth. The Nordics most frequently gave the impression of being a calm, benevolent race brimming with wisdom and compassion. Because of their apparent concerns about mankind's spiritual and physical wellbeing, especially in light of its growing interest in nuclear technology, the Nordics drew comparisons with Angels. Indeed fringe religions began to spring up around them and they were given more respectful names such as the Guardians, the Sky People, the Space Brothers or the Cosmic Brotherhood. One such sect known as the Aetherius Society was founded in Britain in 1954. Its earthly co-ordinator was a man named George King, though he adopted many complimentary titles such as Knight Commander and Metropolitan Archbishop.

By the later decades of the 20th Century, another Alien race however had poached virtually all of the Nordic's limelight and encounters with these beings could hardly have been any more different. These creatures were the Greys, a race of pasty coloured, large-headed, bald dwarves with spindle limbs. Frequently their eyes though have gained particular attention, for often they are described as being liquid black and extremely large. Not all of the given descriptions of Greys coincide exactly but many similar features have been reported from seemingly unconnected encounters across the globe, but especially in the Americas. Some people who have claimed experience of the Greys have considered them to be rather insect-like both in form and behaviour, for many seem to be responding to a swarm mentality or hive-mind rather than independent action. This has provoked further speculation that the Greys may possibly be in the command or servitude of another authority. The coming of the Greys however sparked a major development in Ufology, for as humans who'd previously claimed to have had direct contact with Aliens often became known as Contactees due to the reverent dimension of such meetings, many now became known as Abductees. Claims started to abound and increase that Aliens were now seizing humans, even from their own beds at night. The accounts follow that the human is taken aboard the Alien craft (often by levitation but sometimes by physical force) and made to endure an often-intimate biological examination, before being returned to their homes. Some descriptions of other Alien Abductions relate a longer duration and even stranger turn of events. Sometimes these experiences are remembered instantly but on other occasions it has been stated that perhaps even years may pass before memories of the event are again recollected.

Comparisons have been drawn between the actions of the Alien Greys and those of the Faeries and also other supernatural breeds such as Nightmares. Enough differences between tales of these species occur also for them not to be generally considered as being exactly the same thing. However, researchers who have looked for possible causes of supernatural encounters other than them being actual events, have suggested that similar triggers may account for all such experiences. Whether these be mental, medical or externally provoked is a matter of debate but the proponents of such theories would have that Aliens are a modern interpretation of the same archetypes that once gave rise to tales of Fays and Nightmares. Apart from the bedroom, Aliens have also reputedly abducted humans in remote outdoor locations. This sometimes occurred as a result of the person or persons chancing upon Aliens or a grounded UFO, rather like those in past times who were reputedly held captive in the Otherworld after stumbling across Fairy Rings (see Merry Dancers). At other times it seemed that the Aliens deliberately instigated the chain of events by pursuing cars and causing them to break down, before taking the human occupants aboard their craft. The concept of Missing Time – i.e. the sensation that time cannot be accounted for or instead seems to have passed at an erratic rate (either slower or faster than perceived), is a notion common to both Sidhe and Spaceship.

On occasion Aliens have also displayed a Fay-like mischief and curiosity towards cattle. During the Welsh UFO Wave of the late 1970s, one farmer was shocked and annoyed by the sudden disappearance of his herd of cows and their subsequent reappearance in a different location. Similar events happened several times and always in concurrence with a flux of UFO sightings. However Alien interest in animals sometimes seems to go beyond the merely annoying and inquisitive. Episodes of strange Animal Mutilation have increased in recent times and have often been associated to the sighting of UFOs or other mysterious aircraft. The wounds found on the carcasses of mainly cattle but also sheep, goats and horses are frequently recorded as being surgically precise and appear as if produced by sophisticated tools rather than a predator's jaws. Though various other theories have been proposed regarding Animal Mutilation, UFO exponents have suggested that Aliens may well be responsible, either in their collection of scientific research data or even for food. Animal Mutilations of this type have been reported in these isles, on Dartmoor in Devon and in the Scottish glens.

Angels

According to the tradition of the Biblical Old Testament, prior to the creation of man, God (also known as Allah, Yahweh, Jah, Jehovah etc.) created the race of Angels. These beings were not created from earth or bone like man and woman, but instead from light and fire (and also in Islamic doctrine, from the lustre of precious stones). Following the genesis of man, war broke out in Heaven that pitted Angel against Angel. Pride and /or jealousy are the emotions cited for sparking the rebellion led by the renegade Angel Lucifer / Eblis (see the Devil). Whatever their motivation, the subversive element were defeated in battle and driven out of Paradise by the Angels who had remained loyal to God (see also Demons). The faithful soldiers were led in conflict by the Archangel Michael. The name 'Angel' itself derives from the Greek 'Angelos' meaning 'Messenger'. Acting as intermediaries between God and mankind is an important duty of Angels, but not their only function. In Christian tradition there are nine orders (known as Hosts or Choirs) of Angel which are further arranged into three triads. These are, as follows -
- The First Circle comprised of Seraphim, Cherubim and Thrones.
- The Second Circle comprised of Dominions, Virtues and Powers.
- The Third Circle comprised of Principalities, Archangels and Angels.
The Archangels are the order most commonly known by their individual names. The Christians name these as Michael, Gabriel, Raphael, Uriel, Chamuel, Zadkiel and Jophiel. (Though as these are listed in the apocryphal Book of Enoch, a text removed from the official Bible, the Vatican issued a report in 2002 that only the veneration of Michael, Raphael and Gabriel is permissible. The Muslims also recognise Michael and Gabriel (whom they call Jibreel) but also two others, Azrael (the Angel of Death) and Israfel (the Angel of Music). Students of the Hebrew esoteric system known as the Kabalah (or Q'balah or Cabala), also recognise Metratron the sharer of secrets, as being an Archangel. Of this Choir, Gabriel is important both to Christianity and Islam. He is acclaimed as the angelic messenger that announced to the Virgin Mary that she was to be the mother of Christ and also prepared Muhammad for his role as the scribe of God. Michael is also highly respected as the Prince of all Angels and Commander of the Celestial Army. He is also remembered as being a slayer of Dragons, which holds him in good stead in England (alongside its Patron Saint George, another celebrated Dragon-slayer). In Cornwall alone St. Michael's Mount and St. Michael's Chair are two notable landmarks dedicated to the Archangel.
Amongst the most eminent of the Seraphim (singular – Seraph) are the

Angel of the Apocalypse, Abdiel and Azazel. The Muslims consider Azazel and Eblis (or Iblis) to be one and the same, i.e. none other than the Devil. The Christian view holds that Azazel was the standard-bearer of the rebel forces, but probably a separate figure to Lucifer / Satan, who was himself a Fallen Seraph. The Seraphim that stayed loyal to God were put in charge of guarding the Heavenly Throne. In 'Paradise Lost' , the epic poem of 1667, the writer Milton lists the names of numerous other Angels. Angels are reputed to have remained active in their visitations to this world throughout history and into modern times (though perhaps not as frequently as Demons). Some Saints such as Cuthbert (c. 634 - 687) were said to have regularly communed with Angels, yet British and Irish lay-folk have also at times claimed contact with the Heavenly Hosts also. This most often occurs through the concept of Guardian Angels (also known as Daimonions or Daemons). Many people believe that they have been personally allocated a Supernatural Guardian at birth, which will continue to look over them and protect them throughout their life, until the day that death is due. Depending upon the person's own culture, creed or personal belief system they may see such a being as a Spirit Guide or Protector Spirit (also known as a Psychopompos). Some may feel that their Guardian is a loved one who has passed away or possibly the spirit of a distant Ancestor. For others the Spirit Guide may resemble an animal or have a more unfamiliar guise. Some consider the Guardian Angel to actually be a part of the individual's own spiritual make-up. To others though the Guardian is an Angel in both form and manner.

Angels have also on occasion also acted as portents of death. The Archangel Michael reputedly informed the Anglo-Saxon Saint Wilfrid of the time of his demise. Whilst in 1708, following a three-day long trance, a Norfolk teenager by the name of Sarah Barker related how an Angel had told her of both her approaching death and also of events that would pass in France and England before the end of the year.

Occasionally after enduring severe injury, after surgery or during a long, taxing illness sightings of an Angel or Angels may occur. Sometimes this may be attributed as a side effect of the administration of anodyne medication or as a consequence of the body's own pain-killing mechanism. Whether they be illusion or actual apparition, the appearance of Angels in such a situation may inspire hope, calm and a sense of well being. This in turn could either aid recovery or if the predicament was already too serious, then perhaps make for a more peaceful death. There have also been accounts of Angels actually saving lives. On these occasions they may be either seen visually or a pair of invisible hands may suddenly push a person out of the path of potential danger. It has sometimes been stated that when visually perceived, Angels fulfil the traditional Christian / Judaic/ Islamic image, regardless of the observer's own religion, nationality or preconceptions.

The Christian Church remains cautious about alleged encounters with Angels, as they do with all miraculous claims. Concerning reported observations of Angels and also of the Blessed Virgin Mary (known as B.V.M.s to researchers), Jesus Christ and other Saints, the ecclesiastic authorities first need to ascertain whether the claims are completely fraudulent. If this does not seem to be the case or cannot be readily proved, then they need to determine whether the encounter was actual or visionary. If perceived to be actual, then they would need to check whether there were any other witnesses or any other tangible evidence left behind. If the experience were otherwise considered to be visionary, then the possible source of the image would need to be questioned. It would need to be ascertained whether the vision was influenced by the use of alcohol or drugs, sleep deprivation, a medical or mental condition or from any other discernible source. That done, the Church would deliberate on whether the vision was actually divine and if it appeared to be so, then what its true significance was. This would be especially relevant if the Angel or other Religious Apparition recounted any verbal message.

Even if they conceded that a Supernatural encounter had indeed occurred, they would also need to establish that the entity witnessed was actually an envoy of God. As the Devil is also known as the Father of All Lies, it would be considered conceivable that he or one of his minion Demons would adopt the guise of a holy figure in order to further their own wicked ends. By doing this they could set up a *Honey-trap*, for as honey is said to catch more flies than vinegar, so too may sweetness lure more to sin. For instance the *Angels* that purportedly appeared to the occultists John Dee and Edward Kelly in the 16th Century apparently recommended that the men indulge in a bout of wife-swapping. Therefore the Church would also be cautious of Devils appearing in Angels' clothing as it were. Though the religious authorities may dismiss some uncanny encounters and experiences rather quickly, the decision to venerate others may take decades or even centuries.

368

Demons
(Also known as ~ Devils. Daemons. Tartaruchi. Boh. Orcs.
Lilim.
Includes Fallen Angels. Familiars. Imps. Walk-ins. Inner
Demons.)

The word 'Demon' has its linguistic root in the Greek 'Daiminion'
meaning 'Inner Voice' and in 'Daimon' or Daemon, which referred to
the spirit or soul, or rather to individual parts of a communal world
soul. Some Greek philosophers such as Plato maintained that each
living human possessed such an essence within their being. The Greek
Daemons could also act as protectors and advisers to living people, in a
similar concept to that of Guardian Angels and Spirit-Guides. This is
the concept of the Soul as familiar to many religions, however
regarding the terminology of Daimon and Demon, this is most
significant regarding the concept of Inner or Personal Demons . Before
we examine this notion in further detail, we must first look at the
bigger picture.
With the advent of Christianity the word 'Demon' came to refer
specifically to Evil Spirits, which initially could refer to a vast array of
Supernatural entities including Ghosts and Fays. The word was later
applied specifically to the denizens and servants of Hell. First amongst
their number were the rebel Angels that allied themselves to Lucifer in
the War in Heaven (see also the Devil). Following their defeat in battle
by the loyal Angels, the rebels were driven out of Heaven and thus
began their fall from grace. The worst amongst them fell directly into
the depths of Hell (though were not necessarily trapped there), whilst
others of a lesser malevolence were thought instead to have fallen to
the lands and seas of this world. Though localised folk beliefs ,
encouraged by the Church, held that those that fell to earth included
the Faeries, Mer-folk and their ilk, these creatures tend to be of
ambiguous and unpredictable morals rather than being wholly wicked.
Other Supernatural beings said to wander this world, however could
certainly be accused of being entirely evil and perhaps even be
classified as being Demons. These earth-bound Demons could be either
visible or invisible and display varying degrees of threat towards
mankind. The early Christian Church (amongst other major faiths) also
maintained that the Gods and Goddesses of the Pagan pantheons and
other religions were associated with the Devil and were therefore also
demonised. In addition it was also thought that new Demons could be
created. In Judaic lore, it is said that Eve was preceded as both the
first woman and the first wife of Adam by an enigmatic figure named
Lilith. When Lilith separated from Adam and abandoned the Garden of
Eden, it was claimed that she took refuge in a cave alongside earth-

bound Fallen Angels / Demons and here she gave birth to their children. Not only this but as a powerful Succubus, she would later visit her ex-husband Adam (after Eve and himself were also expelled from Eden) and also other subsequent sons of men and also become impregnated by them. All of her babies (those fathered by Adam were known as the Shedim and the rest were known as the Lilim or Lilin or Liliot) were Demonic and it was claimed that every day she would give birth to hundreds more of these foul progeny. Although three Angels were employed to slaughter her foul progeny, by sheer number many prospered and many were themselves believed able to procreate. In order to ensure further flourishing of her offspring, Lilith was reputed also to murder human infants as they laid in their crib. Like Baal, Moloch, Beelzebub and various other named high-ranking Demons, Lilith may have been previously been worshipped or feared as an Old Religion deity or spirit. Certainly there are strong similarities between her and the Assyrian Lilitu, the Babylonian Ardat-Lili, the ancient Hebrew Laylah, the Greco-Egyptian Echidna and the Greco-Roman Lamia. All of these exhibit both horrific and seductive attributes and are often associated with the night and also sometimes also with storms.

With the exception of Lilith and other eminent Evil spirits said to be constantly active and present in this world, most of the high-ranking Demons are believed mainly to reside in the Hell-realms. Here they attend to their own duties concerned with specific forms of sin and certain sorts of sinner. For instance Asmodeus is ranked as the Lord of Lust, Haborym - the Lord of Arson, Mammon – the Lord of Financial Corruption & Avarice and Aeshma Deva is said to be the Lord of Crimes of Rage. Other notable Demons include Belphegor the slothful, Ashtaroth the Knower of Secrets, Leviathan the Dragon of Envy and Baphomet the Goat of the Witches' Sabbat. It was accusations of holding impious ceremonies in honour of Baphomet that led to the 14th Century Vatican suppressing the Order of the Knights Templar (a troop of warrior monks of French origin that protected Christian pilgrims in Jerusalem), torturing and executing their leader, Jaques de Molay and confiscating their riches. It has oft been claimed that Secret Societies such as the Rosicrucians and Freemasons, which are active in Britain, Ireland and other nations, are strongly influenced by the concept of the Knights Templar.

Though their influence is seemingly ever present, Demons such as these were believed able to visit our world *in person* if deployed by the Devil on a specific mission or if invoked by Sorcerers. Invocation ceremonies could be extremely complex and also very dangerous should some factor be overlooked or performed incorrectly. The Sorcerers would refer conscientiously to spell-books known as Grimoires. The medieval Grimoires would detail and list Demons as well as outlining methods of summoning them. The notion that Sorcerers are Devil-Worshippers can be something of a misnomer, for many sought to invoke Demons, not to homage them but instead to gain power over them and use them to further their own self-seeking ambitions. British and Irish Magicians who have been reputed to have called forth Demons, include Alexander Stewart (the 14th Century 'Wolf of Badenoch'), Gerald Fitzgerald (the 16th Century Earl of Desmond, Co. Limerick) and the 19th / 20th Century Occultist, Aleister Crowley . Amongst the *Demons* Crowley sought to invoke were the ancient Egyptian deity - Thoth (the Ibis / occasionally baboon –headed God of the Moon and Communication) and the Greco-Roman Pan (one of the ancient nature / fertility spirits or Horned Gods). To draw the attentions of Demons is dangerous as some of the many rumours surrounding Crowley testify. One such tale claims that whilst living at Boleskine House on the shores of Loch Ness, during his intense arcane studies Crowley wrote the names of two Demons on the nearest scrap of paper to hand, which happened to be a receipt from a local butcher's shop. Within too long of this inadvertent scribbling it is claimed that the butcher slipped whilst carving a joint of meat and fatally severed one of his own major arteries.

Of the earth-bound lesser Demons, there were some that generally assumed the form of animals (see Familiars and Church-Grims). This appearance may have been their usual form or one that they themselves had created, but these physical vessels may actually be conventional animals by origin. Nomadic Demons, often lacking their own form and sometimes known as Walk-ins would roam in search of a material body to enter, infest and control. This hijacking of body and frequently mind is known as Spirit or Demonic Possession. Animals however are not alone at risk from Possession, for some Demons or Evil Spirits may instead choose to enter and animate corpses or more frequently living human beings. The process of Possession of a live person may occur in various ways. Practitioners of certain faiths such as Voodoo and Shamanism may invite certain spirits, generally of a non-malevolent character to temporarily possess them in order to attain greater knowledge or as a religious rite. This has also been witnessed in some Christian denominations to a lesser extent through the phenomena of speaking in tongues and shaking. Few in their right mind would invite Evil Spirits into their body for they would likely lose all control of their self in this world and possibly lose their soul in the Afterlife. Evil Spirits then would attempt to make their own path into the body. Past theologians have stated that Demons may first turn themselves into a hair or other foreign body and alight on food in order to enter the person through the act of consumption. A person who finds themselves the victim of an uninvited Possession is often known as a Demoniac. Typical symptoms of Spirit Possession generally involved speaking in and responding to unfamiliar voices and displaying uncharacteristic and contrasting personality traits, but sometimes the manifestations could be more profound and sinister, again rather like Poltergeist activity but more definitely emanating from a certain person.

The Church accepted that some Demoniacs may have also unconsciously invited malevolent spirits to invade their body however. This could occur due to acts of sin or through flirting with paranormal and occult forces (Ouija Boards, Seances, the Tarot and even divinations such as reading tea-leaves were considered dubious and dangerous practices). People at a low ebb due to various social, mental and physical pressures may be considered at especial risk of being targeted by Demons. As with Poltergeists, it has been suggested that juveniles on the verge of adolescence may prove an ideal harbour for wandering spirits. Sometimes considered also to be at high risk are people with alcohol or drug dependency. However it could be said that all these conditions could awaken something from within rather than lure in from outside. This brings us back to the original concept of Daiminion - the Inner Voice, which in this case does not relate to a conscience or to a divine spark, but instead to Inner or Personal Demons.

Probably everyone has encountered an Inner Demon at some time, dwelling within the mind and taunting with enduring notions of paranoia, despondency or doubt. Until the Demon can be confronted and laid to rest or at least vanquished for a while then their persistence may cause a lack of sleep or appetite and usher in depression and illness. Those already under pronounced stress may find their Inner Demons causing them to act grossly out of character, perhaps even inspiring violence, blasphemy, deviancy and spite.

Whether the Demons stem from within or without, their influence can be said to be both profound and powerful and it can also be said to sound familiar. In current Western cultures, such symptoms of Possession as expressed above are more frequently considered as evidence of mental illness rather than of Hellish influence. If treatment is then forthcoming, it will usually consist of therapy and medication (in extreme cases possibly also incarceration), rather than Religious intervention.

In the past though , Exorcists would have been called to the scene and through the ceremonial use of bell, book and candle, these Church ministers would strive to expel the Evil Spirits in the name of God. This follows the New Testament account of Jesus Christ exorcising a whole host of Demons out of a single Demoniac ("My name is Legion: for we are many" – Mark chapter 5, verse 9). These he drove into a pig , which was subsequently destroyed. Exorcisms do still occur on occasion within these isles, however under the banner of Deliverance Ministry, they tend to concentrate on buildings , which are seemingly haunted or troubled by a Supernatural presence. The ceremony involved is also more like a conventional blessing rather than the melodramatic ritual of yore or as presented in some motion pictures. Though differing in method, White Witches sometimes also undertake rites of Exorcism. Any apparent Demoniacs cussing, convulsing and foaming at the mouth in Britain or Ireland today would most probably gain the attention of doctors rather than priests. That is not to say that our ancestors were entirely naïve, though through their remembrance of the Old Ways and their adherence to *Fire and Brimstone* Church sermons they were generally more superstitious. Though they recognised mental illness and insanity, many thought their cause could be down to Divine Intervention, Demonic Possession or possibly even due to Fay mischief (the slang term 'Touched' meaning 'mad' comes from the belief that this condition occurred after someone had been actually touched by Faeries or Elves). They were totally aware though of other causes of altered states such as the ingestion of fermented liquids or certain plants and fungi. The use of either could even be sacred, but they would have been aware of the dramatic and enduring effects, over-indulgence could have on body, mind and spirit. The archaic herbalists also had a good understanding of the beneficiary effects of many natural products with regard to health and wellbeing. Modern breweries and pharmaceutical companies owe a lot to the wisdom of the ancients. Even their notions of being 'Moon-struck' (driven insane by the moon) have seen some credence in the work of modern scientists investigating the effects that the lunar phases (and also the weather and turning of the seasons) have on mood and mental health. Also in previous times however, it was also considered that severe illness was a sign that Demons were abroad. Not only would they create malady and suffering for the sake of being spiteful, but again it was thought that the poorly person's resistance would be weakened thus rendering them more permeable to Possession. Sometimes it was

374

thought that Demons would inflict only particular limbs or organs. Charms would often be utilised in a bid to dispel the lingering evil but should that fail, then amputation or surgery may have finally been resorted to. Never pleasant, surgery and especially amputations were extremely grim affairs in the past. People that were obviously close to death were also considered to be at risk from the Demons of the air. When not stirring up storms, these usually invisible fiends were believed to linger above the dying person and taunt them. The Sacrament of the Last Rites and the ringing of church bells were hoped to bring comfort to the dying and to drive away the Demons that may attempt to seize their souls in the last moments.

Demons were also sometimes to be discovered lurking beneath the soil – an occurrence that holds symbolic allusion to Hell being below us (the Underworld). On separate occasions and at separate locations the early Saints, Godric and Columba were both said to have encountered devilish creatures whilst digging in the ground. In the case of Saint Godric, the discovery of a writhing mass of black-skinned fiends with glinting eyes and sharp teeth under the soil of Weardale, County Durham occurred as the anchorite excavated the ground in search of buried treasure. As Christian text tended to demonise virtually all Otherworldly denizens, there remains the possibility that these subterranean oddities were actually Goblins, Mine-Spirits or another supernatural breed rather than true Hell-spawn. The encounter of Saint Columba (who was no stranger to bizarre beasts), held a strange twist. Upon his arrival on Iona, Columba and his brother, Oran, debated upon the true nature of Heaven and Hell. To solve this enigmatic conundrum, Oran agreed to be buried alive in the ground upon the condition that after 20 days he would be exhumed with the intention of delivering his observations from beyond the pale. If he survived the ordeal it would be a miracle to praise but if he indeed died then hopefully he could still retain the ability to speak of what he'd witnessed. Also if he died his act would be an instance of gracious self-sacrifice providing Columba's fledgling monastery with a protective blood-consecration (see also Ankou and Church-Grims). So, Oran was lowered into the ground and after 20 days had passed, Columba excavated the grave of his brother. To his great consternation, an eldritch voice rolled from the Cimmerian depths declaring, " Heaven is not what it is said to be. Hell is not what it is said to be. The saved are not forever happy, The damned are not forever lost." This was not what Columba expected or hoped to hear and concluded that the voice that issued these troublesome words belonged not to his dear brother

375

but instead to some conniving Demon intent on deception. Whatever the case, Columba hastily poured back the soil upon Oran's body and attended to his ministry. Like the cadaver buried in the ground, Columba buried the events and words of that day in the back of his mind.

In the early days of Saint Patrick's ministry it is said that a host of Demons transformed themselves into a monstrous murder of crows and descended upon Ireland. Their reign of devastation only ceased upon the intervention of an Angel, who banished all Demons from the emerald isle for a period of seven years, seven months, seven days and seven nights.

Adding together the members of the Nine Orders of Fallen Angels, plus the Lilim, the Walk-ins and Inner Demons, the Familiars, Imps and Grims; the denizens of Pandemonium far outnumber the notorious biblical Number of the Beast (disputedly stated as 666 or 616). In 1459 the Spanish Franciscan, Alphonsus de Spina declared that there were precisely 133,306,688 Demons in existence then, which leaves many years between then and now for Lilith to continue breeding!

For in addition to those already mentioned there are the dubious Church inclusions of Faeries, Ghosts, Pagan Gods and Goddesses etc. Then there are also the throngs of Hell comprised of the souls of humans sold in Devilish pacts or condemned because of their wicked lives. If this is not enough then there are the Demons particular to other religions and nations. Amongst numerous others, these include the Rakshashas of India, the Shaitan and Djinn of Arabia, the Oni of Japan, the Kapre of the Philippines, the Dibbuk of Israel, and the Daevas and Drujs of Persia (now Iran). The forces of Evil are indeed Legion, for they are many.

The Devil
(Other Names Include ~ **Lucifer (The Morning-Star or Light-Bearer). Satan (Adversary). Iblis / Eblis. Azazel. Diablo. The Black Prince. Black Tom. The Shining One. Avagddu. Robin Artisan. The Old Gentleman. The Tempter. Auld Clootie. Auld Chiel. Auld Sandy. Aud Hornie. Old Nick. Old Scratch. Old Harry. O Bengh. The Div'l. The Divell. Cythrawl. Dera. Diafro. Gwr Drwg. Dewer. Christonday. Plotcock. The Big-Brindled One. Mhor-Ri. Muc Mhor Dubh. The Big Black Pig. Him.**)

Since Christianity pervaded these isles, all paths of wickedness and deviancy (regardless of the apparent culprit and circumstances) have been believed to ultimately lead to one door. Behind which is the Devil. Though the term 'Devils' is often used as an alternative to Demons, *The* Devil as such refers to Lucifer / Satan / Eblis etc. - the instigator of the War in Heaven and commander of the rebel Angels. Upon their defeat in battle, the Devil and his Demonic Host were banished to the blizzards and blazes of Hell (though one theory holds that some also fell to Earth). This Hell realm (also known as Inferno, Pandemonium, Hades, The Abyss, The Underworld, The Netherworld, Tartarus, Niflheim, Gehenna and also has similar equivalents in numerous other religions) is generally regarded as the kingdom where the Devil rules supreme and that sinful human souls are consigned to after death. Though Hell is often represented as being painfully hot or painfully cold in different regions but dismal and brimming with medieval torture throughout, others feel that Hell could be whatever they fear or revile the most, repeated for eternity without any sense of desensitisation or respite. Such personal Hells could include the repeated sensation of drowning, suffocating or burning or it could be being damned to be covered in spiders or scorpions or whatever. The possibilities are endless reflecting peoples' deepest personal phobias or alternately the sinner may be compelled to relive all their crimes and sins they committed in life but this time from the experience of their victims.
However it has also been suggested that in addition to the territory of Hell, the Devil was also granted dominion over the planet earth. That this is so, is indicated in the Biblical New Testament (Matthew chapter 4, verses 1–11). When Jesus Christ endured fast and contemplation in the desert, the Devil arose to tempt him. In exchange for Jesus abandoning his mission and instead bowing down and worshipping him, Satan offered all the countries and cities of the world. Though Jesus refused this bargain, he did not dispute that these things were indeed

the Devil's to barter with. Certainly it seems, that even if not personally present in this world, the power of the Devil holds great sway. Indeed it was ultimately in reference to him, that thousands of *accused* Witches were condemned and executed across the middle ages. Though specifically named and detailed in Britain and Ireland by the Christian Church, equivalents of the Devil could be found amidst the earlier faiths practised in these countries. Virtually all of the world religions past and present heed recognition in some form to the Dark Side of nature and soul, but not always in such dualistic terms of absolute good and absolute evil as recognised by Christianity and other monotheistic faiths. In the Norse / Teutonic myths of the Viking and Anglo-Saxon invaders, the Character of Loki is perhaps their closest equivalent to the Devil. Though in many of the Norse tales, Loki appears as little more than a selfish and petulant Trickster (an archetypal figure common in much myth and folklore), he later revealed the true depths of his character to devastating effect. The Norse apocalypse (known as Ragnarok) was provoked by Loki's insurrection against the patriarchal Odin / Wotan and the other Aesir (Gods). His treachery, assisted by several of his monstrous children brought about the death of the Norse pantheon. The half-black / half-white Goddess of the Norse Underworld however, was named Hel whilst another alternative name for the Christian concept of Hell is Hades. The name Hades referred to the Greco-Roman Underworld (a dismal Kingdom of the dead that certainly compares to the Christian Hell, as opposed to the Fields of Elysium, which is a summer-land Paradise). The name, Hades was also sometimes used to refer to their Lord of the Underworld, a grim figure also known as Pluto or Dis.

The Celts recognised a fair number of malevolent forces, but didn't really seem to name any particular individual as being the specific master or mistress of evil. Even the War Goddesses, though known for being callous and treacherous at times, were not considered evil as such as the Celts relished justified conflict and considered it an honour to die in battle. Celtic Faerie Kings such as Fin Bheara and Gwyn ap Nudd are comparable to the Greco-Roman Hades / Pluto, due to the association of the Faerie Otherworld with the Dead and to the subterranean qualities of the Fairy hills. Though these figures are more specifically connected with the passage of the dead (see Ankou) rather than the mechanics of Evil.

The nature of the Devil, the guises he may adopt and his relevance to Christian doctrine were topics deliberated by the Council of Toledo in 447 A..D. Even then it was widely assumed that in order to tempt mortals along the path of sin he might adopt many diverse forms. The figure that the Medieval Church drew most association to however, especially in Ireland was Cernunnos (and the equivalent Horned Gods of other lands). Though in essence these two figures are worlds apart, the portrayal of the Devil with horns, cloven feet and other goat-like attributes was prevalent in medieval art and has remained a potent stock image to this day. New religions are prone to assimilate whatever similar motifs they can find from the older religion they seek to replace, and incorporate it, albeit somewhat changed to suit their own iconography and teachings. Whatever remains unsuitable and difficult to mould, may instead be demonised and regarded as evil. This is intended to ease conversion to the new faith and deter a return to the old ways under the threat of risking damning their eternal soul to torment. Christianity may very well have reacted strongly to the Horned God in particular because he was such a difficult figure to assimilate into their own creed positively and because the Pagan homage to him was so pronounced and deep-rooted. As Cernunnos represented fertility, not only in the crops of the field but also in sentient creatures, his association to fornication was perhaps also too much for the Catholic Church to tolerate, (especially after it endorsed the vows of celibacy on its clergy and the ban on pre-marital relations for the lay-folk).

The association between the Devil and Goats however runs deeper. In ancient Hebrew text, the Devil is referred to as 'Seirrizim' which means goat, though this may be in reference to their supposedly shared characteristics of being stubborn, lustful and feverish , rather than a physical resemblance. In biblical allegory it has been stated that at the time of reckoning, mankind will be separated as a herder would separate lambs from goats. The lambs symbolic of righteous humans, whilst the goats obviously representing the sinners. The notion of goats being sinful is further indicated by the concept of the 'Scapegoat'. The term scapegoat is often used to refer to a person who bears the full brunt of responsibility in a situation, whilst others escape with the blame that should really have been shared. This is derived from the biblical occurrence of a Jewish High Priest confessing the sins of the people over a goat, thus transferring the responsibility of the crimes into the beast which was then sent into the wilderness. Superstitions regarding goats, claim that it is impossible to constantly watch over one of these beasts for 24 hours for they need to go to visit the Devil each day to have their beards combed. It was also claimed that goats' blood is the best remedy to soften diamonds for crafting and that the presence of a goat amongst a herd of cows will prevent stampedes, miscarriages and poisoning (either from toxic plants or snakebite).

Snakes however were apparently another favoured form of Satan, most infamously his appearance as the Serpent of Eden, the tempter of Eve (though initially this reptile was not specifically identified as being Satan).

There is another theory however that originally the apparent horns of the Devil and Demons were not actually horns at all. The art-historian, Fred Gettings has suggested that early esoteric-symbolist artists might actually have intended these protuberances to represent the points of a crown shaped like an inverted crescent moon. This would represent the Demonic domain of the Lunar Sphere and show the figure to be of a wicked nature and likewise other medieval artworks show holy figures with a crescent moon underfoot, i.e. crushing evil. This symbolism does not seem to have applied during the Crusades with reference to the Islamic Crescent for by this time the crescent moon was regarded in Christian iconography as being symbolic of the Virgin Mary and Christ's ascent from the Underworld. By this point any horn-like extremities painted onto rendered Devils were probably intended to be horns. Both the crescent crown and the moon were associated to the Goddess Isis in ancient Egypt. The Islamic Crescent and Star actually symbolises the communion between the Angel Gabriel / Jibreel and the Prophet Mohammed, as well as representing sovereignty and divinity. The Christian, Judaic and Islamic faiths essentially recognise the same God and the same Devil, and the Old Testament Prophets are relevant also to all three of these religions. However it is difficult to compare the artistic representations of such between Islam and Christianity, as there are very few Islamic examples, for pictorial / sculptural representations of sentient creatures (especially divine figures) are prohibited by Sharia (Islamic law). This is intended to prohibit idolatry but also to prevent people establishing a pre-conceived image of Allah based on human-inspired rendition. It would therefore seem that the Lunar Crown imagery was only really applied by a handful of artists with knowledge of occult symbolism, and that the goat / Horned God association held with more people generally.

The concept of the Devil appearing as a half man / half goat entity, occur mainly in the Witch-trial accounts of Black Sabbats (see also Malefactors, Witch-Hunters and Ceremonial Witches). Many modern researchers seriously doubt whether such Sabbats occurred beyond the fevered paranoia of the Witch-Hunters and the confessions of terrified or mentally confused suspected Witches. Even if a minority of these encounters did actually occur in the material world, then the figures that the Witches greeted with a posterior kiss or actually copulated with may have actually been a conventional goat roped in for the occasion. If the horny being was distinctly more humanoid then it could possibly have been a Warlock wearing a Horned Mask (often known as an Ooser). (Malevolent goat or goat-men manifestations are comparative to forms sometimes chosen by fiends such as Shape-shifting Bogies, Church-Grims and Phookas.)

Whilst the establishing of a pact being made with the Devil was an integral factor to the prosecution and punishment of Witches, why the investigating authorities deemed that such a treaty must be made in person is something of an enigma. Certainly a number of the condemned were likely guilty of assorted wickedness perhaps even Devil-Worship but that is not to say that they ever met the Devil in this life. Likewise, the church clergy could also be said to have made a pact with God in their decision to devote their lives to his mission, but it was not imperative that they arranged this face to face. (Indeed if any of them claimed such a thing they would likely find themselves the subject of a Heresy trial.)

One would assume that scribing the inventories of sin and sinners and providing the condemned souls with eternal torture would keep the Devil very busy in Hell, but there are numerous tales of his visits to earth. He has no need to keep tabs on his devotees or other compulsive sinners for theoretically they will make their own way to his domain anyway. The souls of the virtuous would likely be of greater interest to him, for to tempt or trick a lamb away from God would probably give him great satisfaction. Indeed the corruption and obtaining of one just soul may be of greater relish and value to him than a whole host of Satanists and Malefactors. Though his minion Demons and very many humans will continue to ensure that sin will not go out of fashion, like a lord inspecting his manor, the Devil may tread amongst us himself in person once in a while.

In British lore, The Devil is reputed to be a great musician and an old saying claims that he knows all the best tunes (though this can also be taken to mean that some sins are more pleasurable than virtues). In the mid to late 20th Century, some fundamentalist Christians would insinuate that he had developed a keen interest in the electric guitar and 'Rock n Roll' in general. (A notion that has unfortunately been given some grounding by the blasphemous and murderous crimes of some Scandinavian 'Black Metal' bands { some of whom were actually Odinist rather than Satanist} and also a few demented Rock music fans in nations as diverse as Italy, the USA and Germany.) Traditionally though the Devil favoured the Violin as his chosen instrument (the pressure mark evident on some violinists' necks is sometimes known as the Devil's Crease). A local legend tells that guests at a wedding at

Stanton Drew in Somerset, were so engrossed by the Devil's fiddle playing that they continued dancing into the Holy Day. As a result of this misdemeanour the revellers were transformed into the stone circle that stands there to this day. (Some versions of the tale instead have the Devil playing pipes, but the result is the same.)

The Devil is also thought to be a master chessman and a keen gambler. He would encourage his opponents to continue playing their card game into the Sabbath, therefore causing them to forfeit their soul or perhaps having gambled away all their worldly positions, may invite them instead to wager their soul. The Devil's fondness for gambling is further reflected in the tales of the various Sorcerers who have sought to strike deals with him. Though many of those seeking to bargain their souls from the confines of chalk circles or down at the crossroads at midnight, were of a generally bad disposition already it would seem that they would be destined to end up in his clutches anyway. Granting them knowledge, power, wealth or whatever else they desired in this mortal coil was of no consequence to the Devil, yet he would weigh up the worth of their soul and give due accordingly. Sometimes though the Devil would strike the deal seemingly for the pure sport of it, for many of the soul-traders would try to renege on their side of the bargain or attempt to cheat him.

Such a figure was the 17th Century cleric, Doctor Alexander Colville of Galgorm, County Antrim in Ireland. This Anglican Minister and scholar, was reputed to have offered his soul to the Devil in exchange for his boot and hat being filled with gold coin. However both of these items of clothing had subtle holes in them, through which the riches flowed into tunnels where Colville's servants quickly shovelled it away. Eventually the coin reached the brim of the garments and stopped coming, but not before the minister had amassed a considerable fortune. The Devil took these shenanigans in his stead and fulfilled his part of the arrangement, but Colville was determined to cheat upon his commitment also. It had been decided that Colville would relinquish his soul twenty years after the declaration of the deal, however there was some consternation about the exact date. Colville had purposively suggested December 25th, but the Devil realised instantly that this was Christmas Day – a day when traditionally the powers of darkness held no sway. So instead they agreed that the auspicious date should be the last day of the month of February, a minimum of twenty years hence. In the years interceding, Colville revelled in his ill-gotten gains but more so he added to his bounty by magically assuming the guise of a Crow in order to spy upon his neighbours and subsequently blackmail them over any of their own transgressions. However as the years passed, whenever the 28th of February approached, Doctor Colville would indulge in continuous prayer, fasting, bible reading and hymn singing. This he would continue all the way through the day until the 1st of March dawned. He knew that the Devil could not claim his soul whilst he was embroiled in religious pursuit or on any other day of the year save for the one specified. The time of soul gathering haven past, the twisted cleric would resort again to his nefarious ways until the next 28th of February, when he once again would spend 24 hours devoted to pious pursuit. Thus he thwarted the Devil's advances for several successive years and planned to continue doing so for eternity. One year however, February 28th passed in the now customary fashion with Colville engrossed in fervent prayer. However after the clock struck midnight, he packed away his psalm-book , poured himself a large goblet of wine and joined some associates at a gambling table. Feeling pleased with himself, he laughed how it was a fine March morning. To which one of his comrades commented that it wasn't March yet, but actually the 29th of February. Colville paled at this remark, for in his arrogance he had completely forgotten about leap years. The Devil however had not and so he arrived to seize the soul of the conniving Doctor Colville.

The Devil was not always so triumphant in his visits to these isles however. A 15th Century Welsh minister and suspected Wizard and Necromancer, by the name of Sion Cent or John Kent reputedly had more success in swindling the Devil. Again in exchange for worldly benefits this man bargained his soul with the dark one. However within this particular Satanic contract was the strange stipulation that Cent's soul could only be claimed if his body was buried either inside or outside of his church. To conquer this dilemma, Cent had it arranged that upon his death, his remains were to be laid beneath the exterior wall of the church. Therefore, as technically he was buried neither inside nor outside of the building , the Devil was cheated of his prize.

On another occasion whilst Saint Dunstan (909 – 988) Archbishop of Canterbury and also a proficient metal-smith, was working at his forge in Mayfield, Sussex in England, the Devil appeared to him in the form of a beautiful, sensual woman. Recognising this seductress for what she truly was, Dunstan grabbed some hot tongs from his brazier and clamped her nose. The Devil instantly resorted to a less comely form and manner before finally being released by Dunstan.

It is often said "Talk of the Devil and he will appear", whilst this is generally used to refer to coincidence nowadays , it was once intended more literally. Some of the less reverend terms used to address the Devil may have been intended to ridicule him therefore making him a less attractive focus of worship. Such names include Old Nick, Old Harry, Old Scratch (derived from the Teutonic 'Skratta' meaning fiend) and Auld Clootie (a reference to the notorious cloven hooves). Such names however may have otherwise been utilised to conceal a person's fear of him through mirth or to refer to him without attracting his attention. Also as names such as the Fair Folk, Good People and Mother's Blessing for instance were used as euphemistic terms for the Faeries, referring to the Devil as the Old Gentleman or the Black Prince may also have been intended to appease him. However, if the saying was intended to discourage mention of the Devil, then in these isles it certainly failed in that aim.

The Devil features in numerous superstitions, folk tales and proverbs of Britain and Ireland. Commonly used adages that pay reference to Satan include "Between the Devil and the Deep Blue Sea" (meaning to be caught in a dilemma where neither available choice is particularly ideal), "The Devil dances in an empty pocket" or "The Devil makes work for idle hands" (both of which insinuate that people who have little money or nothing to occupy their time may very well turn to crime or mischief). Even more prevalent mention of the Devil can be found in the given names of many of the megalithic constructions or naturally formed landmarks of these lands. Frequently local lore surrounding these sites will attribute their construction to activities of the Devil. In England so considered locations include the Devil's Frying-pan near Cadgwith, Cornwall, the Devil's Kettles (also known as the Hell Kettles) near Darlington, County Durham, the Devil's Dyke near Hove, East Sussex, the Devil's Chimney at Ibberton, Dorset, The Devil's Punchbowl at Kirkby Lonsdale, Cumbria, the Devil's Bag of Nuts near Alcester, Warwickshire and the Devil's Arse at Peak Cavern, Derbyshire. Elsewhere to be found are the Devil's Hole on Jersey, the Devil's Causeway in Northern Ireland, the Devil's Staine near Dundee in Scotland, and the Devil's Bridge in West Glamorgan, Wales.

In some locations the Devil may have left behind his footprint or rather his hoof-print for it is sometimes believed that even in human disguise, he cannot alter his ungulate feet. It is sometimes claimed though that only one of his feet is thus affected and that therefore the Devil may be recognised by his limp. At Caidair Isis in Gwynedd, by Alwen Reservoir in Clwyd and the Denbigh Moors, all in Wales and also in England at Llanmynech Hill in Shropshire and at Birtley, Northumberland, the Devil's prints are reputed to have been scorched or compressed into solid rock. Fresh Devil's Footprints were reported marked in deep snow on the 8th and 9th of February 1855, in perhaps as many as thirty different towns and villages across Devon in Southwest England. The tracks were reputed to have traversed steep walls, haystacks and rooftops. Nobody claimed responsibility for producing the markings and nobody reported seeing who or what made them. Some locals suspected a deliberate hoax, albeit a clever and elaborate one, with some suggesting that Gypsies on stilts with plaster casts of hoof-prints on the end of sticks were the actual culprits. Others however feared that for some unknown purpose as they slept in their beds, the Devil had indeed chosen to walk amongst them.

The Devil seems able to appear in whatever form he so desires ranging from farm animal to seductive maiden. The bestial forms he has reputedly adopted all seem to be black in colour and include those of serpents, dogs, goats, crows, cats, cockerels and pigs. Rarely however does he seem to chose a truly monstrous form, often leaving such imagery to lesser Demons. He is frequently reported as manifesting as a handsome, well-dressed dark man with beguiling eyes. In order to personally tempt holy men away from their godly path he would at times assume the guise of a beautiful, sultry woman but again this is a practice that may often be assigned to one of his minions.

As the 'Father of All Lies' he may sometimes adopt a form that is contradictory to his nature. For instance in one of the alleged meetings with Alexander Colville (see above), the Devil appeared as a meek middle-aged man with spectacles and rather gave the impression of a parish vicar or accountant rather than the Lord of Damnation. To the same man on other occasions, the Devil is reputed to have appeared as a huge, burly blacksmith covered in soot and wearing a leather apron and also as a noble black man wrapped in a green velvet cloak. A Witch-trial occurring in Edinburgh in 1607 heard testimony claiming that the Devil had appeared to the accused, Isobel Grierson in the form of a naked infant. It has been said that The Devil casts no shadow and is left-handed. Originally, it is assumed that the Devil bore resemblance to the other Angels, but since then his adopted forms can vary as much as the sins over which he presides.

The Owlman

The story of the Owlman of Mawnan in Cornwall began on 17th April 1976 in the grounds of Mawnan old church when two young sisters. Vicky and June Melling claimed to have seen a figure hovering over the church tower. They described the creature as part owl part man and drew pictures of the entity whom appeared to have the head and wings of an owl-like bird, the body of a man and oddly apparently trousers and pointy boots. This avian man-thing apparently emitted strange noises which along with its ghastly visage caused the girls to flee in terror. On 3rd July two other girls Barbara Perry and Sally Chapman claimed to have seen and heard The Owlman in Mawan Woods. Around this same period two young sisters by the name of Greenwood also claimed to have had an encounter with this enigmatic being. Sporadically across the 70s, 80s and then once in the 90s and up to at least 2000 other sightings of the Owlman of Mawnan were claimed.

An oft companion to folklore is fake-lore - whereby something blatantly untrue is proliferated as fact. Sometimes it is the product of a jovial prank, at other times it is conducted accidentally by misinterpretation and further still sometimes as a malicious tool to ridicule or discredit others. Sometimes fake-lore however takes on a life of its own. The case of the Owlman of Mawnan in Cornwall is an interesting incident. It has been claimed that the sci-fi author, artist and magician Tony 'Doc' Shiels whom first 'investigated'the case, may have created the Owlman as a late April Fools . Shiel's connection to the Tom Fool's Theatre of Tomfoolery who were associated to the sea monster Morgawr controversy, would not be incapable of pulling off a fake-loric hoax in this manner but he denied involvement. That is not to say that he doesn't think it could be a hoax but has compared the Owlman to Loplop the bird-headed man created by, (perhaps the best), surrealist artist Max Ernst.

'Hythe Mothman'

In studies of cryptids and UFO alien encounters, The Mothman is a celebrated weird creature made famous by investigator and author John Keel, that apparently first appeared in Point Pleasant, West Virginia, USA in 1966 however 3 years earlier a similar creature appeared between Saltwood and Sandling near Hythe in Kent, England. Whether it was the same creature, of the same paranormal family or just superficially alike is not known, but it is sometimes referred to as the Hythe Mothman in reference to more famous US encounter.

In that November of 1966, rumours abound of strange lights and sounds in the area, and four teenagers walking Sandling Road first saw a glowing light fall from the sky and then a glowing oval object that somehow seemed aware of their presence. Then they spotted a black headless figure with bat like wings that appeared to be carrying something like a storm lantern. Oval lights and apparently sentient glowing mists were then reported by several other young people in the following weeks and on 23rd November the strange being appeared again. The 18 year old male who saw it described it as a bat-like humanoid, with no head and webbed feet. The creature left behind traces in the undergrowth but seemingly was not seen again.

Debate ensued as to whether the being was an extraterrestrial, a ghost, a misidentification or something else entirely. Unlike the Mothman of Point Pleasant, this being did not converse with any people nor did it prophesise any forthcoming calamity in the area.

There have been tales of Other mysterious winged humanoids
reported in the UK prior to this event, but as to whether they were the one and the same 'Mothman' it is not possible to say.

Reynardine
(Also known as Reynard the Fox. Lowrence. Ryner Dyne. Ranordine. Rhinordine. Rinordine. Rossel. Renert. Tod.)

Originating in the medieval ballads and fables, Reynard the Fox was an anthropomorphic trickster figure that had developed a Theriomorphic 'Were-Fox' aspect by the time of the Victorian folk song Reynardine. In this ballad, he is a rakish seducer of women but the implication is that it may not only have been their sex that he desired but also their blood. In Asian lore shape-shifting foxes are very prevalent especially in China, Japan and Korea where there are tales of vampiric seductresses as well as multi-tailed, precious metal-haired, very wise ancient foxes. It is unusual therefore that Reynardine seems to be quite rare amongst British and Celtic theriomorphs, with hares apparently being a much more favoured guise for Witches of these isles and other shape-shifting entities picking a variety of animal forms.

Foxes as predators in the UK and Ireland tend to be opportunistic, more likely to scavenge from dustbins or hunting small wild prey but taking domestic fowl or more seldom weakened young lambs if circumstances allow. For this reason, foxes historically have been the prey of human hunters. There have however been some rare, strange cases of foxes going into houses and attacking people, especially children, as they slept. In a bizarre incident in Glasgow a fox was sighted carrying a human hand in its mouth. This was linked by police to a missing woman case, which later led to a homicide conviction.

Giant foxes were reported in Kent in recent times. One such beast, dubbed The Beast of the Bubble (as in Whitsta-Bubble after Whitstable where it was encountered in 2010), reportedly ate a pensioner's pet rabbit and needed to be battled off with a garden chair and a shovel. Whether this was the same fox that was trapped and killed in Maidstone is not beyond possibility, but this creature, which was thought to have killed a pet cat, was measured at 4 feet long, a little short of The Beast which had been described as standing as tall as a man and as having vivid orange hair.

The Man Monkey
(Possibly Also Known as Old Ned's Devil)

A peculiar encounter with the weird Man Monkey said to haunt the Shropshire Union Canal (also known as the Shroppie or as the Liverpool - Birmingham Canal) was reported on 21st January 1879 whereupon a labouring man was travelled by horse from Staffordshire to Shropshire along the canal path where akin to a Leap-Upon, a bizarre beast covered in hair with glowing white eyes leapt out of the thick foliage upon his steed which panicked and sped off apparently with the man and Man Monkey clinging on. The alarmed worker took to the beast with his riding crop to no avail but somewhere upon the tumultuous journey the entity vanished leaving both horse and rider in a distressed state. Rather than be met with universal incredulity there were those who heard the traveller's tale and greeted it with familiarity for he was not the only one said to have encountered the mysterious Man Monkey. In 1848 aman was said to have come face to face with a shaggy 5 foot tall manimal in the village of Ranton, which after a short while vanished with a burst of light. This latter detail would suggest a supernatural rather than a natural origin of the strange beast, for it would not be beyond possibility that primates escaped from exotic menageries for people of money were known to amass their own private zoos in those days.

In the late 19th Century a man by the name of Ned was traversing a path with horse and cart in the town of Smethwick near Birmingham when, as with the worker travelling the canal paths, a motley beast leapt at them. Again with riding whip a struggle occurred, but this time the strange creature was killed in the violent engagement. The bizarre beast, which has since vanished and with no firm description given thus associating it with Man Monkey simply by regional locale and habit, was reputedly preserved and presented in a glass case in the Blue Gate pub on Rolfe Street, Smethwick and referred to as Old Ned's Devil. It is around Bridge 39 on the Shropshire Union Canal however that further sightings have been reported, Bob Carroll, a lorry driver, reported seeing a strange entity in that area in the early 1970s which instilled him with an uncanny feeling of dread as if the beast emitted an evil aura. In 1982 an encounter with a large gorilla-liker creature was reported from the vicinity of Bridge 39 and likewise in the 80s a man boating along the canal described seeing a hairy man-like beast gazing down on him from the bridge as his barge past underneath.

The Man Monkey shares similarity in its behaviour with trickster Bogie creatures mentioned elsewhere in the book such as the Leap-Upons and even perhaps the Phookas and Kelpies or to the Shug Monkey, a creature part-dog part-ape that haunted the area of Slough Hill in Cambridgeshire, as well as drawing comparison to the British 'Bigfoots' - one of which was reported in Cannock Chase an area noted for strangeness and not so far from the Shropshire Union Canal, which itself, in addition to the Man Monkey is know as a particularly haunted locale.

The Were-Sheep

In 1972 a bizarre being said to be part-man part-sheep was reported creeping out of a house in Hexham, Northumberland. Its sudden appearance (as well as that of reported Werewolf sightings and Poltergeist activity) was linked to the discovery of two small carved stone heads in the region, as when these artefacts were sent south for study, the Werewolf apparently followed. There was initial suggestion that the heads were relics of a Celtic Head Cult (see also Screaming Skulls) but there has since been speculation that the images were actually carved during World War II and actually represented caricatures of Hitler and Mussolini or that a local man carved them as toys for his child in 1956.

The Southend Ratman

There are two urban legends relating to the origins of a mysterious haunting in an underpass at Southend-on-Sea in Essex. The first claims that an old vagrant was sleeping in the underpass when he was viciously assaulted by a gang of juvenile delinquents and as he lay there dying had his flesh devoured by rats. The other tale tells of a former mayor of the town impregnated one of his many mistresses with a child that was born deformed with verminous features, which he had sealed in a subterranean tunnel that connects to the underpass.

Whilst neither story can be corroborated, it is said that at night strange scraping sounds and the screeching of rodents can be heard in the underpass heralding the coming of the bizarre Southend Ratman.

Killer Clowns

The peculiar thing about Killer clowns is that they are unquestionably real in the tangible sense of not being simply 'make-believe' or superstition. They also don't actually tend to be killers, (the infamous American children's party performer and serial Murderer John Wayne Gacy being a notable exception). Coulrophobia - a profound fear of clowns is nothing new but with the increase of bad clowns in movies particularly following the Gacy case, from The Joker in the rebooted Batman movies to Pennywise the Clown from Stephen King's It, the ailment went from a sniffle to an epidemic. This was heightened to an intense degree as waves of Killer Clown panics (or Coulromania) arose with reports of clowns being seen just hanging ominously around streets and other urban areas. Some were said to be brandishing weapons and there were tales of others staring into and tapping on the widows of people's houses. This seems to have began in the early 1980s in America but by the flap of freaky fools in 2016 the phenomena had spread to Britain. The majority of reported sightings seemed to have peaked in October 2016 and was apparently most common to Wales and Northern England particularly it seems across Teesside, County Durham and Tyneside. Reported as Occam's Razor suggests as people in fancy dress costumes playing a joke but both the police and the parents of frightened children took the matter seriously. Regarded in a folkloric sense the clown is representative of the Trickster Spirit- a being that can be found in various forms in many religions sometimes as a mischievous prankster but sometimes of more malevolent intent. In old English culture this can be represented by Reynard the Fox an anthropomorphic vulpine rascal of fables. In the Celtic tradition we are reminded of the Amadan Dubh - the Dark Fairy Fool, a haunter of the Irish hills after sundown who would drive people and even perhaps other Fae entities and old gods to madness or even death with his mischief, pipe music, riddling poems and other potentially fatal challenges.

The Blue Man of Studham Common

On the stormy day of 28th January 1967 a group of young boys were crossing an area known as The Dell at Studham Common, Dunstable when a bolt of lighting was followed by a manifestation of a 3ft tall blue skinned man with a long forked beard, wearing a high domed hat and dressed in overall like attire with a thick belt, in front of which hovered a black cube. The man emitted a blue glow and was accompanied by deep disembodied voices speaking in an unknown tongue.

Slender Man
(also known as Slenderman. Slendy)

Slender Man is unusual and rather singular in the fact that a precise date can be given for his inception into the human psyche. On 10th June 2009 Viktor Surge (real name Erik Knudsen) created a character and an image of that character for an online Photoshop contest on the Something Awful website. The theme was to create a paranormal image and Surge submitted two photographs of groups of children but also featuring a tall, thin blank-faced man in a suit and tie. Surge accompanied these images with text in the manner of short horror fiction known as Creepypasta accounting for the elongated odd figure being an abductor of children and thus Slender Man was born. Inspired by fictional entities such as The Gentlemen from the TV show Buffy the Vampire Slayer and The Tall Man from the Phantasm film as well as modern American folkloric figures such as The Mad Gasser of Mattoon and The Mothman, thus Slender Man was born. Very quickly this character grabbed the attention of many internet users and tales of him spread like wildfire across the web. Inspired users created a mythos around Slender Man giving him a historical presence as well as adding to his imagined contemporary activity.

Within a few short years he made the transition from fiction to folklore. Some people, particularly children came to believe he was real and reports appeared of alleged sightings. Bringing the phenomena into the sphere of this book, several such sightings were reported in England's West Midlands in the Cannock area. The majority of apparent British encounters happened within peoples' houses and when on the edge of sleep associates Slender Man with Shadow People and the Fear Dubh or Dark Man. There is an alleged account of a woman who contacted a parish priest in 1960 in Scotland claiming that the Fear Dubh had been at her grand-children's windows again. One of those children reported seeing a tall sinuous man in his dreams. There are similar bogeymen reported in the lore of numerous cultures around the world, which some see as Slender Man filling the niche for in the digital age whilst others might claim these creatures are real, Slender Man amongst him. There is also the Chaos Magick approach to the Tibetan Buddhism concept of the Tulpa, which is basically the ritualistic process whereby a thought-form or Tulpa becomes materialistic and tangible. Thereby giving the suggestion that The Slender Man was made flesh either by intentional ritual or the consequence of viral exposure creating belief in the figure. The most tragic example of Slender Man belief however occurred in Waukesha,Wisconsin -USA on 21st May 2014 whereupon two 12 year old girls brutally stabbed a classmate to death claiming that they did it to become Proxies for The Slender Man. Proxy is the name given to the servants of Slender Man either by their own choice or through spirit possession. Descriptions of the Slender Man can vary slightly with some descriptions being only subtly different such as the wearing of a Homburg hat but others mention him having vicious teeth or fingers or writhing appendages that resemble tentacles.

Black Eyed Kids
(Also Known as Black Eyed Children.)

Reported sightings of Black Eyed Kids are popularly thought to have began in the USA in the mid 1990s only crossing the Atlantic Ocean to Britain in 2014, but there is an alleged encounter spectral juveniles within these shores that occurred in 1982. Paranormal investigator and author Lee Brickley recounted the incident which concerned his own aunt who was then a teenager. Hearing calls of distress upon Cannock Chase in Staffordshire, herself and some friends went to investigate and found a young girl running through the beauty spot. As the child approached the edge of dark woodland she turned and the teens, to their alarm noticed that her eyes were entirely black. Otherwise the child seemed to be a regular corporeal human.

At the end of September 2014, there was again a sighting of a Black Eyed Child on Cannock Chase - the first of a more recent wave which could suggest the recurrence of a former haunting rather than American lore becoming global through internet communication. In this instance a woman and her child were walking through the Birches Valley area of the nature reserve, when they heard the screams of a child. When they could not see her, they stopped to take a breather and a girl of around ten years old appeared. The child had her hands over her eyes which she dropped to reveal the liquid darkness of her eyes. Since that time other people have reported seeing Black Eyed Kids on the Chase. Tabloids centred on this story and published reports of Black Eyed Children manifesting in the area including also supposedly at the Four Crosses pub in Cannock and also at Scotland, Liverpool and South-west England.

Due to Cannock Chase also being an apparent window for UFO sighting speculation occurred as to whether the children were ghosts or aliens. The ghost scenario is given a tragic weight due to the real-life horror of the Cannock Chase Murders. Margaret Reynolds aged 6 years old went missing whilst walking to school in Aston Birmingham on 8th September 1965 and on 30th December, Diane Joy Tift aged 5 disappeared on her way to visit her grandmother in Bloxwich. The previous year another girl aged 9 was abducted in Bloxwich by a man in a car who left her for dead after being sexually assaulted and strangled but managed to survive. Margaret and Diane tragically lost their lives and their bodies were found together in a ditch at Mansty Gully on Cannock Chase on 12th January 1966. Another body was discovered on the Chase beneath leaf litter and brushwood on 22nd August 1967. This was Christine Darby aged 7, who had been abducted by a man in a car at Walsall three days prior. Following the attempted abduction of a 10 year old girl in November 1968, a 39 year old Raymond Morris was arrested and charged with the murder of Christine Darby. Because of the similarity of crimes he was strongly suspected of the other two murders and spent the rest of his life in prison, dying there in 2014.

As mentioned earlier Cannock Chase is also claimed to have harboured manifestations of Slender Man, UFOs and also for the record,Werewolves, a Bigfoot and a weird Pig -headed man, not considered to be a fae-folk like Jimmy Squarefoot but instead to be an escaped laboratory experiment that took to living feral have all been reported in this beguiling area of natural beauty.

The Hackney Marsh Beast

Like Cannock Chase, Hackney Marshes on the green edge of London, seems to be something of a thin or at leas peculiar place. Within its history it can count reported fears of crocodiles water snakes or aquatic monsters hunting in the River Lea and of Alien Big Cats, but the most infamous of its (urban) legendary inhabitants was the Beast of Hackney Marshes. The first reported sighting seems to have occurred in the winter of 1981 as several young boys playing in the snow became alarmed when a large dark, hairy creature reared upon its hind legs and growled at them. The children were unable to identify the creature but it became associated in the public's mind as being bear-like, especially as weirdly two skinned and decapitated bear carcasses were reported to have been found in the River Lea a year or so earlier. Alleged further sightings continued over the years, with one person claiming that they had seen a 7 foot tall hairy ursine-like hominid run past them on the marshes in 2009. In 2012 a student was walking in the area and managed to take photographs of a strange hairy beas, however weirdly the drummer of the indie band Kula Shaker claimed that she'd likely seen his large, shaggy -coated black Newfounland dog which he exercised in the area.

Momo

As a tool of rationalism the internet can theoretically bring scientific answers to superstitious questions at the touch of a finger via search engines, but when has reality ever listened to rationalism? In moments ideas and images can traverse the globe from computer to computer, tablet to smart-phone. In this cyber-environment folklore and urban legends can go viral and spread like contagion. In this unreal reality Momo was born. Rumour and panic spread that videos were being passed around that featured Momo - a weird entity with lank hair, bug-eyes, female breasts and bird feet and it was claimed that Momo was instructing children to harm themselves or others or even to commit suicide. Whilst any definite correlation between Momo and actual juvenile suicides, and even of the existence of an original authentic Momo Challenge video is still a matter of debate, authorities, including in Ireland and the British Isles took the matter seriously as they feared copycats making videos of there own with the intent to cause harm and of children chancing upon authentic dangerous or disturbing material when out of curiosity searching key-words pertinent to the Momo Challenge. Momo was soon declared a hoax and the creepy image tracked down to Link Factory - a Japanese special effects company. The puppet actually depicted a Japanese ghost known as an Ubeme. They denied any involvement in the hoax that ensued and revealed that the puppet had actually been destroyed.

So from a depiction of an old folkloric entity and through modern technology new nightmare was born and travelled the world instilling fear again in our enlightened minds.

Sleep well ...

Bibliography

Spellbound:
Dominic Alexander, Grange Books - 2002

A Companion to the Myths, Folklore and Customs of Britain.
Marc Alexander, Sutton ~ 2002

Green Man :
William Anderson & Clive Hicks, Harper Collins – 1990

Witchcraft & Magic in Europe: The 20th Century.
Edited by Bengt Ankarloo & Stuart Clark. Atherlone Press - 1999

A Field Guide to the Little People:
Nancy Arrowsmith. Macmillan -1977.

Mythology of the British Isles :
Geoffrey Ashe, Methuen - 2002.

Mary Ann Cotton:
Arthur Appleton. Michael Joseph Ltd - 1973

The Hell Fire Clubs:
Geoffrey Ashe, W.H. Allen & Co. - 1974

The Complete Book of Magic & Witchcraft:
Leonard RN Ashley. Robson Books-1996

The Complete Book of Superstition, Prophecy & Luck:
Leonard RN Ashley. Robson Books-1996

The AA Book of British Towns: / The AA Book of British Villages :
The Automobile Association.

True Life Encounters - Ghosts and Spirits :
Alan Baker. Orion - 1998

Myths and Legends of the British Isles :
Edited by Richard Barber. Boydell Press - 1999

Ghosts and Hauntings :
Dennis Bardens, Fontana -1967

The Book of Werewolves:
Sabine Baring Gould. 1865. Reprint: Senate-1995

A Flower Fairies Treasury:
Cicily Mary Barker, Penguin - 1997

The Real Middle-Earth . Magic and Mystery in the Dark Ages :
Brian Bates, Pan Books - 2003

Dreams and Destinies:
Beryl Beare, Parragon -1995

England, Myths & Legends:
Beryl Beare. Parragon - 1996

The Ancient World of the Celts :
Peter Beresford Ellis, Constable - 1998

The Enchanted Land, Myths & Legends of Britain's Landscape:
Janet & Colin Bord. Thorsons-1995

The Secret Country:
Janet & Colin Bord. Granada - 1982

A Dictionary of Faeries :
Katharine Briggs, Allen Lane – 1976

Ancient Monuments and Historical Sites:
Brockhampton Reference - 1997

Legends & Superstitions of the County of Durham:
William Brockie. 1886. Reprint: EP Publishing-1974

The Alien World :
Edited by Peter Brooksmith, Black Cat - 1988

Great Hauntings :
Edited by Peter Brooksmith, Black Cat - 1988

Incredible Phenomena :
Edited by Peter Brooksmith, Orbis – 1984

UFOs – Where Do They Come From ? :
Edited by Peter Brooksmith, Black Cat – 1988

The Elements of The Druid Tradition :
Philip Carr-Gomm, Element – 1991

The Encyclopaedia of Arthurian Legends :
Ronan Coghlan, BCA -1992

Encyclopaedia of Monsters:
Daniel Cohen. Michael O' Mara Books – 1989

Brewer's Book of Myth and Legend:
Edited by J.J. Cooper. Helicon – 1997

The Modern Antiquarian :
Julian Cope, Thorsons - 1998

Encyclopaedia of World Mythology:
Edited by Arthur Cotterell. Parragon -1999

Illustrated Encyclopaedia of Myths & Legends:
Arthur Cotterell. Marshall/Cassell - 1989

The Ultimate Encyclopaedia of Mythology:
Arthur Cotterell & Rachel Storm. Lorenz Books - 1999

The Creatures of Celtic Myth :
Dr Bob Curran & Andrew Whitson. Cassell - 2000

The Dark Spirit ~ Sinister Portraits from Celtic Folklore :
Dr Bob Curran & Andrew Whitson. Cassell - 2001

Journeys to Heaven and to Hell:
Rodney Davies. Robert Hale Ltd - 2002
The Celtic Saints :
Courtney Davis, Cassell – 2000
The Denham Tracts :
Michael Denham –1846 - 1859. The Folklore Society – 1895.
The Green Man in Britain :
Fran & Geoff Doel. Tempus - 2001
In Fairyland – an Anthology:
Various Poets. Illustrated by Richard Doyle – 1870. Reprinted British Museum Press – 2001.
The Elements of Shamanism:
Neville Drury. Elements - 1989
Celtic Myths & Legends:
O.B. Duane. Brockhampton Press - 1998
The Great Encyclopaedia of Faeries:
Pierre Dubois. Pavilion 1999
Ghost World :
T.E. Thisleton Dyer - 1893. Reprinted - Senate 2000
The Encyclopedia of Ancient Myths and Culture :
Various contributors, Eagle Editions - 2003
A Complete Guide to Fairies and Magical Beings :
Cassandra Eason, Piatkus – 2001
Myths and Legends of the British :
Maude Ebbutt – 1910. Reprinted : Senate – 1998.
Celtic Myths :
Steve Eddy & Claire Hamilton, Hodder & Stroughton - 2001
Timeless Wisdom of the Celts:
Steve Eddy & Claire Hamilton. Hodder & Stroughton - 1999
From Other Worlds:
Hilary Evans. Carlton - 1998
Visions, Apparitions, Alien Visitors:
Hilary Evans. Aquarian Press -1984
A History of Punishment and Torture :
Karen Farringdon, Chancellor Press – 1999
Myths and Myth Makers :
John Fiske –1873. Reprinted - Senate 1996.
An Illustrated Guide To Jack The Ripper
Peter Fisher. P & D Riley - 1996
The Secret Language of Symbols :
David Fontana, Pavilion - 1993
The Illustrated Encyclopaedia of Faeries:
Anna Franklin, Vega - 2002

Nightmare. The Birth of Horror:
Christopher Frayling. BBC Books - 1996
Faeries:
Brian Froud, Alan Lee & David Larkin. Pan Books - 1978
Good Faeries / Bad Faeries :
Brian Froud, Pavilion – 2000
Larousse Encyclopedia of Mythology:
Edited by Felix Guarand. Paul Hamlyn Ltd. - 1959
The Secret Lore of the Cat :
Fred Gettings. Grafton Books - 1989
Visions of the Occult :
Fred Gettings, Century Hutchinson - 1989
The Encyclopaedia of Myths & Legends:
Stuart Gordon. Headline -1993
The Mabiginion:
Translation – Lady Charlotte Guest - 1838. Harper Collins – 2000
Monsters:
John Grant. Apple Press – 1992.
The Irish Fairy Book :
Alfred Perceval Graves. Senate - 1994.
A Dictionary of Ghosts:
Peter Haining. Robert Hale Ltd -1982
The Undead. The Legend of Bram Stoker and Dracula:
Peter Haining & Peter Tremayne. Constable –1997
McX - Scotland's X-Files :
Edited by Ron Halliday. B & W Publishing - 1997
Arthur Rackham ~ A Life with Illustration :
James Hamilton, Pavilion – 1995
Haunted Houses:
Charles G. Harper - 1907. Reprinted - Senate - 1994
Sea Serpents and Lake Monsters of the British Isles :
Paul Harrison. Robert Hale Ltd. - 2001
Understanding Dreams:
Keith Hearne & David Melbourne, New Holland -1999
Folklore of the Northern Counties of England and the Borders :
William Henderson - 1866. Reprinted, EP Publishing - 1973
English Folklore:
Christina Hole. BT Batsford Ltd - 1940
Oxford Dictionary of Saints :
David Hugh Farmer, OUP – 1978

Popular Romances of the West of England :
Robert Hunt –1871. Reprinted - (as

Cornish Folklore and **Cornish Legends**) Tor Mark Press -1969

The Pagan Religions of the Ancient British Isles :
Ronald Hutton. Blackwell - 1991

Ingoldsby Legends :
Thomas Ingoldsby - 1840. Reprinted - Library press - 1916

The Catalogue of Ghost Sightings :
Brian Innes, Blandford -1996

Celtic Fairy Tales / More Celtic Fairy Tales :
Joseph Jacobs - 1892 / 1894 . Reprinted as a single volume ~ Bracken Books -1990

Mysteries of Witchcraft & The Occult:
Robert Jackson, Quintet –1991

The Celtic Image :
David James & Courtney Davis, Cassell - 2000

Haunted Britain and Ireland :
Richard Jones. New Holland - 2001

Encyclopedia of Gods :
Michael Jordan. Kyle Cathie Ltd -2002

The Encyclopedia of Mind, Magic & Mysteries :
Francis X. King : Dorling Kindersley - 1991

Witchcraft and Demonology :
Francis X. King. Treasure Press - 1991.

The Secret Commonwealth of Faeries, Fauns and Elves:
Robert Kirk - 1691. Reprinted: Observer Press –1933

Brewer's Concise Phrase & Fable :
Edited by Betty Kirkpatrick. Cassell - 2000

Vampires - The Occult Truth :
Konstantinos. Llewellyn –1996.

Killer Cults :
Brian Lane. Headline -1996

The Inquisition:
Richard Leigh & Michael Baigent. Penguin -199

Giants
D. Larkin, S. Teale, J. Heller, C. Scrace & J. Wijngaard.
Pan Books –1979

Mythology:
David Leeming. Newsweek Books - 1979

A Natural History of the Unnatural World:
Joel Levy, Carroll & Brown -2000

Ancient Trees:
Anne Lewington & Edward Parker., Collins & Brown -1999

Mythology : The Illustrated Anthology of World Myth and Storytelling :
Edited by C. Scott Littleton. Duncan Baird Publishers - 2002

Lorenz Books ~ Anthologies of Verse & Prose **- Fairies** (1996) **Mermaids** (1998) **Mythical Beasts** (1998)

The Encyclopaedia of Saints :
Howard Loxton, Chancellor Press - 1999

Celtic Mythology :
Proineas MacCana. Hamlyn - 1970

The Middle Kingdom :
D.A. MacManus -1959. Reprinted -Colin Smythe Ltd. 1973

Le Morte D'Arthur :
Sir Thomas Malory, Edited by John Matthews, Cassell - 2000

Dictionary of Classical Mythology .
Jenny March. Cassell - 1998.

The Journal of a Ghost Hunter:
Simon Marsden, Little, Brown & Co -1994

Pre-Raphaelite Women :
Jan Marsh, Phoenix - 1987

Victorian Fairy Painting :
Edited by Jane Martineau, Mereel Holberton - 1997

The Druid Source Book :
John Matthews, Blandford - 1997

The Encyclopaedia of Celtic Myth & Legend :
John & Caitlin Matthews. Ebury - 2002.

Warriors of Arthur :
John Matthews & Bob Stewart, Blandford – 1997

Seal Folk and Ocean Paddlers :
John McAuley, White Horse Press – 1998

A Witch's Guide to Faery Folk :
Edain McCoy, Llewellyn - 1994

Crete and Pre-Hellenic Myths and Legends :
Donald A. McKenzie – 1917. Reprinted - Senate 1990

Mysteries of the Unknown- Monsters, Ghosts & UFOs:
C. Miller, C. Maynhard & T. Wilding

White, Usborne -1977
Silva – The Tree in Britain:
Archie Miles, Ebury Press-1999
Out of Body Experiences:
J. L. Mitchell, Aquarian Press-1988
The Encyclopaedia of Witchcraft and Magic :
Venetia Newall, Hamlyn – 1974
Animal Myths of County Durham :
A.C. Newton, Deorwenta Publications – 1993.
The Folklore of Ireland ;
Sean O' Sullivan. BT Batsford - 1974.
Meetings with Remarkable Trees :
Thomas Packenham, Phoenix Illustrated - 1997
Remarkable Trees of the World :
Thomas Packenham, Orion - 2002
Encyclopaedia of Things That Never Were :
Michael Page & Robert Ingpen, Lansdowne Press - 1985
Sacred Britain :
Martin Palmer & Nigel Palmer, Piatkus – 1997
Myths and Legends:
Neil Philip, Doring Kindersley - 1999
The Faeryland Companion:
Beatrice Phillpots, Pavilion - 1999
Cassell's Dictionary of Superstitions :
David Pickering. Cassell - 1995
Cassell's Dictionary of Witchcraft :
David Pickering, Cassell - 1996
Encyclopaedia of Superstition :
Caroline Potter, Michael O' Mara Books – 1994
Poltergeist Over England :
Harry Price, Country Life 1945
(Reprinted by Senate in 1994 as
Poltergeist. Tales of the

Supernatural.)
Troublesome Things - A History of Fairies and Fairy Stories :
Diane Purkiss, Allen Lane - 2000
William Blake
Kathleen Raine, Thames & Hudson – 1970
Folklore, Myths and Legends of Britain : Reader's Digest - 1973
Myth and Magic in Northumbria
Hazel Reynolds. Coquet Editions - 1992
Unexplained Phenomena- A Rough Guide Special:
Bob Rickard & John Mitchell. Penguin-2000

A History of Torture :
George Riley Scott 1940, Reprint; Senate - 1995
Grisly Trails and Ghostly Tales :
Alan Robson. Virgin Books - 1992
Myths and Legends of the Celts :
Thomas Rolleston - 1912. Reprinted - Senate - 1998
Dragons - A Natural History:
Dr. Karl Shuker, Aurum Press-1995
The Unexplained:
Dr Karl Shuker, Carlton - 1996
British Goblins :
Wirt Sikes –1880. Reprinted - E.P Publishing 1973
The Sword and the Grail :
Andrew Sinclair. Random House -1993.
The UFO Encyclopaedia:
John Spencer, Headline-1991
The Witchcraft and Folklore of Dartmoor :
Ruth E. St Leger-Gordon. Robert Hale - 1965
Exploring King Arthur's Britain :
Denise Stobie, Collins & Brown – 1998
Great British Trees :
Jon Stokes, The Tree Council - 2002
The Complete History of Jack the Ripper :
Philip Sugden. Robinson Publishing - 1994.
Scottish Myths & Legends :
K.E. Sullivan, Brockhampton Press - 1998
Viking Myths & Legends:
K.E. Sullivan. Brockhampton Press -1998
The Vampire (His Kith and Kin):
Montague Summers 1928. Reprinted: Senate-1995
The Vampire in Europe :
Montague Summers 1929. Reprinted - university Books - 1961.
Mysterious Britain ~ Fact and Folklore :
Homer Sykes, Weidenfeld & Nicholson - 1993
Children of the Night - Of Vampires & Vampirism
Tony Thorne. Orion - 1999
Witch, Wicce, Mother Goose
R.W. Thurston, Pearson Books - 2001
Handbook on Witches:
Gillian Tindell, Mayflower-1972

Enchanted World: Series of books - *Dragons. Dwarfs. Fabled Lands. Fairies & Elves. Ghosts. . Giants & Ogres. . Legends of Valour. Magical Beasts. Night Creatures. Seekers & Saviours. Spells & Bindings. The Book of Christmas.*
The Fall of Camelot. Water Spirits. Wizards & Witches.
Various authors & artists. Time Life - circa 1985

Ghosts of North West England:
Peter Underwood, Fontana – 1978

Passport to Magonia:
Jaques Valee. Neville Spearman Ltd –1970

Murders and Mysteries from the North York Moors :
Peter N. Walker, Robert Hale - 1988

A Dictionary of Omens and Superstitions :
Phillipa Waring, Magnum - 1978

No Go The Bogeyman :
Marina Warner, Chatto & Windus - 1998

Encyclopedia of World Mythology:
Foreword by Rex Warner. Peerage Books – 1975.

Dark Nature :
Lyall Watson. Hodder & Stroughton - 1995

Celtic Women :
Lyn Webster Wilde, Cassell - 1997

Albion – A Guide to Legendary Britain:
Jennifer Westwood. Guild-1985

The Devil and All His Works :
Dennis Wheatley, Hutchinson & Co. - 1973

Trees of the British Isles in History & Legend:
J.H. Wilks. Frederick Muller-1972

The Celtic Book of Living and Dying:
Juliette Wood, Duncan Baird Publishers – 2000

The Celtic Twilight : W.B. Yeats - 1893

Celtic Wonder-Tales:
Ella Young -1910. Reprinted - Dover 1995

Chronicles of the Celts:
Iain Zaczek. Collins & Brown-1996

392

Other books by Andy Paciorek ~

drēmour press ~
~The Human Chimaera:
Sideshow Prodigies & Other Exceptional People.
~Black Earth:
A Field Guide to the Slavic Otherworld.
~Outer Space Babe: Jubilee Anthology.
~Art of the Beautiful~Grotesque.

Available from -
www.blurb.co.uk/user/andypaciorek

~~~~~~~~~~~~~~~~~~~~~~~~~~~~~~~~~

Wyrd Harvest Press~
~The Carnival of Dark Dreams (written by Dr. Bob Curran)
~The Wytch Hunters' Manual (written by Dr Bob Curran)
~ Wyrd Kalendar (written by Chris Lambert)

Available from -
www.lulu.com/spotlight/andypaciorek

About the Author / Artist

Andy Paciorek is a graphic artist, drawn mainly to the worlds of myth, folklore, symbolism, decadence, curiosa, anomaly, dark romanticism and otherworldly experience. He is fascinated both by the beautiful and the grotesque and the twilight threshold consciousness where these boundaries blur. The mist-gates, edges and liminal zones where nature borders supernature and daydreams and nightmares cross paths are of great inspiration. He is also the creator of the Folk Horror Revival multimedia project.

For more information and to see further examples of his artwork, please visit the websites ~

Strange Lands
www.batcow.co.uk/strangelands/

Visionary Art Gallery
visionaryartgallery.weebly.com/andy-paciorek.html

Facebook Art Page
www.facebook.com/TheArtofAndyPaciorek

Twitter
www.twitter.com/andypaciorekart

395

CPSIA information can be obtained
at www.ICGtesting.com
Printed in the USA
LVHW090822220819
628183LV00001BC/22/P